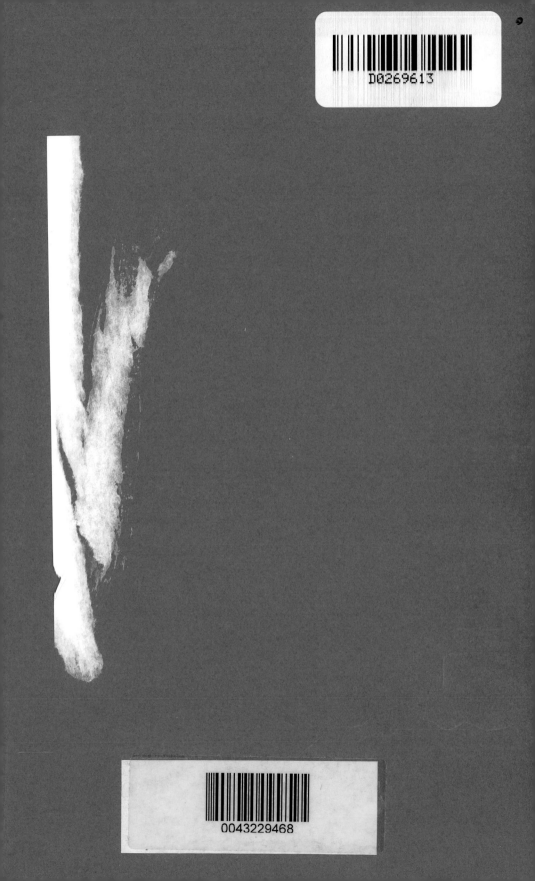

STILLRIVER

Stillriver

Andrew Rosenheim

HUTCHINSON
LONDON

First published in 2004 by Hutchinson

1 3 5 7 9 10 8 6 4 2

Copyright © Andrew Rosenheim 2004

Andrew Rosenheim has asserted his right under the Copyright, Designs and Patents Act,
1988 to be identified as the author of this work

Hutchinson
The Random House Group Limited
20 Vauxhall Bridge Road, London SW1V 2SA

Random House Australia (Pty) Limited
20 Alfred Street, Milsons Point, Sydney,
New South Wales 2061, Australia

Random House New Zealand Limited
18 Poland Road, Glenfield,
Auckland 10, New Zealand

Random House (Pty) Limited
Endulini, 5a Jubilee Road
Parktown 2193, South Africa

The Random House Group Limited Reg. No. 954009

www.randomhouse.co.uk

A CIP catalogue record for this book is available from the British Library

Papers used by Random House are natural, recyclable products
made from wood grown in sustainable forests. The manufacturing processes
conform to the environmental regulations of the country of origin

Typeset by SX Composing DTP, Rayleigh, Essex
Printed and bound in Great Britain by
Clays Ltd, St Ives PLC

ISBN 0 09 180037 4

For my brother Jim
and for Clare, Laura and Sabrina

One

1

As he had driven north through the high orchard country he had seen the last sliver of sun slip into Lake Michigan, but here enough light remained for him to make out the birch tree on the corner of the lot, the towering twin maples next to the house, the long expanse of white pine boards and green-shuttered windows that was the house itself. And a patrol car in the drive.

He parked his rental car and got out slowly, stretching after the drive from the little airport in Muskegon and looking around for a minute before going inside. The rough ryegrass (they had never had a silky lawn) was high – why hadn't his brother been round to cut it? He looked across at the Wagners', and was surprised to see four cars parked under the cedar trees there. Then he remembered it was now a bed and breakfast. Tourists up for Memorial Day, hoping that, like a rare restaurant meal served ahead of expectation, summer would come early to dispel this wet, cold weather. There was no sign of the Wagner twins.

He heard the back door groan as it opened, then slammed shut, and he turned round to see Jimmy Olds standing on the porch. He was in blue-grey uniform, and had the crescent moon shades of a motorcycle cop pushed back on his head, covering the top of his balding forehead. He was an improbable policeman – short, skinny, quite the opposite of his predecessor, Jerry Dawson, who had been a bear-like barrel of a man, an ex-marine well over six feet tall and very tough with it.

'Hey Jimmy.' He was trying to sound friendly but could tell his tone was merely resigned.

Jimmy nodded. 'Michael.'

Michael walked to the porch and climbed the steps to shake hands.

'You've had a long trip,' said Jimmy.

'You could say that.'

'Europe, right?' Pronounced *Yurp*. 'How long you been over there?'

'Almost six years.'

'You must like it.'

Michael looked across the street, this time at Bogles. The front yard was surprisingly tidy. He nodded absent-mindedly. 'It pays the bills,' he said.

'That's what counts,' and they both nodded in mild agreement at the banal correctness of this. They were silent for a minute and Jimmy looked down at his black leather boots. 'Well,' he said, lifting his chin. 'I expect you want to go inside.'

He followed Jimmy in, staring at the walnut grip of his holstered pistol. Jimmy's father had been a local builder, not very successful, one step up really from a handyman. After high school Jimmy had joined him, until the day he announced to his father's chagrin that he had passed the necessary exams and was joining the state police in Fennville. When Jerry Dawson died of cancer Jimmy had become the town's policeman – actually, now one of three of them, since despite a virtual absence of serious crime, Stillriver's governing council, flush with tourist property tax, had decided the community was underpoliced. Although Jimmy was the senior officer, there was a morose quality about the man, an air of mild disappointment, as if he had expected that by stepping into Jerry Dawson's shoes his feet would grow correspondingly. They hadn't.

They walked through the kitchen, which had always been the cosiest room in the house, with its wood-burning stove, and the radio tuned to Blue Lake while his mother bustled around and Michael sat after school reading the *Chronicle*. After she'd died, the room assumed a colder, functional air. His father would come in and make supper quickly, Michael and Gary would join him when the meal was ready and the trio would eat methodically – meat, vegetable, and potato; or stew, rice and salad; sometimes just plain stew – seated around the soft-pine kitchen table, talking only occasionally. Gary and he would do the dishes, then quickly go their separate ways, like a pair of cats let out of their carrier basket after a trip to the vet. In the rack by the sink now there was a plate, a glass, knife and fork – the only sign of his father's last supper.

He followed Jimmy into the dining room, a large square with an old-fashioned, heavy-looking mix of dark wainscoting and cream plaster walls, like the interior of an early Frank Lloyd Wright house. An old oak table and matching chairs were grouped in the middle. When his mother was alive they would sit down formally for supper and, at weekends, for lunch as well. But now the table was bare, and dusty from disuse.

On to the living room, again tidy but cold: three soft armchairs, a sofa the colour of groundfall plums, and a maple rocking chair formed a circle around the Mojave rug. Behind the sofa stood the mahogany grandfather clock, ticking with a metronomic resonance. It was an heirloom from Michael's mother's family that his father had wound religiously each Sunday evening. Michael made a mental note to wind it in two days' time – it seemed wrong even to contemplate winding it sooner.

Then to the stairwell, on one side of which was the small study where his father had taken to sitting, reserving the living room for company. Michael was pretty sure that lately there had not been much of that.

Jimmy stopped at the bottom of the stairs. 'You know he's not here any more, right?'

Yes, of course he'd realized that – it had been almost two days since they'd found his father – but Jimmy's bluntness unnerved him. 'He's in Fennville now,' Jimmy went on. 'At the hospital.'

They climbed the steep stairs and Michael gripped the thin rail of the banister, worn smooth by years of little boys' hands sliding along it. The stairs had been daunting when he was little – one family legend had him pitching down them head first, aged three, only to be caught at the bottom by his father. *Another time he saved my ass*, Michael thought wearily.

On the landing Jimmy turned left but Michael went right. Jimmy called out to him: 'He wasn't in the master bedroom.'

5

'I know.' His father had moved to the spare room at the back of the house during the last month of his wife's illness, and when she had died he hadn't moved back. *So why am I going here first?* wondered Michael. Maybe to feel some hint of his mother's past presence in the house – there was virtually none in the cold rooms downstairs; maybe somehow to ready himself for the fact that, with his mother long dead, now his father was gone, too.

He opened the door slowly and looked in. The light outside was fading fast, but he could make out the big double bed with its high mahogany headboard, and his mother's oval dressing table, where her set of ivory brushes was lined up carefully. Then he softly closed the door and walked down the hall to Jimmy, who was waiting outside the back bedroom.

'Did Henry usually sleep back here?' Jimmy asked.

'Once my mother died.' Michael sounded formal even to himself.

'The room's been sealed. I'll open it, but don't touch anything. We had the state police in and they've done the forensics – dusting fingerprints mainly – but they may want to come back.' Jimmy peeled back a thick ribbon of yellow adhesive tape. Then he turned the door knob and, reaching in, switched the light on.

There was an armchair of cracked brown leather by the window, with a reading lamp on an adjacent small table. His father's clothes from the day still lay on a wooden kitchen chair near the closet: trousers folded on the seat, his shirt hooked over the uprights of the chair like epaulettes on a store window mannequin. The closet door was open, and Michael could see a few pairs of shoes neatly lined up, some shirts on coat hangers, a fading sports jacket doubtless bought at Vergil's in Fennville. There was an old man's smell in the air – of clean but ageing clothes, of foot powder applied after a bath.

He was avoiding the bed to his right, but eventually forced himself to turn and see what was there. Not his father, he knew, and no longer any bedclothes. 'They've stripped the bed,' he commented flatly.

'They took the sheets away for analysis.'

'Analysis?'

Jimmy sighed. 'Blood. They need to make sure it was just your father's blood.'

'Oh.' He hadn't thought about the blood. 'Was there a lot of it?'

'A fair amount,' Jimmy said quietly.

'Tell me,' he said, keeping his back to Jimmy, 'was there any sign of a struggle?'

'If it's any comfort, Michael, I doubt he knew what hit him.'

'So he was asleep when it happened?'

'Well, he had sat up in the bed. We're pretty sure of that.'

'How do you know?'

'Because he got hit right on top of his head. If he'd been lying down he wouldn't have got hit that way.'

'And that's what killed him?'

Jimmy was silent for a moment. 'He got hit more than once.'

Since he'd first been told, on his mobile phone as he sat in a rowboat inspecting the beam encasing under Anfernachie Bridge, through the hours and hours of travel that got him here, all Michael had been able to imagine was his father's body, inert on the bed. It was the stillness of the image, a snapshot, which held firm in his mind's eye.

But now he could visualize his father startled from sleep, sitting up in surprise, turning towards the door and seeing, seeing exactly what? His killer? Heading towards him, weapon already raised, perhaps already descending – which would leave just enough time for his father to understand that he was about to be hit, about to be killed, in fact. Just enough time to feel the bone-shaking panic of a man about to die. *Christ.*

He had seen enough. He turned around and faced Jimmy. 'What did he get hit with?'

Jimmy shrugged. 'We don't know. So far there's been nothing. No prints, no sign of forced entry—'

'He never locked the back door.'

'The doctor thought it might have been a lead pipe. Something heavy.'

'Doctor Fell?'

Jimmy shook his head. 'He's retired. There's no doctor in town now. This is some guy from Burlington.'

As they left the room Michael switched off the light and closed the door, then watched as Jimmy patched back the strip of yellow tape. They went down the stairs and walked through the ground floor until they again stood under the covered porch side by side as rain and mist came down in a fine, almost invisible mix. The air felt moist and heavy, and the lights from the Wagners' house seemed to quiver like buoys bobbing at sea.

'Is Gary coming by?' asked Jimmy.

Michael shook his head. 'I told him to come round in the morning.'

'Come here?' Jimmy sounded surprised.

'I'll sleep here tonight. I don't imagine they want to kill me, too.'

Jimmy looked so shocked at this that Michael almost laughed. 'Don't worry, I'll lock the door.' But then suddenly his studied diffidence dissolved. 'Who would have done this, Jimmy?'

Jimmy took a stick of gum from his shirt pocket, unwrapped it and popped it in his mouth. He chewed thoughtfully for a few seconds. 'They told me to ask you, did your dad have any enemies?'

Me, when I was a mixed up kid, he wanted to say, but instead replied with exasperation, 'Jesus Christ, Jimmy, he was a retired schoolteacher.'

'Told 'em that. Taught me three years running. Or tried to anyway.'

'So what do they think – he flunked Oscar Peters twenty years ago and made a lifelong enemy?'

'Oscar's dead.'

Oscar Peters had been the town's closest approximation to a village idiot. 'You know what I mean.'

Jimmy said nothing and when Michael spoke again, his

8

voice was softer. 'All right. I know what they're thinking. Obviously *somebody* didn't like him. But I can't think of anyone obvious. How could I? I haven't been here in six years. Anyway, when was the last murder in this town? I've never even *heard* of one.'

Jimmy looked pensive. 'There was Andy Everitt.'

'That was a mercy killing, as you know perfectly well. He just put her out of her misery. What did he end up serving anyway? Two years?'

Jimmy shrugged. 'Something like that.' He chewed some more on his gum. 'Ronald Duverson *tried* to kill somebody once. That I know for a fact.' He turned and looked blank-eyed at Michael.

Michael heard his heart start to thump like thunder in his ears. He tried to sound calm, almost nonchalant. 'Is that right?'

Jimmy nodded. 'But he's in Texas now. Safe and sound.'

'How do you know?' He tried to keep the urgency out of his voice.

'Because he's sitting in the penitentiary. Down there he *did* manage to kill somebody.'

'Well, that rules him out,' Michael said, his voice pitched high enough for Jimmy to look at him again. 'Seems to me,' he said, his natural deeper tones reasserting themselves, 'that you're looking for a loony.'

'Or fanatic.'

'Meaning what?'

'Hang here a minute.' Jimmy walked down the porch steps and went to his patrol car. When he came back he held a heavy black flashlight in his right hand. 'Come look at this.'

Michael followed him around to the side of the house, where a bough of the peach tree extended almost to the wall. He could smell the incense of the cedars that, mixed with mulberry trees, formed a hedge separating the lot from the Jenkinses next door. Jimmy stopped and swung the flashlight's beam on to the white boards. Michael moved closer to look.

What he saw seemed oddly out of place and time, depicted in

9

black paint strokes on the overlapping edges of five or six of the thin pine boards:

'*What?*' is all he could say.

'Michael.' Jimmy's breath smelled sweet from his chewing gum; his voice was embarrassed and mild. 'Was your father some kind of a Jew?'

HE SLEPT WELL, though he woke long before dawn, since his body's clock thought it was ten in the morning. He lay in his old room, listening as the birds began to stir and whistle in the dark, and a car started as one of the Bogles went out early.

He had slept with his own door open but the back door downstairs locked. He'd found three beers in the fridge and drunk them all – enough to sail him through the night undisturbed. If they were going to kill him too, he had decided, he didn't want to wake up when it happened. He had drunk the beers in the kitchen, reading an Edinburgh mystery novel he'd bought at the airport in London. He hadn't wanted to explore in the house until morning – he didn't know why he felt this way, but knew he did.

He got out of bed and a little dizzily did seventy-four pushups, then stood and stretched for several minutes. In the bathroom there was an old set of scales that told him he weighed 192 pounds, which sounded about right. He had gained five or six pounds since the Scottish job had begun, but looking at himself in the mirror he found no noticeable paunch. He hadn't been to a gym in ten years, but kept very active on the job. He showered, noticing that the wallpaper in the bathroom was starting to peel, and that the low, light-blue curtains still hung in the little window next to the toilet, leaving anyone sitting there visible from the waist up to the houses across the street. His mother had never used this bathroom but had complained nonetheless about the indelicacy of this exposure; his father would chide her gently for her prissiness. 'I wave politely each morning to Mrs Decatur, and she waves back at me. Nothing wrong with that.' Even his mother would laugh.

Michael dressed in corduroys and an old, soft, blue work shirt. Looking around his old room, he found only the wallpaper was familiar from childhood. A Van Gogh poster he had never seen before was the sole picture on the walls; his own pictures – what had they been? He could remember only a photograph of the Mackinaw Bridge – were gone. The bookshelf on the wall above his bed held overflow history books from his father's study downstairs; where were his own books on baseball, his Robert Ludlum novels, and geometry texts? Had they still been here on his last visit six years before? He couldn't remember – it was memories of the room of his childhood that provided the contrast to his surroundings now.

He searched the chest of drawers but found only Gary's old clothes until, at the back of the bottommost drawer, he felt a soft, bulging pouch of chamois. As he drew it out, its contents rolled and clicked. Opening the drawstrings, he looked inside and saw his old friends – blue, aquamarine, green and clear marbles. How odd a source of comfort they had been. He started to reach inside the pouch, spying the chipped deep blue marble he always made the leader in his imaginary games with them. *Jesus,* he thought, *how old are you now precisely?* He pulled the drawstrings tight and put the bag back in the drawer.

Buoyed by the imminent prospect of daylight, he walked through the other rooms of the second floor. Gary's bedroom was also almost stripped of belongings, though a few photographs remained on the walls: an ensemble shot of Gary's high school graduating class, a pennant of the Detroit Tigers, and the famous poster of the blonde woman tennis player, taken from behind as she hikes up her skirt and scratches her backside.

He stopped outside his father's room and thought for a moment. If they had already dusted for fingerprints, then, provided he was careful, he couldn't do any forensic damage. He undid the tape and opened the door, looking quickly around and going to the chest of drawers. One drawer down he found his father's wallet, which held a driving licence, one credit card, a membership card for the town library and, to Michael's surprise, over $300 in cash – six fifties and some singles. Why this surfeit of cash from a man who had rarely carried more than twenty dollars with him at any one time? He assumed the police had seen it already, although he was surprised they hadn't taken it away. Then he realized: *the killer didn't want his money.*

Before going downstairs he stopped again in his parents' bedroom. It faced north, and had tall windows still flush with dark. He felt for the bedside lamp and turned it on. The room had been kept unchanged, down to his mother's bedtime reading: novels mainly, always hardbacks, in the little book-stand next to her side of the bed. He ran a finger along the glass top of the dressing table – clean. His father must have dusted regularly. Or did someone come in to clean?

His father's study downstairs, a small room with just one window on the front side of the house, was the first room that felt lived in. The far wall was ceiling to floor bookshelves, which held his father's American history books. In the corner sat a soft armchair, covered in scarlet plush, positioned to face the portable television sitting on a low coffee table in the middle of the room. His father's mahogany desk sat by the window, with a padded swivel chair that faced the front yard.

On the desk he found a stack of old bills, presumably paid, which were held down by an oval piece of jade Michael had sent his father from the Philippines. A tin can held pencils and pens, but otherwise the desk was bare. In the drawers he found more bills, a protracted correspondence with the IRS about a tax refund, the annual letter from Adlard Ferguson, a local timber merchant, offering to cull trees on the Half, and a mimeographed copy of a short history of the county's Indian population, which his father had produced for the local historical society in the days before photocopying. And, tucked beneath a ledger book, he found an unfinished letter on a piece of stationery. It was dated three weeks before in his father's hand, and read in its entirety: *Dear Patsy, I was very happy to hear about the float.*

Patsy who? A girlfriend? It seemed unlikely, for his father had never shown the slightest romantic interest in any woman after Michael's mother died. Yet who knew what his father had got up to in the six years since Michael had last visited? Though if 'Patsy' were a girlfriend she must not be local, since why else was he writing her a *letter*? And what was *the float*?

Michael put the letter back under the ledger and went and sat down in the armchair, turning on the television with the remote control to catch the morning news. He found nothing but static except for one Pontiac channel, which was broadcasting a cartoon. *Too mean to put in cable*, thought Michael, then regretted his own lack of charity. For his father had been necessarily frugal, was hardest on himself, and simply never had much time for television. He read a lot instead, very slowly (odd, perhaps, for a teacher), mainly local and Indian history, sometimes large tomes about the Civil War. No fiction.

He walked out to the kitchen. Opening the freezer on top he found frozen hamburger, French fries, peas, even ice-cream – enough for a short stay. In the fridge below there was little other food and the milk smelled borderline sour.

He hated black coffee. Nothing would be open in town, but there was a new twenty-four-hour gas station by the interstate exit, which he had passed on his way in the previous evening. So he went outside and drove with his lights on in a daze of sleep and jet lag through the persisting dark. He filled up at the gas station, and bought a quart of milk and a replacement six-pack of beer from a bemused teenage boy behind the counter. On the way back it was suddenly lighter, and as he drove down the hill towards the Junction, the very top of the sun had just touched the horizon line.

The Junction was not a meeting of roads, but the precise point where the two branches of the Still river met at the bottom of a bluff, flowed as one under the bridge, and emerged into the wide flood plain of Stillriver Lake. The bridge itself was a standard beam-and-slab job, a Butler's Tray as it was known in the business (his business after all), a simple plate of reinforced concrete slapped across three perpendicular bents. Crossing the bridge, his rental car made a flat, metallic sound, like driving over tin, and he looked down to see the water level of the river – it was high for May, so it must have been a wet

14

spring. As his eyes moved up from the water to the bridge's balustrated side he saw that the concrete was pitted and cracked and beginning to flake. Not good.

He drove along the winding road to town that hugged the shoreline, looking out first at the flood plain, then, as he passed the causeway to South Beach, at Stillriver Lake itself. Inland lakes abounded in the county, but were mainly small, mild affairs, rarely more than twenty feet deep and therefore warm and good for swimming. On any map of Michigan they looked like tiny spots of paint, thrown randomly on to the canvas of the state. Stillriver Lake was bigger, a proper lake, over three miles long and almost a mile across at its widest, continuing up to and around the southern border of the town until it flowed through a thin channel into the great cavern of Lake Michigan, which the locals knew simply as the big lake. In places the smaller lake was as much as three hundred feet deep, and it would freeze over completely only in severe winters, when ice fishermen would materialize with saws for cutting holes, put up wood shacks, and build fires inside that were kindled without fear, such was the thickness of the ice.

As he drew closer to town, he saw, in the small strip of shoreline between road and lake, new summer cottages that developers had somehow managed to put up, many of them hanging out on stilts over the water like stacked dice. It was hard to imagine that none of their sewage made its way into the lake. The cottages had been erected after a loosening of the zoning regulations ten years before, when the town planning board had decided physical expansion was the only pre-emptive strike available against economic stagnation. Through gaps between the cottages he could see that, like the river, the lake's waves were grey, with small whitecaps from the wind the only variance to the monochrome. *No diamonds today*, he thought, remembering his mother's name for the points of light that sparkled on the surface, jewel-like, when the sun was out and the lake flushed blue as a girlfriend's eyes. *My old girlfriend*, he thought ruefully.

The road curved up the hill away from the lake and suddenly

he was in a tunnel of trees, swaying poplars planted years before. The road swung ninety degrees west, heading straight for the big lake at the other end of town, and he saw new houses sitting where even recently there had been only scrappy woods and a field of high, uncut grass that seemed to say *Gophers live here undisturbed* and *SNAKES*. Coming into town from this direction, his father would ask, 'Back way or Main Street?', and now Michael faced the same choice. He chose the back and quicker way, for he didn't want to run into anybody, not until he had got to the house and seen – seen what? He remembered again that his father wasn't going to be there.

He drove by Alvin Simpson's house, separated from the road by an acre of neatly-tended grass. Alvin's son had never pushed a mower in his life, exempt on account of his putative prospects as a baseball player, so Alvin had operated a sit-on tractor affair throughout Michael's childhood. Michael half-expected his former boss to emerge now, although he knew perfectly well that Alvin had been dead four years.

At the stop sign he turned left past Kyler's house (Kyler was the town's one-man band of maintenance), saw the City truck, used for everything from ploughing snow in winter to transporting the town's mowers in summer, then saw Kyler himself through the kitchen window reading the paper while his wife cooked breakfast. At the next street he turned right, driving past the empty sandy lot, once the site of the town's school, now clotted with patches of scrub grass, weeds and wild flowers, and took a deep breath as he got closer to his block, his home.

There, as he made a pot of coffee, he looked out the window into the backyard. A clothes line, full of pegs hanging down like swallows, stretched from the spruce tree to the old chicken shed door – the chickenless chicken shed, for within living memory it had only been used for storage. His father kept his tools there; it was where Gary and he had stored their bikes, their baseball bats, and their fishing gear. Occasionally, as little boys, they would even sleep out there in its windowless confines, leaving the door open and lying next to each other on camp beds.

16

He took his mug and went outside to sit in a solitary deckchair under the spruce. Its lower boughs had been lopped off years before to let the light in, and the sun was just high enough over the chicken shed to start to warm him in the slight morning chill. He looked in the daylight at the houses around him. *The neighbourhood.* This early, the street was still silent: there were no kids playing, no one mowing a lawn. Nothing stirred and the deceptive peace held.

When his ex-wife had phoned him two days before with the news, he had kept asking 'What did he die of? What did he die of?' Until finally, in exasperation, she had shouted down the line: 'Michael, I've said it three times. Somebody's killed him. He's been murdered.' And all he could say, feebly, was, 'You must be joking.' Even now, drinking coffee less than a child's stone's throw from the scene of the crime, he found the fact of homicide unreal. Death was real enough; a chapter had closed, about the biggest chapter left other than his own. But murder seemed the odd, peripheral accessory to death, a supplementary feature he had yet fully to take in. Why would anyone want to kill his father?

He didn't know how he was supposed to feel, and when he tried tracking his own emotions, they seemed to have disappeared. Maybe he was in shock. He remembered how once, in Germany, he had watched as a young local engineer slipped and fell from an uncompleted cantilevered span into the river thirty feet below. They had managed to fish him out, unconscious, just before he would have drowned, and two hours later the young man was sitting in the site's Portakabin wearing dry clothes, munching a *wurst*, and discussing the next day's work. Everyone was impressed, until three days later the engineer was found holding a blueprint and sobbing uncontrollably. *No sign of that in me*, Michael thought without surprise, figuring that he was just being his now-normal, unaffected self.

A car slowed down in front of the house and for a moment seemed about to turn into the driveway. Michael stood up and stared, but it was no one he knew – a man and woman in a

Passat, staring at the house. They noticed him, and drove on.

Five minutes later it happened again, this time an elderly man on his own. When another car repeated the process – slow down, stare, move on – Michael grew irritated. In summer cars often went by slowly, the passengers looking at the house appreciatively, for it was a large classic of its kind. But not this often, and not these people. They had come to see the murder site.

He felt he had to stay busy, but there was no point ringing the Portakabin in Anfernachie, because on a Saturday afternoon (the time there) Jock and the crew would already be in the pub. But he had to do something, preferably out of doors. Things inside could wait.

His mother had been an avid grower of flowers, exceptional in a town where usually only lawns and vegetables were cultivated with intensity. So inspecting the grounds, he noticed with dismay that his father had let the yard go, or rather let the garden recede to yard. The flowering bushes all around the house – forsythia, philadelphus, white- and purple-flowered lilac – now were ragged and overgrown. Around the front door his mother had trained a Rambling Rector rose that now looked to be dying; he'd prune it hard and hope for the best. Almost all the flower beds were gone; even the once-neat bed of iris that stretched in a trench all along the house side of their fence was empty, gone to scratchy grass. And the lawn itself had always been a struggle; between the hard play of two young boys and soil that tended to sand, even ryegrass had trouble establishing itself in anything but clumps. As he wondered whether any wild flowers still bloomed in the high grass behind the house – there'd been ox-eye daisies and fleabane and dog fennel – he suddenly remembered there was a swastika painted round the back.

Jimmy had said the forensic people were done with it; they'd photographed it from twenty-three angles or some such, then scraped and taken away samples of its paint. In the chicken shed Michael found an old can of white primer (not a perfect match but it would do) and a stiff brush that softened when he poured thinner in a bucket and let it soak while he looked around the shed. Everything was neatly arranged: the gas mower, a spade hooked on a pegboard by its handle, two rakes, a wooden wheelbarrow, a gas can.

It took two coats to mask the black paint effectively, and while he waited for the first coat to dry he inspected his handiwork and wondered what the swastika was meant to signify. Could it have been there before the murder? No one would have seen it, here on the back side of the house, sheltered by the cedars. But his father would have, surely. He had still been active about the place – his hands hurt from arthritis but he was otherwise in no way infirm. He would have seen the swastika and painted it over as Michael had.

So it had been put there after the murder. But why a Nazi symbol? What did it mean? Was there even a US Nazi party any more? There'd been one in his childhood, he could dimly remember – Rockwell, wasn't that the leader? Wasn't he assassinated? They caused trouble in Chicago with blacks, and one of their leaders turned out – naturally – to be a secret Jew.

But there weren't Nazis any more; as far as he knew there had never been any up here anyway. No Klan, either. The Michigan Militia had a decade before been much in the news, along with other emergent paramilitary organizations, but it had never prospered here and even its strongholds elsewhere in the state had largely wasted away after the Oklahoma bombing of 1995.

No, this was not fertile ground for the lunatic fringe. Although Atlantic County was overwhelmingly rural, Republican and conservative, it had never been a home for extremism. It was full of decent people, by and large, tied to an upright life by the demands of making a living – if you worked hard you didn't always do well, but if you didn't work hard you *never* did well – and by religion. Lutheran, Methodist, Dutch Reform, Baptist, a handful of Catholics, and a few stuffy Episcopalians – there were not many variants of Christianity unrepresented in Atlantic County. And few heretics to get between them and their God, for the bogeyman stayed in the cities, where, according to the pervasive local wisdom, nobody worked or went to church, and everyone was a welfare cheat.

So who in this comparative haven of peace would want to kill his father? He'd had few close friends, especially after the death of Michael's mother. There were the Fells, the local doctor and his wife, a bond strengthened after they had lost their only child, Ricky, a contemporary of Michael's who had been killed in a car accident the summer after graduating from high school. There was Charlie Anderson, the postmaster, who had fished for years with Michael's father on the very upper reaches of the Still's north branch, using worms for brook trout. But Charlie got grumpy and Michael's father's arthritic hands hurt – Michael doubted they would have fished together once in the last ten years.

His father had been an intensely private man, but there was nothing sinister about him, and he had led a life without controversy. If he held a mild disdain for the holders of public office (shared, in Michael's experience, by most people who saw life as essentially a private affair), he was nonetheless no recluse, and took pains as a citizen to meet his civic obligations: a veteran of Korea, he had paid his taxes, supported bond issues, and voted, as far as Michael could remember, Republican in the semi-automatic way of virtually everyone else in Atlantic County. He had broken no laws of consequence (only fishing without a licence when he forgot to buy one) and had served until old age in the town's all-volunteer Fire Department.

What else? Well, he drank sparingly, was kind to animals that strayed onto his property, and was always on cordial terms with his neighbours, even when the Bogle boys were raising all kinds of hell. True, the Bogles had been weird for a little while, especially after their own father had died. They'd had a banner on their porch, *FIND THE MIAs* – soldiers in Vietnam whose bodies had never been recovered but who might, if you listened to the Bogles, still be held prisoner in remote jungle encampments, more than twenty years after their capture. But so what? The MIAs stayed missing, the banner came down (certainly there was no sign of it now) and none of this had anything to do with his father who, in any event, had always got on with the Bogles. But then, his father had got along with pretty much everybody.

Of course, it was a staple of American mythology that behind the picket fences and neatly painted shutters of a small town like Stillriver lay abiding hatreds, sexual deviation, passionate longings and psychopathic obsessions, all nursed secretly behind closed doors. Michael had seen the films of David Lynch. But if he knew one thing from his own upbringing, and his adolescent years working at the town's hub of news and gossip (the drugstore) it was that yes, all these feelings existed – no question there – but *none of them was secret at all*. For a small town was by definition *small*; over the months and the years, you couldn't hide anything. If it was privacy you wanted, much less anonymity, you moved to a city, where your secret appetites could be indulged yet stay secret.

So as Michael tried to come up with candidates for the murder, he drew a blank in the neighbourhood. Who then? A former student? Yet his father had never been a tyrant of the classroom, not as far as Michael knew, though he'd never had his father as his own teacher. Henry Wolf had been a fairly formal pedagogue of the old school, Michael supposed, and possibly a little daunting; he had, after all, been a big man, powerfully built with the shoulders (as Michael's mother once said) of a moose. But the occasional hint of gruffness hadn't really disguised an essentially warm nature – he had always seemed to like the kids he taught. To get an 'A' grade from Henry Wolf was difficult – you had to be smart *and* work hard. But it was much harder to get an 'F'. Michael had once heard his father explain to a cousin of his mother's: 'You've got a not-too-bright kid with no money and no prospects. Life for him will be a downhill road. Is there any point in my jump-starting the process?'

It was hard to see how anyone – ex-student, neighbour – could have worked up so great a grievance against the man to want to kill him. And Henry himself had been thoroughly non-

21

violent, despite his hefty physical presence and obvious strength. He wouldn't even raise a hand to his own children, a rarity in small town family life where spanking, smacking and the odd slap were the staple instruments of parental discipline. Only once in Michael's memory had his father even threatened violence, and that was only to protect his son.

He left the paint outside in case the swastika needed yet another coat. As he walked round the house by the back door he smelled the acrid fumes of a cigarette – since quitting ten years before he'd grown especially sensitive to tobacco smoke. He moved slowly towards the back porch, suddenly nervous for the first time. Who would go into his father's house, make himself at home, and light up? He moved cautiously up the porch steps.

'Don't worry,' a voice called out. 'It's only me.'

He opened the screen door to find Gary sitting at the kitchen table with a cigarette in one hand and a bottle of root beer in the other.

'You scared me.'

Gary raised his eyebrows. 'Lock the door next time if you don't want company. You told me to come round this morning. Where've you been, anyway?'

'In back,' said Michael, then went and wiped his hands on some paper towel from the holder above the sink. His father's plate still stood there, dry and clean in the rack. He turned around and put a hand out to shake. Gary shook it but did not get up. 'You want some coffee?' Michael asked.

'Nah.' Gary gestured with his root beer bottle. 'This'll do me fine.'

'Breakfast, huh?'

Gary shrugged. 'Whatever.'

Michael pulled out a chair and sat down across from his brother. He hadn't aged much, and was still skinny, lanky really, shorter than Michael and bonier, more fragile-looking. Where Michael had their father's brown hair and medium complexion, Gary had inherited their mother's fair skin and straw-coloured hair. He looked especially pale now, wearing

22

blue jeans, a white T-shirt with the logo of a heavy metal band, and dirty track shoes.

'Haven't seen you in a long time,' Michael said, trying to sound friendly.

Gary nodded evenly, and Michael sensed he wasn't inclined to make things easier. He felt the same irritation with his little brother that he had always felt – since when? *Since day one, when Mom and Pop brought the little fucker home from Fennville wrapped in a flannel blanket.*

'Jimmy said the body is in Fennville. At the hospital.'

Gary nodded.

'I was thinking I should probably go see him.'

'Why?'

'I don't know. Do they need the body identified or did you already do that?'

'There wasn't much need for a formal procedure,' Gary said sourly, 'seeing as I was the one who found him in the first place.'

'Of course,' said Michael. 'That was Thursday morning?'

Gary nodded. 'I came round to cut the grass at about nine – if I cut earlier the Jenkinses complain. As soon as I walked in I knew something was wrong: there was nothing out for breakfast, no coffee. I went upstairs and found him, then I called the police, if you can call Jimmy Olds "the police". I tried reaching you through your old work number in New York, but they weren't much help: they didn't even know which continent you were on. So then I found Sarah's work number in Pop's book and I called her. I didn't have any choice.'

'Don't worry about it. She tracked me down all right. Anyway, maybe I should go see Pop to say goodbye. Something like that.'

'I wouldn't recommend it.' He took a swig from his root beer. 'Not a pretty sight, I imagine. They've had to perform an autopsy. Always do in murder cases, apparently.'

'Why didn't you say so?' Presumably all there would be to see was a nice assembly of parts. Michael got up and poured himself a glass of water from the tap. What he really wanted was one of the beers he'd bought, but it was too early. He wondered if there were any more booze in the house. He drank the water and turned towards Gary. 'So I guess there's a lot to do.'

'Like what?'

'Well, the funeral for one thing.'

Gary leaned back and seemed to suppress a yawn. 'Relax, big brother. All taken care of. The funeral's on Tuesday. I assume you can stay that long. Family only. No flowers please.'

'Family only? What, you and me?'

'No such luck. The GR clan will be here. Said they wouldn't miss it for the world.'

His mother's family from Grand Rapids, cousins he hadn't seen in years. 'Where?'

'At the cemetery. Pop's plot is right next to Mom's.'

'I know. He told me he bought two when Mom died. What else have we got to do? What about his will, do you know if Pop left a will?'

Gary shook his head. 'I did call Steve Atkinson.'

'What did he say?'

'He didn't. He's away. Can't be reached.'

'Can't somebody in his office check?'

'He hasn't got a somebody in his office. And his wife says he can't be contacted. Seems he's being dried out in Kalamazoo. Your average twelve-point plan and then some. No visitors, no phone calls, no emails, no messages. Nothing. Zip.'

'Steve Atkinson? I didn't know he drank.'

'Then you're the only one who didn't.'

The bush telegraph of a small town. 'Shit. When's he due out?'

'Another two weeks.'

Michael thought for a moment. 'Well, maybe there's a copy here, but I haven't seen it, and I went through his desk. I'll look some more. Now what else have we got to do?'

Gary suddenly put his head in his hand. 'Jesus, Michael, Pop's barely been dead two days. I'm still trying to get my head around it all.'

'I'm sorry.' Michael looked at the clock and saw it was only ten thirty.

'Even you have to admit it's pretty incredible.'

'I know it is. I guess the only way I can deal with it is by doing things.'

Gary smiled. 'You haven't changed much.'

Michael smiled back. 'Neither have you. How's Beverly?' That was her name, wasn't it? He had trouble enough rubbing along with Gary not to cause gratuitous offence.

'I threw her sorry ass out. I'm on my own now.' He paused and added, 'She moved to Detroit, anyway.'

'Season started yet?'

'Next week. Dig the pits again this year, then line them. I'm a partner now.'

'Congratulations,' Michael said, meaning it but seeing right away this spoiled it somehow for Gary. Whatever he said Gary would feel patronized.

'Some partnership. Fifty per cent of a trading loss.'

'Cherries still that bad?'

'They're coming back. At least people are replacing orchards when the old trees die. For a while they were actually digging good ones up to plant asparagus.'

'Where you living?'

'You remember Sissy Farrell? Next door to her parents. The bungalow, where nobody ever lived. 'Til me.'

'This place looks in good shape,' said Michael. The fruit business shut down from November until May, and Gary's money never managed to last until spring. Their father provided subvention in return for small repairs the old house increasingly required.

'Windows are going. I was going to do them this fall.' The *was* hung in the air between them.

'Might as well do them.'

'Let the next owner do it.'

'Who knows? You might want to live here yourself. And if we do sell it, you'll get a better price if the window frames aren't falling to pieces.' When Gary still looked doubtful Michael realized what the problem was. 'Don't worry, you'll get paid. It can come out of the estate.'

'So I'd be paying myself?'

He suppressed his irritation. *Remember*, he told himself, *this must be harder on him than on you*. 'It can come out of my share. Okay?'

Gary nodded. After a moment's silence he said, 'Did Jimmy ask you about Pop?'

'How do you mean?'

'Like who would have done this?'

'I didn't have much to contribute. He always seemed to get on with everybody pretty well, wouldn't you say?'

Gary shrugged. 'It could be anybody. Some nut. And I don't mind admitting it – I'm scared.'

'Why are *you* scared?'

'What do you mean, why am *I* scared? What's wrong with you? How do I know they won't kill me, too? It could be anybody,' he said again. 'The whole town's freaked out.'

'Well, it's not Mrs Decatur. And the Mean Man's dead too.'

Gary didn't smile. 'His son's there now. He's about as friendly.'

'I don't think it's the Bogle boys. They liked Pop.'

'Yes, they did.' He briefly pursed his lips. 'The thing is, the police won't leave me alone.'

'Why is that?'

'I don't know,' he said with agitation. 'I gave a statement to Jimmy, then a detective from Muskegon came and went through it with me, and now they say they want to go through it again.' He started to say something else but stopped, looking so miserable that Michael was moved to reassure him.

'That's just the way they are, Gary. Don't let it bother you. I've got to see them again, too, and I wasn't even in the country when it happened.' He paused. 'Jimmy did ask me one thing. He wanted to know if Pop was a Jew.'

Gary looked startled. '*What*? That's crazy.'

'Well, if he was, it's sure news to me. I think Jimmy was asking because of the swastika. You saw it, didn't you?'

Gary nodded. 'Pop always said he was an American. That was enough for him.'

'I guess so. Though Sarah once asked me—'

Gary's voice rose. 'What would your wife know about anything west of . . . what's it called?'

'Bloomingdale's?' said Michael, then added, 'My *ex*-wife.'

'Big difference.'

'It is, actually. She's got remarried.'

'She has?' Gary looked briefly contemplative. 'Man, it has been a long time. Last time you were here you weren't even divorced yet. Who'd she marry this time?'

'Some guy she grew up with. She probably should have married him in the first place. He's a banker.'

'So he's rich?'

'Colossal.'

Gary guffawed. 'I'm not surprised.'

'Whatever makes her happy.' He paused for a moment. 'I didn't.'

'Have you painted over the swastika?'

Michael nodded. 'Can't say I understand it. The only Nazi sympathizers I ever heard of in Michigan belonged to the Militia. But I thought they'd disappeared.'

'It's not called the Militia any more,' said Gary sharply. 'And they're not Nazis. They're just against the government. Who isn't? Why should Washington tell us what to do.'

'I didn't know it did,' said Michael gently.

'Ninety per cent of what I pay for gas goes to the federal government. And then where does it go? Harlem? Detroit? It doesn't come here, I tell you. And if you want to see *real* poverty take a drive out east of thirty-one. Just because nobody's rioting doesn't mean they have enough to eat.'

Inwardly Michael sighed. There wasn't much point discussing this kind of thing with Gary, who had always been quick to fall back on the adages of the disgruntled: *If you outlaw guns only outlaws will have guns*, etc, etc. There was always a hint of grievance, a slightly paranoid view that others were profiting by gouging him – him, and of course the 'little man', the one who didn't have *fancy lawyers on call* or a *sweet-talking manner* . . . this sort of stuff was actually produced as an argument. Even his father, always protective of his younger son, would grow tired of Gary taking this kind of tack.

'Cheer up, Gary. Where I've been living, gas is six dollars a gallon.'

'You don't look like you've been suffering.'

Oh, not that too, thought Michael. The sibling refrain had begun really only when they'd both grown up – Michael had been to college, Gary hadn't; Michael got married and Gary didn't (*lucky Gary*, thought Michael); Michael made a pretty good living, Gary scraped and took backhanders from their old man; Michael had got out, Gary hadn't. On and on, in a brew of competitive bitterness, which was part true, part fantasized grounds for some larger, unspecified resentment. Yet it was Gary who had been the apple of their father's eye. *Some apple*, thought Michael. *Go easy*, he told himself again, struggling not to rise to the bait, and he heard his mother's voice from years before, telling him to be nicer to the awful youngest Bogle boy, because *he hasn't had your advantages*.

So now with a show of mock-emotion he said, 'My suffering's all inside.' To his relief Gary laughed.

'Say,' Michael added, 'who is Patsy?'

'What do you mean?'

'Pop was writing a letter but he'd only just started it. It's in his desk. Says "Dear Patsy" but that's about all.'

'He didn't know any Patsy, not that I'm aware of. Patty Betts works at the Dairy Queen, but since she's about sixteen years old I don't suppose he was writing to her.'

'No. Well, that's one more mystery to solve.' He looked at his watch. 'Have you been out to the Half?'

Gary shook his head. 'Not in ages.'

'Is Sheringham's open for the season yet?'

'Yeah,' said Gary, 'but just asparagus.'

'I was thinking I might drive out to the Half, then go by there. Get out of the house for a while. You want to come?'

28

Gary shook his head. 'I'll come back at suppertime, unless you've got plans.'

'Hardly.'

Gary stood up to go but then hesitated. He looked slightly embarrassed. *What is it now?* thought Michael. 'Say Michael,' said Gary awkwardly.

'Yeah?'

'Could you maybe lend me a little money?' He looked like he would almost rather have starved than ask. *Almost* being the operative word. 'You see, Pop was going to pay me . . . honest, Michael, he hadn't paid me yet.'

Michael thought of the money remaining in his father's wallet upstairs – *that's why he had so much cash.* Suddenly Michael's cynicism melted away. 'Of course,' he said. 'Will a hundred do you for now? I didn't change that much money. I'll go to the bank after the holiday and get some more.' He couldn't bear the thought of taking money from his murdered father's wallet.

3

HE DECIDED TO go for a walk before driving anywhere. He went out the back door and through the yard, between the two maples with their bark scars where, with his father's permission, the Bogle boys would tap the syrup each winter, along with the three maple trees in their own backyard and any others they could get away with, out in the woods east of the interstate.

He looked across the street at Mrs Decatur's small bungalow, now inhabited by her grandson. She had been a small, quiet woman, ancient even in his childhood, memorable only for her insistence on cutting the grass with an old-fashioned push mower well into her eighties. Across the street, kitty-corner from his father's home, a mass of dark foliage and thin hardwood blocked out the house sitting back from the road. He couldn't remember the owner's name – he and Gary had simply called him the Mean Man. Their own father had warned them: 'Stay away from there and don't play on that side of the street. I don't want your ball ever going in there. Understood?'

He crossed the street, walking by Benny Wagner's new bed and breakfast, where there were now five cars parked in the driveway. There was still no sign of the twins, and he found himself missing them. 'Idiots-savants', his father had once called them, to the young Michael's mystification, then qualified this: 'though if you ask me they're mainly idiot.'

They had never been girls in Michael's memory, had been too old for school even when Michael was a little boy, though they were tiny creatures, standing as adults just over five feet tall, with the small hands and feet of pre-adolescent children. Born identical, they had very slowly moved apart in appearance over the years, though only to those, like Michael, who knew them well: Daisy got fat and Ethel's moustache matured. Adopted, they had outlived their 'parents', and when their adoptive

30

father died they had been put into a state institution until rescued by Benny, their sort-of brother, who came back from Florida to live in the house. They were occasionally annoying and consistently harmless, which is why most people in the town treated them with the tolerant condescension shown an idiot like Oscar Peters, rather than with the gratuitous cruelty often inflicted on borderline oddballs who live in small towns.

Obsessives, they had filled their days with unvarying routines, which included once a week taking all their neighbours' garbage cans down to the street for collection, an act of altruism that would have won greater appreciation had it not taken place at six o'clock in the morning. They were also compulsive readers (and re-readers) and had virtually all of Louisa May Alcott by heart, as well as much of Bret Harte, and they could act out between them most of the numbingly trite dialogue of the two eponymous brothers in the Hardy Boys mystery series. But the problem was that these literary leanings were mixed with such an autistic incompetence at simple things that you couldn't leave them alone for twenty minutes in case they accidentally burnt their house down.

Michael had never paid them much attention until Cassie had befriended them, and Ethel had subsequently taken to following her around like a puppy dog. Thereafter he had made a show of being attentive, bringing them Lifesavers from the drugstore when he remembered to, until in time he came to know them well and his interest became authentic. So he wondered where they were now, worrying that perhaps the reconstituted Wagner *ménage* had not worked out. Benny might have found them unmanageable without his father's firm hand to help. And what would paying guests have made of them?

He nearly tripped over a tree root that had erupted through the concrete pavement, so moved out into the street, which was lined all the way to Main Street by enormous maple trees, the few gaps in the avenues created by lightning strikes or disease. This was the oldest part of the town, and the houses remained mainly the original ones erected in the years after the town's founding during the Civil War, when the empty lots of the master grid were gradually filled in, like a game of checkers played backwards. The houses were built from the white pine lumber that provided the original incentive for people to settle here, and they sat on disproportionately small residential lots – rarely more than a quarter-acre. As if in devising that original grid, the town's settlers wanted to huddle together in a defensive measure against the elements (the local Indians had never been a danger), knowing that however snowbound and storm-struck a winter proved, you had neighbours almost within touching distance to help.

As he walked, Michael saw that many of the houses now bore plaques with the date when they were built. *1871, 1866, 1882.* It was a recent affectation: on his last visit, people had just begun to put them up, at the instigation of the local historical society which provided owners with a 'certified' date. His father had been contemptuous: 'Bert James came here to sell me one of those gewgaws and had the date wrong by fifteen years.' But then, his father had always found the local historical society insufferable, usually returning irritated from its meetings, which were attended chiefly by retirement residents of the town, interested only in the pedigree of their own properties, and indifferent to the town's real history: the eviction of its Indians, its rise and fall as a lumber town, its commercial rebound after World War II as a tourist Mecca.

It had become famous for its prettiness, this small lakeside town of old houses and tree-lined streets, but Michael had only come to recognize its quiet beauty after seeing it through someone else's eyes. *Someone else.* He intended to walk down Calvin Street, but two blocks shy of its reaching Main Street found himself moving over to Henniker – he couldn't help himself. There on a corner he saw the same small gable over Pastor Gilbert's front door, the same neat strip of lawn in front. But everything else had changed. The house had been painted, changed from traditional bone-white to a light mocha he didn't like at all. There was a new balcony outside the main bedroom – the pastor's bedroom – with pale oak struts coming out from the house to support it from below. Sound engineering, hideous effect. A further ground-floor room was under construction in the back, and there was a second garage where once there had been flower beds full of roses.

She must have sold up at last, he thought, feeling feeble about the sadness that threatened to fill him. And just an hour before, he had thought he couldn't feel much about anything or anyone. *Let it go*, he told himself.

He walked towards home on Fromm Street, cheered to see that at least Anthea Heaton's house was unchanged – the big porch with the swing was still there, where, as just a freshman in high school, Kenny Williams had taken off all of Anthea's clothes while her parents sat not twenty feet away inside watching television.

At the next corner Michael turned left, passing the one old brick house in town, where Reverend Parker had lived with his 'ward' in the days when openly homosexual life was unknown. At the corner sat Marilyn's bungalow, a long, low wooden structure, only one room wide, which had small cotton awnings over the south side windows. She'd had a stroke several years before, and according to his father's report was totally incapacitated, so he didn't stop to say hello.

He started to turn for home then decided to extend his walk, remembering how exposure to daylight was supposed to be the best antidote to jet lag. Nearing the eastern perimeter of the town, he passed the vacant lot owned by Harold Riesbach – still not built on – where in a far corner he and Donny would brave an immense tangle of brambles to pick a few choice wild raspberries. The old dairy still sat unoccupied next door, but a chalet-style summer house was going up on its east side. Now he was on the very edge of town, and came to Alvin's, which he inspected on foot more closely than he had from the car that morning. There was a new cyclone fence running along the property line, and several lilacs planted to replace the vast single bush which even in his childhood had gone woody. As always, the lawn was lush and thick and a rich, velvet green. He saw a little boy riding his bike in the yard, coming towards the fence. 'You must be Phil's little boy,' he said, but the kid just looked at him, mystified.

'*Hey!*' The shout came from the screened porch of the house. Then a man in cotton shorts and T-shirt charged out and ran down the steps, then sprinted towards them. With a hammer in his hand.

Keep calm, thought Michael. Probably the man had been nailing replacement siding onto the back of the house, or tacking down linoleum on the porch floor, but Michael was grateful nonetheless for the cyclone fence between him and the approaching figure. 'What do you want?' the man demanded, a little breathless as he neared.

'Nothing,' said Michael, holding his hands out as if to emphasize his harmlessness. 'I thought I was saying hi to Betty's grandson, but I guess I was wrong.'

'Who the hell is Betty?'

'Alvin's Simpson's widow. She used to live here. I thought she still did.'

The man shook his head but seemed less tense, and he relaxed his hold on the hammer. 'I bought the house from her son; she'd already moved to Florida. Sorry to be shouting like that, but we're all a little jumpy – there's been a murder in town.' He looked at Michael for a moment, and his suspicion seemed to return. 'Who are you, anyway?'

'My name is Wolf,' said Michael quietly. 'It was my father who was murdered.' He extended his hand across the top of the steel fence.

The man stared at it, slightly shocked, before slowly extending his own. 'I'm so sorry,' he said as they shook, then added, with Michael wondering how often in the days ahead he would hear this formulation, 'and so sorry for your loss.'

He drove the back way out of town, discovering more new houses stretched out along Park Street, even at the Twin Kilns, where his father had taught him to shoot, throwing clays with a hand device for Michael to fire at with the smaller .410 shotgun. He crossed over the interstate which ended ten miles north in Burlington. It had originally been meant to stretch north all the way to Traverse City, but construction had stopped during the lean years of the 1970s and never resumed.

Where the road curved left and north towards Burlington Michael went straight and east, onto what had been a sand surface but was now paved. The sun was high overhead and the day warm for May; here, entering the Back Country, the temperature could be ten degrees higher than by the lake. The older farmhouses had large hardwoods planted around them for shade, and lines of trees, oaks or maples, planted carefully in west-facing rows from the side of the house (to block the sun at noon) all the way to the end of the lengthy drives (to block the sinking sun of late afternoon). But the ubiquity of air conditioning made these traditional strategies unnecessary: by the iron bridge of the north branch of the Still there were many new houses, some no more than trailers hoiked up on blocks, positioned on the baking sand of the cheapest treeless land.

He decided not to go to the Half, for he realized he'd been fooling himself – it was Sheringham's he wanted to see. As he moved south the land began to roll, and turning onto Polk and heading east again he came to considerable hills. Polk was *The Roller Coaster Road* – his father's name for it when as a family they'd come back from the Half. He dipped down into a valley with horses grazing on one side, and halfway up the far side pulled over. The Sheringham house was at the top of the hill, but the stand itself was lower down, set back from the road in a half-moon drive, with a field immediately behind it full of asparagus, and orchards in the distance further back. There were three cars parked in front of the stand and a tractor approaching from the field towing a large box of asparagus.

He saw Nancy move out of the barn to the open shed where asparagus lay upright in racks, tied in bunches by rubber bands, two dollars per bunch. It was too early for anything else to be on sale, but soon there would be strawberries, then cherries and raspberries, salad onions, peppers, followed (in July) by the first corn, zucchini, then more corn, and pickling cucumbers and peaches galore, until finally the season ended with an autumn burst of apples, pears and hard squash. She and Lou had less than one hundred acres and Nancy had to substitute teach to make ends meet, but they sold a lot to the food middlemen in Fennville and at the height of the season the stand was busy with customers from early morning until suppertime.

As he neared the shed Nancy saw him. She looked unchanged – tall and big-boned, wearing overalls with her straight blonde hair cut shoulder-length. She had never been a beauty, never in fact a pretty girl, but she was strong-willed, lively and smart, and she drew many men to her – not least Donny, Michael's best friend in boyhood. He had gone out with her throughout college only to have her drop him after graduating for Lou, a farmer's son from Shelby. She had married Lou within a year and moved out of town to farm here, in the middle of the county. Unusually for these parts, she had kept her maiden name, and her own friends knew the farm by her rather than Lou's surname.

Now she finished giving change to a lady in pink pants and came over to him. She did not look surprised to see him. 'Michael, I was so sorry—' she began.

He held up a hand. 'I know,' he said. 'Thank you. It's good to see you, Nancy.'

'How long's it been?'

'Six years. Thanks for your cards.' Christmas cards, every year, with news about her family and, until the recent years, about Cassie, too.

'Thanks for yours. The girls always like to see where you've got to.'

He pointed to an apple-cheeked girl who looked about ten years old and was taking money from a fat woman in slacks. 'She's one of yours, isn't she?'

'That's Ellie. You've seen her before.'

'Sure. When she was all of four years old. Where's the other one? Hilary,' he said, risking the name, fairly confident he had it right.

'She's at basketball practice. Hoping for a scholarship. She's

36

taller than me but got my build, poor kid. No messing with her under the boards. She always asks about you when we get your postcards.' He usually sent one from wherever he happened to be working. Saudi, Germany, the Philippines, Sweden, Ireland, England, most recently Scotland. 'You *have* travelled. Makes us seem pretty provincial. Mind you,' she said with a laugh, 'we took the senior class all the way to Chicago last year.'

'That's pretty adventurous.'

'I'll say. I got dizzy at the top of the Sears Tower. One of the kids had to hold my hand all the way down in the elevator. So are you still mending bridges?'

'Fixing them. I fix bridges. I think you'll find it's fences that get mended.'

'I stand corrected,' she said with a short laugh. 'Gary said you were working in Scotland now.'

'That's right,' he said. 'It's nearing the end, though, so I'm leaving right after the funeral. I have to get back.'

'Aren't there things to tie up?'

He shook his head. 'Gary can do it easy enough.'

'Don't the police want to talk to you?'

'Jimmy Olds already has. I expect they'll want another session, but there's not much help I can give them. I haven't the faintest idea who would have killed my father. Absolutely none at all.'

'I'm surprised you're not staying longer.'

Why was she pushing him on this? 'I'll be back at some point. Maybe Christmas to make sure Gary's okay. The will should be through probate by then – I can't believe there's anything complicated. Gary can decide whether we should sell the house or if he wants to live there. I don't know. It's not like this is home any more.'

'Scotland is?' she asked with a dubious cast to her eyes.

'Nancy,' he said with a laugh, 'I'm glad you weren't ever my teacher. You don't let anybody win an argument. You haven't changed a whit.'

But Nancy wasn't smiling. 'This isn't an argument. I just thought you'd want to see her before you left.'

'Who?' He was genuinely puzzled.

'Cassie. Who else?'

'*What?*' he said for the second time in two days. 'Jimmy said they were still in Texas.'

'She moved back last summer with the kids, just before school started.'

'How old are those kids?' he asked, though he knew. *Calm down*, he told himself. *It doesn't mean anything.*

'Sally's ten and Jack's six. They're nice kids, they come out here a lot. Jack's a little hard to handle, but hey – that's what boys are like, right?'

'I heard Ronald killed somebody.'

'That's right. Not entirely on purpose, I guess. He just hit somebody too hard. You know Ronald.'

That I do. 'When did it happen?'

'About three years ago. I'd have told you, Michael, but I figured Cassie would tell you herself if—' and she left the sentence unfinished.

If she'd wanted me to know, he thought. 'Why did she move back?'

'She never liked Texas. Ronald's not going to die in prison – they convicted him of manslaughter, not murder – but the son of a bitch did get ten years. Excuse my French. Actually,' she said, seeing a city lady waiting impatiently with money in her hand, 'excuse *me* a minute.'

When she returned he asked, 'Is she back for good?'

'She's glad to be here, I know that. But she hasn't got a job and Ronald's not exactly in a position to pay her child support. She sold her daddy's house a while ago, and she's got some money left, but not a lot. She's living next to Turner's, near the wireworks, renting.'

'Has she divorced him?' He tried to sound calm about it.

'No.'

'Is she going to?'

Nancy reached over, took a bundle of asparagus from the racks, and gave it to him. 'Here, don't even think about paying for it. As for your question, ask her yourself.' She looked at him full on, her big cheekbones already showing freckles from time spent out in the fields. 'If you got to go back right away, fine, go ahead. But you come back, Michael, you come back soon. It's best for everybody. I don't want a foreign Christmas card this year, do you understand?'

He avoided the interstate on the way home, skirting around Fennville, the county seat. He drove by cherry orchards still in late blossom, then swept down the steeply angled slope of Happy Valley, not its official name (*was there one?* he wondered) but how the small, lush valley was known locally. At its bottom, the road crossed the south branch of the Still as it flowed from Fennville Lake towards the Junction and Stillriver. He crossed the simple wooden bridge of thin pine planks, with the river only a foot or two below; the river was slow here, and wider than upstream.

There was a black pickup truck parked in the lay-by and as he passed a man stepped out from its far side and waved at him urgently. Mystified, Michael pulled over. When he got out and walked back towards the river and the truck, he saw it was Donny, wearing hip waders and carrying his fishing rod.

'I thought it was you!' Donny was beaming, his vast features – fat cheeks and a wide grin – almost engulfing his tiny nose. As Donny stomped towards him, Michael thought, *He must weigh 250 pounds*, remembering the beanpole kid of his childhood. Donny was six foot three but seemed shorter now. Was it the extra weight? Maybe the hair, which had been cut as short as the crew cuts they had sported as kids. Back then they had been inseparable, which meant that Michael was happy enough to wallow now in the soft soap of reunited buddies, though as far as he was concerned there was a piece or two of grit in the lather.

'Don't tell me,' said Michael, pointing at Donny's rod, 'you've become some sort of "fly" fisherman. I never thought you'd switch from worms.' Donny's face changed expression. As he started to speak, Michael interrupted him. 'Don't you say how sorry you are. I couldn't stand it.'

Donny shook his head. 'But I *am* sorry. You all right?'

'I'm okay. To tell you the truth, I don't think it's really sunk in yet. It all still seems a little unreal.'

'I bet it does,' said Donny, laying his rod down flat on the back of his truck. 'Believe me, none of us can believe it either.'

Michael wanted to change the subject, so he pointed at the bridge. 'Water's high.'

'I'll say. You seen the Junction?' Michael nodded and Donny shook his head. 'I've been telling them for three years they've got to do something about it. They've scheduled a rebuild.' Then he hissed, 'For *2006*.'

Michael stared at the wooden bridge while thinking of the larger, concrete one downstream. 'It's got cracks and water stains and signs of spalling.'

'What's spalling?'

'Oh, nothing much,' he said dryly. 'Just concrete buckling where the internal reinforcements have corroded. I bet the piers are worse than the deck since they're sitting in the water. If *they* move, the beam may go and the whole thing will collapse.'

'Maybe you should be telling them instead of me.'

'It wouldn't take that much for them to go.' By which of course he meant something extraordinary would have to happen – a grocery truck, heavy-laden, skids and hits the railing. Or a speedboat, perversely going upriver instead of staying in the lake, strikes the pier full on. Or . . . who knows, who can predict a disaster made terrible precisely because it is so unpredictable? And the bridge gives way, entirely unexpectedly, and against all odds – which are of course phenomenally remote. Risk analysis was a 'discipline' with which Michael had enjoyed some contact, as in: *Mr Wolf, all things being equal and the political situation in the Sudan attaining equilibrium, would you say the odds of the Utaki Bridge collapsing within two hundred years were less than 0.5%?* It had always struck him as a futile exercise, for what did 0.5% mean? To his impatient way of thinking, either disaster happened or it didn't; either a bridge collapsed, a causeway slithered into the sea, a river flooded and drowned a city's thousands, or . . . it didn't. Simple enough, but then, he wasn't in the business of reassuring insurance companies.

He looked at Donny. 'Is money the problem? I thought the economy was booming. I thought even Oscar Peters could get rich from the internet.'

Donny looked contemplative. 'Oscar died, you know. Choked to death on a chicken bone.'

'Jimmy Olds said so.' There was a pause, then Michael asked, 'So how have you been?'

'Good,' said Donny. 'Brenda's fine, kids are okay, though they'll be teenagers soon enough. Still, the kids in town don't seem to smoke dope the way we used to, and thank God there's not much hard drugs here. Who can get mad at them for drinking beer? You'll have to come by and see us all. How long you here for?'

'Funeral's Tuesday, then I got to get back. I'll try and come round tomorrow. If not, I'll be back again.'

'What else did Jimmy say? They got any idea who did it?'

'No.' He told Donny about the swastika. When he'd finished Donny was silent for a moment. Then he said, 'Ever since they discovered that one of McVeigh's accomplices was a Michigan Militia member the authorities have started seeing para-militaries behind everything.'

'I thought the Militia barely existed any more.'

'It doesn't. But there's a splinter group up here. Though how you have a splinter of a splinter is beyond me.'

'Who are they?'

'You remember Raleigh Somerset? You know, the kid in Fennville who went to school here for a little while.'

'Oh, the dumb guy with the big ears.' He remembered him from junior high. Raleigh was bigger than the rest of them, even bigger than Donny, but awkward with it and very stupid, given to bragging about the exploits of his father and brothers in almost moronic fashion: his daddy knew the President, his brother had flown on Air Force One. Stupid lies, like the fabrications of a grade school braggart, entirely unconvincing to an audience who possessed the scepticism of early adolescence.

Even Michael's father, usually scrupulous not to comment on his students, found Raleigh preposterous. 'Imagination is a good thing to have, but young Raleigh kind of overdoes it.'

'That's him,' said Donny. 'The one who almost drowned.'

'Ronald saved him,' Michael interjected, so Donny wouldn't feel he had to avoid the name of Raleigh's rescuer.

'That's right. Ronald jumped in and pulled him out of the channel. Anyway, Raleigh moved to Detroit and joined the Militia down there. He got in some trouble; I heard they had him before a Grand Jury. Then he moved back here – he's got a place out by Walkerville now, not far from the Half – and started holding meetings. He doesn't call it the Militia any more; he calls it the Michigan Marines.'

'Membership booming?'

'Of course not. I mean, honestly, nobody admits to *liking* the government, but what exactly does that mean? Almost everything's state or local government, and it's kind of hard to get very worked up about the Post Office. But a bunch of them get together out by Spring Valley, and it's Raleigh who organizes things. To be honest, I think it's mainly social. If they're not out in the woods playing war games they're sitting around drinking beer.' Donny looked thoughtful for a moment. 'I don't think the swastika has anything to do with them. I mean, why would a bunch of rednecks want to hurt your dad?'

'Jimmy asked me if Pop might have been a Jew.'

'Your father?' Donny looked surprised. 'I thought he was Episcopalian. You used to go to church when we were kids.'

'Sunday school. He'd only go once in a while – Christmas, Easter, that kind of thing. It was my mother who cared about it.'

'Yeah, but he did go. He wouldn't have if he'd been Jewish, would he now?'

Michael shrugged. 'He'd have been hard-pressed to do much about it if he was a Jew. I haven't seen any synagogues around here lately, have you?' Michael looked out across the flood plain and could just make out a duck blind that sat halfway across the vast basin of grass and water. 'I never knew a lot about my father's background. He didn't ever talk about it. Not that we talked very much the last few years.' He fell silent at this. *Does a letter count?* he wondered, remembering the last surprising communication from his father, just a few months before.

'That's no more your fault than his. You'd have got close again.'

Again? He and his father had never been close. Michael sighed. 'I feel bad I'll never know. Anyway, all I really know is that he came from Detroit, and couldn't wait to get out of there.'

'Well, whatever he was, he wasn't a Jew while he was here, was he? If his own son didn't think he was it doesn't seem like the Marines would either.' Donny took off his waders and threw them in the back of the truck, then retrieved his work boots and put them on without bending down, standing there with the laces untied. 'It's good to see you, Michael, but I got to get going or there won't be anyone home to look after the kids. Try and come by tomorrow. Please?'

'I will,' he said. 'But relax, I'll be back soon anyway.'

'What's soon mean? Christmas? You going to spend the new millennium night with all of us here?' Donny laughed.

Michael shook his head. 'No, I'll be back before then.' An image of Cassie on the beach entered his head, wading into Lake Michigan wearing oversized basketball shorts and a T-shirt, laughing at him laughing at her. 'You'll see me this summer,' he said, fully aware he'd said Christmas to Nancy.

'Good,' said Donny, climbing into the truck. He started the engine and put it in gear. As he started to roll away he stuck his head out and suddenly stopped the truck. 'Michael, have you been out to Sheringham's yet?'

'I'm on my way back from there. Why?'

Donny looked uncomfortable. 'So Nancy told you, right?'

Donny was the last person he was going to confide in. 'Yeah, she told me all right.'

'That's okay then. See ya.' And he drove away in a spray of gravel, as Michael thought, *Yes, everybody, I know she's back,* and then turned and looked for fish under the bridge.

4

ON SUNDAY A detective named Maguire came up from Muskegon to conduct a formal interview. They sat in the living room while Jimmy Olds hovered, a little embarrassed, in the kitchen.

Michael had not expected someone out of Raymond Chandler, but Maguire still came as something of a surprise. The surname matched an expectation of ethnicity derived from the television of Michael's youth – *Kojak, Banacek, Mannix* – but there seemed nothing particularly Irish about the young man who now sat across from him. He was trim and had the build of a lightweight boxer – long hanging arms, almost simian, wide shoulders and a dancer's tiny tapered waist. He wore a blue blazer, white shirt, spanking yellow tie, and tasselled loafers; the effect was natty, and reinforced by his hair, which was straight and neatly styled with a part on the left side. Although probably only half a dozen years younger than Michael, he looked just out of his teens, for despite the addition of a neat moustache his face was youthful and unlined, and his expression managed to be alert and polite at the same time. He looked the kind of young man you would happily allow to take your teenage daughter waterskiing. *Waterskiing?* thought Michael, imagining the snobbish snickers of his east coast friends and his east coast ex-wife. *Yes, waterskiing. Fuck them.*

Maguire taped the interview, and began with the kind of formal questions – 'Please state your full name and current address,' – which made Michael feel as if he were a suspect. When he asked about Michael's whereabouts on the night of the murder, Michael got out the stub of his plane ticket and showed the dated stamp in his passport. There was a faint but perceptible relaxation in Maguire's manner.

Maguire said, 'I was hoping to get a better sense of your father. Where did he come from?'

44

'Detroit, though I'm not sure what part of the city. He moved up here a few years after the Korean War. He served in that.'

'Is there family still down there?'

'None that I know of. He was an only child. His father left when he was a boy and his mother died after he came back from Korea. He never mentioned any cousins. I think his mother had a brother but he never talked about him. I'm pretty sure they weren't in touch.'

'So he didn't have any family at all?'

'No. We just knew my mother's family.'

'Was your mother local?'

'Grand Rapids.'

'And there is still family there?'

He thought of his myriad cousins. 'Lots of it. They were lumber people, then lawyers.' *Why am I telling him that? Slow down*, he told himself, since Maguire's questions were coming right on the heels of his replies.

'Did they get on with your father?'

Meaning did they dislike him sufficiently to murder him, twenty-odd years after his wife, their relative, had died? 'Well enough, I think.'

'How did your mother and father meet?'

'My mother's parents had a house on South Beach – that's the other side of Stillriver Lake. There's an association, sort of a compound, with Grand Rapids people who built summer houses there a long time ago. My mother would come up here every summer with her folks. She met my father at a Yacht Club dance, one thing led to another and they got married.'

'And that was okay with her parents?'

Michael looked at the youthful detective. *The man is only doing his job,* he told himself. *Don't get mad.* 'There was nothing unrespectable about my father. He just didn't have any family.'

'Okay,' said Maguire. 'But he does sound a little unusual.'

Michael shook his head. 'I wouldn't put it quite that way.'

'Would others?'

'He always got along with people. He was friendly, and he

45

liked living here.' He remembered once asking his father why he hadn't wanted to teach in a bigger school, a bigger town. His father had snorted. 'Why eat crackers if your pantry's full of dinner rolls?'

Maguire stared at Michael, then asked, 'Yes, but did he fit in?'

What are you, an anthropologist? 'There was nothing eccentric about him. He was simply a little – and I stress the word "little" – reserved. Even with us.'

'Did he get on with your neighbours?'

'He did in my time; I'd be surprised if that had changed. You must have spoken to them.'

'I have.' Maguire took out a small spiral notebook from his jacket and flipped through its pages. He spoke rapidly as he looked at his notes. 'The Jenkinses say he was the ideal neighbour. They heard nothing the other night. Billy Decatur said he'd known him all his life – his grandmother used to live there. He and his wife were asleep. Harry Montague and his wife were at a crafts fair in Mount Pleasant and spent the night there.'

'Who is Harry Montague?'

Maguire looked surprised, then pointed with a thumb in the kitty-corner direction. *Oh,* thought Michael, *the Mean Man's son.*

Maguire continued, 'Benny Wagner had two sets of guests staying in his B & B; we're still checking them, but they were couples and seem ordinary enough. Same goes for him. The Bogles, well,' and he looked up and grinned, 'they're something, aren't they?'

Michael said, 'We never had any trouble with any of them. Believe it or not.'

'Actually, I believe you. In any case, all the brothers were in Baldwin that night. We've checked their story and it's true. Their sister was the only one here. There are others I talked to if you want to hear about them, but I've done the neighbourhood pretty thoroughly, and it looks clean to me.'

'That's fine,' Michael said, thinking he hadn't asked for any of this.

'Tell me something,' asked Maguire. 'Were you close to your father?'

'Well, not recently. I hadn't seen him in six years.'

'Was your brother closer to him than you when you were kids?'

'Yeah. He was my father's favourite.'

'Did you mind that?'

'No.' *Are you being a psychologist now? I only minded after she died. I was* her *favourite.*

'Six years is a long time not to see your father.'

'I work overseas. It's not easy to get back.'

'Still,' Maguire said, and looked at Michael, letting the word hang in the air.

'There was no bust-up. We just didn't see each other. I called him once in a while – on his birthday and Christmas.'

'Was he Jewish? I'm only wondering because of the swastika.'

'Jimmy Olds asked me that already, and I told him not as far as I know. He wasn't especially religious, but he sometimes went to church. He certainly never said he was a Jew.'

'Your brother told me categorically your father *wasn't* Jewish. Does that mean you might have thought he was?'

'It never even crossed my mind.'

'You're separated, right?'

Gary must have told him that. 'Divorced.'

'Are you still in touch with your ex-wife?'

'She's the one who called me about my father. Gary rang her because he couldn't track me down.'

'Your brother indicated that your wife didn't seem to like your father very much.' *Thanks, little brother. What else did you tell this guy?* 'She barely knew him.'

'Still, did she have any grounds for disliking him?'

'Only the grounds of social superiority.' Michael laughed for the first time. 'She was from the kind of family who thought that the slaves should be freed in order to become domestic servants. That's not the kind of attitude that would endear her to my father. He disliked all sorts of things, but he was never a snob, and he never liked labelling people. When folks started publicizing their roots – you know, "I'm proud to be Polish", that kind of thing – my father was contemptuous. He thought the whole point of America was to forget about that stuff.'

'Was he prejudiced himself?'

'Well, like I say, he didn't like groups or labels. But he wasn't a Nazi if that's what you're getting at. *He* didn't put the swastika on. There was a black family in town. My father always went out of his way to be nice to them. A lot of people did the opposite.' *Yeah, and what did that really count for?* He remembered a stand-up comic in New York announcing, 'Some of my best friends are niggers . . .' The audience had sat in stunned silence, until a black man near the stage started laughing. He looked at Maguire. 'Which are you thinking he was anyway, a fascist or a Jew?'

'I was hoping you'd tell me. What about the Michigan Marines?'

'What about them? Until yesterday I'd never even heard of them.'

Maguire nodded. 'How would your father have felt about them?'

'He'd think they were a sick joke.'

Maguire's eyes widened. 'And your brother?'

Your turn to tell me, he wanted to say, since he sensed he was being drawn on something Maguire already knew. He waited until the detective added, '*He* doesn't seem to think they're a joke.'

'I don't think it's something he feels especially strongly about.'

'Strong enough to attend meetings, I understand.'

Gary, you idiot, he thought, and found himself growing irritated. 'Well, in that case you understand more than me.'

Maguire changed tack. 'Was your father a popular teacher?'

Michael thought for a moment. 'I'd say respected rather than popular.'

'For his intellect?'

Michael laughed for the second time. 'Probably more for his size.'

Maguire persevered. 'But he was pretty intellectual, wasn't he? I mean, that room,' – he nodded his head towards the study – 'it's just full of books.'

'He read a lot. I wouldn't have called him intellectual.' He felt weary of the questioning. 'I'm not sure I'm helping you much, Detective, so let me ask you something.'

'Shoot.'

'Do you have any idea who did this?'

Maguire shook his head. 'Not really. The one thing I would have to say is that this was a very violent crime.' Seeming to remember that he was talking to the son of the victim, he suddenly stopped talking.

'It's okay,' said Michael. 'Jimmy told me my father was hit more than once. It seems a pretty messy way to kill somebody.'

'Exactly,' said Maguire. 'And yet it must have been carefully planned; the doctor thinks it happened at three in the morning, give or take an hour. Whoever did it wasn't staying here – at least, there weren't any indications that your father had an overnight guest. But I would bet my bottom dollar this was not a burglary. Nothing got stolen. Whoever did it snuck in quite deliberately. Either he knew your father always left the door unlocked, or he was going to force his way in and just got lucky.'

Michael said, 'If you wanted to kill a man, this wasn't the most reliable way to do it, was it? You'd use a gun, maybe with a silencer. Or you'd use a knife.'

Maguire nodded, and Michael concluded, 'So whoever did this had more hate in him than sense.'

Maguire looked at Michael thoughtfully. 'I hope you're right there, because that will make it a lot easier to catch him. The problem is, this person was really very careful. We haven't got hammered shit to work with: forensics haven't found a thing. So I'm sorry to have asked all these nosy questions, and I appreciate your patience with me, especially when I must be barking up quite a few wrong trees. But to be honest, that's about all I can do right now: bark, and then hope something falls out of the tree.'

TUESDAY EVENING HE sat in his car with the lights out underneath a large sycamore tree outside Buckling's Gun Shop, which was a dirty shack of a place, filled with stray ammo and shotguns and rifles held in badly-fitting racks and old cupboards. The shop was closed and the night was moonless dark, but if he peered carefully, with his window rolled down, he could see quite clearly into the kitchen of the low bungalow across the street, where an overhead light bathed the room in a honey-coloured glow.

He watched as she set the table for breakfast, carefully arranging three places, then putting out two big boxes of cereal. Finished, she began ironing, setting up the board next to the stove, taking each garment out of a purple plastic tub of clean laundry.

The soft black hair was shorter now, cut just above the shoulders in back with a straight fringe in front that brushed her eyebrows. She wore blue jeans and a long-sleeved flannel shirt that looked far too big for her. As she ironed, she bit her lower lip with her front teeth, a sign of intense concentration he had liked in her from the start.

The little boy came in, dressed in pyjamas, and she put the iron down and hugged him, then took him by the hand and led him out of the kitchen. After a few minutes a light went off in a room at the side of the house, and he decided she was saying goodnight to her son. In a minute she returned to the kitchen and resumed her ironing until her daughter appeared, also dressed for bed, and the same ritual was repeated.

He watched, and wondered what had brought him here, why he was sitting outside spying – that was, after all, what he was doing. He was very tired and had a long trip ahead of him the next day (and the day after that) back to his reconstructed bridge on the west coast of Scotland. And before he left, he would still have one final conversation with the police. *It's only Jimmy Olds*, he told himself, and he could imagine the language of the autopsy report: *a bisectional trapezoid concussion of the left cranial quadrant measuring 3.23 inches by .65 inches . . . Blah blah blah.* What they really meant to say was *somebody smashed his head in.*

He would also need to make plans with Gary about what had to be done, and try to find out without a major fight just why his little brother would, of all things, attend local meetings of the Michigan Marines. Then he'd have to go downtown to the bank to sort out his father's accounts, and leave a note for Atkinson the lawyer to call him about the will (if there was a will) whenever Atkinson returned from drying out, and no doubt there would be countless other chores he hadn't even thought of yet. But despite, or perhaps because of all these things to do, he was happy now to sit in the car watching through her kitchen window as she continued ironing.

It seemed both as if he'd been back for months and as if he had barely been back at all. The funeral had been simple and straightforward, conducted in a light drizzle by an earnest young Episcopal minister he had never met, on a slope of the new part of the cemetery unsheltered by trees. He had felt upset only when the minister mentioned the proximity of his mother's grave to the freshly dug one in which they were about to put his father.

Other than that brief moment, he had felt . . . well, nothing much at all, not even when the cousins had come back and tried to make friendly small talk with him and Gary (who had cried during the service), trying to disguise their manifest curiosity about this old wooden house where their relative – his mother – had elected to come and spend her life, clearly struggling to understand why she would have left the fine lawns and large modern rooms of a Grand Rapids suburb to live with the slightly mysterious man they had just buried.

He hadn't gone by Donny's house, not because he didn't want to see his boyhood friend, but because he didn't want to see another family's happiness right then. After her sole visit to

Stillriver, his ex-wife Sarah had declared, 'I wish I'd known your family while your mother was alive . . . Because now it's totally dysfunctional.' And Michael had snapped back, 'It's not dysfunctional. It doesn't function at all.'

He was, he knew, a master of repressed emotion. Repressed? In his day-to-day life now, there was almost nothing he felt strongly about; he had no emotions to repress. And what he did feel was always tied up in his past, visiting him on occasion, unbidden, unwanted. Why, if his father had managed to send his own past away, or leave it, couldn't his son do the same? So he was surprised to be struck for the second time since his return by an almost overpowering feeling of sadness, though he was too well trained and too self-conscious to yield to it, even here alone in his car – as an adult, he had never been able to cry. With the sadness came a powerful sense of regret, one that seemed to sweep through his past as he surveyed it. Regret that his mother had died when he still needed her so badly, regret that his father had died before the two of them had made their peace, and regret that he had not been here to save his father as his father had once saved him. Finally, and achingly, regret that she was there inside, while he sat outside, alone in a rental car. *I am wifeless, childless, loveless,* he told himself, not for the first time.

But at least I am here, he told himself, *at least I still care enough to spy.* And as he recognized this in himself, for the first time in . . . how long? Six, seven years? For the first time in that long he saw at least the remote possibility that the cloud he felt around him – the cloud he thought of as the past – might lift, and that just possibly, in time, he might find himself able to live in the present. *Present and well accounted for.* He looked through the window and saw that Cassie was no longer there, then the kitchen light went out.

Two

HER NAME, ACCORDING to Donny, was Cassie Gilbert. 'Funny kind of name,' said Donny.

'Gilbert? What's funny about that?'

'Not that name. Cassie. What's it stand for?'

'How would I know?' asked Michael, and changed the subject.

He hadn't really noticed the new girl in class because he was entranced by geometry. He had always been good at math, but found 'tinkering with numbers' (his father's phrase) too finicky to inspire him, and somehow soulless. In geometry he found a purity that made him feel clean.

He noticed her after this, and would have eventually anyway, since she was pretty, and the students in his year comprised only sixty-five teenage boys and girls. But the quiet, attractive girl who dressed so demurely – knee socks (knee socks for God's sake!) and skirts or corduroy pants – was not going to intrude in his world. He didn't want a girlfriend anyway, he told himself, though part of him did. The problem was simple: he knew enough, even just turned sixteen, to sense that any girl he was interested in was going to suffer by comparison to his mother two years dead.

Still, he proved easy prey when Nancy Sheringham cornered him at break one morning, a little over a month later. 'What are you doing tomorrow after school?'

'Working.'

'No you're not. It's Wednesday. Store's closed at one.'

He had forgotten what day it was. He looked at her suspiciously. 'So?'

'There's something I want you to do for me. A favour.'

'What's that then?'

She hesitated for the first time. 'Well, it's not exactly for me, you see.'

Nancy was never this coy. 'Oh?'

'A friend of mine needs help with the math test on Friday, and you're elected. That's the bad news.'

What was going on? It didn't work that way, as he wanted to say to Nancy. Sure, you might help your friends on occasion – but on something *specific:* how long was the Rio Grande, say, right before a quiz, or *tell me the plot of the story I didn't read.* There was even mild cheating in the classroom itself, like when Candy Simmons dropped the contents of her purse all over the floor so Mr Walwicki's attention was diverted while Louise Grade flipped her chemistry notes to Sarah Fane during the end of term exam. But an hour? Unheard of. Nancy must be out of her mind. Now he said as much to her.

'Ah, but you haven't heard the good news yet, buster. Your pupil is the nicest girl in class. Probably the prettiest too.'

Cathy Stallover was the prettiest girl in the class by miles, but in the lowest fifth percentile when it came to nice. She was also in a different league socially – her last boyfriend had been a marine. He looked at Nancy, who seemed strangely confident he was going to do what she asked, and said, 'If you're feeling sorry for Lindsay Morag again,' – Lindsay, who might have been pretty if God had omitted to put a hump halfway down her back – 'you can find another sucker.'

Nancy was shaking her head. 'What a way to talk,' she scolded. And then she laughed, a loud laugh that for some reason always reminded Michael of munching apples. A harsh but happy sound. 'No, it's not Lindsay Morag. Would I do that to you?'

'Without batting an eye. So who is it?'

'Cassie Gilbert.' And she stood back with visible pride to watch his reaction.

Which, inexplicably, was to blush, something he usually did only when he was trying to insist a lie he'd told was true. 'Since when is she your friend?' He hadn't even seen them talk together, much less act like bosom pals.

'Since she came out for basketball. She's good, too.' High praise from the women's team captain and high scorer the year before. 'She was all-county reserve her last year of junior high. That was down in Saugatuck.'

'That's what she says.'

Nancy shook her head. 'I saw the photograph at her house. They're living in that little house across from the Episcopal Church.'

'Why did they move here?'

Nancy looked at him. 'Her mother died last spring. Her daddy took early retirement after that and they moved to Stillriver because he wanted to. But I don't think he's very well either – Cassie has to go home every day to make his lunch. Not that he sounds grateful. I think he's pretty tough on her. That's where you come in.'

'How's that?' As was often the case dealing with Nancy, he was starting to feel slightly jello-like, being shaped and reshaped to accord with her requirements.

'He won't let her play basketball unless she gets all As and Bs. She said the way it's going now she won't even get a C in geometry – she almost flunked that first quiz. So over to you, Mr Math Whiz.'

'You expect me to spend my free time helping your new friend so she can play basketball with you?'

Nancy looked him right in the eye. 'That's right.' She put a hand on his shoulder and pushed him playfully. 'It's not so bad, Michael. Who knows? Maybe she'll think you're cute.'

And for the first time in more than two years, Michael found himself looking forward to something.

When his mother died, he was in the eighth grade and not quite fourteen years old. Later, he could never remember much about the first few months after her death in April.

He had gone back to school after the funeral, played baseball that spring, but his days seemed completely empty, direction-less, pilotless. For he had lost his lodestar. It was not that he had been a clingy child, or in any sense a 'mama's boy'. Rather, he had been so favoured by his mother, so instilled with con-fidence, that he could use her – 'use' was the word; he felt guilty about this – as a touchstone to which he could return from his forays, increasingly adventurous, into the world. He had been like a puppy charging ahead on an extendable lead, full of a happy illusion of complete independence, knowing in the back of his mind that the lead was there if he got into serious trouble. And then the lead had snapped.

At school he kept to himself, not speaking much even to Donny, going home every afternoon and sitting in his own bedroom, listless, unwilling to do his homework, unable to read anything else. He had tried listening to music, he had tried listening to himself – thinking about thinking he grew to call it – but nothing helped. Time passed like molasses with sand in it, infinitely slow yet abrasive and painful. He thought: *I have to get out of here before I die too*. But where could he go? He had exactly forty-three dollars saved and not even a prospective haven in his head. His uncle's place in Grand Rapids? He'd ship him back the same day. The streets of Chicago or Detroit? No thanks, forty-three dollars wouldn't last long there. No, he was stuck in Stillriver at least until the end of high school. *Four more years*. It looked like a century to him.

In the absence of his mother, Michael might have grown closer to his father, particularly had there been any overtures from him. But instead his father withdrew, growing even more aloof, managing to double his official territory as a parent (since he was forced to assume his dead wife's responsibilities as well) while actually shrinking his emotional range. Henry Wolf hunkered down into a routine that was deliberately solitary: he read during virtually every spare moment he had outside of teaching and the cooking and household chores he now did. And walked, long walks out Park Street, usually on weekend mornings, though sometimes also in the evenings during spring and summer when the light held late.

Years later, Sarah showed Michael a story she'd read by a man in New York who had grown up in the Midwest and lost his mother as a little boy. Every evening after supper, he and his father would walk round and round the dining room table, the father's arm slung loosely over the little boy's shoulder, walking

58

away their grief in a daily ritual. Michael had thought, *Why couldn't my father have done that with me?*

What interest his father did take in his sons seemed confined to Gary; sometimes he took him along on his walks, while Michael went over to Donny's house. This upset Michael more than he would admit even to himself, and it also mystified him, since he found Gary just plain irritating. He didn't play baseball, he didn't like to read; all he seemed to want to do was hog the television and watch his dumb-ass cartoons. And he was a little thief, too, as Michael discovered when he caught Gary red-handed, taking three dollars out of his chest of drawers. When Michael exploded their father had come into the room, but it was Michael he shook roughly before Michael had a chance to explain.

That evening his father had called him into his study and Michael had thought, *Maybe he'll say he's sorry.* But there had been no apology for grabbing him, only more expressions of concern about his younger brother: 'He's just a little guy. I need you to help me watch out for him.' Which Michael assumed was supposed to flatter him and make him feel grown up. But he didn't feel grown up at all. *Don't I need watching out for too?* he had thought. His father wouldn't even help him with his homework: 'Son, it wouldn't really be right,' he'd claimed. 'I teach there after all.' And Michael had thought, *So what? You're my dad, aren't you? Mom would have helped me.*

It didn't seem a family any more. The three of them ate together (unless Michael went for supper at a friend's house, usually Donny's), sometimes shopped together, and twice a year (Christmas and Easter) attended church together. But in their time together there was no joy for any of them, and there were no more outings of the informal kind that marked his childhood – trips to the Half and long rides through the Back Country, picnics on the banks of the south branch of the Pere Marquette, a sudden decision to turn off the record player and go to the movies on Saturday night. Oddly for a man of his generation, his father had always left the driving to his wife. In her absence now he drove only when absolutely required to, and spontaneous fun had become an impossibility. On Michael's birthday that first summer, his father gave him a cheque instead of a present.

Even baseball failed to lift his spirits, associated as it was with his mother. She had always encouraged him to play, and though completely ignorant of the intricacies of, say, the infield fly rule, was happy to let him expound on its complications for hours. In the year after her death, he stuck like glue to his memory of her at the school baseball diamond, the image of her standing by the bleachers as he took infield practice: a tall woman with straight, corn-coloured hair that came to her shoulders, in a blue dress of light cotton that was almost diaphanously thin, and sandals the colour of caramel. A pretty woman (to Michael beautiful), who never made the slightest effort to look good – no make-up, no nail polish, no jewellery except for her gold wedding band. Freckly skin that turned pink in the early summer sun and was only slightly tanned by Labor Day. A striking face, with high cheekbones, a sliver-thin nose, and eyes the colour of lapis lazuli. The effect was decorous until she laughed, with that crooked lower tooth and lips that seemed to stretch from ear to ear. When she smiled at him out on the field, Michael felt he could do anything.

She attended all his games; his father never did. His father hadn't even played catch with him as a little boy, and when he'd once asked him why had said only, 'I don't know how.' Which proved, strangely enough, to be the truth. Unlike the other teachers at school, Michael's father coached no sport, took no interest in the teams, extra- or intra-mural, attended no basketball games, watched no track and field events, did not help raise money through a summer bazaar to build the school new tennis courts. This distanced him slightly from most of the other teachers; more important, in Michael's view, it distanced him from Michael. His mother tried to explain: 'Your father didn't have time to play sports when he was young. He had to go to work.' Doubtless this was admirable, but Michael wanted only to have a father who would play ball with him.

The summer after his mother died, Michael was too old for

Little League, but he made it into the Colts, playing against older boys. He was used to playing shortstop in Little League, pitching on those occasions when fat Ronny Buell ran out of steam and got shellacked. He was an okay fielder with a strong arm but what he could really do was hit, not for power (he had grown two inches in the last year but still weighed all of 124 pounds), but solidly, always making contact, drawing lots of walks, batting well over .400 in his last year of Little League.

Now against these bigger boys in the new league he was demoted to right field and batted seventh in the order. He played well enough, but found it joyless, being younger than his team-mates and therefore not their social equal, spending innings in the field trying not to think about his own misery, counting cracks in the dugout's mud floor when there was no prospect of batting soon.

He was nonetheless hitting a more than respectable .326 when they faced Shelby under the ancient lights in that town's park. They were losing 2–1 in the second inning when he came to bat against a tall, lanky kid he'd never seen before – later he learned he was seventeen years old, a vacationing ringer called in for the night who'd already had Big League scouts watching him at his high school in Flint.

He took a fastball strike that absolutely zipped in. As a team-mate said in the first inning, 'It comes at you like a raisin-sized piece of piss.' He stepped out of the box, ignoring the catcher who was laughing at his obvious discomfiture. He swung far too early on the second pitch, missing altogether a slower breaking ball he should have waited for and punched to right field. Cross with himself, he tensed up now, the count 0–2, and watched as the next pitch came out of the pitcher's hand like a fastball but with obvious spin.

SLIDER, his mind registered, which was all he remembered after the ball failed to break and hit him square in the left ear, precisely where the ear flap would have been if he hadn't worn his lucky helmet, which didn't have an ear flap.

He never lost consciousness, but he was severely concussed. Stretchered from the field, he spent a night in Fennville Hospital for observation. When he woke up in the early morning, he found his father sitting on a metal chair reading a history of Michigan Indians. Michael felt dizzy and nauseated. 'The pitch didn't move,' he complained.

His father looked up briefly from his book. 'Apparently, neither did you.'

He missed the last four games of the season, but was relieved at this. For he was scared now, frightened at the prospect of facing pitchers again, though he felt he could tell no one of his fears. *I could have told Mom.* He knew that somehow he should go to the batting cage in Burlington and face the Iron Mike there, set it at top speed. Wasn't that what you were supposed to do, get back on the horse when it had just bucked you off?

His depression was gone, replaced by fear. At first, baseball was the obvious source, but soon he couldn't have said what he was afraid of; only that arbitrarily, quite out of the blue, an unsettled feeling would come on which escalated into a sense of vulnerability that had him looking around, as if under attack. Even on the beach, where he had always loved to swim, he could grow frightened, finding the sand sweeping into water somehow intimidating and scary in its expansiveness. It seemed that, with his mother gone from the world, she was also gone from her supporting position in his head – as if some inner mother had disappeared too. The first time he woke up in the middle of the night, badly frightened – of what? Burglars? Ghosts? he was never really sure – he had gone to the door of the small bedroom where his father now slept. 'Pop,' he called out, tentatively.

He heard the heavy frame of his father roll over in bed. 'What's the problem?'

Michael hesitated. 'I thought I heard something downstairs.'

There was a pause. 'Well, you didn't,' his father said. There was another pause. 'Now go back to bed. You've got school tomorrow.'

After that when he woke up in the night he turned his light on and read (baseball books: he finished all the works the school library held by John R. Tunis in six months of broken nights). If he concentrated hard enough on the book the fear would subside; if it was especially bad, he'd turn on his transistor radio as well, tuned low to a Detroit talk show – the company of voices was more comforting than music – until he'd suddenly wake up at daybreak with the bedside lamp on, a book on his chest, and a voice describing the traffic jams near Cobo Arena.

It was strange, this fear, especially for a once-confident boy growing up in a small town. So where did it come from? He wasn't sure; he knew only that it had arrived with the slider that didn't break, that shattering pitch that seemed to have told him, *You are exposed. And there is no one to hide behind.* He felt small, and vulnerable, and afraid. He did not see how he would ever be able to become a man.

He wanted to huddle, secure in his small bedroom, clutched up like a neurotic war veteran suffering from shell shock. And what he did was a variant of this, for he spent the afternoons, sitting on the carpeted floor of his bedroom, playing imaginary games with marbles his mother had given him years before. He divided the marbles into two teams, and had them play an odd kind of football game between them; sometimes, they divided into warring nations, with heroes (his favourite was the blue marble with a slight chip) leading squads into battle against marble foes. Strange? Of course, and a childlike reversion that gave him some comfort and a feeling of protection. He didn't want to go anywhere; in his room he was safe. *I am becoming peculiar*, he told himself, using those very words, *but I don't know what else to do.*

Oddly, it was his father who changed things. 'You busy today?' he said one Saturday morning at breakfast. It was halfway through autumn, cold now but too early for snow, and a little more than six months after Michael's mother had died. Michael shook his head. He was never busy now. His father picked up his newspaper and began reading the front page. As he turned the page he said calmly, 'You might want to go down to the drugstore and talk to Alvin. He's looking for somebody to help out there. Might be time you got a part-time job.'

He didn't make it downtown until almost noon, torn between curiosity and resentment at his father's suggestion. Not, actually, at the suggestion itself, but at his father's making it. *The one time he has an idea for me*, Michael thought, *and it's intended to get me out of his hair*. When he walked in the store he saw Alvin Simpson at the back, serving someone at the liquor counter. Michael knew Alvin to say hello to, and remembered standing as a little boy in the store holding his father's hand, while the two men loomed above him, deep-voiced, sometimes laughing, while he tried to keep patient, hoping he would be allowed to pick out a sucker or roll of Choco-mints on the way out.

Now Michael looked down the store and wondered how even to speak to the man without his father present. What did he know about Alvin Simpson, except that he sat on the school board and that Michael's father would talk to him when he shopped in the store? What had his mother once said? Something about Alvin's similarity to Pop, that Alvin too had picked Stillriver instead of letting it pick him. Whatever that meant.

Michael walked slowly round the store, trying to gather his nerve; he didn't understand why, but the fear was there again. Cigarettes, candy, gum, newspapers, magazines, paperback books, the soda fountain, sun tan lotion, shaving cream, beer in the twin iceboxes – like Alvin, they all looked different now, oddly alien, as if bathed in a new kind of light. Suddenly he was at the liquor counter and found Alvin looking at him.

'Mr Simpson, I heard you were looking for someone to work here.'

'That's right.' He looked amused. 'Anyone you can recommend?'

Flustered, Michael started to stutter until Alvin spoke again. 'Pay is a dollar seventy-five an hour. I take taxes out at source. I want you four to six on weekdays, nine to six Saturdays and eight to one Sundays – I need help putting the papers together.

Summer hours are longer. You can start tomorrow. How's that?'

There goes baseball, he thought with relief. 'Okay.'

'Let me introduce you to Marilyn.'

They walked up to the front of the store where a thin old sharp-jawed lady in a white uniform stood behind the peanuts counter, her back to the cigarette racks. She was smoking herself. 'Marilyn, this is Michael. Henry Wolf's boy.'

She crushed out her cigarette and shook his hand. 'We know each other, don't we? A little anyway,' and she flashed a smile at him.

He smiled back a little nervously, but there was nothing scary about Marilyn – she quickly took Michael under her wing and showed him what to do. And he took to the job at once. For the first time Michael was in a world altogether outside his family; even the world of school had the dubious benefit of his father's presence. Here in the drugstore, no one ever mentioned his mother; no one asked him if he was scared, or how he got on with his father, or whether he liked his younger brother. People weren't unkind (Marilyn in particular seemed to keep a mildly maternal eye on him); it was simply that they assumed his personal affairs were his business and not related to the business of the store, their joint enterprise and connecting link. He was treated, for the first time in his life, as an adult.

Which was unnerving and did sometimes frighten him, in the essential emotional coldness of its premise – no substitute mother here. But he got used to it, and in any case was usually too busy to let it bother him. In the job itself there was a pleasing alternation of the finite with the open-ended. The finite had to do with stock: replacing liquor, loading beer into the coolers, opening fresh cartons of cigarettes (the extra-longs were a pain, and did not fit the racks). It took Michael all of three days to break the letter code – DFC, say, for $1.29 – which showed the wholesale price on the label, and discover the mark-ups involved: gargantuan for the ephemeral summertime products (sun tan lotion, ice-cream, and charcoal), modest for items full-time residents needed, or thought they did (medicines, cigarettes, and razor blades).

Open-ended, on the other hand, was the relationship with customers – town regulars, expending a munificent two bits a day for a newspaper; sleek summer folk buying high class booze for their beach parties; poorer visitors from the trailers in the State Park, bitching about the prices. So he was never bored and always busy, since Marilyn made sure, even when the store was empty, that nobody ever just stood around; if there was nothing that needed restocking, there were always shelves to dust. At home nothing seemed to happen any more; in the store, life was an endless series of episodes.

And there was also the matter of Alvin. An intelligent man, he ran his store with a savvy industry that would have seen him prosper in a more sophisticated business. He was, unusually, a Democrat, who couldn't bring himself to vote for McGovern in 1972 but had voted for Carter even though Ford was a Michigan native. Alvin loved politics and baseball. Coming from a home where politics rarely got a mention and his father didn't play sports, Michael found talking about these subjects – and with an adult – a marvellous novelty. Alvin's own children were grown up: Marie, who lived in a suburb of Detroit, and Phil, an executive for a Chicago sporting goods firm who had never taken any interest in the store and even as a boy had never worked there. This was something Alvin had accepted, according to Marilyn, but felt sad about. 'Alvin's built this business from nothing,' she said, 'but he's got nobody to turn it over to.'

The only problem was that Alvin turned out to have a bad temper, which scared Michael. Alvin would become suddenly, unpredictably enraged by a smart-ass kid fingering the candy, or a summer lady complaining about prices, and retreat behind the raised pharmacy counter where, standing, he would pound out prescriptions on his Hermes typewriter, his lower lip quivering as he talked furiously to himself. Interrupting him in such moments was almost fatal, since even the most anodyne request could reignite his rage. Though this fury rarely lasted more than five minutes, Michael still found it excruciating trying to explain to a baffled customer why no, not for all the tea in China was Michael willing to go on their behalf at just that moment and ask the pharmacist about anything.

Yet it was not the awkwardness with customers that bothered him most when Alvin flared up, it was his own fear. *He's not going to hit me*, he'd tell himself as Alvin's lips began to quiver, but knowing this rationally did nothing to make him less afraid. One morning – Sunday, so it was an early start – Larry Bottel failed to pick him up at quarter to eight as arranged. Michael waited and waited, then ran all the way downtown, entering the store out of breath to find Alvin standing behind a stack of half-assembled Sunday editions of the *Chicago Tribune*, lip quivering, jaw jutting, absolutely furious. Michael had the full brunt of that particular blow-up, for by the time Larry sailed in at nine thirty, hungover but acting perky, Alvin's temper had subsided. He was actually laughing at Larry's insouciance while Michael simmered with resentment at the injustice of Larry going scot free when an hour before, thanks to Larry, Alvin had seemed ready to kill the hapless Michael.

But then, Larry wasn't scared of Alvin anyway. Neither was Debbie Waller, who worked full-time until she converted a date with a Dutchman from Grand Haven one summer night into a backseat pregnancy and left her job and town on the same day. And Mary Joe, Marilyn's niece, who lived in the trailer park with two other girls and saved her money for her marriage, though she didn't have a boyfriend. There were others in the summertime, when the store hours were longer and business was most intense.

It was Larry he grew to know best, for they were the only males working in the store (other than Alvin) and therefore had the heavy chores assigned them: loading the cases of liquor or taking the charcoal in and out each day from the front sidewalk. Larry was a high school senior whose father owned the bakery, where Alvin and most of the Main Street business-men met for coffee every morning. Three years older than

Michael, Larry smoked Old Gold Filters and acted towards him like a man of the world introducing a kid brother to it. How Michael admired Larry's confidence, his sureness with girls, his lack of fear of Alvin, and his sophistication, especially about sex. No one had ever talked to Michael about sex so explicitly before. Larry even had a girlfriend, a summer resident named Ursula Lowy, who kept her mouth closed when she spoke because she was embarrassed by her too-prominent front teeth. But she also had beautifully long tan legs, which Larry liked to describe in loving detail when he regaled Michael with next-day accounts of his multiple acts of sexual congress in the back seat of the Bonneville, handed down by Larry's father. 'I fucked her 'til she whimpered like a dog,' he proclaimed one day, and thereafter this became his catchphrase for any expression of carnal longing. 'Like a dog!' Larry would exclaim, in not so *sotto* a *voce*, as a bikini-clad girl would skip into the store in search of a Coke or a pack of Vantage Lights.

Larry's was such a sexualized world that Michael wondered what arid planet he had himself been living on. He saw the same girls as Larry did, coming into the store showing their swelling breasts under their skimpy tank tops, their naked midriffs above their cut-offs – and their brown legs, so smooth that he wanted to lick them like ice-cream. But to Michael these girls were remote objects of unfulfilled and – since he felt too young and shy and unwanted – *unfulfillable* desire. Yet in the world according to Larry they were *all* available, all consumed by a lust that Larry painted as ubiquitous and usually deviant. By his account, no one was innocent of a susceptibility to outlandish sexual behaviour: he'd slam the register drawer, hand over the change, say a beaming 'Thank you,' then as the customer left with her aspirin announce in a stage whisper that 'She'd feel a lot better if she fucked one guy at a time.' Or, of some virginal sixteen-year-old girl Michael had served, buying a pack of mints, her bathing suit still wet from the beach, 'Don't even think of asking her out. Not unless you want a dose of clap the size of a Winnebago.'

At least for the first two years of working with him, Michael believed everything Larry said. Larry was so *confident* it seemed unimaginable that any of this was the product of a fantasist. To Michael, Larry seemed to have the world by the tail (*like a dog!*). He had the easy charm of a precocious salesman, and Michael never saw the cockiness falter. Except once, and then it had nothing to do with girls.

It was a hot weekday afternoon in August. The air-con back by the liquor counter was on high and the fans up front were revolving full-speed in a blur of blades. Everyone was at the beach, and Michael hadn't rung up much more than five dollars in the past hour. 'First you need enough sun,' Alvin would say, 'to get them to come to Stillriver in the first place. But then you want enough rain to drive them off the beach and into town.'

A man came in, wearing soiled jeans, work boots, and a sweat-stained, grimy white T-shirt. He looked about fifty, slightly over average height, with hair cropped so short that Michael couldn't tell if he was bald or not.

He wanted cigarettes, and Larry served him, making his usual small talk, looking cool in a neatly pressed cotton shirt, with chinos and expensive loafers. While he searched for a new carton, the man stood silently, leaning against the counter with both arms. His biceps and forearms had muscles bunched like the knots of a sailing rope, grouped so asymmetrically they could not have come from any gym.

Finally Larry stood up holding a carton. 'Got 'em,' he said. The man didn't reply. As Larry rang up the transaction, his voice took on a folksier, back country tone. 'Sure is hot today, ain't it?'

'*What?*'

'I said, kind of hot today.'

The man snorted. 'Hot?' he said, his voice rising. 'You're *hot?*'

Larry stood back, startled, and didn't say anything.

'Poor baby. Poor baby's hot.' The man picked up his cigarettes. 'If it gets any hotter, your mama's going to have to iron you a new shirt.' And he strode out of the store.

Larry looked at Michael as he tried to regain his composure. 'Did you hear that?'

Michael nodded.

'I should have told him to shove it up his ass.' His voice was scornful. 'He puts up pole barns for a living. No wonder he's so cranky. Shit, anybody who puts up pole barns *deserves* to be hot.'

For once Michael detected a false note.

'I'm sure you'll meet some nice girls.' His mother, in between naps near the end. He would come home from school and peek into her bedroom, usually finding her dozing. That day she had been napping but must have heard him at the door. 'Come in,' she'd said, and smiled, though even her smile seemed weaker now, as if it were a strain to move her lips that much.

He'd helped her sit up a little to take a drink of water from the glass on her bedside table, then sat at the end of her bed to talk. He had told her about school and how his day had been, and started talking about his next baseball game when suddenly she'd looked at him and interrupted: 'I want you to promise me one thing.' And he'd nodded and said, 'What's that?' and his mother had said, 'Promise me you'll see more of this world than I ever did. Stillriver's a nice town and I'm glad you're growing up here. But don't get seduced.' He'd thought *seduced*? and he must have looked puzzled, for she'd chuckled, then made her remark about his meeting some nice girls. And then she'd added, 'But be sure and take your time. I don't want you getting stuck here because of some girl. Always remember that calf love never lasts.'

There seemed little danger of anything failing to last when nothing had even begun. His relationships with girls were largely confined to his own fantasies, especially in summer when they trooped half-naked through the store. He had all the yearnings of boys his age but found girls a mystery, one deepened by living after his mother's death in an all-male house. He found the prospect of intimacy with a girl completely shy-making; he could no more tell a girl about what he really felt than he could fly. Not that he was now altogether without sexual experience.

There was a girl from Walkerville named Susie Mest, known of course as Susie Breast since she was well developed. Although she was a year older, he had found himself in the ghost train with her at the Fennville County fair only the year before, sitting side by side in an open-topped train car contraption as it entered a darkened, meant-to-be spooky world of plywood and tin. As soon as their rickety car went through the entrance flaps and into pitch dark, Susie Mest had opened her mouth over his, stuck her tongue halfway down his throat and put her hand right on the bulge in his blue jeans, oblivious to the dangling rubber masks that popped up in front of their racing railway car and the skeletons that waved bony, illuminated arms as they took a sharp corner. When – too soon, too soon – the train had emerged into the garish light of the nighttime fairground, she'd looked at him wide-eyed while he waited for his excitement to subside enough to allow him to stand up and leave the train car. He had to wait a long time.

When he next saw Susie Mest, selling squash at her daddy's roadside stand, she was seven months pregnant and three months married, and he thanked God for the brevity of the ghost train ride at the fair.

Then there had been Tina, a half-Mexican girl, who had kissed him and let him feel her left breast (why only one? he often wondered subsequently) in the back seat of her brother's car in the parking lot of Custer Dance Hall, while Kenny Williams was talking his way out of a fight with a farmer's son by the club's front door, with Donny standing by protectively in case Kenny's mouth made things worse.

But these were encounters; anything that involved knowing a girl as a *person* seemed impossible. 'Thank you,' he could just manage to say when they paid for their candy or ice-cream or sun tan lotion. How he dreaded it when a girl would try and engage him in conversation, finding himself tongue-tied and blushing if she asked so much as the price of a postcard.

It was so much easier to see girls in groups, and in the next year he started to see the same gang of kids more or less every weekend and sometimes after school. There was Donny Washington, his closest friend (at the age of seven they had tried the Indian blood exchange, but the jack-knife proved too dull), whose mother fed Michael supper almost once a week. Donny had shot up in the last twelve months, and was suddenly over six feet tall and getting broader. Donny liked Nancy Sheringham, partly (Michael felt) because she was big, with powerful shoulders but good legs, and partly because she had a self-confidence Donny lacked.

Ricky Fell was the doctor's son and made Nancy seem modest, so happy was he with himself. For he was good-looking and knew it, and had great success with girls. 'I shot a deer with that rifle,' he'd declared to an impressionable brown-haired summer girl one June night while a bunch of them drank beer in Doctor Fell's living room (the Fells were in Traverse for the weekend). Despite Michael and Donny's incredulity at the hokeyness of this pick-up line, it had worked – half an hour later Ricky was doing the deed with the girl from Evanston in his father's outboard, which was moored to the dock outside on Stillriver Lake.

Then there was Kenny Williams, a year behind them all at school, which nobody minded because he was so outrageous and so funny. Unusually articulate, he had Ricky Fell's success with girls, but it rarely lasted once they discovered he had just turned fifteen (though Anthea Heaton hadn't seemed to mind). Anthea was pretty, but stuck up and occasionally pretentious – she would drop the group at a moment's notice for a better invitation. Her snobbishness was kept in check by teasing, especially after she unwisely confided in Kenny that she never ate asparagus because it made her pee smell – an admission Kenny was never going to keep to himself.

What did they do together? Hang out, which in a town the size of Stillriver was, for nine months of the year, mostly all there was to do. The boys played sports, and the girls did too, and they all had jobs of one sort or another. By tacit agreement they did not sleep together, although there was the hilarity of

72

Kenny's partial seduction and complete disrobing of Anthea Heaton on her own swing porch – that occurred before Kenny really became a member of the group. They managed to resist teasing Anthea about it. Managed, in fact, in an untypical kindness for adolescents, never to let on to her they knew at all. The asparagus issue was a different matter altogether and not subject to immunity.

They drank some, mostly beer, although for heavy drinking the boys would go off on their own. The summer before, Donny had pitched a pup tent at the State Park and drank a bottle of Seagram's Seven in four and a half hours, then been embarrassed half to death when Nancy had shown up and found him retching in the sand. They smoked dope on occasion – Nancy in particular liked it and always promised to grow it on her father's farm, though she never did. Once Kenny tried acid, but acted so weird that it put everyone else off and kept him from doing it again, in their presence at any rate. No one had a car, and though Donny and Nancy were able to borrow their parents' on occasion (pickup trucks for both), Michael's father almost never let him use his – he acted as if his own aversion to driving should be shared by his son. This general lack of wheels meant that recreation after school was limited in terms of venue; usually they spent it downtown by the bandstand, or making one lemon Coke last two hours at the drugstore soda fountain (Alvin Simpson and Marilyn were very patient).

Was he happy now? Well, with his life widened by the job in the drugstore and a circle of friends, he was less *miserable*. And he was no longer quite so scared, particularly of Alvin, whom increasingly he enjoyed talking with and increasingly admired. Alvin was a businessman with *principles*. When Michael asked him why he hiked up prices for the summer people, Alvin said, 'I price in winter for need, in summer for desire.'

And so he got through his freshman and sophomore years of high school. He knew now that he would see his time through, graduate from high school, then obey his mother's words and *go*. Though now, at the beginning of his junior year, he found Alvin taking an interest in him.

'You started thinking about college yet?'

Michael shook his head. *I'm just a junior*, he thought, *why's he talking about college?* 'Maybe U of M,' he said, just to be saying something. 'If I can get in.' He'd have to go to a state school, he knew that, for there was no money to go to a private college. U of M was good, anyway.

Alvin nodded. 'Good school,' he said, but then added, 'you should think about Ferris. You've got the grades.'

Michael was mystified by this; Ferris was a dump in the dreary middle of the state. The University of Michigan in Ann Arbor was Arcadia by comparison, and a famous university. Puzzled, he told his father about Alvin's remark.

'Ah,' said his father with a knowing smile. 'Ferris, the pharmacist's friend. It's famous for it.'

'But what's that got to do with me?'

'I've never seen a pharmacist go hungry. People will always need medicine.'

So that's what this is about. 'I'm supposed to become a pharmacist? What, and take over from Alvin when he retires?' He remembered what his mother had said – *don't be seduced.*

'There could be worse fates. Alvin does real well.' His father's voice turned slightly sarcastic. 'Or are you itching to get out of here? You'd prefer Grand Rapids, I suppose. Or the beauty of Detroit.'

'What's so bad about Detroit?'

His father looked at him without sympathy. 'Son, you have many virtues, yet a sense of irony is not among them. Having clawed my way out of that shithouse, it would be pretty peculiar to have a son of mine try to claw his way back.'

2

THE DAY AFTER Nancy cornered him he looked at Cassie Gilbert in math class and she smiled at him. After school he walked home and ran into the twins, all excited about some TV show they'd watched that morning. He paid little attention, being so preoccupied himself. Sticking his head into his father's study, he found his father reading the paper. 'I got to go out for a while. I'll be back before supper.'

Lowering the paper, his father looked at him with slight surprise. 'Where are you going?'

'Helping somebody with math. There's an exam.'

'Donny struggling again?'

'No.'

His father smiled to himself and put up the *Chronicle* again. From behind the spread he said mildly, 'She must be pretty.'

He half-ran to Cassie's house, since he was already late. He rang the bell and heard a soft, distinctive two-tone note inside. *Dee-dah, dee-dah.* (Years later ringing a doorbell at a foreman's house in Stockholm he heard exactly the same *dee-dah*, and could hardly speak as the foreman's wife opened the door.) After a minute, he heard feet running down the stairs, the door opened and Cassie stood in front of him, a little breathless. 'Hi,' she said, 'come on in.'

She'd changed from school clothes – those knee socks – and was wearing blue jeans, white sneakers and a red flannel hunter's shirt with the sleeves rolled up to her elbows. When she smiled there was the faintest hint of an overbite, and a slight imperfection to one front tooth that sometimes caught the light. To his mind these just made her prettier, and he liked the little point to her jaw, and the small straight nose between the startling high cheekbones (almost American Indian). And then the eyes – big, round and cornflower blue – he had never

75

realized a pair of eyes could make such a difference, turn something pretty enough into a face of extraordinary beauty. With her black hair tied back in a pigtail, the eyes seemed even larger.

He followed her into the living room. It was simply furnished with a brown, thinly-cushioned sofa no one would ever want to get kissed on, a mahogany coffee table, and two handsome but uncomfortable looking Windsor chairs. The one concession to comfort was a leather recliner chair, sitting next to a standing lamp by the now-unused fireplace. Presumably her father sat there, for on the table next to the chair was a book about biblical excavations in the Middle East.

He followed Cassie into the kitchen, which was light and cheerful, where the living room was just this side of dour. White canisters with stencilled flower patterns of blue lined the counter below the sideboard cupboards. In the middle of the room there was an oval pine table and wooden kitchen chairs, and Cassie stopped at the fridge and pointed to them. 'We can sit there,' she said. 'Would you like something to drink?'

'No thanks,' he said, and sat down, carefully moving aside a large arrangement of dried flowers, then opened the geometry textbook he'd brought. 'We better get started.'

She was nice, she was pretty (and, since opening the door, beautiful), so he somehow expected that she would have to be dumb. And at first she didn't disappoint him. What he liked about geometry most was its interconnection of the visual with the logical and verbal. You saw the symmetry, say, of two triangles superficially unalike, then set about to prove their congruence through a verbal reasoning. This kind of proof would be a large part of the exam, and he quickly drew two triangles on a piece of paper, using a table knife as a straight edge for his pencil. By the third step of the proof he could tell that he had lost her. 'Confused?'

She nodded and blushed. 'I don't mean to be so stupid.'

'That can't be helped,' he said automatically, then tried to apologize. *Thank God, she is laughing.* He tried to explain away his outburst, but she cut him off.

'Don't worry,' she said, 'you're probably right. I think I was born with a spatial deficit disorder.'

'A what?' he said.

'You know how some people can put things together,' she said, 'even without the instructions?' He nodded. 'Well, I can't do it even with the instructions right in front of me. My father's even worse, which means I'm the one who gets to try. He bought a barbecue in Burlington when we moved up here and I spent a whole weekend this summer putting it together. It's still not right.'

'Show me,' he said. 'I'll fix it for you.'

'Not now. It's out in the garage. Besides, I've got to get through geometry. First things first, though with me it looks like first things third.'

So they ploughed on, and after half an hour he felt that though she didn't understand noticeably better, she was quick enough to memorize the moves for what he was confident would appear on their exam. As they continued, he did almost all the talking, and he found that once his slight self-consciousness had gone, he enjoyed it. But he also wanted her to talk, though not about geometry.

Finally they finished. There was no reasonable way he could prolong the lesson. He looked up and was astonished to see the kitchen clock read 5.15; it hadn't seemed half that long.

'Nancy says you're a good basketball player.'

'I like it,' she said.

'You must be good. She said you were all-county down south.'

'Just reserve,' she said quickly. 'I wasn't trying to brag.'

'I know,' he said reassuringly. 'Nancy can get anything out of anybody. Kenny Williams, do you know him?' and she nodded. 'Well, he calls Nancy "the dentist". He says she gets secrets out of people like a dentist extracts teeth. Gently if possible, but with brute force if she has to. Like the dentist in *Marathon Man*.'

They were both laughing at this image of Nancy when suddenly Cassie stopped and looked at the doorway. When

Michael turned he found a slightly-built man in his sixties standing in the doorway, frowning. 'Doesn't sound to me like much geometry's going on.'

Michael stood up. Cassie said, 'This is Michael Wolf, Daddy.'

'I'm Parson Gilbert,' said the man, staying in the doorway while Michael stayed awkwardly standing by his chair.

'We're almost finished, Daddy,' Cassie said. 'I'll be up in a minute.'

'Take your time, my dear,' her father said, and Michael could tell both that the man didn't mean this and that he didn't like the man. He wasn't sure which thought came first. As her father turned and walked away, Michael noticed he was wearing bedroom slippers. 'Pleased to meet you, sir,' he called after him, realizing he didn't mean this either. Cassie's father turned his head and nodded, then walked away.

'Well,' said Michael, gathering his book and sheets of notes, 'I'd better be going.'

'I've got to go out too,' she said. 'I need something from Dumas's.'

'I'll go with you,' he said eagerly and without thinking, since Dumas's was in the opposite direction from home.

She smiled hesitantly. *I shouldn't have said that*, he thought, feeling geeky and futile. 'The thing is,' she said, more hesitantly still, 'it might be best if you left first. Then I could meet you outside.'

He nodded dumbly but didn't really understand. She motioned upstairs with her head, then flicked back the hair from both sides of her face. 'He worries.'

Got it, he thought. *The parson won't approve.* And with a sudden, furtive joy, he found himself saying goodbye as the parson came halfway down the stairs.

Cassie's father nodded curtly. 'I'll be down presently, Cassie,' he announced.

Outside Michael waited by the corner, out of sight of the living room window.

When she joined him she was wearing a down vest. They

stood silently for a moment, then she pointed down the street. 'Look at that,' she said, 'isn't it beautiful?'

Look at what? he wanted to say, seeing only Lonergan's modern ranch house and the raspberry patch in back where, when he was little, he and Donny had snuck fruit on Wednesday evenings when the Lonergan clan went as a family to midweek service at the First Baptist Church just up the block. They had done it two weeks running and doubtless would have picked the raspberry patch clean if Mrs Donovan across the street hadn't seen them in the late-August dusk. She'd called Donny's father, who had scared the living hell out of them both by telling them what he would do if they so much as walked on the sidewalk next to the Lonergans'.

'The houses here,' said Cassie, 'are wonderful.'

Michael didn't know what to say. No one in his family other than his mother had ever used the word 'wonderful'. And what about the houses? They were, it seemed to him, just houses.

'You like it here?' He tried not to sound incredulous.

'Of course. Don't you?'

Michael shrugged. 'I don't know. I guess I'd like to see somewhere else for a change.' *I want you to see the world*, his mother had said. *Stillriver's not the be all and end all.*

'You must have been to a big city.'

He thought of his uncle's house, not seen since his mother had died, located on the outskirts of the city. 'I've seen Grand Rapids.'

Dumas's loomed ahead of him across the street. *Don't push your luck.* 'Well,' he said, 'I hope the exam goes all right.'

'Thank you so much for your help.'

'Let me know how you do before you thank me too much.'

She was looking away. 'I usually go for a walk each day at five.'

Why tell him this? And then he understood it was an invitation, as awkwardly put as his own offer to accompany her here. 'I'm working then,' he said. 'I work in the drugstore.'

'Oh,' she said with a false brightness to her voice. 'I guess I'll see you at school then. Thanks again.' She started to cross the street as he saw the one truly hopeful thing in his life start to disappear.

'I don't work on Wednesdays,' he shouted as she reached the far sidewalk. She turned around and waved. *Did she hear me?*

A week later he announced at ten to five that he needed to go to Dumas's, ignored his father's questioning gaze, and walked towards Main Street. When he didn't see Cassie on the street that stretched from the Gilberts' house down to the Main Street intersection, he walked around the block. Then he spied her, a block ahead of him, as he passed by her house for a second time.

'Hey!' he shouted, forgetting altogether his plan to meet her 'by accident'.

When he caught up to her she was smiling. 'I was hoping I might see you,' she said. 'Gosh it's cold.' She dug both her hands into the pockets of the green parka she was wearing. It made her look like a model in an ad for a ski resort.

'Let's keep moving,' Michael said, and they started walking without an agreed destination, which proved to be no problem since their conversation was at once so easy – yet somehow so intense – that it overshadowed the issue of where the two might be headed. She walked quickly, he noticed, her long legs striding out with the loose grace of a filly happy for exercise. But then he forgot her legs as she began to talk, first about the math exam ('I got a B plus!' she said excitedly, giving his arm a sudden two-fingered pinch), then basketball, and then Stillriver, which she seemed to like so much that Michael began to wonder what he had been missing all these years, then more about some book she was reading, which he decided he had better read too. And suddenly he started talking, and over an hour later as he was describing the twins to her (how had they got on to Ethel and Daisy?), he found they had ended up three doors down from the Lonergans' and four from Cassie's own house, so they stopped (as if tacitly agreeing they did not want to be seen by her father), and stood there under one of the tallest maple trees in town. 'Gosh it's late,' she said, looking at her watch.

He nodded and said, 'I'd better get home,' then paused, uncertain of what to say next.

'That was fun,' she said, and flashed a big open-mouthed smile. He saw her teeth were wonderfully white and her mouth was so expressive as she laughed that he felt waves of prickles spread all over his skin.

'We could do it again,' he suddenly blurted out, looking away and wondering where he had found the courage to say *that*.

And she laughed, reached out and pinched his arm again, lightly and playfully. 'Same time, same place?' she asked. He looked up at her and saw that her eyes seemed to be dancing, such was their sparkle, and he found himself smiling back and laughing too. And he watched as she strode away, noticing again how quickly her long legs moved, and when she got to her front door she turned and waved once, real quick, before sliding into the house.

As he walked home he whacked himself hard on the chest with both fists because his heart was beating so fast (*thump, thump, thump*, like the drum in the high school marching band) and he wondered if he felt the mixture of adrenalin and warmth because, for the first time in as long as he could remember, his heart was full.

After this, he could be sure of seeing Cassie by herself at least once a week, though getting to know her was a gradual process of discovery, made slower not because she was putting up a deterring façade but rather, he sensed, because she was . . . well, just taking her time. On their walks, Cassie talked more than he did, but she wasn't gushy; in fact, what he liked right away was the mix of slight reserve and utter absence of affectation. She had a light, soft voice which, when they were walking in winter weather, Michael had to strain to hear. And once in a while she would sing, without embarrassment – usually something folky, a Joan Baez song taught her as a child by her Berkeley aunt, or a favourite from The Band, 'The Night They Drove Old Dixie Down'.

He liked it when she sang. In fact, he found very little in her that he didn't like, except that he couldn't get to see her often enough. He liked the fact that she made him laugh, and could laugh at herself. He liked the fact that she liked fruit as much as he did, though her favourite was cherries, his peaches. He liked that she read novels mainly, usually by authors he had never heard of. Who was Lawrence Durrell? He liked the fact that she liked to cook, since he didn't, and he wondered why she ate so little meat; she drank wine too, or at least a little bit, even though the parson was teetotal. He liked her small hands, though she was tallish, and that she sometimes bit her nails (he was chronic), and the way she liked wearing men's shirts, though the shirts in question came from her mother, one of the few references she made to her. He liked, when he got to know her pretty well (it was summer by then) the fact that she waxed her legs, and he even liked the fact that she once declared she wouldn't ever sleep with anyone she didn't love, because he thought (she was still seeing him wasn't she?) that this some-how kept him in the running

Intentionally or not, Cassie moved effortlessly into his tight circle of friends, helped by the fact that she was already a team-mate of Nancy Sheringham. Cassie was quiet with them, not talkative as she was with Michael, which made it easy for the circle to accept her. They might have closed ranks against a pushier person. And like most of them, she was a fairly normal kid without a normal family: Nancy Sheringham's father drank and, though Nancy didn't talk about it, hit his wife and kids; Kenny Williams had no father, and his mother ran a beauty salon in the basement of the unfinished house his father was building when he dropped dead while she was pregnant with Kenny; Mrs Fell, Ricky's mother, was confined to a wheelchair; Michael's mother was dead. Only Donny had two ostensibly normal parents, and it was accordingly Donny's house where they often gathered, and where Mrs Washington fed them without complaint. So Cassie, sports-playing, mother dead, father odd (and ailing), fit in right away.

From the beginning, however, Michael had the wonderful if

fragile sense that it was he and not the others who mattered most to her. For she took such an obvious *interest* in him, even seeming to be interested in the doings of the drugstore. She didn't hang around there, didn't make it tough for him by wanting him to pay her attention when he was working, but she would ask him later about the job, and laugh when he told her stories about Alvin's explosions, or about Larry's most recent ridiculous boast (though he did not mention *like a dog!*). He could tell her about more serious things, too, even painful things: one afternoon he must have talked about his mother non-stop for an hour and a half, describing her, in effect remembering her out loud, for the first time since she had died.

Soon they weren't just meeting on Henniker Street on Wednesday afternoons; sometimes on Sundays, after the drugstore closed at lunchtime, she would come by his house (though only for a little while) during the parson's afternoon nap. With Michael's father, she seemed so much at ease – straightforward (grown up, really) and polite – that even his father began to unbend and initiate conversation with her. To Michael's mild disbelief, she had snot-nosed Gary eating out of her hand by the simple expedient of pretending to care what he thought. 'You don't have to be so nice to him,' Michael had told her, and she'd just smiled and said, 'That's all right. Your brother's not so bad.'

And she especially liked the twins, managing to persuade Michael (though not his father) about their specialness without going on about it excessively. They adored her, and Ethel in particular complained if much more than a couple of days went by without their seeing her.

Michael was almost never inside the Gilbert house, since Cassie's father grew no friendlier. When he came to the store to get his paper he was civil to Michael, but only just. He seemed to hover around their relationship like an oppressive girdle, for he was very demanding of Cassie and strict about her going out. Yet Michael was left in no doubt from the beginning that Cassie's tending of her father always came first. He was not well, Michael was made to understand, and Cassie saw her job – well, her duty anyway – as looking after him.

Michael asked his father early on, 'What exactly is a parson?'

'An old-fashioned word for minister. Like reverend.'

'You know anybody nowadays who calls himself Parson?'

'No. I thought it died out with Parson Weems a hundred and fifty years ago. Though come to think of it, there was a horse's ass known to your uncle in Grand Rapids. But he died years ago. Never heard anybody use the title since.'

That Sunday morning as Michael gulped hot coffee before rushing late to work, his father came down in his old bathrobe, terry cloth worn smooth from age. 'I thought you might be going to church today.'

'*Church?* You know I'm working. I *always* work Sundays.'

'Reverend Taverner's away and Cassie's father is preaching today. I'm sure he'd be pleased to see a friend of his daughter in the congregation.'

Michael had shrugged – he was going to work. *What's it to you anyway?* he wanted to ask but didn't. And then he wondered, *Is he teasing me?*

As spring came and the weather turned warmer, he and Cassie would walk across Main Street and down to the shore of Stillriver Lake. Past Dr Fell's, over to Mr Nelson's dock and up the boathouse stairs, where they would stand under the high cedar and lean against the rails, looking out at the lake. It was illicit – actually, it was illegal trespass – but since the Nelsons were gone during the week they could go there undisturbed. And if any neighbour noticed them, Michael and Cassie must have had their blessing, since no one ever challenged their right to be there.

It was a long time before he and Cassie were anything but friends, and his encounters with Susie Mest and the Mexican girl helped him not at all. *I should have tried to kiss her at the beginning,* he told himself; *if she had said no then I wouldn't have been losing anything.* For it was the loss of her he feared, and which checked him from trying. He couldn't read the signs at all. Sometimes she'd put her hand on his shoulder for a

84

moment and once, standing at Nelson's, she stroked his hair. But that was all.

Until one day, talking about grammar of all things (*Why is she talking about this?* he thought) he suddenly listened hard as she explained a gerund to him. 'Like kissing instead of kiss,' she said, and his heart began to pound. 'Daddy says there's a gerundive too – that's when you add "able" on.'

'Like kissable,' he said at once, determined not to let the door close – if in fact it was open.

'Well,' she said, 'that's poss-ible.' They both laughed.

'And even prob-able?'

And she leaned over and turned her mouth to him, and just before they kissed she said, '*Yes.*'

She laughingly called him *fast mover* after this for weeks, but she was very slow to let him do anything but kiss her. Then one Saturday early in July, he was working a split shift, with the afternoon off. When he came out of the store he found Cassie outside. 'What are you doing here?'

'Daddy's gone to Grand Rapids with Reverend Taverner. I offered to go with him but he said I should stay and do my homework.' She grimaced. 'It's too nice out for that.'

'I'm free all afternoon. You want to do something?'

'I want to go to the beach.'

'Okay,' he said hesitantly, and they walked down Main Street past the Dairy Queen and turned along Beach Road. Now they walked in the street like everybody else; you only stayed on the shady sidewalks, with their split concrete and obtruding tree roots, if you were trying to be low key.

The State Park was packed with cars and the beach was crowded. The chalk board on the back of the lifeguard station said 78, and there was virtually no wind off the lake.

'Grand Central Station,' said Cassie. 'I wish the Nelsons weren't here weekends – we could go there.'

They walked over to the channel and climbed onto the long, thin concrete pier. 'What's over there?' asked Cassie, pointing across the channel.

'South Beach.'

They watched as two Coho fishing boats moved through the channel, then a succession of smaller craft, one of them heading out to waterski. A voice came from left and below them, and looking down Michael saw Larry Bottel entering the channel in his father's speedboat, his girlfriend Ursula beside him in a bikini. 'Hey there,' shouted Larry, 'we're going out on the big lake. Want to come?'

Michael looked at Cassie, who shook her head. Then she said, 'I know, let's get him to give us a ride over there.' And she pointed across the channel to South Beach.

Michael called down to Larry, who manoeuvred the boat next to the iron rungs on the side of the pier and idled while first Cassie and then Michael climbed aboard and stood in the well. 'Come on,' he said, 'come out with us for a while.'

Michael hesitated but Cassie shook her head. 'No,' she said firmly, 'drop us over there will you?'

Larry kept looking at Michael. 'Come on,' he said again, 'the big lake's like glass today. We can really let her rip.'

Cassie's voice grew harder. 'No. Please just drop us over there.'

Larry shrugged. 'Suit yourself,' and he swung the boat hard, gunned the engine, then immediately eased off as they approached the matching ladder on the other side of the channel. 'Have a good time,' he said a little sarcastically as they clambered up the ladder.

Up on the pier Michael and Cassie watched Larry and Ursula move out towards the larger waters. 'Why didn't you want to go out there?' he asked.

'I want to be with you,' she said, taking his arm. 'Besides, Larry gives me the creeps.'

'How's that?'

'Sometimes a guy looks at you,' Cassie said, 'and seems to like what he sees without your minding at all. And sometimes he likes what he sees and makes you feel like a piece of meat. That's Larry.'

They clambered over the rock fill that divided the channel

from the beach, then moved down onto a wide expanse of sand that stretched south ahead of them all the way to Sable Point.

'Look at the difference,' Cassie exclaimed, and Michael nodded. Perhaps half a mile down the beach he could see three or four people running into the water; otherwise, the beach was theirs. 'It's amazing,' she said. 'Or is this private?'

He shook his head. 'I'm sure some people would like it to be,' he said, pointing towards one of the old cedar cottages up in the dunes to their left. 'But it's not. No beach is.'

'But why isn't anyone here? You'd think with the State Park so crowded some of the people would want to come here.'

'They'd have to swim across the channel. Or drive all the way round, and even then, there's nowhere to park. All the property between here and the road is private.'

They were walking quickly now, though Cassie would stop to look up at the houses, shrouded by brush and high pines above them. Then he stopped to look as well.

'What are you staring at?' she asked.

'Nothing much.' *Go on and tell her.* 'See that house up there with the green shingles? That was my grandfather's house.'

'Really? Is he there now?'

'No, no. He's been dead for years. It's my uncle's now.'

'Do you want to go up and say hi?'

He shook his head. 'Not especially. Anyway, he's probably not there. He rents it out a lot.'

'Do you see him much?'

He shook his head. 'We used to. When my mother was alive.'

'He doesn't get on with your daddy?'

'I wouldn't say that. But my father doesn't like coming over here. He never did, and now that my mother's gone he doesn't have to. My uncle still drops by our house when he's in town.'

'At least they get on. My father hardly speaks to my mother's family any more. My aunt in Berkeley had to pay my fare when I visited.'

'Maybe he didn't have the money.'

'He has more than she's got. He just didn't want me to go.'

He doesn't want you to go anywhere, he thought. 'Your father,' he started to say, shaking his head.

'Hush,' she said, and pressed her fingers to his lips. They felt cool and dry. 'I know what you were going to say. Please don't. I have to look after him. I promised my mother.'

'Oh,' he said, and thought of his own mother in those last days, between the alternating sessions of pain and sleep. She hadn't asked him to look after anybody. *Just don't get stuck here.*

'Like you did?' he'd managed to ask.

His mother had shaken her head. 'If I hadn't lived here, young man,' she'd said with the mock-formality she used to tease him, 'you wouldn't be here today to listen to me.'

'Earth to Michael Wolf,' and he looked up to see Cassie staring at him.

'Sorry,' he said dully. 'Say, tell me, is your father unhappy that we see each other?'

'He doesn't know we do.'

'What?' he protested.

'Keep walking,' she said, and took his hand. After a minute she said, 'What do you miss most?'

'What?'

'About your mother. Go on, you can't get mad at me. I lost my mother too.'

He looked down at the sand. 'I miss the way she'd listen to me.'

'I did too. Until I met you.'

'I didn't mean you don't listen to me.'

'I know. Let's swim.'

'I don't have trunks. And what about you? We can't go skinny-dipping in broad daylight.'

She was tying her hair up in a ponytail with a rubber band. She started to take off her shirt. She undid her buttons with a provocative movement of hands until he could see she had a T-shirt on underneath. She unbuttoned her jeans to reveal basketball shorts instead of panties.

'Go on,' she said. 'I'm not swimming without you.'

'I told you, I don't have trunks.'

'You wear underwear?' she asked, not without reason, since many of his friends didn't. He nodded. 'Well, then we can go swimming. Anyway, we're going to have to swim back across the channel, aren't we?'

How could he say *I'm scared*? So he took off his jeans and shirt, gritted his teeth, and followed her into Lake Michigan, running across the first tier of sandy bottom, with ridges like the corrugated surface of an old-fashioned washing board, until they reached the sandbar.

'Come on,' she called, and he turned and watched her swim out towards the second sandbar. He had always loved to swim – *my water rat* his mother had called him – but he saw at once that Cassie had a grace in the water he could never match. She flutter-kicked and lifted her arms high and slow in a crawl that propelled her with a surprising speed. Her feet flashed white in the air, and he could glimpse her thighs as she moved, sleek and porpoise-like, through the water.

As she swam further out, he felt a flicker of his usual panic, which recently came less often than before and less deeply, although whenever he thought it had gone for good it would inevitably reappear. Now he turned round to face the shore and found this comforting, for it was the endless expanse of the lake merging into the distant horizon that most unsettled him. He tried to distract himself from his anxiety by scanning the dunes, looking for his uncle's house, which was lost, hidden in the towering pines and hardwoods that had never been cut for lumber. Suddenly Cassie's arms were around his chest. 'Come on in,' she said.

He shook his head, unwilling to turn round; even the thought of it brought the edge of panic back again.

'What's wrong?' she asked. 'Is something the matter?'

He shook his head again, and she tightened her grip. 'Go on, tell me,' she commanded. 'I can tell something's wrong.'

Frightened as he was of telling her, he was more frightened still of what would happen if he turned round, the shakiness he sensed he'd feel if he tried to swim out with her, the panic he could anticipate as his throat would tighten and adrenalin surge through his nerves like electricity. 'Do you ever get scared?' he asked, almost in a whisper.

'All the time,' Cassie said at once. 'I get scared I'll flunk math, I'm scared I won't get into college, I'm scared—'

'No,' he interrupted her. 'I don't mean those kinds of things. I mean just scared generally, scared about everything.'

She held onto him and he could feel her breath tickle against his back. 'Oh, you mean being scared without knowing what you're scared about.'

'Sort of.'

He felt her lay her cheek against his back; it felt warm against his wet skin. 'I used to, after my mother died. Why? Does that happen to you?'

He couldn't say anything and just nodded.

'Were you scared just now?' she asked. 'Is that why you wouldn't turn round?' When he nodded again, she leaned up and put her lips close to the side of his head. 'The next time that happens, just tell me, okay?' She lowered her clasped arms and hugged him gently, until he felt himself growing excited. Then she kissed him on the back of his neck, small tender kisses. She must have sensed him growing, but she kept her hands clasped around the front of his boxer shorts. 'Not *all* of you feels scared to me,' she said with a light laugh.

'Don't tease me like that,' he said.

'I won't.'

'You're driving me crazy. You've got no idea.'

She laughed. 'Yes I have.' She grew serious. 'I'm not teasing you. It's just that it's my turn to be scared. I've never done it before.'

Done what? he started to say, then stopped.

Cassie laughed. 'You know what,' she said. 'You're probably an *expert* on the matter.'

He started to blush, and was glad she couldn't see his face. He wanted to reassure her she was wrong, yet felt embarrassed by it – it seemed slightly sissy to be a virgin still. 'You probably know all about it,' she continued. 'You think it's amazing that

I don't. The prissy parson's daughter – that's what you think, isn't it? Go on, admit it.' She seemed to be getting cross the more she went on.

'You're wrong,' he admitted, telling the truth but not sure he should.

'Am I?' she asked.

'Yes, goddamnit. Now stop it,' and he unclasped her hands.

She stood up and came round to face him. 'Look at me,' she commanded, then kissed him lightly on the lips. 'I know you want to,' she said calmly, 'and what you don't know is that I want it to too. But I want it to be right. Trust me, it'll happen.' She laughed. 'I guess we'll have to show each other how.'

Which is exactly what they did, early one Friday night in his own bedroom when his father was having dinner at the Fells' and Gary was on a sleepover. He didn't know what scared him most, anxiety about what to do or the prospect of his father coming home early. He had taken a box of Trojans from the drugstore, snuck that very afternoon while Marilyn was serving up front and Alvin was writing payroll cheques in the office.

Now Cassie insisted on reading aloud the written instructions tucked into the box. 'Expel all air before unrolling,' she commanded in a gruff voice. 'Remove immediately after ejaculation.' She was naked under the covers, having taken off her clothes quickly while Michael tried not to stare after his first long look at her: the tan legs the colour of sun-soaked apricots, the dark bushy triangle of soft hair, her flat stomach with an almond slit for a belly-button, and her breasts – white, curved rounds with nipples like the small buds of pink roses. She seemed so entirely beautiful to him, as he sat on the edge of the bed in his boxer shorts, that his hands trembled as he struggled with the foil packaging.

Suddenly Cassie threw the instructions onto the floor. 'Let's do it together,' she said, reaching out for him. 'Because at the rate you're going I'll be here for breakfast.'

Soon enough he lay down beside her, breathing hard, elated by what they had just done but feeling utterly peaceful as well.

He didn't care if his father did come home early. Cassie cradled her head on his chest and he stroked her silky hair. 'You okay?' he said.

'Never better. Say,' and she sat up suddenly, 'what time is it?' He told her and she grinned as she lay down again. 'We've got plenty of time for round two.'

'Cassie,' he said, trying to keep all emotion out of his voice. 'You said once you'd never sleep with anyone you didn't love.'

'I did,' she said cheerfully. 'So I did.'

3

ONE FEAR REMAINED, one he could not tell even Cassie about.

It was a hot and breezeless Saturday, with a kind of inland mugginess which had people hanging around the air-conditioned store until ten o'clock closing. Saturday night meant that by the time the drugstore closed none of his friends were still around. Cassie had gone to a play reading on South Beach ('a play what?' he'd asked) with the parson, and by the time she got home it would be too late to call in there.

He walked down Main Street, looking through the park surrounding the bandstand for friends, but not finding any. There would probably be people he knew down on the beach, but it didn't seem worth the walk to share a joint or half a can of beer with a dozen guys staring at the two or three girls sitting by the driftwood fire.

He took the long way home, by the Dairy Queen where Main Street met the Beach Road. Here he found Kenny Williams sitting on a bench, drinking a malt, and talking to a tanned, blonde girl in shorts and a tank top who could not have been more than thirteen years old. The girl was leaving as Michael walked by, and Kenny waved him over.

'She looks even younger than you,' said Michael as they both watched the tan calves move across the street. 'Jailbait or what?'

'It's like erecting a house, Michael,' said Kenny in his precocious fashion, 'and I am building the foundations.'

'She's a foundation?'

Kenny shook his head. 'No, no. Our conversation is. She's thirteen years old and comes up every summer. Next summer we might make it to the ground floor, like on the living room sofa, then the summer after it's upstairs to the bedroom. All thanks to a little groundwork done tonight. And she even paid for my malt.'

Michael could share the logic of this, if not its supreme

self-confidence. He bought a snow cone and rejoined Kenny on the bench. They watched the cars turning off Main Street to cruise the beach, and waved to the drivers they knew (most of them) and stared hungrily at the girls in the cars where they didn't. Michael had to work the next morning, which involved an early start to assemble the Sunday papers, and he was about to walk the few blocks home when Dicky Millicent joined them on the bench, obviously drunk.

He was a summer kid whose parents had a house in town, down near the Yacht Club, across from Dr Fell's place on the town side of Stillriver Lake. He had a pint bottle of Canadian whisky with him now, which he made a great show of furtively sipping. Michael was about to leave when he remembered that Dicky's father had killed himself the summer before; he wasn't sure why that was a reason to stay, but he did.

He sat listening as Dicky half-ranted and half-talked, alternately exuberant and cranky. Where Kenny and Michael looked out eagerly at the cars that passed, looking for friends, Dicky sneered. When a pickup with two guys in the cab turned off the Beach Road onto Main Street in front of them, Dicky stared at the driver, and the driver stared back, not pleasantly. It was then that Michael recognized Ronald Duverson in the passenger seat. He didn't know him really, though he'd been in the *Chronicle* for saving Raleigh Somerset from drowning when Raleigh, a non-swimmer, had decided that somehow, some way, he could swim after all.

And Michael knew Ronald's younger brother Mex – called that for his dark, curly hair and walnut-coloured complexion. Mex was a wiry, little guy, but Ronald was big and fair-haired with a freckly face. He must have been eighteen years old, and had left school as soon as he could – the only one in his class who didn't wait to graduate – to work construction. He put up pole barns, which were cheap and easy to build.

'Fuck them,' said Dicky loudly, continuing to stare at the driver as he slowly drove on. Michael figured the driver would have heard him but he didn't stop. Dicky shook his head. 'Who are those sorry assholes?'

94

Kenny looked over at Michael and raised his eyes. 'Take it easy, Dicky,' said Michael. 'We know one of them.'

'That's your problem,' said Dicky, and took a long pull from his pint bottle. He offered some to Kenny and Michael, but both shook their heads. Dicky shrugged. 'More for me then,' he said, and was taking another pull when the pickup returned, heading the other way so that this time the passenger seat was nearest.

'Say something?' It was Ronald speaking.

Dicky jerked the bottle from his lips and with liquor still in his mouth nodded, swallowed, then spat out, 'Sure dickhead. Whatever you like.'

Again the truck didn't stop but turned sharply down Beach Road, out of sight behind the Dairy Queen building.

Kenny stood up quickly. 'Come on, Michael, time to go. I'll walk home with you.' He was lifting his eyebrows again.

'Okay,' said Michael, and got up with deliberation to disguise his own sudden anxiety. 'See you, Dicky.'

They crossed the street quickly and started to cut through the empty lot on the corner. 'I don't really want to be there when those guys come back again,' said Kenny.

'It's not our fight.'

'You try explaining that once they start throwing punches. Don't you know Ronald?'

'He's Mex's brother. So?'

'He's not like Mex, I tell you that. Ronald *likes* to fight. I'm surprised he's in town tonight. Usually he goes to the tavern in Spring Valley and breaks chairs over the pickers' heads.'

'Hey, wait up!' They turned and saw Dicky walking across the street. It was dark here, in the middle of the lot. Then from behind them – they must have circled around – the pickup appeared and braked sharply in the soft, sandy edge of the street, not forty feet away. The driver got out and walked towards them. He was short and powerfully built, and looked like he could give even Ronald ten years in age, much less the two younger boys he now faced. He wore khaki shorts and combat boots, and his arms swelled out of a tight, dark T-shirt.

His clothes, and a crew cut so bleached it looked white in the darkness, gave the overall effect of a faintly camp marine – had he not looked both so strong and so angry.

'What were you saying?' he demanded. Both his fists were clenched.

Michael turned to see what Dicky would say, but discovered to his amazement that Dicky had disappeared. Then he reappeared in the yellowing arc emanating from one of the overhead streetlights, heading back towards the Dairy Queen. *Shit*. Michael turned back. 'Mister, *we* didn't say anything.'

'*Yo no hablo Ingles*,' Kenny piped up, and Michael could have killed him for choosing this time to crack wise.

The stranger's head turned sharply towards Kenny. 'Listen, little asshole. Do you see these hands?' He held them up in the air, karate-style. 'I was in 'Nam. I was a Green Beret. And these hands are *lethal*, these hands are *registered weapons*.' Statements at once so preposterous and frightening that Michael's chief concern was that Kenny would start laughing. But then all three of them were distracted by the sound of the pickup truck, which was now moving along the street towards Dicky Millicent with Ronald at the wheel.

When he saw the truck approaching, Dicky lifted a fist high up into the air and began shouting: 'fucker' was the only distinguishable word. Even before the truck came to a complete stop, the driver's door opened with a jerk, and Ronald launched himself out of the cab and ran at Dicky. Dicky must not have been that drunk, for he waited until Ronald got close, then simultaneously threw a left kick and a right-handed punch. The kick missed Ronald altogether, and with his arm he easily blocked the punch.

And then Ronald laughed, a harsh, shitty-sounding laugh that broke through the air like a loudspeaker in a waiting room. Suddenly, as the last notes of this noise died down, he hit Dicky with a right hand that came up and out like the head of a sledgehammer, its weight perfectly balanced to maximize its impact. Dicky fell straight backwards, and as he fell he emitted a strangely feminine-sounding 'oh' before his head hit the turf with a thud. *Jesus*, Michael thought at once, how hard had Dicky fallen if you could *hear* his head hit the moist ground?

Fight over, or so Michael thought. But Ronald wasn't done. He walked behind the prone figure and turned around. As Dicky involuntarily flexed and sat halfway up, his legs stretched before him, Ronald walked deliberately towards him and swung his foot like an old-fashioned field goal kicker, planting the left leg, then swinging *boom* with his right. He caught Dicky square on the back of his head with the steel-capped point of his boot, and Millicent's head snapped down like a guillotine. *He's killed him now*, thought Michael, and looking up he saw the Dairy Queen's neon sign shimmering in the hot and bug-swarming air.

'You want more? You want more?' Duverson shouted at Dicky beneath him, and started to plant his left leg again, ready to score three more points with his right. The Vietnam vet suddenly materialized behind him and wrapped two stubby arms around Ronald's chest and whispered something in his ear. With one sideways roll of his shoulders, Ronald freed himself, then turned and walked back and got in the cab, where he sat on the driver's side impatiently, as if waiting for a friend to finish filling up at the gas pump.

The rest of them surrounded Dicky Millicent and collectively breathed a sigh of relief as he slowly regained consciousness, indicated at first by a telltale moan, then by his ever so gradually beginning to sit up. Dicky rubbed the back of his head and explored the left side of his face with one careful hand. 'What happened?' he asked weakly.

There was silence for a moment. Then the Vietnam vet with 'registered hands' spoke up. 'Boy, you got on Ronald's bad side. I've seen that mistake made before, and I recommend you don't make it twice.'

Michael and Kenny Williams told Donny all about it on Monday, during recess. Kenny said, 'I've never seen anything like it. It was scarier than shit.'

Donny shrugged. 'I wouldn't be scared of him.'

Michael looked at his friend. 'Oh really?'

Donny wouldn't meet his eye. When he did he laughed, a little nervously. 'Well, I might be a little scared.'

'I hope so. Otherwise, you're either crazy or stupid or both.'

This seemed to touch a nerve. Donny wrinkled his nose and said, 'I've got no problems with Ronald. If anybody ought to be worried, it's you.'

'What?' He asked with a sudden sense of dread.

Donny was nodding his head. 'That's right. Ronald's a big fan of your friend.'

'Who's that?' asked Michael, feeling weak and a little sick, for he sensed he knew the answer to his question already.

'Cassie, that's who. He told Daryl Flynn he had his eye on her. Flynn said she was tight with you, and Ronald just laughed.'

'Let's go back in,' said Michael, seconds before the bell rang.

Three

'SEEN A GHOST?'

It was Jock, joining him on the steel stairs outside the
Portakabin where Michael had taken refuge when his mobile
phone had rung. Inside the crew were playing a noisy game of
cards while they waited yet again for the rain to stop.

The two men stood in the drizzle, looking out over the grey
loch. A low bank of dark cloud moved in from the west, further
darkening the colours of the Western Isles in the distance,
muted greens and flint blues. The amazing speed of weather
fronts in Britain; little wonder the weathermen were so often
wrong. In the Midwest fronts came in from the West in slow
motion – a thunderstorm over the Rockies usually took three
days to reach the Great Lakes, its arrival predictable virtually to
the hour.

He turned to Jock, who was struggling to put on an oilskin,
and said, 'It was Atkinson, the lawyer from home. My father
left me the house.'

'You're surprised?'

Michael nodded. 'Completely. I'd always assumed he'd leave
it to my brother. I think my brother assumed that, too.'

'Did your father leave him anything?'

'The Half.'

'What's that?'

'It's some land my father bought a long time ago. It was
supposed to be ten acres, but they got the survey wrong and it
turned out to be ten and a half. So we call it the Half.' He
remembered his father's glee over the mistake.

'What's it worth?' Jock was nothing if not beady-eyed.

'Not much. But that was the whole point of it: the day it's
worth something is the day it's not worth having – it means
civilization is getting close.'

'Did he leave much else?'

Michael shook his head. 'There are some shares, I guess, and maybe something in Detroit – I think that's what Atkinson said. Most of that goes to Gary, but it can't be very much.' He sighed.

'When did you last see your father?'

'Almost seven years ago.'

'Well then, it's not as if it's your doing, is it?'

'I guess I better call Gary.'

When he did, his brother sounded half-drunk, even though it was an early weekend afternoon in Stillriver. Michael rang from the living room of his rented bungalow, looking out towards the Kintails looming huge and impossibly green to the east.

'*Fucking Atkinson*,' Gary began almost at once. 'When I asked him *when* Pop did this he said five or six months ago. When I asked him *why* he did it, he said it was covered by client confidentiality.'

'What's that supposed to mean?'

'How the hell do I know?'

'Listen, we should talk about this.'

'What's there to say? I stay here looking after Pop, and what happens? *Gary gets fucked.* So what else is new?'

Nothing is new, he wanted to say, *since you're doing the same old whining. And Pop looked after* you. 'When I get back we can sit down and sort things out. I'm not going to screw you.'

Gary laughed harshly but Michael sensed he was close to tears. 'There's no need to screw me, Michael. Pop already has.' And Gary put the phone down.

He loved bridges: like geometry, they held a magic that intimacy did nothing to dispel. *How does it stay up?* That was the question he'd first asked himself when as a college sophomore he'd seen a photograph of a voussoir arch, Roman-built but still intact. In a sense, all of his training as an engineer – undergraduate major, the first job in the East, his Masters degree, all the travel and projects of recent years – had been his search for the answer. Intellectually, of course, he knew exactly why some bridges worked and some – the ones he was paid to encounter – threatened not to. But nothing, not all the computations of load-bearing force, or differential equations plotting tension/compression ratios, or slump tests to measure the viscosity of concrete, adequately explained the feeling of witnessing a simple miracle, on the very first day in Engineering 101, when he saw the picture of the bridge and thought, *How*? Like the theorem of Pythagoras, or even the smaller miracle of a curve ball in baseball, the beauty of bridges stood defiantly outside explanation. Bridges were geometry's miracle made real.

He'd taken this Scottish job partly out of time-bred sympathy for Jock, who had uncomplainingly assisted him in half a dozen foreign projects that took him far from his home in a suburb of Glasgow. Jock was rising seventy, squat and square, with arms like clubs from his early days as a brickie's apprentice, when he'd carried countless pails of wet mortar. He was famously direct, although he also had a sentimental streak that took the form of a loyalty to Michael and kept him working; with Michael this had a counterpart in his own unwillingness to insist Jock call it a day. Jock's knowledge of engineering was practical rather than book-learned – and thus most useful for those problems that had no obvious technical solutions. If he'd been less valuable, he would have been put out to pasture by the company three or four years before, when his wife Annie, a veteran of projects around the world, decided she was no longer willing to travel on the job with him, staying in Glasgow instead, where she read women's novels and learned Gaelic at the Adult Education Centre.

Yet for all his fondness for Jock, Michael was uncomfortable in Scotland. He was in magnificent country, but the persistent rain seemed to carry an emotional greyness, and it was hard to admire the view of anything, however conventionally breath-taking, when your socks and underclothes were soaked within minutes of stepping outside. The food, moreover, in the attractive phrase of an English contractor, was 'terrible shite', stodgy and lukewarm and visually unappealing. Too many root vegetables and greasy stews and sticky mashed potatoes. The beer in the village pub down the road was excellent, but the owners were visibly displeased if more than two members of the crew set foot in the place. Unless they were local.

And this too had surprised him – the hostility of the Scottish members of his crew. A surly nationalism seemed rife among those recruited locals who constituted the manual part of his labour force. They were junior in the job's hierarchy to the skilled assemblers he had brought from England, and no amount of nationalist triumphalism could obscure the fact that they were being paid to take orders from their despised Sassenach neighbours. The result was sulky, uncooperative behaviour that slowed down the job and soured the atmosphere. Michael had looked forward to working with men who spoke English for once, but he found instead that a shared language merely facilitated the communication of complaint. And Jock seemed to feel personally responsible, no matter how much Michael tried to reassure him.

Yet the biggest problem for Michael was not people, but the weather, and the fact that the job was being done on the cheap with no allowance from the local authority for any delays. They could curse and kick and scream all they wanted, but there was nothing Michael could do. He specialized in the mix of cement and water and ballast that constituted concrete, which provided the irony – for all that concrete was the newer, stronger, cheaper, and more flexible material – of putting him at the mercy of the elements in a way steel or even iron would not have. Because no advance had yet managed to allow concrete to be poured easily when it was raining.

Job aside, the rain imposed an inactivity in which he had too much time to think. He dreamed about Stillriver for the first time in years, often having the same odd, geographical dream which found him walking the town streets, usually heading towards the drugstore, just as he had in real life during those teenage years when he'd been too young to drive yet felt too old to ride a bike (because it made it obvious – and how uncool – that he wasn't old enough to drive). The dreams were almost sensuous in the tactile feel of the streets he walked; he could have drawn a mental map minutely detailing their slightest variations in grade – a gradual incline here, a slow downhill street there – even if he could not remember all their names.

Increasingly, as the days passed, he brooded on his father's murder, and found his bafflement at *why* he'd been killed as great as his wish to know who had done it. He sensed somehow that the answer to both questions (if he were ever to find answers) would be stunningly obvious, or completely incomprehensible – a lunatic killed his father on his way through town. Curiously perhaps, he felt he could live more easily with a senseless killing than a murderer with a 'reason' to kill, which only something in his father's past could explain. A past which Michael didn't know how to begin to explore. *I don't understand him even when he's dead.*

He was used to thinking about his mother, especially alone late at night when he tried to sleep, or later, in the middle of the night, when he couldn't. It had always brought a soothing if temporary comfort, though the memories were set-pieces, frozen against addition by her death so many years before: picking wild flowers with her at the Half or in the Meadows just up from town; watching her, the time he stole second base in the first inning and stood up to dust off his uniform, as she sat, surrounded by baseball fathers, and beamed at him, her pride moving across the diamond like a laser.

But it was a novel experience to think so much about his father, the mysterious figure about whom he knew so little. Even Henry's antecedents were a closed book to Henry's son. 'Pop,' Michael had asked as a little boy, 'What did your daddy do?' And his father had said, 'Not much,' then changed the subject. Michael had tried a different tack: 'What was your mom like, Pop?' This time Henry Wolf had smiled, then shaken his head. 'Oh, she died before you were even born, son. Even before I met your mother.' After that Michael gave up.

'Was your father some kind of a Jew?' And Michael had

replied to Jimmy Olds, 'Not that I know of.' Which was the truth. Growing up in Stillriver, Michael hadn't really known what a Jew *was*, other than a term of abuse – *you jewed me, don't be such a jew.* Jew wasn't a person; Jew was an unpleasant synonym for avarice, the vernacular form of a casual anti-Semitism which, along with mild abuse of anything coming out of Washington, an aversion to homosexuality, and slight suspicion of anyone whose surname ended in a vowel, constituted the standing prejudices of rural Michigan. So had his father been among the reviled? Michael racked his brain for evidence, telltale signs he may have missed. But like the Jews of Atlantic County, there weren't any. Unless, of course, his father had been a single, unrevealed exception. But why would that explain his murder?

The reason for the murder was not the only mystery he pondered, as the rain continued and he found himself undis-tractable by his detective novels, or by meals in the pub and occasional walks with Jock. Why, for example, had Michael been left the house? It would have seemed almost a joke from the grave if it had not caused such hurt for his brother. Why would his father have turned against Gary? There was no doubting his brother's ability to alienate virtually everyone, but his father's tolerance had seemed lifelong, ironclad; something very dramatic would have had to happen to shake that. And nothing during Michael's quick trip to Stillriver after the murder had suggested any such thing.

And if Michael got the house, what was he supposed to *do* with it? All right, so he was going back to Stillriver for a while – if he were honest, he had known that from the moment Nancy Sheringham told him Cassie was back in town. But for how long? Did he think he was going *home*?

He didn't need a home, hadn't for virtually his entire adult life. New York, even though he'd liked it, proved too alien for him to adopt and ultimately he had given up trying. Then his recent globe-trotting years, where he was happiest unfettered, until he decided he should at least have a base, a home in theory if not emotional practice. And so he'd bought the flat in Ealing, a suburb on the west side of London. It was near the High Street, on a quiet road of small houses, most of them still single-resident.

Why Ealing? Well, a two bedroom flat there remained affordable; it was also near Heathrow and transportation into London's centre was good. Which was the way to rationalize the fact that he simply hadn't known where to go. If it had been up to Sarah, his ex-wife, he wouldn't have had a roof over his head anywhere. There had been something almost perversely refreshing about her searing avarice during the divorce proceedings, especially since it was her family who had money, not his.

It was therefore a good thing that Michael didn't need a lot to live on. He was paid well, if erratically, and his outgoings were modest: accommodation was provided on the remote locations of his jobs, and often food – there had been an early job in the Philippines which hadn't been within fifty miles of a store. So when his wanderlust had subsided, or at least was tempered by the desire for a base, he had been able to scrape together the down payment for the Ealing flat, then take on the ninety-five per cent mortgage he felt too old to have.

He was happy enough to stay in the flat in between jobs, mooch around the Ealing neighbourhood, travel into central London centre for a show or a dinner with friends or colleagues who might be passing through. But it certainly wasn't *home*. Lack of which had never bothered him before. So why now – more sophisticated, better educated, altogether more worldly than the young man who once drove out of Stillriver 'for good' – was he beginning to feel that deep at heart, in his innermost core, he was utterly and completely the product of the town he'd fled? He had always known you couldn't go home again. But no one had ever told him you couldn't ever really leave it, either.

Ten days later it was still raining when Maguire, the detective from Muskegon, called him. 'Are you planning on coming back here anytime soon?'

'I was, but the weather's not exactly cooperating.'

'What's the weather got to do with it?'

'I'm replacing three quarters of a bridge over here. It's concrete. You can't lay it very easily when it's raining. We haven't had a wholly dry day since I got back.'

'That's funny. Neither have we. Maybe it's global warming.'

'Well, whatever it is it's keeping me here for a while. I was hoping to get back for the fourth of July, but at this rate it will be August. Have you found out anything?'

'No big breakthrough, but some leads.'

'Like what?'

'We think the killer was barefoot.'

'Really?' Michael said, but thought *so what?*

'He left a smudged shoe print on the porch by the back door but it's not very clear – Forensics think he took his shoes off before entering the house and left them on the porch.'

'Why would he do that?'

'Because he was being very careful. He not only planned this, he also knew what he was doing. There are no fibres from his clothes that we could find inside.'

'So he was naked?'

'Or not far from it. And he must have worn gloves because there weren't any strange prints. In fact, the only prints they found upstairs were your father's and your brother's.'

'So the killer was barefoot, half-naked, and didn't leave any fingerprints. Really narrows things down, Detective.'

Maguire ignored this. 'Can I ask you about your father's will?'

'Is it one of these leads of yours?'

'I want to know how it affects your brother.'

'Why don't you ask him yourself?'

'He's refusing to talk to us.'

'Why?'

'I was hoping you might tell me that.'

Ping-pong. *I ask this, you say that. So I ask something else.* It was starting to get annoying. 'Is my brother in trouble?'

'I hope not. But I need him to come clean with us, especially about his friends in the Marines. I think he got more involved there than he lets on.'

'Are you seriously trying to tell me he had something to do with my father's death?'

Maguire's voice now grew more assertive. 'I'm saying I'd like to clear him once and for all so I can concentrate on other areas. Without his cooperation that's proving hard to do.'

Michael sighed. 'I'll try and talk to him. But believe me, he's not hiding anything.'

'I'd feel more certain of that if I thought you'd told me everything, too.'

'What's that supposed to mean?'

'Why didn't you tell me about Patsy?'

'Who?' but Michael knew. There was a long silence until Michael grudgingly filled it. 'You mean the letter?'

'Why didn't you mention it?'

'I'm sorry. I meant to tell you but I forgot. Then I meant to call you but what with one thing or another I hadn't got round to it. I don't know who she is.'

'Well, neither do we. So if you get any creative thoughts about it, this time don't keep them to yourself.'

'I hear you,' said Michael. Then feeling chastened he said, 'Listen, I'll try and reach my brother, though the way he's feeling right now he doesn't want to talk to me, either.'

'Do that,' said Maguire. 'And let me know when you're coming back.' There was a long pause. 'Please.'

His conversation with Maguire stoked Michael's curiosity about the Michigan Marines, and he tried to learn more about the outfit from the internet. It seemed sensible to start with its progenitor, so using Google, he rapidly found the Michigan Militia website. What he discovered, however, was almost disappointingly pallid; there was no sign of neo-Nazis at work, or of extremists preparing themselves for insurrection. The emphasis instead was overwhelmingly *educational* – courses, exercises, training, all conducted at weekends throughout the state, most of them outdoors. The usefulness of the instruction struck Michael as a little questionable – he didn't know a lot of people who were commonly caught in the wilderness without food, transport, shelter and a method for making fire – but as far as he could see the ethos espoused was firmly Boy Scout rather than Hitler Youth. There were repeated injunctions about behaviour (no unauthorized weapons, no distribution of literature; failure to obey any instructor's orders would result in instant expulsion) which suggested real efforts being made to distance the organization from its less savoury former association, in the public's mind at any rate, with supremacist groups. And in justification of all this traipsing around the Michigan woods no particular ideology was invoked, other than a general alarmist view that the world was going to hell and the only sure way to survive the inevitable if unspecified catastrophe to come was to pass Level Three Sharpshooting & Sniper Skills.

His heart leaped when he found a link to the Michigan Marines, which he immediately pursued. The homepage he arrived at listed three branches, one of them in Atlantic County – *Commander: Raleigh Somerset*. The rest of the site (not that there was much of it) consisted of listings of impending exercises and 'military manoeuvres', and 'Events', which Michael soon realized really meant barbecues and picnics (*Bring the family*, the site exhorted). The Atlantic County list had not been updated for three months.

He widened his search, and began poking around groups further out on the fringe, looking for far-right organizations in the Midwest. There was plenty there, most of it inflammatory and very angry indeed; he hadn't realized you could use epithets on the web (*nigger, kike, rag heads* were not uncommon) which anyone would shy away from putting into print. Google only got him so far, but its selection of semi-respectable URLs (only a *demi-monde* of the lunatic fringe, not the truly subterranean) provided further links to more rabid sites, and in these he began hunting for Raleigh Somerset.

After several hours' hard work on an expensive phone connection he found him at last, participating in a chat room operating in the anodyne-sounding *Populist States of America* website. From an editorial mention on the main site, he discovered that Raleigh was a frequent contributor to these online discussions, and Michael tried to find out what sort of thing Raleigh talked about. The problem he immediately encountered was that to enter the chat room you needed not only a handle and password, but also had to provide a real name and address (for mailing purposes the site claimed). *Michael Wolf, Anfernachie, Scotland*, seemed a little revealing for the son of a homicide victim, so after some thought, Michael substituted the name *Luke Appleby* and gave *72 Nixon Road, Elbridge, Michigan*, as his address.

Three days later, returning from fishing one of the small lochs, he found a terse email in the dummy mailbox he had set up. There was no Appleby listed either in the local Atlantic County telephone directory or the electoral roll, the message informed him; furthermore, a chat room member who lived locally had, at the site postmaster's request, done some investigating and had reported that there was no such address on Nixon Road. Wondering if this local member were Raleigh, Michael came to the email's concluding sign off: *Access Denied*.

Suddenly, at the beginning of August, they got six days of hot, sunny weather with barely a hint of breeze, and they worked virtually round the clock mixing and pouring until the seal on the final layover was complete and he stood in a cherry-picker extended high above the span, looking down on a finished job.

He stayed the night at Jock's in Glasgow, and took him and his wife to dinner in the city centre, an old restaurant in a cellar, with leather booths. They sat for a long time over coffee and liqueurs, reminiscing about the places they'd worked in the past six years. 'So how long are you going to be away?' asked Annie suddenly, and Michael sensed Jock's eyes on him.

'I don't know. It may be some time.'

Annie was as direct as Jock. 'Have you got somebody back there?'

He smiled weakly. 'I did have, Annie. But that was long ago.'

'I'm taking a break myself,' said Jock, and Michael and Annie looked at each other. This was as close to a retirement statement as anyone would get from Jock. 'At least until you come back,' he added.

Michael nodded. 'Sure, Jock. I'll keep you posted.'

He caught an early plane for Heathrow and took a taxi to the flat in Ealing. He called Gary and again got the answering machine – he left a message asking him to turn the heat on in their father's house. *My house now*, he said to himself, but it sounded unnatural. There was no point calling the house itself since there was no answering machine; it had been hard enough in recent years even to get his father to pick up the phone.

He put on his one suit – Brooks Brothers, dark blue, chosen by Sarah almost a decade before – and travelled by Underground to the company's headquarters in the City. There, in the squat block near Liverpool Street Station, he found most of the personnel had changed. Streatley, his former boss, was long gone, having moved with his second wife and their new baby to a rival based in Stuttgart, and Michael found himself talking to an Englishman whom he had never met.

'No completion bonus, I'm afraid,' the man announced before Michael had said anything. 'If anything the Scottish authorities would like some money *back*.'

'I suppose they think the weather is a Sassenach plot,' said Michael.

'Anyway,' said the man, looking through a thick sheaf of papers, 'I've got a delamination job in Denmark, pretty short term that, and a longer one in Dubai. They say Dubai's rather nice, actually. You're not a Jew, are you?'

Michael shook his head. 'I'm going back to the States for a little while. I've got some family business back home to attend to.'

For the first time the man across the desk scrutinized Michael. 'For how long?'

'Hard to tell. Three or four months, maybe longer.'

The man shook his head. 'Don't make it longer than a month if you can help it.'

'Why's that?'

The man was shaking his head, as if in sorrow at Michael's myopia. 'Business is booming,' he said. 'I've got more jobs than I can fill. But it won't last. And then you may not find it so easy to get back into the game. You freelance people have to understand that it's all very well to be independent, but when push comes to shove we're going to be looking for people who are *reliable*, people who will take jobs when we need them. People who act just like regular employees.'

Michael looked at the man benignly. 'There doesn't seem much point being freelance if you end up running around like a chicken with his head cut off – just like any "regular employee".'

The man waved a dismissive hand. 'I'll give you a month to make up your mind. I can't keep the job open any longer than that.'

2

As he drove over the Junction bridge he found the river just as high, which was surprising for August. There was scaffolding on one side. *About time too.*

The house was cold and empty. Either Gary hadn't got his message or he had ignored it. Michael had not spoken with his brother for six weeks, since the angry conversation about their father's will. Michael had had no opportunity to ask him about his involvement with the Michigan Marines.

He managed to light the boiler in the dank basement and gradually the house warmed up. Upstairs he found Gary's room completely bare now, and then in the kitchen he discovered the freezer empty, and all the canned goods in the cupboards gone. His heart lifted when he saw a solitary beer in the fridge, but it was open and completely flat.

This time he sat in the living room, where years before his father would sit reading, while his mother knitted next to him or read herself as they listened to music. Michael and Gary would sit on the floor, playing a board game spread out on the Mojave patterned rug his parents had received as a wedding present. He sat now in his father's chair and tried to read the *New York Times* he'd bought at the airport in Chicago, forcing himself to stay up to beat jet lag. But why? What precisely did he have to do? And why was he assuming he would be back for a while? He looked around the cavernous living room and thought, *This is no house for a single man. What am I doing here?*

He was still dreaming about Cassie when the pounding woke him. His first thought as he tried to extricate himself from the sticky web of sleep was that piles were being driven into a dry river bed; the second was that someone, bizarrely, was at the front door downstairs.

Looking at his watch he saw that his anti-jet lag strategy had worked, for he had managed to sleep until almost nine. As he moved carefully down the steep stairway in his boxer shorts and a T-shirt he saw through the fan window above the tall front door that the day was fine and sun-filled. As he turned the knob the pounding stopped, but the door was stuck. He used brute force and pulled, and suddenly it came free. 'Christ!' he exclaimed, just getting out of the way of the heavy swinging door.

Donny, standing back on the steps, laughed loudly. 'About time,' he said.

'The last person to use this entrance was a UPS driver twenty years ago.' He shook hands with his friend. 'How'd you know I was here?'

'I didn't. I just saw the car. Getting paranoid are we?'

Michael stood aside to let him in, and they walked into the living room and sat down. 'There's no coffee, there's no bread, there's no milk. I only got here late last night and discovered Gary's cleaned the place out. You want a glass of water?'

Donny stood up. 'Tell you what. You wake yourself up while I run downtown and get some Java. What do you want to eat? Toasted bagel?'

'Bagel? In Stillriver?'

'New York comes to the Midwest.'

He showered, shaved and dressed and finally felt awake when he joined Donny in the kitchen. 'So how's the summer been?'

'Terrible. It rained most of July, then started again last week. It only stopped yesterday.'

'I thought I'd be getting away from the rain coming here. It must have put a dent in business if the weather's been that bad.'

Donny shrugged. 'I guess so. To tell you the truth, it's been an odd time anyway.'

'Because of the murder?'

Donny nodded. 'The police say they're exploring all sorts of leads, but they haven't given out any news or seemed to make any real progress. On the surface, life's gone back to normal – what else are you going to do? But it isn't really the same. People are scared, and they'll stay that way until they find your dad's killer.'

'*If* they find Pop's killer. You know, it might have been a drifter, some one-off burglar who isn't even in Michigan any more.'

They pondered this in silence, until Donny said, 'Listen, I've got a problem with the Junction bridge. Me and my boss can't seem to agree. I was hoping you might be able to give me some advice.'

And as Michael ate his bagel, Donny explained. He was in charge of the small crew repairing the Junction bridge and was following the plans of his superior, the county's one qualified engineer. 'The thing is,' explained Donny, 'I don't think Cassavantes knows what he's doing. Only I'm not an engineer so I can't really challenge him.'

'What do you think he's got wrong?'

'He's only resupporting one side – the upstream side – because he says it's the current flow that's weakened the concrete of the supporting piers there. I think the whole thing's wonky. But if I'm right they'd have to close the entire bridge – the way it is now only one lane will get shut down. And nobody wants the bridge out of commission, especially in summer. You've got four miles detour to come into town the other way.'

'So how can I help?'

'Come have a look and tell me what you think.' Donny paused. 'Just a quick look,' he said awkwardly. 'Unofficial. I can't pay you anything.'

'*You can't?*' said Michael in mock outrage. 'Don't you understand who you're talking to? Why, I charge seventeen hundred dollars an hour to look at some of the world's most famous bridges. So you expect me to look at a lower peninsula piece of pissant work for free?' He felt he was just warming up. '*Gratis* as the Romans would say? *Pro bono* work? You think I'm running a charity, boy?'

Donny was smiling by now. 'Is this what they call jet lag?'

*

116

What Michael had not appreciated, flying back, was that he was arriving in time for Homecoming weekend. Now he found himself, late that afternoon, walking with much of the Washington clan – Donny, Brenda, their two younger kids on bikes – to watch the parade. Other families were also hurrying downtown in a quick-moving, ragged procession of T-shirts and shorts and bicycles and strollers. It was an entirely unsinister version of the crowd scenes of sci-fi movies of the '50s, in which inhabitants moved *en masse* towards the Town Hall to discuss how to combat the giant blobs threatening to invade their small town Eden.

They passed Cassie's old house, where the new extension was still under construction. 'Who did she sell it to?' he asked.

'Summer people with deep pockets,' Donny said loudly.

'Hush,' said Brenda, but she laughed. She was a big woman, whose vast thighs filled her Bermuda shorts, but with oddly petite features – a button nose, jujube lips and eyes like small collar buttons. She had a pretty face and a sunny disposition, which had been the perfect antidote to Donny's broken heart when Nancy dumped him. Brenda sometimes teased Donny that he still carried a torch for Nancy, which was probably true, and made Michael admire her even more and think her right for Donny. His friend would have hated farming. He was too sociable: Donny liked having neighbours within shouting distance, with half the children of the neighbourhood playing with his own kids in their backyard.

'A lot of building going on,' said Michael, for he could see several other houses along the street that were now being turned into modular hodgepodges of affluence. 'More money than sense,' Alvin had liked to say about any obvious excess, and that is how Michael felt about these supplementary constructions. For the enlarged houses dwarfed their lots, and lost their former elegant simplicity of line and material (wood, wood, and more wood). Improvements in the manufacture of aluminium siding, formerly available only in telltale thick nine-inch board, meant it could be used to ape the thin lines of the original white pine in a sleek, modern mockery of the old

117

wood's rough grace. It seemed typical of the pseudo-preservationists whom his father had despised that they put commemorative plaques on buildings whose spirit they were effectively destroying.

'You know,' Michael announced as they neared Main Street, 'when I was back in May I never got downtown. Not even to drive through. I expect it's changed.'

'I'm not saying anything,' said Donny as they turned onto Main Street by the Methodist church. Crowds were already beginning to line both sides of the street, and Michael felt the strongest sense of déjà vu as he began to walk down the street. It was as if he were wearing bifocal, sometimes even trifocal glasses, with different lenses for different eras. For what he saw now was paralleled by a visual memory of what he had seen as a boy, then as a young man. The different presentations seemed to run as separate strands, like the multiple applications of his laptop, except that here the different windows merged in a mysterious confluence of memory and time.

'What happened to Dumas's?' he asked, pointing at its former corner location, the excuse for his first assignation with Cassie.

'Dumas's?' asked Donny, dumbfounded. 'That's a long time ago, Michael. You've been back since it changed.'

'I guess you're right,' he said slowly, starting to remember what had initially replaced it – a retail storefront for a talented wood-carver, who sold oak candle holders and elegant maple boxes in summer. During the rest of the year he might make the occasional commissioned piece, usually a Christmas present (one year Alvin Simpson had given his wife a walnut wardrobe; some lady in Burlington had commissioned three blanket chests), but was forced to supplement his income by working as a carpenter for a local contractor. It must have always been a touch and go enterprise; now Michael could see that 'go' had triumphed in the long run. In its place stood a shop of such elegant pretension that he thought for a minute he was in London's South Kensington, or taking a break in Stockholm after a job on one of the western islands. *Gourmet coffee has come to Michigan*, he thought with a smirk, looking at the hand-painted canisters high on a shelf carrying coffee beans from all over the world. Takeaway cups of *latte, cappuccino and espresso* were all on offer, and fancy baked goods behind glass. Time was, the only choice in coffee in this small town was with cream or without. 'They'll never make it,' said Michael, thinking of his youth, when a few stores utterly reliant on summer trade would open and inevitably fail. 'Here in May,' Alvin would say, shaking his head as another T-shirt shop opened its doors, 'but not to stay,' as he gleefully watched them go bust during the cold months out of season.

'Actually,' said Brenda mildly, 'they've been going about five years. The owner says business is better than ever.'

'Really? There must be more money around than there used to be.'

'There is,' said Donny firmly.

'Hey stranger,' a voice boomed. He looked up and Larry Bottel stepped in front of him, holding out a hand. He was wearing a blue shirt with thin stripes of alternating white and orange – the effect was dizzying.

They shook. 'Hi Larry, how've you been?'

'I'm back here now, selling real estate. And business is *good*,' he said. 'Listen, I was real sorry about your dad. Never knew a nicer man.'

'Thanks, Larry. He liked you, too.' Had he? He'd never said one way or the other about any of his friends, had simply seemed to accept them, and that was that. Except for Cassie. He'd made that clear, though not by saying very much, just once remarking, 'Your mother would have liked that girl.'

Larry now grew confidential, moving his face in closer to Michael's. The skin on his cheeks was puckered and bumpy. Too much sun? Booze? 'Michael, I heard about the house. I don't know what you're planning to do, but if you decide to sell, I hope you'll remember your old buddy from the drugstore. And don't worry, we can handle rentals too, if that's the way you want to go.'

How did Larry know the house was his? If it wasn't Atkinson

himself, it was someone Atkinson had blabbed to. There was no point getting irritated about this – the inevitable leaks of a little town. 'Sure, Larry. But I'm not going to do anything right away.'

'Okay,' said Larry. 'Hope that means you'll be around for a while.' He scanned the street, a hand over his eyes to shade the sun. 'Listen, I've got to scoot and meet my kids. But come round some time. We're down near Viner's cottage, just next door. And bring your family, too.' Suddenly he leaned forward confidentially again, 'Hey, your old girlfriend's back in town.' Michael didn't say anything. Larry slapped him on the shoulder. 'Don't worry – I won't tell your wife.' He laughed hard at this.

'Jesus,' said Michael appreciatively as he rejoined the Washingtons.

'Some things *don't* change,' said Brenda.

'Larry's not that bad,' said Donny. 'He just can't help himself. You're playing cards and having a few beers and suddenly he tries to sell you a mobile home. But he's not like Jeffers.'

Jeffers had been a wheeler-dealer whom Alvin had spotted from the beginning. Michael remembered Alvin standing by the cigarette rack, picking at his own cashews from the rotating machine and saying, 'I give Jeffers two years. Then he'll be bust or in jail.' Jeffers managed both within eighteen months.

He had been a Gatsby-like exception; what other wealth Stillriver had then contained was solid, low key and hard won. *No one used to be rich here*, thought Michael. Strictly speaking that wasn't true. They'd found oil on Paskett's forty acres years ago, which bought Paskett a swimming pool (where Michael and seemingly half the town's small children had taken swimming lessons) and eventually an expensive divorce. But otherwise wealth was uncommon, and rarely flaunted. When Alvin had bought a Cadillac, he'd felt the need to explain to Michael that he was merely fulfilling a vow he'd made to himself as a boy in the Depression. Not precisely plutocratic. Who else? Lonergan was well off – his emporium had always thrived in the summer months, but as a strict Baptist Lonergan only splurged on a finer grade of grass seed for his lawn.

'Let's go down by the City Hall,' said Donny. 'The kids can stand on the wall there and get to see.' So they kept walking along what was becoming an increasingly crowded Main Street. Every now and then Michael noticed someone staring at him; once an old boy in a straw hat tapped his wife and pointed him out with a bony finger. Feeling self-conscious, Michael concentrated on looking at the storefronts on either side of the street, and discovered that virtually every one now pandered to the summer tourist trade. Again, he felt himself in a parallel universe, switching between the new commercial realities and the Main Street he remembered from boyhood. In two blocks he counted six realtors where formerly there had been only Harold Riesbach, who had also sold insurance to make a decent living. The bakery was now a clothes shop, the hardware store was divided into three upmarket boutiques; the former dime store sold expensive-looking teak carvings; the movie theatre had been divided into offices.

It had long been a resort town, and in the other, non-season nine months the town drew into itself perfectly happily, using the money summer brought in the way a hibernating bear draws on his reserves of fat. You bought groceries at Dumas's or Schiffer's, your paper in the drugstore, drank coffee and ate terrible sweet rolls in the bakery, filled up your car at the Standard station (the Shell station was more expensive on gas, better at repairs), and saw the doctor (Dr Fell for over forty years) in the brick one-storey building he'd put up in 1959, next door to the funeral home you paid him to keep you out of.

The difficulty was that you could do none of these things now – buy groceries, get gas, see the doctor. So what kind of life could you have in this town outside the summer months? What good was a T-shirt or ice-cream shop in late November; how much of a January morning could be spent looking at wood carvings?

'Changed a bit, huh?' asked Donny.

'I'll say,' said Michael. 'At least the park's still here. And the bandstand.' Scene of Thursday night concerts all summer long.

'Remember how we used to roll down the hill as kids? Well, you can't do it any more. The place is *packed*. People get here two hours early just to find a place for their folding chairs.'

As drums from down the street signalled that the parade was on the move behind them, he came to the drugstore. Six years earlier Alvin's store had been on its last legs. He knew that Alvin had sold it at last, to a beer distributor from Detroit who fancied himself a retailer. It was hard to see why: entering the store, Michael saw changes everywhere, none of which made any commercial sense. The neat aisles were gone, replaced by standalone units that wasted space and made the store look messy. Newspapers were now by the front door, violating the fundamental retail principle of drawing the purchasers of inexpensive items deep into the store, where they would pass many other things to buy.

And then, taking a minute to overcome his disbelief while he figured out what was missing, he realized it wasn't a drugstore at all any more. Mr Beer Distributor had decided to dispense with a pharmacist, which rather defeated the underlying purpose of what was traditionally known as a drugstore. *Marilyn would have died at this*, he thought, and felt awash in memories, the thousand incidents and minor episodes that built a corpus – yes, it seemed heavy as a body to him – of sights and smells and noise. The comical incidents were naturally the most enjoyable to remember: the evening Frank Conroy, who lived in the squalid apartment upstairs and worked at the wireworks, had bought and drunk three pints of Rocking Chair bourbon after his half-day Saturday shift, then marched through the store just before closing, singing a song about a French-Canadian whore. Or when an intensely nervous Michael had sold prophylactics for the first time, to a construction worker who came in from the bar next door and must have been surprised, on opening the bag Michael had so discreetly handed over, to find three *dozen* condoms rather than the three he had asked for.

There were also poignant moments, as when the ancient, almost historical farmers would come into the store, on what for many was one of only two or three trips to town each year. Marilyn knew them all and would insist on serving them herself. 'Hello Claud,' she'd say to an old man in a clean pair of overalls, his face mahogany-coloured from years of working in the sun. 'Marilyn,' he'd acknowledge shyly, before using a big, calloused hand to extract his money from a deep pocket, then count the coins out on the counter with painstaking care while Marilyn handed over the pouch of chewing tobacco or pack of Lucky Strikes or Pall Malls. Even to the young Michael they seemed to be the last vestiges of the county's past, as they shuffled in and out like the black-and-white figures he'd seen at school in a documentary about the Dust Bowl in the Depression.

There were bad memories too: the time Margaret Mercy, a middle-aged recluse who refused to take her epilepsy medication, suffered a fit just there by the perfume counter; or when Oscar Peters walked through the second and perpetually locked glass front door (he needed one hundred and seven stitches); and the tension in the air the time a Detroit lady complained about the smell when a family of Mexicans stood in the aisle looking at the rotating Timex watch display. It had taught him to avoid generalizations about human nature, for just when you decided that people were essentially good, Mr Nice Guy turned out to beat his wife with a tuning fork. Before your cynicism took over completely, however, you discovered that some exemplar of wickedness was a secret philanthropist, paying the school tuition of Korean orphans and reading on the sly to the residents of an old folks' home.

Looking around him now, Michael felt as if the location of his own life's unofficial schooling had been knocked down. *Jesus Christ almighty*, he said to himself, or so he had thought until a woman in plaid pants frowned. 'Sorry,' he said, but she had left the store. He walked out into the oncoming distraction of the Homecoming Parade, remembering the look on Alvin Simpson's face when he'd told him he was switching majors from pharmacology to engineering.

'You okay?' asked Donny.

'Yeah.' He motioned at the store. 'It's just changed so much.'

'And it's about to change again,' said Donny. 'I hear he's going bust.'

The grim state of the store bothered him. Why? If he wanted his past behind him, why care that the *scene* of that past had changed? Perhaps because one of the very things he had escaped from was no longer there to flee. It was like encountering a long-lost love, one held immutably in the imagination for many years, only to discover that they had changed so completely that the person you were in love with *didn't exist any more*. He didn't want to think what Cassie would be like now, though this was not an avoidance he could sustain for long, since within sixty seconds of leaving the drugstore he had spotted her, standing with her two children, deep in the crowd across the street.

At first he assumed his imagination was simply being over-active. Years before in New York he had suffered agonizingly from phantom sightings of her, outside Paul Stuart on Madison Avenue, at the bar of Gallagher's restaurant off Broadway. All illusory, of course, which made him doubt what he seemed to be seeing now. But there she was, crouched down in her blue jeans and sneakers, with an arm around the little boy – Jack, wasn't that what Nancy had said? – whom he'd seen from his car outside Buckling's Gun Shop. Next to Cassie was a little girl. *That must be Sally*, thought Michael, watching as Cassie pointed down the street towards the advancing parade. He knew he wasn't hallucinating when he saw her upper teeth bite down on her lower lip.

He was confident she hadn't seen him, and soon he could no longer see her, for the parade had reached them and blocked his view. He was relieved, for he felt his blood was rushing every-where inside him, and his arms twitched, and a tic had suddenly declared its presence with short, repeated strokes above his left eye. In an effort to slow his breathing he forced himself to watch the parade.

God knows, there was plenty to look at. For if in his

childhood the parade had been a pretty limp affair – the high school band blaring John Philip Sousa, one solitary majorette, the Homecoming Queen waving from a chair on a flat bed towed by the town's fanciest car, and that was that – now it was a larger, virtually professional production.

Why don't you join the band? had been the standing insult when you dropped a pass or lost a fly ball in the sun, and the band in his high school years had been the bolt-hole for geeks and losers. But now it clearly enjoyed greater status, since half the high school seemed to be in it. They marched by, spruce in their gold and purple uniforms, playing 'Tie a Yellow Ribbon' at an accelerated clip. They were followed by members of the American Legion in a mix of uniforms, veterans from World War II, a few of Korea, and two guys he recognized who had been in Vietnam. Then a succession of store-sponsored floats – the *Wild Thyme Shop*, *The Emperor's Ice-Cream Store*, *Pot-pourri and More*, *Bottel's Bakery*, the *Dairy Queen*, and the *Atlantic County Bank*. Two of them had teenage girls sitting on top, wearing two-piece bathing suits and throwing taffy candy, which small kids scrambled for on the pavements. On others sat the families of the business owners, from babies to grand-parents. And one – the bank – had nobody on the float at all.

Then came a series of antique cars – a Model T, driven by a South Beach man Michael recognized, its honking horn sounding like a goose in pain, two pre-war Dodges, a Studebaker, then a mini-convention of Corvettes from the early 1960s. A cavalcade of Shriners followed, fat middle-aged men riding large three-wheeled motorcycles and wearing maroon uniforms with gold trim and commanders' hats with white plastic bills, weaving wide-wheeled figures of eight in an intricate motorized ballet. The float with the Homecoming Queen came next, a tall blonde girl with a toothy grin, wearing a ball gown of blue taffeta with long white gloves unrolled up to her elbows. Then, incongruously, the Collinsville Clown Band, announced by a blast of Dixieland jazz. They were famous for their outrageous costumes, heavy boozing, and adroit musicianship – in roughly equal proportions.

Which made the group behind them all the more peculiar. Four men marched together, side by side, their faces cast with fixed expressions of a disturbing, solemn grimness. Each carried a rifle, slung over the shoulders by a strap, and they all wore camouflage hunting fatigues and short-sleeved shirts of combat green, the sleeves just long enough to bear a badge, a large black '**M**' in a circle of white.

There was something ridiculous about them, but something sinister too. The tallest, a heavily-muscled man with a reddish tan, a blond crew cut, and wide, innocent-looking eyes, seemed to be the leader, for he very slightly preceded the others, marching in crisp strides that smacked of the parade drilling ground. Michael poked Donny as the weird quartet passed by. 'That guy looks familiar,' he said, pointing to the tallest one.

'Sure he does. That's Raleigh Somerset. And that,' he added, taking in all four with a sweep of his hand, 'is the famous Michigan Marines you were asking about. All *four* of them,' he added scornfully.

'They don't belong in the Homecoming Parade.'

'Of course they don't – nobody thinks so. But when they tried to keep them out they threatened to go to court. It seemed easiest just to let the dumb shits march.'

A hand touched his shoulder, and he turned round to find Jimmy Olds standing behind him, in his uniform of blue starched shirt, dark tie and dark sunglasses. 'Hey Jimmy.'

'Nice to see you back. Here for long?'

Michael couldn't see his eyes through the dark glasses; Jimmy's tone was friendly but semi-professional. 'Don't know yet. Any news?'

Jimmy shook his head. 'Afraid not. Still interviewing people. We've talked to just about everybody we can think of. Even students of your daddy from forty years ago.' He shook his head again, then seemed to recognize how hopeless he was making his efforts sound. 'Something will turn up,' he said feebly. 'Say, Maguire wanted to know if I'd seen you. You called him yet?'

'I got here yesterday, Jimmy. Let me catch my breath, will you?'

'I was just asking.'

'He does push it a bit,' Michael said.

Jimmy nodded. 'I know he does. Fact is, if he weren't a fellow professional, I might even describe him as an aggressive little prick.' When Michael laughed Jimmy allowed himself a small smile. 'I'll let him know you're back, Michael. Look after yourself.'

When he turned round the parade was ending. He looked but could not see Cassie or her kids in the dispersing crowd across the street. He scanned up and down Main Street fruitlessly, finding many familiar faces, but not Cassie's.

Wasn't that Kyler's daughter, and hadn't she got fat? Look at that lady in the wheelchair – could it really be Mrs Fell? God, Candy Simmons looked old. And, up by the ice-cream store, wasn't that Ethel, about the size of a twelve-year-old girl but with a woman's face? But where was Daisy? And what was Ethel doing here alone? The final squad car moved gently through the crowd with its roof light flashing, strobe-like. He walked around and behind it, looking for Cassie, but she had disappeared. *Just as well*, he thought, since he had no idea how she would react to seeing him. He looked again for Ethel, but she was gone too.

'We're going home now,' said Brenda as he rejoined them in front of the drugstore. 'Why don't you come to supper?'

'Thanks, but I've got a lot to sort out.'

'You sure?' It was Donny.

'Yeah, I'm sure. But thanks anyway.'

'You should take your time, you know. There's not a lot to do in Stillriver that can't wait.'

There was no real other side of the tracks to Stillriver. Even if you included the trailer park, no one lived in outright squalor; only the Back Country had people on the margin, the invisible rural poor who scratched out an existence which no one made documentaries about and politicians found demographically insignificant. In Stillriver itself, the four square blocks around the wireworks were about as close to a low-rent district as the town allowed. They contained single-storey breezeblock bungalows, erected by the wireworks company on land it then owned in an effort to attract new employees during its sole period of expansion just after the World War II. Other than the shoreline, this was the lowest-lying part of town, sitting next to a long trough of swamp which separated the town's perimeter road from the neat grid of the town's residences. Stillriver's sewage had drained into the swamp from one side; from the other water came down from the higher land of the Meadows; the result was a vast, primitive cesspit, its grey ooze studded here and there by scraggly cedars, the one species of tree that could live in such revolting liquor. Long after a processing plant had been built on the other side of town, the swamp's smell had lingered, sulphurous and sour as a paper mill.

Gary had said he was living across from the parents of Sissy Farrell, so Michael had no trouble finding him. 'A pink place kitty-corner from the Malcolms' or 'you know, the white house on the lake side of the old school' – these were the designators he had grown up with and remembered. With no home delivery of mail, there was not any identifying value to a numerical street address: if Gary had said 325 Cedar Street, Michael couldn't have placed him with confidence within three blocks.

Opening the front screen door of the bungalow, Michael stepped into a low-ceilinged living room full of magazines and newspapers and dirty glasses. Hearing a television set from the back of the house, he walked through a wood-panelled galley-style kitchen that was surprisingly tidy. 'Anybody home?' he called. In the back he went down a step into a screened porch, which looked out over ratty yellow grass and a low wire fence towards a virtually identical bungalow.

Three young men were watching television, one sprawled on a sun lounger, the other two leaning back on a sofa with their feet up on a bamboo coffee table. After an initial glance his way, they kept their eyes glued to the television.

'Football this early?' he asked, looking at the screen.

'Exhibition game,' said the guy lying on the lounge chair. Michael looked at him. He was long and skinny, wore jeans and a white T-shirt with cowboy boots, and had a mouth, thought Michael, like a small asshole. On his forearm there was a purple tattoo of a mermaid entwined in an anchor.

He turned to the two on the sofa. One had a boy's face with the improbable adornment of a bushy, ginger moustache. Next to him sat a fat, sandy-haired man with slick-backed hair, who was draining a can of beer. Both of them paid no attention to Michael, so he tried again with the guy on the lounger. 'Is Gary here?'

The tattooed cowboy stared at the screen. 'Who wants to know?'

Enough was enough. 'I do,' he said flatly.

'Hear that?' said the guy on the lounge, craning his neck to look at his two friends. 'Bubba,' he said with a smile, looking past Michael.

Michael turned round and faced a newcomer who walked in from the kitchen. *Bubba?* he thought. *Who are these guys?*

'Say what?' said Bubba, in a voice so deep it could have been bought from the classified ads section in a bikers' magazine. He was a little over six feet tall and must have run close to three hundred pounds. He had the long, greasy, black hair of biker mythology and wore a blue jean jacket, tan workpants, and clunky work boots.

'This guy says he's looking for Gary,' the cowboy announced. 'Says he's called *Eye-Do*.'

'Actually,' said Michael, changing tack, since he could see no percentage in playing tough guy, 'I'm Gary's brother. Anybody know where he is?'

Bubba seemed to find this funny, for he guffawed like a cartoon bear. He walked through the room, still chuckling, opened a door in the far corner, then went through and closed it behind him. Coming out again a minute later he signalled with his head. 'Find him in there.'

Gary was lying on the bed on his back, with his clothes on but his shoes off. 'You all right?' Michael asked as his brother slowly opened his eyes and took him in.

'All the better for seeing you,' said Gary, using their father's favourite greeting. Then he closed his eyes again. There was a glass of something brown and watery next to the bed, with a long cigarette stub in it, half-floating, half-submerged.

'Who are those guys next door?'

'Friends,' said Gary. There was a leaden note to his voice.

'Not real friendly friends.'

'I didn't say they were *your* friends,' he said, growing slightly more animated. 'They thought you were a cop.'

'Why?'

'Because of your clothes.'

Michael was wearing pressed chinos, a blue cotton golf shirt, soft loafers – the same clothes he'd worn, along with a sports jacket, for his farewell dinner with Jock and his wife. He looked down at his brother, who was keeping his eyes closed, and said, 'Speaking of cops, Maguire wants to see me. You know what that's about?'

'No.'

'I had a feeling it had something to do with you.' He thought of the 'friends' next door. 'Maybe it's the attractive company you're keeping.'

Gary snorted. 'I thought a man was still allowed his own choice of friends.'

Leave it alone, he decided. 'You missed the parade.'

Gary now opened one eye. 'I had my own celebration last night.'

'So I see.' Even by their usual standards, Michael thought, the two were conducting a pretty desultory dialogue. 'Why don't we get together when you're feeling better? Come round to the house. I'd give you supper but I've got to shop first. You cleaned me out.'

'Sorry about that.'

'Can't you afford your own groceries?'

Gary put a hand over his forehead.

'I thought you were a partner now. That's what you said.'

'We never signed the papers.'

'And you had a falling out with Harold?'

Gary's hand moved down over his mouth. His words came out from between his fingers. 'Something like that.'

Oh, Christ. 'When'd you last get paid?'

'June.'

'Why didn't you tell me? I've been calling you for weeks now.' He didn't expect an answer and didn't get one. He tried to control his irritation as his brother now put both hands over his eyes. 'Come over when you get up. I'll buy you supper at the Poplar.'

'Pop said they'd fucked it all up. He wouldn't go there any more.'

'They still serve whitefish?'

''Spose so. Why?'

'It's pretty hard to fuck that up. Anyway, come by the house. I'll lend you some money. Then I'll talk to Atkinson. We'll sort something out.'

As he left the trio were still watching football. In the kitchen the big guy named Bubba was making peanut butter sandwiches. As Michael passed by him Bubba said, 'Y'all come again, ya hear?' like a racist comedian doing black folks, then gave another guffaw.

Thugs, he thought as he left the bungalow, then thought again. He had not supervised construction crews throughout the world without some acquaintance with the kind of hard guys who were always happiest with violence as a solution (or resolution) to anyone crossing some internal line of cussedness that was their (the hard guys') *raison d'etre*.

But these guys had seemed more punk than thug. There was something strange about the set-up, odd as well as unpleasant, that he couldn't really put a finger on. And then he got it. These men were young but grown-ups: *not* teenagers. Yet there was an overwhelming sense of 'boys' night out' about them all; there was not the smallest suggestion of women in their lives, even deep in the background. What had Gary said about his girlfriend? *I threw her sorry ass out.* Creepy, definitely creepy. What was this all about?

And then he suddenly wondered, would his father have changed his will if he'd discovered Gary was gay?

He waited until eight for Gary to show, then went and ate dinner by himself at the Poplar Inn, the town's first hotel, built around 1900 on the top of a dune next to the State Park. It had new owners, well-heeled ones from the looks of things. On his table, a brochure for the hotel boasted about the recent renovation of the bedrooms: a double room cost $135 and *brought back turn of the century charm with today's comforts;* the honeymoon suite (price on request) was decorated with *authentic antique Shaker furniture.* On the walls hung photographs of the nineteenth-century Stillriver, sepia stills culled from somebody's ancient scrapbook or a volume of local history. One showed the original sawmill on the shore of Stillriver Lake; another the ferry crossing at the lake's shortest ends, close to where the channel was later dredged and lined. Then a shot of two moustachioed men cutting ice with a long two-handed saw, while a cart horse, hitched to a wagon full of sawdust, stood waiting for its load.

No wonder Pop didn't like this place any more, thought Michael, for it seemed to embody the ersatz historicism his father had loathed. Considering his almost obsessive interest in local history, it was funny, thought Michael, how much his father had resisted recent efforts to promote it. Was it because it seemed so artificial, and so out of place? So *un*Midwestern? Yes, that was it – these new owners seemed intent on recreating the ambience of a New England inn, as if in some superior way they believed that there was a historical grandeur to the town which, until the owners came on the scene, had gone completely unappreciated by the ignorant locals.

And that would have infuriated a man who, having killed off his own past, had been passionate about that of the town where he'd come to live. Henry Wolf had held a timeless, romantic vision of the Midwest, based on an ideal that presumably had first drawn him to Stillriver. His father had created his own mythology, thought Michael as he examined the vast menu, full of food previously unknown to the state of Michigan (*Belgian* frogs' legs), and this mythology rested on the purely American building block of the melting pot. *Be what you want to be, not what you were born as. Be American*, which came full circle back to *be what you want to be*. But ultimately the mythology was about the Midwest – where plain men rode tall, or walked that way at least, and women were gentle and kind, and the region drew its strength from a quiet, unaffected pride in its inhabitants, who were, well, quiet and unaffected.

And where nobody banged on about their ancestors, unless one of them had done something funny or outrageous, or spectacularly brave, and nobody gave a shit about what ship their family had sailed on to come to America or whether they prayed in a simple nonconformist church with an elegant white bell tower or rolled about in more opulent pews, sniffing incense and lighting candles. Where first names were the stuff of '50s sitcoms – Darren, Bruce, Debby, Kim – and last names potentially anything – Walwicki, Meisenheimer, Buryk, Jabot – without being in the least regarded as socially indicative. In other words, the Midwest of lore. That's what Michael's father had believed in.

And the problem was, as Michael was coming to recognize, however much he didn't want to as he finished his Lake Michigan whitefish and good green beans (he held out against the importuning owner, who was functioning as sommelier, and stuck to beer), then walked home in the muggy air, just beating the thunderstorm; the problem was, as he opened the locked back door then relocked it behind him, and the wind outside picked up and the rain came down, first like a gentle sprinkler then, picking up volume, more like bucketfuls dumped from the heavens, and he turned off the brass standing lamp in the living room and went upstairs; the problem was, as he got into his bed with just a single cotton sheet over him and yet another Edinburgh paperback mystery to read as two Bogle boys squabbled across the street and a car door slammed and someone raced by on a bicycle, the wheels hissing on the now-slick surface of the street and the wind whistling through the turning spokes; the problem was, as he thought of his father's almost wilful negative distortion of the life to be had anywhere else, his sentimentality about Stillriver, his provincial romanticizing and fundamental unshaken belief in the virtue of a Midwestern life; the problem was, as Michael thought of his own nomadic recent past, the far-off places he'd worked in, the rootlessness that no flat in Ealing was going to cure; the problem was, thought Michael, *I'm beginning to believe in it, too.*

He woke up and wondered if he had dreamt the sound of thunder, close by, virtually simultaneous with a lightning strike, a mixture of *boom* like a cannon fired at close quarters and then *crack,* sharp as a whip. The rain had stopped, and the wind came through the window in a cool flow of small, rippling waves over the sheet. The bedside clock said half past three.

Or had whatever wakened him come from inside the house? The thought unnerved him, and he lay still, breathing as quietly as he could, listening carefully. A small creak – was that the stairs, someone moving slowly up them? The faintest of thuds – the boiler, perhaps, but what was it doing in the middle of the night?

There was nothing for it but to get out of bed. He turned on the light, went out into the hall, opened the closet and found his father's sixteen-gauge Winchester shotgun. Feeling faintly ridiculous but also nervous, he turned on lights as he went and toured the entire house. In the basement he found the fishing rods of his childhood; his father had hung them and his own waders from nails pounded into the side of one of the enormous overhanging floor beams. Behind them he found a window open. It was a very small window, just above ground level, and faced towards the street in front; it was hard to see how anyone larger than a small boy could get through it. But he closed it just the same.

Emerging upstairs he repeated his tour in reverse, this time more warily. There was nothing. Returning to the kitchen, he poured himself a hefty belt from a bottle of Maker's Mark he'd bought at Duty Free and took the glass and the shotgun upstairs. Standing outside his bedroom, he put down his drink on a bookcase, broke open the breech of the shotgun, and discovered it wasn't loaded. *That would have done a lot of good*, he thought.

He rummaged through the closet and found an open box of shells. He took two of them, loaded and closed the gun, then carefully put it standing up in the closet of his bedroom, half-hidden behind one of his jackets. He felt uneasy about keeping a loaded gun in the house – what if kids came in? *Whose kids?* he asked himself, trying not to think about Cassie and her children. But he took the shells out and put them back in their box, then placed the empty shotgun on its side, high up on the shelf above the hangers, just as the first birds began their early call for dawn.

LATER THAT MORNING he drove to Meijers in Burlington and spent $245 equipping the house and buying food. There was a certain adult satisfaction in buying cleaning stuff – Windex, paper towels, sponge-headed tubes with washing liquid inside, a new mop head, washing powder – but it was a childish delight he took in buying the food.

For he had forgotten the sheer abundance of the American supermarket. There were fewer differences between America and Britain than he had expected, chiefly because Britain (or London at least) seemed to him so surprisingly wealthy. He had gone there expecting to find it infinitely poorer than America, misled by his colleague Streatley's memories of an England many years before – little heating and less hot water, fridges the size of a laptop computer, dinky-sized cars and waxed toilet paper.

Still, there was the constant sense there that space, physical space, was at a premium, not to be wasted. He remembered how driving through Sheffield he had been amazed to find sheep grazing on a green hillside just above a steel mill, and how British greenbelt policy kept a rural ring around each town, giving a sense of space in a country smaller than Minnesota. In America, paradoxically, you could drive for miles through the asphalt peripheries of even small-sized cities before finding open countryside. The availability of so much space meant it was exploited to wastefulness.

As in the cavernous arena he entered now, with a ceiling so high that once inside he didn't notice it any more, and floor space the size of several football fields. There was a pizza parlour at the front – *Eat Here or Take Away / Makes no difference to what you pay* – a drugstore (one more nail in the coffins of the small town likes of Alvin Simpson), an optician, an ice-cream shop, a hardware store, and, just inside the food store itself, a bakery. Having made the expensive mistake of coming shopping while hungry (he'd had just coffee for breakfast) Michael now cut loose.

He began with healthy priorities in the fruit and vegetable section. He remembered shopping with his mother, her fixation with large salads – *healthy food for my healthy boys*. He and Gary had called it rabbit food – behind her back so as not to hurt her feelings. Now, captivated by a sprinkler system dripping pearls of ice water on the lush-leaved heads, he bought three different kinds of lettuce, then a cellophane bag of peppers the size of softballs, fire engine red and the yellow of hotdog mustard, beets scrubbed down to vermilion, baby carrots the size of his little finger, a long, fat cucumber with shiny skin, and a bunch of radishes with diameters the size of golf balls.

Always mad about fruit, he started to buy blueberries and peaches, then realized he could get them fresher at Sheringham's, as well as new-picked corn, so he contented himself with a quarter-watermelon, dazzled by the crescent-shaped rim the colour of Key Lime pie and the flipside flesh, which looked like a trough of pink, studded with raisin-black seeds.

Lamb stew, beef stew, pork stew, even ghastly chicken stew – the relentless succession of watery broth, mushy carrots and deconstructed onions of his father's cooking had given Michael a perpetual appetite for unadorned cuts of meat. At the counter he stared at the mitts and flaps and mounds, pink and crimson for the beef, the dull beige marble of pork, and he succumbed like a child unable to stop eating chocolate. He bought a sirloin steak the size of a first baseman's glove, two pounds of lean hamburger, and a flange of skirt steak; he remembered how, years before, Cassie had grilled it, on one of the few occasions she had cooked for him when her father was away. *Delicious*, he'd declared, and she'd beamed with pleasure before admitting it was the only thing she knew how to cook. Now he also picked up a pack of four griddle-marked cube steaks, two long racks of spare ribs, veal escalopes, a cut-up frying chicken, three packs of local hotdogs, a small plastic tray of pork chops, and finally, in case he hadn't done enough for his cholesterol count, a bag of frozen jumbo shrimp from the Gulf.

He felt he was past the point of no return in this plundering swoop through the supermarket, and to wash it all down, he added jug wine and a twelve-pack of Stroh's beer, fifths of bourbon and Scotch, then threw in Gilbey's gin and bottles of house brand tonic water – in case a cousin from South Beach should drop in. He liked to drink, unlike his father, who had confined himself to the occasional beer; or his mother, who was really pushing the boat out when she allowed herself a weak highball.

Potatoes came next: a big bag of Idahos, then a string sack of onions, boxed garlic, and he was just eyeing a bag of frozen French fries, thin and particularly adept at grease absorption, when a voice said, 'Hello neighbour.'

He looked into the thin, pinched face of an old lady, neatly dressed in an old calico dress with patterned roses. This old-fashioned modesty was punctured by a pair of spanking white gym shoes. For the briefest moment, he thought that Mrs Decatur had risen from the dead, then realized he was face-to-face with Mrs Jenkins, his father's neighbour on the other side of the cedar hedge.

'How nice to see you,' he said automatically – *be polite*, his father's stricture since he was four years old. He had been standing stock still by the freezers, so he courteously did not move on, though he yearned to. The Jenkinses were polite and pleasant people (she was smiling now), who had retired to Stillriver from Lansing, where Mr Jenkins had worked for a large insurance company. They'd seemed almost excessively grateful to move to Stillriver, vocal to the point of absurdity in their appreciation of the merits of small town life (they'd been among the first to put a plaque on their porch). Stillriver was their Pleasantville, that Disney creation of picket fence and homemade lemonade served in Grandma's favourite pitcher.

So it had taken a while to realize how unbelievably nosy the Jenkinses were, how relentlessly they interfered in other peoples' business, how tenaciously they worked to ensure their neighbours lived up to the Jenkinses own high standards. Even the Bogle boys found themselves being pushed around by these elderly new arrivals: for the first time the boys actually used the green plastic boxes provided by the town authorities for newspaper collection, started parking their many cars neatly parallel to the street, and made unprecedented efforts to rein in Ralph, their half-blind mutt, who was long accustomed to claiming all the local backyards as his own.

Mrs Jenkins was looking with interest at the contents of Michael's shopping basket and her eyes lingered on the booze. 'Saw you'd come back,' she proclaimed. 'It's nice to have a neighbour there again.' She seemed to sense her tactlessness, adding, 'We do miss your father, you know. God bless him.'

It was a sincere smile Michael could give to this, since he knew that if his father were enjoying one emotion at the moment, wherever he might be, it was relief to be out of range of the obtrusive neighbourliness of the Jenkinses. 'I am sure he has you in his thoughts.'

'May they find the man who did that to him, soon.'

Amen, he almost responded.

Mrs Jenkins said, 'That detective seems *awfully* young.'

'Who's that?'

'Maguire is the name, I believe. He said he'd spoken to you.'

Don't say a word, he told himself, or it would be halfway round town before he went to bed that night. He could hear her hushed account: *I have to say Michael Wolf didn't seem very impressed with the efforts of the police.* Or would she say 'constabulary'? He looked down at his purchases, feeling childlike again, caught with *both* hands in the cookie jar. 'I thought I'd better stock up,' he said weakly.

'I didn't know you had a family,' she said pointedly, then her face brightened again. 'I take it you'll be staying a while. It will be good to have the place tended again. Goodness knows what your father would have said about the yard. He was such a tidy man.'

Better than Gary, he thought, *that's for sure*. He stared at a large, frozen blueberry pie while Mrs Jenkins kept talking.

'Like us, your father was very disappointed when they let Benny open up the B & B. But you know, it hasn't been that bad. And at least he got those two girls out of there.'

Benny had two girls? Then he realized she meant the twins. So they were gone after all. *Shit*. 'Ethel and Daisy aren't so bad, Mrs Jenkins.'

'Never noisy, that's true. But hard to control. You've been away a long time, young man. I think they drive the people in that home crazy, if you ask me.'

'What makes you say that, Mrs Jenkins?' He was trying to stay polite but also trying to understand what had happened to the twins.

'Why, because they keep running away. Benny takes them back, then they run away again. Especially that Ethel.'

That explained why he had seen Ethel at the Homecoming Parade. 'Maybe they don't like it there.'

This was obviously not what she wanted to hear. 'I'll let you get on with your shopping. We'll be seeing you, I'm sure.'

He lifted the pie with relief and put it in his cart, then added a half-gallon carton of vanilla ice-cream from the vast freezer section in the centre aisles. He moved to the aisle of ancillary condiments – A-1 sauce, ketchup, dill pickles and a jar of relish took care of that. He finished at the bakery counter with a tray of fresh dinner rolls, a bag each of hotdog and hamburger buns, two loaves of still-warm bread and a pecan coffee cake. His trolley was overflowing, and he wheeled it with cautious dispatch to the checkout counter.

'Having a party?' asked the woman behind the till, 'or just got growing kids?'

Not you too, he wanted to say, but only smiled non-committally as his English credit card went through and he found himself signing a screen with a graphic pencil. Steering his overloaded cart out on to the baking, softened macadam of the vast parking lot, he found that his emergence into the sudden envelope of heat triggered the memory of a two-month

140

consultancy in Riyadh, the single hottest place he had ever been. He dismissed the memory as best he could, but wondered if his reimmersion in America, and return to Stillriver, were why he was acting like a kid in a candy store.

He was unpacking his groceries in the kitchen and wondering who on earth was going to eat all the food he'd bought when a slow wail began to fill the air and he almost jumped out of his skin. The town's daily siren, what the inhabitants called the Noon Whistle. As he confirmed this with a glance at his watch and relaxed, he heard footsteps on the porch and a little boy's complaining voice. He went to the screen door and opened it just as a hand was starting to knock.

'Sorry,' he said for the small collision, then looked into Cassie's big blue eyes.

'Hi,' she said a little shyly. 'I heard you were back. I missed you last time. I wanted to say how sorry I was.'

'Thanks,' he said, moving his eyes away from hers, feeling unprepared for the almost banal actuality of meeting once again what he had assumed was gone for good, the slight unreality of seeing in the flesh what he had seen only in his head for more than six years. Eager for distraction, he looked at the little boy holding Cassie's hand. 'You must be Jack,' he said, and got a toothy grin in reply. 'And you're Sally, right?' he called out to the girl in the background. The girl nodded solemnly.

'Coffee?' he asked Cassie.

She hesitated, then Jack piped up. 'Can we play outside, mister?'

'Sure you can.'

'You stay right around here,' Cassie commanded. 'I'll be in the kitchen.'

Inside he spooned coffee into the percolator while she stood by the sink looking out the window at her children. 'This room's just the same,' she said, turning and looking around.

'The whole house is just the same,' said Michael. 'It's like a museum; I should charge admission. Pop didn't redecorate *anything*.'

'I always liked this house,' said Cassie. 'It has a lot of character. Big rooms. And high windows.'

'It's mine now.'

She didn't seem surprised. 'What are you going to do with it? Sell it?'

'Maybe. I thought it was going to be Gary's problem and I'd just get left with the debts.'

'Are there many of those?'

'None at all. I was surprised. His pension couldn't have been very much.'

'How's Gary taking the business with the house?'

'Badly.' When Cassie nodded, he said, 'I was thinking of asking him to live here. No point paying rent when a house this big is going empty.'

'You going back soon?' He could detect nothing from her tone; she might have been making polite conversation with a visiting tourist.

He shrugged. 'That depends.'

'On what?' When he didn't reply she said, 'Oh, on how soon they catch whoever did it. They must have *some* ideas.'

His tongue clucked like a cricket against the roof of his mouth. '*I've* been cleared, apparently. Even high technology wouldn't let me bash my father's head in from Scotland.'

Cassie shuddered. 'Don't.'

'Sorry. Frankly, I don't think they have any idea who killed my father. And neither do I.' He wanted to change the subject. 'Anyway, what about you?' he asked, moving next to her and looking out the window. The girl Sally was sitting in the director's chair, reading, while her little brother ran round and round the spruce tree, whooping noisily.

'What about me?'

'You here for good?'

'I'm not going back to Texas, if that's what you mean.'

He kept looking at Sally. 'They're going to let him out some time.'

'That's nothing to do with me.'

'Does he know that?' he asked, still unwilling to look at Cassie.

'He does. I told him to his face, in case you're going to start feeling sorry for him.'

'Cassie, I'm not likely to feel sorry for him.' He smiled sourly. 'How did he take it?'

When she didn't reply, he said, 'I thought so.'

Outside the boy suddenly slipped on the grass by the spruce and fell hard, scraping his knee on a paving stone. He started to cry and his sister came out of her chair, dropping her book. Cassie started, then put both hands down on the edge of the sink as her daughter comforted her son.

Michael stared at the boy. 'He looks just like Ronald, doesn't he?' She nodded, compressing her lips, and he added, 'Why did he ever think he could be anything but his?'

Cassie sighed. 'Maybe he knew I wished it were that way. But please, let's not talk about it.'

He poured the coffee into dark blue mugs and got the milk out of the icebox. He walked over to the door and called out through the screen, 'Jack, there's a wagon in the shed over there you might like to play with.'

The boy stopped crying. Michael came back and stood by Cassie, and together they watched as Jack pulled the old PF Flyer out of the shed. After a moment Michael said, 'Jesus, that was a grim place.'

'What was?'

'That motel.' He remembered the room's sterility, the depressing certainty he'd had that its bright colours and fabrics were endlessly repeated in thousands of identical, loveless cells across thousands of the motel chain's bedrooms across America. They had been able to see the runway of LaGuardia, barely more than a mile away, and feel the shudder as airplanes took off, then watch them disappear into the smoky cloud that had hung like a bad mood over the New York area.

'We didn't have much time as I recall. Sorry.'

'It wasn't your fault. I wasn't thinking of blame.'

143

'Really?' She looked at him and he saw how little she'd aged since he'd last seen her, waving goodbye as she got into a taxi and he'd held back the curtain of the bleak hotel room and stared down at her, certain he would never see her again.

'I never blamed you for any of it.'

She laughed, but not happily – there was a mixed note of weariness and cynicism in it. 'That's a relief. Pity my husband never saw it that way.'

'I hate it when you say that.'

'What?'

' "My husband".'

This time she reached down and took his hand in hers. She interlocked her fingers with his and squeezed hard. 'I am so glad to see you.'

She came back the next day for lunch with the children, having agreed to help Michael make a dent in his mountain of groceries. He felt peculiar all morning waiting for her, then realized that what he felt was simple happiness. Which made him wary, for he was gun-shy. *She only squeezed my hand*, he told himself, like a teenager debating the signs in a first provisional courtship. He was leery of his sudden, bubbling hope, the tingling anticipation he felt knowing he was about to see her again. There had been a time not so very long ago when his life seemed to have meaning only because of Cassie; he knew that because when he'd had to live without her his life had seemed meaningless. *Seemed?* he thought cynically; *it's still that way.*

When she and the kids showed up just after the Noon Whistle, they all sat outside next to the wooden fence at the picnic table, which his father, when first retired, had spent an entire summer sanding down and varnishing. They ate cube steaks on buns with tomato slices and lettuce, and he and Cassie drank white jug wine while the kids drank milk.

'You know, I saw you at the parade,' he said. 'But when all the floats had gone by you weren't there any more.'

'Dairy Queen,' she said and laughed. 'I promised Jack an ice-cream.'

'Butterscotch dip?'

'They don't sell them any more.'

He put his hand on his heart. 'Too much change. I barely recognize the place. A tourist trap now, pure and simple.'

She picked up a piece of lettuce. 'It's still a pretty town, Michael. Whatever you say. And the money helps everybody. The school's a lot better than when we went there.'

Feeling slightly chastened he changed the subject. 'Tell me, was I imagining things or did I see Ethel at the parade, too?'

'You might have.' She smiled slyly. 'But how do you know it wasn't Daisy?'

'Ethel has the five o'clock shadow.'

'Don't be mean.'

He gestured with his head towards the cedar hedge. 'Mrs Jenkins said they're in a home.'

'Haven't you seen Benny?' He shook his head and she went on. 'He put them in the home at Fennville last year, after he started up the B&B.'

'Which place are they in? They're too young for a nursing home.'

'They're in Fennville Acres. You know, the one on the side road by Happy Valley.'

'You mean they're in the *poorhouse*?' The county place for indigents, a Victorian relic he had assumed had long been put to bed, replaced by modern if equally horrible places for the homeless or chronically drunk or mad – anyone with a bad enough complaint would do, provided the complainant had not even a nickel to rub between their hands. When he was a boy, his father had joked about Fennville Acres: 'Mind you don't put me there when I'm old and grey.' Back then there wasn't even indoor plumbing in the place.

Cassie said wearily, 'I know. I've been to see them. It's terrible.'

'Are they mean to them?'

Cassie shrugged. 'Hard to say. Mainly I think they just ignore them both.'

'Do you visit them very often?'

'I've only been twice. It's hard for me to get there because of the kids; I wouldn't want to take them with me. That place is *grim*. Benny goes. Once in a while.'

'Jesus Christ, Cassie. Can't we do something?' He looked at her, then realized the fatuity of his words. 'I know, I know,' he said, 'it's none of our business.'

But most of their conversation, over lunch and then on into the afternoon, as Sally read her book and Jack played in the old iris bed, was unremarkable: Stillriver – how it had changed, how it had stayed the same; the kids; her search for a job. 'I think I may have something now,' she said.

'Ah,' he said, remembering how Nancy had told him how hard it had been for her to find work.

'Miss Summers retired. Remember her?'

'How could I forget her?' The second-grade teacher. Prim, even in her younger days, teaching Michael almost thirty years before. In her spare time, a gifted creator of dried flower arrangements – 'How fitting,' he'd once heard his father say to his mother, 'seeing as she's dry as dust herself.'

'They had a replacement lined up from Lansing, a young woman.'

'Oh, and you're so old?' He was glad to see she still blushed when teased.

'You know what I mean. Anyhow, she's decided to get married and stay at Lansing.'

'And they've offered you the job,' he said, happy for her but somehow discomfited too. *She's not going anywhere then*, he thought gloomily.

She was shaking her head. 'Not yet. They're going to advertise again. But the principal says I've got a good chance.'

'Fingers crossed,' he said, trying hard to smile.

Without ever really discussing it, they managed to see each other every day that week. The amount of food he'd bought provided a standing excuse to invite her over, and they ate hotdogs or sandwiches for lunch at the picnic table, or ate early supper inside at the dining room table, which hadn't been used in years. Although usually awkward with children, he liked her two kids, and with the easy grace of their young age they were soon no longer shy of him. He especially liked Sally, who was a sombre-faced girl, much given to reading – with a little encouragement she would tell him about her favourite books and show him two of her 'special' dolls. Jack was easier on the surface – all little boy, running around, playing cops and robbers by himself. He also loved the PF Flyer wagon, and would cajole his sister into pulling him round and round the big spruce tree in Michael's backyard, then recruit Cassie when his sister got bored, even pressing Michael into service until he too flagged, his arm heavy as lead. But there was something less innocent in the boy as well, something a little meaner than you usually found (at least in Michael's limited experience) in the average child. When his sister teased him Jack would go quiet, a sure preface to going for her, and when he made his run it was with a steely, murderous anger that chilled Michael. For he knew just where Jack had got that from.

With Cassie, surprisingly, Michael felt awkward, and they avoided those topics of conversation that might prove thorny, such as how long he was back for or what he might do next; such as Ronald, who wasn't mentioned again after their initial exchange. They didn't even talk about his father's murder or who might have done it, not even after Jimmy Olds came by the house to give a self-conscious report (ninety-three people had been interviewed to date and seventeen phone calls received, of which two were anonymous), which managed to convey both the extensive activity and lack of progress of the police investigation. And though Michael had left a message for Maguire with the police in Muskegon, he had yet to hear from the detective.

His feelings for Cassie had been so long dormant that he had imagined them extinguished, but he knew now that had never really been the case – why else had he come back to town so urgently this summer? He could see how in a matter of days she was already beginning to colour his life again, to the point where even the smallest plan he made – to run even the most pedestrian errand – had him taking Cassie and her brood into mental account.

He did not find her greatly changed, for there was the same easy grace about her, evidenced in how she *did* things: he liked to watch her perform even the most everyday tasks, from washing the dishes to cleaning the barbecue with an old toothbrush, or just to watch how she laughed when Jack spilled ice-cream all over her jeans. As ever, she always had a book on the go, inevitably a novel – Anne Tyler, Diane Johnson, Joan Didion. Michael liked it when she'd describe them, talking about their characters rather than the plots he relished in the formulaic thrillers and detective novels he read. She still liked wine, but now bought him bottles from states where he had not realized grapes could prosper – Washington, Texas, even Michigan itself.

Yet it wasn't clear any more to him what she was *feeling*, and he was not confident that she wanted the same closeness again. Sometimes she behaved as if she were spending time with a member of her family whom she actually didn't know that well. But then why was she seeing him again, and so often? Why, without ever mentioning it, had she fallen so easily into a daily routine of visiting him?

Curiously it was a spat that dissolved the tension. At the beginning of the following week he went to her house – 'It's time we fed you,' she declared. He came in through the back door of her bungalow, stepping down onto a freshly waxed linoleum floor as the screen door banged shut behind him, to find Jack going *bam bam bam* with the fingers of both hands wrapped around a stick, like a television detective pointing his weapon. Cassie gave Michael iced tea in a plastic glass full of ice cubes, and he stepped into the living room, surprised to find it an absolute mess. Cassie apologized and he said, 'Don't worry,' but it annoyed him – this annoyance serving to annoy him further, since he knew he was unnaturally orderly in his childless bachelordom. *You don't have kids*, he told himself. *Remember that. You have no idea what it's like.* But something of his irritation got out, for he looked at the crooked mountain of video cassettes and the web of wires and attachments and adaptors that lay like so many black snakes on the rug underneath the television and hi-fi and tape deck and God knows what else, and asked, a little tetchily, 'What is all this stuff?' Was this how Ronald had taught her to live?

'Don't be stuck up,' she said.

'I'm not. I'm not a snob.'

'How do you know?'

'Because I was married to one. So I can recognize the breed.'

Cassie looked at him sceptically. 'Well keep an eye on the mirror, pal. You forget, Michael, it's a long winter here.'

'I thought Sally likes to read, just like you do.'

'Kids can only read so much; you can only play so many games of cards. And when Jack gets too much – you know, stir crazy with all that energy – then I thank God for videos and I thank God for cable TV.' She looked at him and added crossly, 'so don't you go acting sniffy with me until you spend another winter here.'

'*Don't you go* . . . ?' he asked with a smile. 'Your father never talked that way.'

'You know exactly what I mean.'

He shrugged. 'Don't listen to me, Cassie. It's not for me to criticize.'

Though she seemed to accept his apology, her mouth, firmly set, said *no it isn't.*

And when he left that night, not late but well after the kids had gone to bed, and he tried to prolong their kiss goodbye, she broke away and shook her head. 'Let's get one thing straight, okay?'

'Sure, Cassie,' he said, but his voice was light and nervous.

'We're not the same as way back when. If that's what's in your head forget it.'

'I know that, Cassie. It's not like we haven't seen each other since then.'

'Six years ago,' she said flatly. 'And that wasn't for all that long. You know, when I saw you that first time again in Texas, I thought it didn't matter that we'd each changed, because some

149

part of us – you, me, and us together – had survived. Now I'm not so sure.'

'Why? Are you that different now?'

She looked at him in surprise. 'Me? No, whatever Ronald did to change me happened long ago and you've seen it. But *you've* changed.'

'No I haven't,' he protested. 'I am what I've always been.' When she shook her head he felt suddenly almost desperate. What he didn't feel he could say was that yes, he knew he had changed, and that deep within him now there was a coldness that had not been there before. But *she* had put it there. Six years before. Didn't she realize that? 'You loved me way back when,' he said plaintively. He added, 'And I'm still the same.' Not daring to state where the logic of this was intended to lead, but hoping she would do that herself.

'I loved you then for a lot of reasons.' She paused and laughed. 'Because you were smarter than you knew. Because you were cute but didn't know it. Because you were shy.' She looked at him knowingly. 'Don't try and tell me you're shy any more.'

'You're making me shy,' he said, like a kid wheedling pocket money.

'Tell me about it,' she said curtly, but with a small smile. Then she grew serious. 'What you are now is a cynic.'

'No. I'm just not sentimental.'

She looked at him almost pityingly. 'Michael, *all* Americans are sentimental. That's what this country is about. That's what being an American *means*.'

'Okay, so I'm just not naive any more.'

She snorted. 'Bullshit – excuse my French. You haven't been naive since your sophomore year in college.'

He had no answer to this and his face must have made that clear. Cassie took a step back into the kitchen. 'I'm not trying to be hurtful, but the way you've been talking since you came back makes me think you're on some expedition down Memory Lane. Maybe you're nostalgic instead of sentimental. Donny said you acted surprised Dumas's wasn't there any more. *Honestly,* Michael.'

STEVE ATKINSON DIDN'T look like a drunk, but then, Michael charitably concluded, that was because he wasn't a drunk any more. Michael had called and left a message for him during the week, and was surprised when the lawyer called him back late Sunday morning. 'I'm in the office today,' he explained, 'catching up on things.' He didn't mention his extended absence from town. 'Drop by if you like – I'll be here 'til three.'

Cassie and the kids were at Sheringham's, so Michael ate lunch at home by himself. As he came out of the back door to go downstairs, he saw yet another car slow down in front, its occupants pointing at the house. Gary had told him that the town was 'freaked' by his father's murder, but so far Michael has seen as much curiosity as fear – these cars slowly cruising by, the people at the Homecoming Parade staring at him, then quickly looking away.

He disliked being the object of public interest, but he could not avoid contact with his neighbours, and he had already received a number of unsolicited visits from them, usually on the pretext of their offering to help: Mrs Decatur's grandson came by with a toddler in tow, bringing a plate of chocolate chip cookies; Mr Jenkins, his way eased by his wife's encounter with Michael at Meijers, came and talked a mile a minute about town affairs with only the briefest of references to the murder, then offered the loan of his lawnmower in case Michael wanted a 'finer cut'. Even three Bogle boys made a showing at the back door, cleaned up for the occasion in fresh T-shirts, extending their condolences and offering to keep an (armed) eye out for unwelcome visitors to the Wolf residence.

It was all kindly meant, Michael knew, though he suspected it was as much designed to help evacuate their fears as to assist him. He was not surprised to learn from Donny that since the murder the households of the town had taken to locking their doors at night, and that Buckling claimed his gun sales had doubled.

He walked downtown, where Main Street was full of tourists window shopping. Atkinson's office was in a low building of yellow brick, built badly in the '50s on a concrete base that was now cracking, two doors down from De Witt's Funeral Home. Michael found him sitting at his desk in the back room of his office.

Atkinson wore chinos and a brown golf shirt and talked in a deliberate, somnolent way that reminded Michael of the first time he had worked with a colleague on Prozac. Atkinson's father had driven the school bus in New Era; possibly as a consequence, the son was at pains to let you know he had *professional* qualifications.

Now from his desk he drew out a copy of Henry Wolf's will and put it on the desk between them. Michael pointed at it and said, 'Gary told me my father changed that six months ago.'

'That is correct. Though now it's actually been eight months. He came in here a little after New Year.'

Since Gary had also said that Atkinson wouldn't discuss *why* their father had changed his will, Michael was surprised to find him perfectly happy to say *what* had changed. 'Basically, your father simply reversed the earlier disposition of his properties.'

'Reversed?'

'Swapped, if you like. So what you got in the earlier version is now Gary's, and *vice versa*.' He pronounced the vowels at the end of both words.

'So up until January Gary would have got the house, and I would have got the Half.'

'Correct. You also would have got the lion's share of his other assets.'

'Which are nothing much, are they?'

Steve allowed himself a shrug, not wishing to deprecate the value of his dead client's holdings. 'There's some Common-wealth Edison stock, a couple of downstate utilities, a few bonds – I figure they come to about six thousand dollars. Then there's this Detroit company.'

'What is it?'

Atkinson pursed his lips. 'I regret to say that I haven't been able to discover that. Your father says in the will that he wants his holding in the company divided four to one between you boys in Gary's favour – and it said just the opposite for the earlier version. But I can't trace the company.'

'Doesn't he give its name in the will?'

'Sure he does. Fine and Son – with a P.O. Box in Detroit but no other address, and nothing saying what the company does, or who to contact. I've written to the P.O. Box two times now. No reply.'

Michael shook his head in dismay, and Atkinson took this as criticism. 'I know, I know, I should have caught it when your father changed everything, made him spell it out. But I didn't,' he said defiantly, as if he were being wrongly accused. 'Frankly, I wasn't expecting anything to happen to your father.' He paused as this sentence seemed to curdle, then added, 'I assure you it wasn't because of my own problems.'

'I didn't think it was,' said Michael. 'I was shaking my head because the whole thing is mystifying. And I don't know how we're going to find out what or who this is. Should we hire a private investigator?'

'I wouldn't recommend it myself. The fact is, I don't know what they'd discover that we can't. The Post Office aren't allowed to tell us who holds a box number, and a box number is all we've got.'

'And the name – Fine and Son.'

For the first time Atkinson smiled. 'Somehow I think there's more than one Mr Fine in the city of Detroit.'

He walked home, and as he crossed the driveway he saw that Jack had left the PF Flyer underneath the spruce. One of its wheels was loose, and Michael got a screwdriver from the tool box his father kept at the top of the basement stairs and tightened the screws. As he put the screwdriver back he heard a creaking noise below him in the basement. He took out the screwdriver again and held it as he slowly walked down the stairs, feeling alternately scared and ridiculous. At the bottom of the stairs the air was musty and slightly sour, a trigger for memories of being sent down here as a boy by his mother to fetch mason jars full of peaches she'd pickled, or white asparagus spears.

To his relief, he found that he had simply failed to close the small window properly when he'd come down here at three in the morning. He shut the window, then looked around the room. Behind the waders he found a kiddies' blue inflatable wading pool – bought for whom? The grandchildren his father had never had? – folded flat on the concrete floor. By the boiler there was a tarpaulin crumpled in the corner, a mouldy softball and two baseball bats, one of them a red plastic bat for playing whiffle ball on the beach. The wooden bat had *Roger Maris* written in black on its fat, bleached, vanilla-coloured barrel. He'd been given it as a birthday present by his mother. He picked up the bat and tentatively swung it through its web of associated memories. He checked his swing and stared at the end of the bat, then brought it, still extended, closer to the bare light bulb where he looked at the faint reddish smears he could just make out in the faded grain of the bat's ash wood.

He went upstairs and out the back door, bat in hand, his heart suddenly pumping thunderously. Sitting down, he thought, *How could they have missed it?* It was right under their noses: what *had* they been doing? Searching the bushes, dragging the channel, enlisting bloodhounds from inland counties? When right in the basement, almost directly beneath the murder scene, lay what looked very much to Michael like the weapon that had killed his father.

Call Jimmy, he thought, looking again at the dark strands of blood. Putting the bat down carefully, he got up and went inside, started to make the local call, thought for a moment, and dialled Muskegon instead.

Maguire showed up two hours later in a Subaru, wearing jeans and white running shoes and looking about sixteen years old.

'Sorry to interrupt your weekend,' said Michael.

'You didn't. I'm working.'

Michael pointed at his clothes. 'Is Sunday dress down day?'

Maguire looked a little embarrassed. 'I was on a drug case hoping to bust a dealer. He didn't show.'

'I thought you were Homicide.'

'Homicide is not exactly a full-time occupation in this part of the country. Now, you want to show me this bat?'

'It's right behind you,' said Michael, pointing to the base of the tall spruce where he had placed the bat standing up.

Maguire nodded, then went to his car and returned with two large plastic bags and a pair of rubber gloves. As he put on the gloves he asked, 'Whose bat is this?'

'Mine.'

'When did you last see it?' Maguire was putting the bat handle in one bag, the bat end in the other.

'I don't know. I haven't been here in nearly seven years and I doubt I saw it then. I was with my wife and we only stayed a night.'

'You didn't see it this spring when you came back?' He taped the bags together where they met in the bat's middle, then carefully balanced the package on the seat of the director's chair.

Michael exhaled, thinking back. 'I'm sure I must have gone into the basement to have a look around; but I don't remember seeing it.'

They went inside and down to the basement, where Michael pointed towards the boiler in the corner. 'Right back there, next to the whiffle ball bat. But I just don't know if it was here when I came back after the murder.'

'I do,' said Maguire. 'And it wasn't. I searched here myself the following day. And Jimmy Olds had already been through the day before. We were looking for a blunt, heavy weapon – believe me, I wouldn't have missed a baseball bat, not sticking out like that.'

'So who put it there?' Michael asked, turning off the light and climbing the stairs. He saw a questioning look come into Maguire's face. 'And whatever you say,' said Michael, his voice

155

rising, 'don't say "I was hoping *you'd* tell me that". I couldn't stand it.'

Maguire's expression changed to one of amusement. He held his hands up in mock-surrender. 'Okay, you win, I won't say it. Say, I don't suppose there's any chance of a drink of something, is there?'

'Cold beer?'

'Perfect.'

They went into the kitchen and Michael took two cans of Stroh's out of the icebox. They sat down at the kitchen table to drink them.

'You play a lot of baseball as a kid?' asked Maguire.

'Just when I was younger. I didn't play in high school. How about you?'

Maguire nodded. 'High school. Then junior college. I was hoping for a while I might get drafted by the pros, but looking back I think I thought I was better than I was.' He took a long swig from his can.

'Where are you from?'

'Dublin.'

'Dublin? You've sure lost your accent, then.'

'Dublin *Ohio*,' he said with a smirk.

'Oh,' Michael said, mildly embarrassed. 'I thought because of your last name—'

'I am exactly one-sixteenth Irish. But because of the name, everybody assumes I like potatoes and go to mass.'

'You live in Muskegon now?' he asked, imagining life for a snappy young policeman. A condo, probably, in a singles complex, where Maguire could lie back in summer on a lounge chair by the communal swimming pool and pick off the poolside beauties one by one. *Actually,* he'd say with disarming modesty, *I'm a detective.*

'No,' said Maguire. 'I own a small holding in New Era with my sister. She raises horses and has a riding school. I'm in charge of the peach trees.'

'How did you get to Michigan in the first place?'

'A girl from Newaygo.'

'Sounds like a song.'

'A sad song,' said Maguire and smiled ruefully. 'She dumped me three weeks after I got here.'

There was something likeable about that, and perhaps that was the point, for now, wiping his mouth on the back of his hand, Maguire returned to business. 'Did your brother use the bat too?'

'I'd be surprised. He never played ball,' said Michael, wishing they could talk about peaches instead. 'Is he really still a suspect in this?'

'Officially, yes. But I don't think he killed your father. I never have. He might know the person who did. Without knowing that he knows, if you catch my drift.'

'Is this the Michigan Marines we're talking about again?'

Maguire nodded and finished his beer.

'And just how is Gary involved?'

'He knows a lot of the members, hangs out with them. That's established. And he's been to meetings.'

'I saw some of his friends.' He described the three watching television, adding, 'and there was a big guy. Looked like a biker.'

'Bubba.'

'That's right. Real charmer.'

Maguire didn't respond to this. He held out his empty beer can and slowly crumpled it in his hand. 'I don't know. For a while, I thought maybe this was some sort of racist murder, because of the swastika. But nobody thought your father was a Jew, maybe because he wasn't.' Maguire smiled.

'Why couldn't it have been some nutcase? That seems to me to make as much sense as any other theory.'

Maguire shook his head. 'It was too carefully planned. Things like taking his shoes off.'

'Someone with a grudge, then?'

'That's more probable, though everything we've learned about your father makes it seem very unlikely it was just a personal thing, like an ex-student convinced his life had been ruined by your dad. He just wasn't like that, was he?' When

Michael nodded reluctantly, Maguire said, 'So then I started to think maybe it was a political thing. Even if your father didn't seem to have any politics.'

'If anything he was conservative.'

Maguire nodded. 'Exactly. And it seems your father went to a Marines meeting or two.'

Michael was astonished. He pinched his lower lip between his fingers and sat shaking his head.

Maguire explained. 'They have events sometimes. It's usually a barbecue – something with food because it helps get the crowd. You know, five bucks and all the chicken you can eat. Then somebody speaks.'

'Who was speaking?' Perhaps this had been the draw for his father – a historian speaking, perhaps, or a scholar of Native American culture. *But at a Marines meeting?*

Maguire shrugged his shoulders. 'Don't know anything more than I told you.'

'Well, who told you?'

Maguire looked at him coolly and said nothing. *Oh*, thought Michael, feeling slow on the uptake, *an informer told you*. 'You have ways of making them talk, eh?'

Maguire grimaced impatiently and said, 'So that's where your brother comes in. You see, we've almost had enough to put the local leader of the Marines away on two occasions.'

'That's Raleigh Somerset?'

'That's right. Once downstate—'

'I heard about the Grand Jury.'

'You are well informed. And once up here. We searched his place and found several sticks of dynamite. That's a federal offence.'

'Dynamite? That sounds pretty retro.'

'Retro?'

Michael wondered if he'd used an Anglicism – too much time in Ealing. 'Old-fashioned. I thought fertilizer was all you needed.'

'A single-shot rifle's old-fashioned too, but it works. And so does dynamite.'

'What happened?'

'We couldn't prove the link with Raleigh. We didn't find it in his house but in a corner of the property. The DA said that wasn't good enough.'

'So what about my brother?' he asked a little fearfully.

Maguire shrugged but it seemed a disingenuous gesture, almost coy. 'You better ask him.'

'But why would the killer put the bat back, if it is the weapon?'

'Hard to say. But I'd bet you the earth that whoever killed your father won't have left prints on the bat.'

'Meaning what?'

'Meaning they put the bat back for some other reason. I haven't figured out yet. But it means the murderer is still around, or at least wasn't just quickly passing through.' Maguire looked at the back door behind Michael. 'You lock up here at night?'

'I do now.'

'You got a gun here?'

'My father's shotgun.'

'Know how to use it?'

'It's not exactly rocket science.' He remembered being taught – *you can swing with the bird until you cover it or you can lead it. Either way will work.* Which was true – he was a competent shot, except when he tried both methods at the same time. 'Should I be preparing to shoot someone?'

Maguire was back in professional mode and didn't smile. 'I think you should be careful. After you left last time one of your neighbours called in to say she thought she'd seen a light on in the house here – at three in the morning. We checked with Gary and he said he hadn't been here then. Who knows? But best to take care, okay?'

'Who was the neighbour?' Michael asked, with more curiosity than apprehension. He had spent so much of his youth feeling scared that he seemed incapable of being very frightened now – the reserves of fear in his emotional batteries had been so drawn down over time that they could no longer supply much of a charge.

'That was the funny thing. The call was anonymous. But it was a woman's voice.' He stood up now. 'Anyway, thanks for the beer. We'll check that it *is* blood on the bat first – not much point doing anything if it's just some paint. If it is blood then I reckon we can assume it's your father's. We'll do the DNA tests to make sure, but they take time, up to thirty days. In the meantime we'll check for prints and run them through the database.'

For once Gary answered the phone and, seeming to appreciate the urgency in Michael's voice, he came over right away. When Michael told him about his discovery of the baseball bat, Gary immediately grew agitated.

'Where is it now?' They were sitting in the living room, slouched in the two armchairs like caricatures of their parents. All that was missing, thought Michael, were two small boys playing on the Mojave rug on the floor in front of them.

He said, 'Maguire took it away. They're going to check for prints.'

Gary shook his head. 'Oh shit.' He rubbed his eyes with both hands.

'What's the matter?'

'What if they find my prints on the bat?'

'What if they do? Doesn't prove a thing. The point is whether there're any other prints on it.'

'That's what you say, but what if there aren't? What happens then? Shit,' he said again, only louder. 'I haven't seen that bat for years. *You* were the baseball player.'

'Calm down, Gary.'

'But how could they miss it? Didn't they search the place?'

'They didn't miss it, Gary. That's the whole point. It wasn't there when you found Pop. Somebody's put it back there.'

'*Somebody?*' Gary's jaw went slack and his eyes widened. 'You mean . . .?'

His brother looked so pale and scared that Michael tried to reassure him. 'Who knows? It's another mystery. Let Maguire try and sort it out. They're not even sure it's the murder weapon.'

'The way you describe it it's gotta be. But why would they put it back? What good does that do them?'

Them? 'Let's wait and see what the forensics people find.'

'Great. We'll wait while this murderer makes fools of the cops and picks us off one by one.'

'If you're that worried, you can come stay here. Get out of that dump while we figure out what to do.'

'About what?'

'The house. You know, do I sell it, do I rent it? Or do you live here?'

'You're talking about the house when there's somebody out there, maybe gunning for me.'

'The way I look at it, if he wanted you, he'd have already killed you, too.' He took a deep breath. 'So tell me about the Marines. And no bullshit.'

Gary distanced himself at once. 'It was never a big thing,' he said. 'I went to some of their barbecues. Shit, you know me Michael, I'd listen to anybody for free beer.'

'What about those guys the other day? Are they Marine members?'

Gary shrugged. 'Not any more, same as me. Bubba was the most involved. But even he got tired of the politics.'

'I thought the whole point of it was politics. "Freedom! Keep the government off our backs." That kind of thing.'

'There's more to life than politics,' said Gary with a loftiness Michael found infuriating.

'Maguire said that you took Pop to one of these meetings. Is that right?'

'No. He went on his own. Maybe he was interested.'

This seemed improbable. 'Oh, and was he?'

'He got into an argument with Raleigh. Said he'd always been plumb stupid in high school and he was disappointed to see how little had changed. Something complimentary like that.'

'Why did Pop get involved? He didn't care about politics.'

'Says you. How do you know what Pop cared about? You haven't been here. You don't know what it's like. People are fed up.'

'Not here in town they're not. I've never seen so much money around. And this wasn't exactly the local Rotarians, meeting to bitch about property tax. These people are extremists. Raleigh Somerset had *dynamite* on his land, for Christ's sake. He's lucky he's not in jail.'

Gary was startled. 'How did you know about that?'

'Why? Is it meant to be a secret? Maguire acted like you knew all about it.' *You better ask him.*

Gary stared at him with an expression of mixed amazement and fear. Then the phone rang.

'I'll be right back,' said Michael, moving quickly towards the kitchen to answer it.

It was Larry Bottel, asking to come round and visit, a prelude presumably to engaging Larry to sell the house for him. He put him off and started to go back to the living room when the phone rang again. What had Larry forgotten to say? But this time it was Nancy Sheringham, welcoming him back and inviting him to a barbecue the following week. 'And could you give somebody else a lift?'

'Sure, Nancy.'

'She's got kids, but you've got room, don't you?'

'Who is it?'

Nancy gave her apple-crunching laugh. 'You know who it is. See you Thursday.'

He walked back through the dining room. 'Sorry about that,' he proclaimed to an empty living room. Where had Gary gone? He went to the bottom of the stairs and called up. Nothing. Then he realized the front door was open. For the second time in twenty years, somebody had used it. Gary had run away.

'WATER'S HIGH,' HE said, as he waded out towards the Junction bridge's central pier, trying not to slip on the river's gravel bottom and to keep the swirling water from tipping in over the top of his waders. They were Donny's and too big for him, but he was grateful for the extra inch or so of latex that separated him from the heavy, icy flow. He'd first put on his father's, fetched from the basement, but they were full of holes that cracked and widened even as he tried them on.

They'd gone by Gary's house on the way out of town at Michael's request. His car wasn't there and a folded note was pinned to the front door. *Bubba*, it said, and Michael was worried enough about his brother to feel no compunction about reading the note. *Something's come up and I'm out of here for a while. I'll call you. G.*

Where would his brother have gone? And was it fear driving him away? He couldn't gauge the tone of the message for Bubba. He walked around the side of the house until he came to his brother's bedroom window. The blind was down most of the way, but by getting on his knees and shading his eyes from the sun with his hand, he could see into the room. The bed was made and the room was tidy – surprisingly tidy.

He got back in the truck with the note in his pocket. 'Not there then?' said Donny as they drove past the wireworks, past the old sewage swamp and onto the highway leading out of town.

Michael shook his head. 'You know this guy called Bubba?' Donny gave a wry smile. 'Who is he?'

They moved through the avenue of poplars at the town's edge, then followed the sharp curve of road down towards Stillriver Lake. 'You remember those dances at Custer we used to go to? And how sometimes some bikers would show up, kind of stray Hell's Angels with nothing better to do than pick a fight at the dance hall?'

'I remember.' And Tina, the Mexican girl in the back seat of a car when he'd been all of fifteen years old. Later, he and Cassie had only gone once, partly because Cassie could rarely go out on Saturday night, thanks to her father, and partly because on their one visit she had hated the place.

'Well, Bubba's one of those strays, only younger than the guys we used to avoid. Kind of a cross between the hippies and the rednecks.'

'And weird?'

'Little bit, I guess.'

'Sexually weird?' asked Michael. It seemed strange using the word.

'I guess. Or so they say.' He looked awkward. 'Shit, Michael, times have changed. Nothing's meant to be weird any more.'

They were coming to the bridge and Donny pointed to the scaffolding on the upstream side. 'See, we've started. Let's get to Fennville quick and come back here. I'll be interested in what you think.'

They took the back road to Fennville, eight miles away, rather than the interstate. They passed a new charter school, set in a large clearing carved out of the woods. The woods gave way to farmland, and he saw the small stand where his father had always bought plums and you left your money in a lunchbox. Then meadowland before the road curved and moved down to the north branch of the Still river. As they took the bend Michael said, 'They took the tree down.'

Donny grunted. 'They should have done it years ago.' It was an enormous oak that served as a marker for the sharp curve of road. One night in the summer of their senior year Ricky Fell failed to take the curve and drove straight into the tree at ninety miles an hour, instantly killing himself and a girl from North Beach.

'I saw Mrs Fell at the parade. I hear the Doctor's retired.'

'Yep. Spends most of his time hunting now. I don't think they ever got over it.'

They drove in silence for a while, Michael thinking about Ricky Fell. Suddenly Donny piped up: 'I shot a deer with that

164

rifle,' – Ricky's most famous pick-up line – and they both laughed.

As they dipped down through Happy Valley Michael saw the sign for Fennville Acres, and the small road to the left that led to it, the county poorhouse. He would go see Ethel and Daisy, he decided, take them a couple of presents, but only if Cassie would go with him. Maybe Nancy could look after the kids; he'd try to arrange it when he went to Sheringham's next week.

Donny drove into Fennville, passing the cemetery. The town sat over ten miles from Lake Michigan, hot and dusty, and few tourists ever came there. It survived, if not exactly prospered, because it was the county seat, holding the courthouse, jail and sheriff's headquarters, all housed in a new low building of yellow brick. Formerly the jail had been next door, a four-storey edifice of dark granite, the tallest building in the county if you didn't count silos and water towers. When they'd had occasion to come to Fennville, his father would have Michael's mother drive by the jail so that Michael and Gary could wave to the prisoners staring out through the upper storeys' barred windows. His father had loved Fennville, the essential Midwest mustiness of the place.

Parking by the dime store, Donny went off to the bakery to buy sweet rolls while Michael walked to Cameron's, the sporting goods, gun and hardware store. Inside it was busy with a Saturday morning traffic of farmers and fishermen. The counter and walls were plastered with pro-gun posters and stickers, and there was an NRA-sponsored petition on the counter. Michael bought a resident's trout licence from a boy who looked to be Cameron's son (the same dimple in his chin) then moved to the hardware section, where he found a thin enough chisel, some high-tensile wire and a small, light hammer. There was a sale on inflatable wading pools, and he bought a loud blue one – he'd promised Jack he would, after they found the one in the basement was as full of holes as his father's waders.

When he got back to the truck Donny laughed at the pool tucked under his arm. 'You hoping to float round the bridge?'

'It's for the house.'

'Cassie's kids?'

He nodded. 'Good,' said Donny, the first time he'd indicated he knew they were seeing each other. 'Let's go by the lake. I want to show you something.'

They drove the other way out of town, past the old gravel yard and into a small park on the far shore of Fennville Lake. The land was owned by the town and there were picnic tables scattered through some second-growth woods around a central group of brick and iron barbecues. A track wound its way through the park and they followed it, catching glimpses through the trees of the water down below them. They came to a high chain fence with a padlocked gate.

'I'm getting too old to climb a fence that high,' said Michael.

'Sit still,' said Donny and, producing a key, went and unlocked the gate. He came back and drove through it, leaving the gate open behind them. 'I'm an important man locally,' said Donny, 'worth seventeen hundred dollars an hour.'

The track meandered through low bushes on either side that scratched the truck, until suddenly the terrain opened up, and they drove onto a flat pan of hard-packed sandy dirt, which ended in a long concrete slab – over a hundred feet wide – at one end of the lake.

'That the dam?' asked Michael, and Donny nodded. 'I've never seen it before,' said Michael, getting out of the cab, for it was tucked away in this recessed corner of the lake, out of sight of Fennville. The lake itself was small, less than a mile across in any direction.

They walked out onto the narrow slab on top of the dam. 'What's that?' asked Michael, pointing to the last forty feet or so of the dam's top. It was lower and darker, the colour of olive fatigues.

'That's clay. That's from the original dam here.'

'You have got to be kidding.'

'Haven't you seen it used before?'

'Sure I have,' said Michael. 'In the Philippines just before a monsoon washed it away. Tell me, is the lake always this high?'

166

He pointed at the surface of the water, which was only about a yard beneath their feet. On the other side, there was a good twenty-feet drop to the river, which was fed by water gushing from two drainpipes jutting out the side of the dam. From here the river ran for eight miles until it reached the scaffold-covered bridge at the Junction and then flowed into Stillriver Lake.

'No, that's why I wanted you to see it. The water's higher than it's ever been. If we get much more rain, it's going to go right over the top. Back there,' Donny said, pointing to the far end of the lake, where the Still entered from the east, 'the river's burst its banks in a couple of places.'

'What happens if it comes over the top here?'

Donny shrugged and turned round to face the river beneath them. 'It's never happened before, and there's been a dam here since before the War.'

'Shit, it's not going to take a lot to get it over. Think what it's going to do to the river level. That little bridge in Happy Valley will be under water.' His voice started rising. 'And by the time it gets to Stillriver Lake, Christ knows how high the water will be. It will knock your scaffolding all to hell, and probably shake the piers. If they move, the beam will go and the deck with it. Goodbye bridge. Jesus!'

Donny was scratching his head and looking pained. 'Hell, Michael, don't start shouting at me. Why do you think I brought you here?'

Now, standing in the Still with both hands against the dense pier of the Junction bridge, he thought hard about what would happen if the dam gave way. The resulting flow would be immense; if less catastrophic than he feared, it would none-theless do damage on its way downstream to anything standing near the bank. And then reach this bridge, where from even superficial inspection he could see prospective problems. The abutments on either side of the bridge had been designed to sit on dry land, but now their bottom halves were below water. The current flow was fast along the banks, and signs of vortices suggested eddy flows which could scour away the sandy gravel surrounding these piers until the piers gave way.

He'd brought his laptop with him from England, and with it he had access to some fairly basic analytic tools, but he'd left his field kit behind in a closet in Ealing four thousand miles away. He couldn't conduct even a basic salinity test on the deck of the bridge, or use ultrasound to detect lethal internal voids below. So he tapped thoroughly and systematically with his hammer on the upstream side of the bridge and saw at once why they were replacing the concrete base of the piers since at least half of his strikes sounded hollow – sure sign of an internal void. They'd need to use properly reinforced concrete this time, with epoxy coating to inhibit corrosion. But the real issue lay in the other, downstream side, the one on the lake side, not now under repair. He knew he should wade back up to the bank, climb up in his dripping heavy waders, then climb down again on the far side. But the short cut under the bridge was too appealing, and he stepped tentatively forwards.

This was a mistake. Even one step under the bridge was too many, for the current here, concentrated in the sudden narrowing passageway, was much stronger. He could not step back at all against the intensified flow; in fact he struggled not to be swept off his feet and carried downstream. The water absolutely *thundered* here, the noise magnified and reverberating within the tunnel formed by the piers. If he shouted out for help he doubted that Donny, standing almost directly above him on the road surface of the bridge, would hear. And if Donny did hear him, what could he do, since they hadn't brought a rope?

He moved very slowly, almost counter-intuitively, since the pull of the water made each step so easy to make – it would be fatal to accept its implicit invitation to move quickly, since within a matter of steps the pace would accelerate until your feet were literally racing ahead of you, unable to stop and grip the bottom, and all pretence to control would be swept away as *whoof*, they were swept out from under you. In the middle of the bridge the bottom sloped down sharply, and he gasped as water rushed in over his wader's tops and moved quickly downwards to his boots, shocking him with its icy touch through his cotton shirt. Just as suddenly the slope bottomed out, and he found himself moving slightly uphill towards the far end.

Then he was through, and used all his strength to move sideways against the current until he was out of it, safely behind the thick, protective abutment. He caught his breath and heard movement up above him, which turned out to be Donny, now leaning over the downstream, unscaffolded side of the bridge. 'All right?' said his friend, and Michael waved weakly to signify he was okay.

After a minute he felt his strength return, and from his fishing bag he took out the chisel and the hand drill he'd found in the drawer at the top of the basement steps, laid neatly with the other tools – most over forty years old – that his father had stored there. With the chisel he knocked a thin chip out of the bridge's side, a foot or so above the water level. He worked the hand drill in with a quarter-inch drill bit and drilled for about thirty seconds, astonished to find the interior amazingly soft and easy to pierce. He extracted the drill carefully, then looked at the soft powder worked around the bit. There was no point taking the sample home, since he didn't have the right tools to analyse it anyway. But it was worryingly, dangerously soft. And there were cracks in the surface of the pier, several looking fresh and capable of widening. Using some of the wire, he worked lengths of it into the cracks, pushing until the pre-stressed wire would go no further. He bent each piece of wire at right angles to their bend marks, then clipped them and deposited them with his tools inside his bag.

He looked up at Donny and nodded to indicate he was done. He took a big, safe step towards the shore, but instead of finding gravel found soft mud. Lifting his wader boot with a jerk he put his other foot forward and found a hole, a sudden absence of bottom which simply shocked him, until he realized he had stepped into a river void.

His waders filled at once and somehow, suddenly, he was

moved back into the mainstream rush, just below the bridge. He felt the intense cold of the water and its pushing, sudden weight as his legs sank suddenly into the void, and the boots of his waders scraped the bottom. He managed to keep himself from rolling over face down but then found himself turning sideways to the current and sinking into the river. He sensed he was in the very middle, too deep to touch bottom even if he could manage to stand up, which he couldn't, and again he had to struggle to keep himself from rolling over.

As he gasped for air and inhaled some water instead, he suddenly realized that he was very likely to drown, and saw only strands of dark blue around him, skeins of colour almost purple in their darkness. He felt a surge of panic, which was followed by a sudden burst of concentrated thoughts – *Don't try and take the waders off* – then a sudden image of Cassie walking on a Stillriver street – *which one?* – and then the face of the German engineer after he'd fallen off that bridge into the water and they had gone in to pluck him out and for the first time the man had seen that help was coming and no, he wasn't going to die. And then a voice, shouting hoarsely, what memory was this? he asked himself almost whimsically. But it was Donny's voice, and he was shouting the same thing again and again. *What's he saying?* he wondered as he started to turn over again, and this time he could not resist the roll, his feet swinging round upstream and behind and his head turning over into the water, face down between his outstretched arms, and as he sensed this fatal final move into the river's depths he suddenly thought *swim!* Donny was shouting *swim!* And he awkwardly kicked his right leg and then his left and lifted an arm up into the air and pulled back at the water, not daring to try and breathe, certain he would only inhale river, and he did this again, and discovered he was now moving himself as much as being moved, and then risked a large gulp of air that proved blessedly water-free and, already tiring, closed his eyes and moved his arms, the wader straps tangled and restricting his movements, and then *kick kick kick* and his right hand jammed into slimy ground, almost breaking his thumb, and he was safe.

He crawled on all fours onto the little hillock of marshland that jutted out into the river here, and looking up he saw Donny running along the bank, his big boots splashing in the shallows. Michael stayed on all fours, like a panting dog, recovering his breath, too tired to disentangle the wader straps from his arms or take the waders off. Donny got to him, reached down and extracted his fishing bag, which was somehow still lopped over his shoulder, then helped him unravel the curled and twisted straps of the waders. Very slowly Michael stood up, supported by Donny, and let the waders slip down, water sloshing out of them. 'You had me scared there for a minute,' said Donny.

Michael exhaled noisily and took a deep breath. 'You weren't the only one.'

'I'm not quite sure what I would have told Cassavantes we were doing here. Much less explain to Cassie how I let you drown.'

Michael stepped out of the waders one foot at a time, then picked them up by the boot end and turned them upside down until what seemed a bathtub full of water had cascaded onto his feet. 'Well,' he said cheerfully as he looked in some wonder at the river now flowing so unthreateningly beside him, then at the bridge upstream that had caused it all, then further back to the headland bluff of dense woods and brush, 'you could always tell them I died for my county.'

He said nothing about the river to Cassie the next day when he collected her and the children, and they drove north and east through the Back Country until they crossed the county line and moved into the national forest. They parked a quarter-mile off the road by the remains of a camp fire, and walked down along a soft needle path through a pine stand until they reached the south branch of the Pere Marquette river.

He'd found one of his grandfather's fishing rods in the basement, an old fly rod of Tonkin cane, whippy from years of wet fly fishing in fast rivers, and brought it along with a kid's rod he'd also found in the basement. The last thing he wanted to do was wade in the river, but he forced himself, and after lunch spent twenty minutes in its fastest part, casting into a big pool on the far side until he felt at ease again. *Get right back on the horse that threw you off.*

He got out and found Cassie sitting on the bank, reading the kids a story. 'Catch anything?' she asked with a smile, and he shook his head.

He rigged the kids' pole, and because he had forgotten a spade, took a kitchen knife from the picnic basket and cut out a large patch of soft turf, then dug down quickly and pulled out two worms before they got away. He baited the hook of the kids' rod, and started with Jack, but the boy was soon bored and preferred throwing rocks to staring at a fishing line. Sally, on the other hand, took to it at once; she didn't want to stop when Cassie said it was time to go. Michael commented he was surprised by her fervour.

'Why?' Cassie demanded. 'Can't girls like fishing too?'

'Sure,' he said quickly. 'Why not?'

She was frowning a little.

'Cassie,' he said plaintively, 'don't be like that. I didn't mean anything. I'm just not used to *girls*. I didn't have a sister. Once my mother died we were all boys in our house.'

She nodded, but was quiet on the drive back. When they arrived at his house, she didn't want to stay, and had her kids get into her car while she said goodbye to him. 'Will I see you tomorrow?' he asked.

'Most likely,' she said, and he saw that something was still wrong. She shook her head. 'I'm sorry, Michael. I don't mean to be this way.'

'It's okay, Cassie.'

'No, it's not. Let me ask you something. Is this what you want?'

'What, seeing you? You know it is.' He scratched his chin in a parody of thoughtfulness. 'I could stand a few additions to the process, but I'm not complaining.'

'Additions?' she asked suspiciously. 'What, you want other people around?'

'No. But I was thinking it would be nice if maybe you

stayed over one night. The kids wouldn't mind a sleepover, I bet.'

She shook her head. 'I can't do that.'

'What if I stayed with you, then?'

She shook her head again, to his great disappointment. 'Not yet,' she said.

'I don't know,' he said wistfully, with an air of resignation he didn't truly feel. 'In high school you made me wait ten months before you went to bed with me, so I guess I can't complain about a little delay this many years later.'

'Is that what this is about? Going to bed with me?'

'Sure,' he said, not willing to let her treat him like a blind date.

'You just want a fuck for old time's sake?'

He stared at her with disbelief. 'You don't have to talk like that to me, Cassie.'

'*Excuse me,*' she said sourly. 'Sorry to offend your ears.'

He caught her by the elbow, then thought better of it and let her go. 'Listen you, where do you think I spend my time working? I work on *construction sites*. You can't teach me much about bad language. It's like Eskimos with all their words for snow. I can give you seventy-three words that all mean blow job.'

Cassie laughed. 'Well, what do you want then, if not sex?'

'Who said I *didn't* want it – among other things? Though I have to say, in my present condition of sexual deprivation going to bed with you is miles and away at the top of the list.'

She had dropped the hard-ass pose. 'I just feel old, Michael. I'm tired half the time and my bones ache and I'm worried about the kids and I'm worried about money and I'm worried about everything. You *can't* want me that much.'

Oh, are you wrong, he thought. For he positively ached for her, found in the very ageing that she cited as a fault something infinitely sensuous, lying in some zone of mixed libido and love. 'Gi-rl,' he said in the kind of Motown jive accent Kenny Williams had used as a teenager to make them all laugh. 'I want to eat you up, bones and all. The best chicken is an *old* chicken.

173

That's what the man said, and I think you owe it to the man to let *this* man find out.' He was glad to find her smiling. 'I'll phone you in the morning,' he said normally, and watched as she drove away.

As he stood by the fence – he would have to get to work on the yard soon – he looked at the house, suddenly picturing its rooms and the lives that had been lived in them. He saw the window on this side of his parents' old bedroom, its blind pulled down, and pictured his mother lying there in the enervating final months of her illness. 'Calf love never lasts,' he heard her say, and he wondered now how he could be sure that his feelings for Cassie had survived both the years and the hurt she'd caused him. High school, their abbreviated time in college, Texas and those furtive rendezvous – they looked like the tick marks on an emotional graph of their involvement. How could he be absolutely certain that he was in love with Cassie as she was now? How could he be sure that he wasn't seeking what was no longer there?

He was more aware of his resistance to change than Cassie or Donny would credit, and this awareness meant the changes in town – the kinds of stores on Main Street, the recent influx of retired people, the unprecedented prosperity of the place – jolted him but were also, he knew, *good* for him, since they knocked his nostalgic inclinations on the head. It was the same with the way he felt about Cassie. Enough of the coltish, funny, pretty girl remained to demolish any suspicion that she was now a different person altogether, but there were enough alterations that he could not conceivably think of her as the teenage girl he had first fallen in love with. She spoke her mind more forcefully than before, but her manner of speaking was almost always gentle, even when sassy, and her voice was still soft. She had kept her generosity about other people, and seemed able to live without envy, despite fifteen years of little money and no encouragement from Ronald to enjoy even those things money isn't needed for: books, or her music, or the always-free enjoyment of looking around at the world she daily walked through. Her rampant curiosity remained, and she seemed to

174

want to know everything about what she didn't know and hadn't seen. She had an *appetite* for life that Michael, not hungry for years, found energizing. For all his recent travels, all those years in the sophisticated epicentre of New York, he knew that he was learning more from her than she from him.

Maguire phoned that night as Michael was eating a second piece of broiled chicken and drinking a glass of surprisingly good red jug wine. The detective came right to the point: 'It's blood on the bat all right. We've sent it for DNA analysis to confirm it's your father's, but I think we can assume it is.'

Michael was not surprised, but the fact still chilled him. He remembered the heft of the bat in his hand. 'And the prints?' he asked.

'There're some of yours of course, but it also looks like your brother played more baseball than you knew. His prints are all over the bat.'

Shit. 'That doesn't mean a thing. It would have been odder if they weren't there.'

Maguire hummed lightly on the other end of the line. 'Maybe so. But I need to talk to him. Any idea where he's gone?'

'You know where he lives.'

'He's not there. Neighbours say he hasn't been there for a while. Jimmy Olds went by and says the place is spick and span, like he'd gone away for a while.'

'I saw him two days ago, not long after you left.'

'And?'

What do you want me to say? I mention Raleigh Somerset and the dynamite and he takes off like a frightened deer. 'He seemed fine to me, even when I told him about the bat.'

Maguire snorted. 'I need to find him ASAP. Don't hold back on this one. That's official.'

Official? He didn't require this warning. 'I understand,' he said insincerely.

'Good. Don't you want to know what else we found?'

'Go on, surprise me,' he said. 'Oscar Peters' palm prints everywhere.'

'Who's Oscar Peters?'

'Never mind. What did you find?' asked Michael, suddenly thinking, *he's going to say 'no one's'.*

Maguire paused, as if to heighten the effect. 'We found eight prints: some smudged, a couple really clear, all belonging to the same individual.'

'Who is?'

'Beats the hell out of me. There isn't a match in the database, and we checked the Washington one too. But that's not surprising.'

'Why? I thought they had millions of fingerprints stored.'

'They do. But they're almost all *adult* ones. And the prints we pulled, according to the technician, seem to belong to a child. There's no way to tell gender, and we can't be precise about the person's age, but there's no way these are the fingerprints of a grown man. How do you figure that one, Mr Wolf?'

Four

1

HE WAS IN Burlington at Mitchell's lumber and hardware store on route ten. His father was talking two-by-fours with Mr Mitchell while Michael walked up and down the aisles, looking at paint ranges and hoping for a glimpse of Mitchell's daughter, who was pretty.

Well, not pretty – *sexy*. She was a couple of years older than Michael, quite short, with streaked blonde hair, a stub nose, a Bardot *bouche* of a mouth, and breasts that bounced like beach balls underneath her tight pink T-shirt. If she caught you looking at her (and she usually did) she would glance back with a flirty, fleeting look of her own that seemed to say *I know how you are feeling about me, and maybe I feel likewise.*

As he moved past paint to nails and screws, he asked himself, *Why am I trying to find her?* and felt guilty about Cassie. They had made love the day before, in the soft grass of the meadow out at the Half, and here he was lusting for someone else within twenty-four hours. Was that supposed to happen? *Maybe when you're married that all goes away.* He turned the corner and managed to bump right into Ronald Duverson.

'Sorry,' he said faintly.

To Michael's astonishment Ronald's voice was warm and relaxed. 'Oh, it's you,' he said. 'How you doing? I hope your friend is all right.'

Donny? Larry Bottel? 'Huh?' he said.

'You know, your friend at the Dairy Queen. I didn't mean to beat him so bad.' Ronald shrugged with a kind of aw-shucks modesty.

'He wasn't my friend,' Michael blurted out, and immediately regretted it. *Sorry Dicky.*

Ronald's eyes widened and then he laughed, rich and deeply from inside his chest. 'Well, that's okay then.' Michael saw that his front teeth were chipped.

'Ronald.' The voice was low and heavy and came from a man who suddenly appeared behind Duverson. Michael looked at his hard face and suddenly saw him elsewhere – by the cigarette counter, mean-looking, perspiring. *Hot? You think it's hot? . . . Poor baby's hot.*

'Coming Pa,' said Ronald. 'Good to see you,' he said amiably to Michael, and slapped him a little too hard on the shoulder before leaving the store with his father.

'He was *nice* to me,' he insisted to Donny.

Donny shook his head knowingly. 'A snake says hi to a mouse. Then *Pow!*'

His SAT scores came as a surprise. The entire class took them late, in autumn of their senior year, and Michael received 580 in English, which was respectable, and 750 in math – the only score over 700 in his year.

'I knew you'd do well,' Cassie crowed, happier than Michael, who was slightly bewildered by his score. He tried to affect an air of nonchalance, but she was having none of it. 'My genius!' she exclaimed, though she had done well in English, scoring 680.

'I bet we like Ann Arbor,' he said, for they had agreed that summer to go to the same college, and to make U of M their first choice.

'We'll see,' said Cassie smiling. 'Don't count your chickens.'

He had good grades – an A-average – and was working hard to keep them that way that first crucial term. He saw Cassie every day at school, but despite their now-official status as boyfriend and girlfriend, Michael saw her less often elsewhere. For her father seemed constantly to be ill, and although Michael was not precisely barred from the Gilberts' house, he visited infrequently and briefly when Cassie's father was at home, and then only when the parson was resting upstairs.

His own house became something of a refuge for Cassie, and she would come for breaks from looking after her father, growing so comfortable at Michael's that sometimes she would drop by even when she knew he was working in the drugstore. He would come home to find her playing cards with Gary (trying for the hundredth time to teach him Hearts) or talking with his father; Michael still found it astonishing how easy she seemed to find it to talk to his father, and even more astonishing the way his father would let her tease him. He even let Cassie plant flowers in the patch in back by the cedars which he had left untended since Michael's mother's death. Ethel would come over, following Cassie around like a lapdog, and together they planted sunflowers and zinnias and, at Ethel's insistence, two rows of pink carnations.

Michael was surprised by how obviously Cassie felt at home; he admitted to her that he hadn't felt comfortable in his own house since his mother had died. 'So does it bother you?' she asked.

'What?'

'That I like your house. It's so big compared to ours. The ceilings are so high. And I like Gary, and I like your father. Is that okay with you?'

'Of course,' he said insincerely, for though he was happy that she fit in so easily, he was slightly irked that this meant he spent more time at home in the company of his brother and father.

'Your father's a good man.'

'Sure,' he said sarcastically.

'I know you're not close, but he does care about you.'

'He didn't when I needed it,' he said, for Cassie knew that he felt a lingering resentment about his father's detachment.

'Maybe you weren't there for him either,' she said softly.

'*He's* the father.'

'He suffered too when your mother died. More than anybody. Remember that.'

He looked at her thinking, *He suffered more than me? How would you know?* Cassie was looking at him calmly; he could not get angry with her. 'I'll try,' he said quietly.

They could find the time and privacy to sleep together only with careful planning – when her father went to one of his meetings at Marshall College, near Grand Rapids, a Baptist school of 600 students where he was the token Episcopal Trustee; less often, when they could be sure Michael's father and Gary were out of the house. It was rarely more than a couple of times a month. She seemed unperturbed by this, which bothered Michael; they had the easy contact of the closest friends, but what he wanted more of was the intimacy of lovers. He hated sharing her or, specifically, hated the feeling he was ever sharing her love. The very gentleness which had first attracted him, almost drove him crazy when it was extended to others in any way that seemed to threaten his primacy in her affections.

One afternoon, when his father had gone to a teachers' convention in Whitehall and Gary was busy at a boy scouts' meeting at a friend's house, Michael had led Cassie upstairs to his bedroom and, having laughingly removed all of her clothes, was about to join her in the bed when a loud, continuous wailing came from outside on the street. He closed the window but the noise continued. It was Ethel, bawling her heart out in the wake of some unkindness from her foster-father or foster-brother Benny or twin sister Daisy or somebody, since God knows even a romantic novel could upset her and make her cry. And having taken off his own clothes by now, Michael joined Cassie under the sheets and tried to kiss her, ignoring the sobs below. But Cassie pushed him away, not roughly but with firmness, and within thirty seconds she was out of the bed, dressed and moving towards the stairs. He knew that there really wasn't any point even hoping that Cassie would ignore Ethel's misery in order to satisfy his lust.

But at college there would be a different kind of life, and his agitation at the prospect of leaving Stillriver was reduced by knowing Cassie and he could enjoy a real privacy. In the drugstore he said nothing about his plans to go to Ann Arbor. Larry Bottel had gone off to college that autumn, intending to major in real estate somewhere near Grand Rapids ('That's a *major*?' his father had said) so Michael was often alone in the store with Marilyn and Alvin. He told Marilyn he was applying to Ferris, knowing she would tell Alvin, and he duly did fill out its application form, along with ones for U of M and Michigan State. He did not consider any college outside the state, but then no one in his class was going to leave Michigan, except for Cathy Stallover, whose parents were paying to send her to modelling school in Milwaukee.

He still wasn't old enough to sell liquor, but otherwise knew the store so well by now that he could even place the order with Charlie, the candy salesman, one afternoon when Alvin had gone to a funeral in Elmira and it was Marilyn's half-day off. *Too many Lifesavers*, Alvin had commented when the order arrived, but he was teasing, and Michael knew he trusted him since he had to cash out the registers and lock up two days running when Marilyn was on vacation.

And then Alvin got sick in December, seriously ill with gastric ulcers that put him in the hospital and kept him off work for almost two months. Leonard Scopes, a retired pharmacist from Shelby, came in four afternoons a week to fill prescriptions, and Alvin's wife Betty, a clever woman with a taste for fine clothes and jewellery, kept up with the books in a primitive way and signed the pay cheques. But otherwise the store was run by Marilyn, and she made it clear she needed Michael's help.

He had a driving licence now, though with no car of his own he only got to drive on the few occasions when he had the grudging loan of his father's ageing station wagon. But with Alvin out, he had to take the store's pickup truck each Saturday morning to the state liquor store in Burlington, load the liquor cases, drive back and stack them in the store's dank basement. To help Marilyn, he took over replacement of the stock. The greater the detail the more he liked the job; he was glad to think he would be working summers there during college.

The snow had come early, just after Thanksgiving, and stayed, packing down into a frozen hard layer on the street, supplemented after Christmas by several new falls. For the first time in years, Stillriver Lake was completely frozen, and one Sunday afternoon when Michael and Cassie walked down and stood on the deck of Nelson's boathouse they saw families skating on a large circle of ice. They'd brushed off the snow, piling it up in a low wall that surrounded their temporary arena. Further down, by the causeway link to South Beach, the ice fishermen sat on folding chairs outside their shacks.

In the cold weather Cassie's father became virtually housebound, and soon they had no place to make love, since Cassie adamantly refused to in his father's car on the very rare occasions he could cadge the use of it. 'It's just too trashy,' she said when he'd first proposed using the back seat. So *I can't wait for spring* became his catchword for the time when they could sleep together again in the high grass of the Half, or, after dusk, on a blanket among the marram grass and sand cherry of the dunes north of town. Cassie would smile when he said the words, and he would momentarily forget his frustration and feel a deep love for her.

But in the absence of a sex life he found his sexual fantasy life virtually unceasing – he felt guilty when he thought about other girls, but think about them he did. *I have sex on the brain*, he thought, which was one reason (the sheer busyness of his life was another) that he had forgotten about Ronald Duverson – his surprising friendliness in Burlington, as well as Donny's remark that Ronald had taken a shine to Cassie. Until one Saturday afternoon, in the glum days of early February, when he was working in the store but had arranged to take the night shift off.

He had somehow managed to wangle the car from his father, and planned to pick up Cassie from New Era where she was playing basketball. Alvin was back in the store, but he had lost a lot of weight. Once a big man in Michael's eyes, he now seemed to have shrunk overnight. Suddenly, at six feet, Michael was taller than Alvin, and no longer stick-like against the man's bulk. Michael had begun to fill out where Alvin seemed to have withered.

After lunchtime Alvin suddenly said he felt faint, and he looked terribly off-colour. Alvin was not normally a complainer, so Marilyn right away called Betty, who came and drove her husband home before calling Dr Fell. Knowing Michael was due to pick up Cassie, Marilyn said she could hold the fort on her own, but he knew that even on a slow February Saturday night this would be exhausting for her. So he called the New Era High School and, getting through to someone still working on a Saturday afternoon, asked them to get word to Cassie or at least Coach Brower, that he wouldn't be there to collect her. He stayed and worked that night, which was just as well since it was busy and he didn't see how Marilyn could have managed alone. When he got home after closing his father said that Cassie had rung when she'd got home to let Michael know she'd got back all right.

And that would have been all, except that Sunday morning Anthea Heaton, who was also on the basketball team, came in to buy the *Free Press* for her parents. 'Who won the game?' he asked her.

She looked at him. 'Didn't Cassie tell you?'

'No,' he said, 'I haven't seen her. I couldn't pick her up.'

'But she wasn't on the bus.'

He shrugged, trying to disguise the fact he was surprised. 'She must have got a ride,' he said, and turned to the other customers waiting to pay for their papers.

He went by Cassie's house after the one o'clock closing, hoping her father was napping. When Cassie answered the door she hugged him spontaneously, then kissed him for a long time, and he thought, *What am I worrying about?*

They sat in the kitchen and she made the peppermint tea she liked on these cold afternoons.

'I hear you won yesterday,' he said, as she gave him his tea and sat down across from him.

'We did.'

'How many points you get?'

'Fourteen,' she said with a slight smile.

'High scorer?'

She thought about this. 'I'm not sure. Nancy played really well. Maybe she was.'

'Bet you were.' He blew on the tea, which was too hot to sip.

'How did you get back? Anthea Heaton said you weren't on the bus.'

'Mex gave me a lift.'

Ronald's brother, a sophomore. He stared at Cassie. 'Mex's not old enough to drive.'

'I didn't say he drove. His brother was there. He drove us both back. And Janie Waters.'

'Ronald drove you back?' He was flabbergasted, aware of the gulf between what he knew about Ronald and what Cassie did, and uncertain how to bridge it. *Take it easy*, he told himself, and promptly burned his tongue on the tea. 'Shit,' he said sharply, then covered his mouth with his hand. 'Sorry.'

Cassie laughed. 'Daddy's sound asleep.'

'Why did you go back with them?'

'I don't know. Janie seemed to want me to.'

He felt he was digging himself into a hole he wasn't going to like being in, but he also felt he couldn't help digging. 'I just don't like it. He's not a nice guy.'

She knew he didn't mean Mex. 'I know people say that. But he seemed very nice to me. Very polite.'

'You sit in the front?'

Cassie gave him a look. 'As a matter of fact I did. What's the matter with you? Are you getting *jealous*?'

He shrugged. 'Should I be?'

'Of course not.' But for the first time she looked uncomfortable. She ran a hand through her hair.

'Did he ask you out?'

'Honestly, Michael.'

'Did he?'

Her expression hardened. 'He asked if I was seeing anybody. I said I was. Then I thanked him for the ride and got out of the car. That's all.' She reached over and placed her hand on his. 'Stop being silly, okay? I don't like it.'

'Okay,' he said, with an artificial brightness. There was no point asking any more questions of Cassie, for it was Ronald who held the answers. Why was he asking Cassie out when he already knew she was Michael's girlfriend?

*

After this he became aware of Ronald Duverson floating in and out of the fringes of his daily life. He was not a major presence, but not forgettable either. It reminded Michael of how, on learning the meaning of a new word – *intuition*, say, or *perspicacity* – you suddenly couldn't pick up the newspaper without finding it littering its columns.

Michael knew little about him, but gradually – from an overheard remark here, a casually placed question put there; the kind of information that his job in the drugstore made him almost uniquely qualified to gather – a picture of sorts emerged.

Ronald still lived with his parents in a brick bungalow east of town, built by Ronald's father on the north branch of the Still river. As well as a younger brother, Mex, who was small and friendly and dark like his mother, Ronald had an older sister who'd gone away to Detroit and not come back. His father was a hard man and hard on Ronald; his mother was – at least two people said much the same thing with much the same pitying sigh – *a gentle, decent woman* who kept quiet and stayed deep in the background of her husband.

Ronald had left school as soon as he legally could, at sixteen, and was now either nineteen or twenty. He worked with his father, building pole barns in fall and winter, switching to erosion construction for lake cottages in the warmer seasons. It was heavy work and he was built for it – six foot one, about one hundred and ninety pounds of labour-generated muscle.

It was as a young teenager that he had saved Raleigh Somerset from drowning in the channel, and been feted as a hero. This might have been the only (and commendable) noteworthy thing about Ronald, had he not during the following years shown a growing, chronic addiction to fighting. This was remarkable, if only because Stillriver wasn't the South Side of Chicago; it was actually a very peaceful place. The sandlot fistfights of teenage boys were rare and undangerous – nobody would have dreamed of using a weapon. Once in a blue moon there would be a ruckus in one of Main Street's two bars, but it was invariably confined to some drunk taking umbrage either because they had cut him off at the bar or because he had decided someone smaller was eyeing up his wife.

But Ronald didn't have to be drunk or wait for someone to push him into a corner. He was game and ready to go at the first look on somebody's face he didn't like, the merest gesture or word that offended his sensibilities, which for all their lack of refinement were trigger-quick to sense a slight. Ronald liked fighting so much in fact that he often went looking for it – in the tavern at Spring Valley on Saturday night, at Scotch Haven, the snowmobile resort, when there were big, rowdy dances, in the Mexican-only bar in Fennville where he won the fistfight but only just avoided getting stabbed, and even, since opportunities were apparently thin on the ground, outside a Dairy Queen in Stillriver one hot and muggy summer night.

He had put people in hospital and been there himself, and once spent three days in a Wayne County pokey. He had fought older men, bigger men, men his own age, and two smart-ass high school kids who had unwisely given him lip. The only exemptions to his relentless, persisting love of violence seemed to be small children, men suffering from acute physical disability, and women. So chronic was his preoccupation, this waging of a one-man amateur war, that it was almost funny.

Almost but not quite, for behind the semi-jocular currency of anecdote – and a general willingness, given his heroism saving Raleigh, to cut Ronald more than an average share of slack – lay a darker undercurrent, a sense that Ronald's behaviour was a step or two (or three) beyond sheer feistiness, was in fact the conduct of someone so well out of order that he constituted a menace.

Having seen Ronald approximately once a year through the course of a decade and a half, Michael now found him popping up all the time, on the periphery perhaps, but visible just the same. He didn't exactly camp out in front of Michael's house (or Cassie's for that matter), but for someone who didn't live in town he now seemed to spend a lot of time there, usually cruising in his vanilla pickup truck. And Michael knew enough about himself to know that Ronald scared him half to death. It was the same kind of fear he'd felt in the anxious emotional wake of his mother's death, but now his former inchoate, panicky timidity was focused on one instigating agent. Michael wasn't scared of Ronald all the time, but he wasn't ever free from fear for long.

Yet there wasn't anything Michael could do about this, for he did not live in a culture of complaint. *Take your medicine, be a man* – spoken out loud, the sobriquets sounded ridiculous, but their force was still there. His father had never been given to macho displays, despite his size, or flaunted an aggressive masculinity, but there was a quiet strength to him. And anyway, what exactly could Michael complain *about*? Ronald wasn't actively harassing him or Cassie, wasn't even following them, and when met he was always so friendly. Passing Michael and Cassie on one of their walks, he smiled shyly at Cassie, then grinned at Michael. 'How's it going?' he said, and went by. In the drugstore, where to the best of Michael's memory Ronald had never come in before, he'd pick up a *Chronicle,* then seem to wait to make sure it was Michael who served him. 'Thanks, little buddy,' he took to saying. *Little buddy?* Michael was almost as tall as Ronald and, though about forty pounds lighter, no longer thought of himself as little.

Nor did he feel able to say anything to Cassie, who seemed unaware of the ubiquitous presence of her admirer. She had been so understanding that day on South Beach when he had told her about the panic attacks that would sometimes still seize him. But his fear of Ronald was different; it touched at the very core of what he assumed made her want to sleep with Michael, indeed made her love him: his masculinity. She was a girl, and although after living in an all-male household Michael found something wonderful and strange and sometimes daunting in this simple fact of otherness, he also had a fundamental sense that women wanted to know they could be protected. And from this it seemed logical that if he showed too much weakness, Cassie would herself feel weakened and under threat – and would despise him for it.

As the snow melted and spring came, Michael found himself

increasingly bothered by Ronald's lurking presence. It was as if the release from winter's restrictions on movement somehow made the spectre of Ronald even more anxiety-inducing, in the way that depressives suffer more in the longer, lighter days of spring precisely because their own internal winters persist. Michael found much of the satisfaction he had always derived from the drugstore now eroded, since he never knew when Ronald might make one of his casual forays in for a newspaper or cigarettes. Even the pleasure when Michael's admission letter from the University of Michigan coincided with the one Cassie got too was soured on his way home, when Ronald passed in his pickup truck, waving at him happily like an old friend.

Fortunately, he knew that the sense of menace he felt would go away in the autumn, when he and Cassie would be in Ann Arbor. And early in the summer it went away in any case – he didn't see Ronald or hear anything about him for six weeks. As the days passed, and the source of his agitation failed to make an appearance, Michael gradually relaxed. Business was good at the store and Alvin's health largely recovered; Cassie and he could make love again now that the weather was good, and the summer proved warm and sun-filled. He caught himself thinking *I wish this could go on for ever* as he walked downtown one day to work, passing the Gilbert house, and for the first time he felt a twinge of regret that he would soon be leaving.

Then in late July Ronald was back. Minimally at first – Michael only saw the taillights of his truck as it turned off Main Street two blocks ahead of him – but it had the effect of even the smallest cloud when it blocks the sun in an otherwise cloudless sky. And the next day Ronald bought a *Chronicle* in the drugstore. 'How you been little buddy?' he said with a big smile as he handed Michael the money.

Michael felt his anxiety return almost two-fold, so much so that he almost didn't notice the change in Cassie's house. For on one of his rare visits there, as he went to use the downstairs bathroom, he saw that there was a bed in what had been the parson's study, and his slippers were on the floor beside it.

'Is your father sleeping downstairs?' he asked Cassie as they left the house and went for a walk down to Stillriver Lake.

'The stairs are too much for him,' she explained. 'He gets so breathless he can't get to sleep. So I moved him downstairs.'

'It's *that* bad?'

She nodded, then changed the subject. But something niggled at the back of Michael's mind, and when about an hour later he kissed her goodbye and went back to the drugstore, he realized what it was. If the parson was too ill to climb the stairs, he was too ill to look after himself. And Michael thought, *Who's going to look after him?*

'I am,' said Cassie firmly, sitting in the kitchen of Michael's house. His father had walked downtown to get the mail and Gary was cutting the grass outside. The way Cassie was twisting her hands belied the confident tone of her pronouncement. 'I am,' she repeated. 'There isn't anybody else.'

'What about Ann Arbor? How can you look after him when you're there?'

She stared down at her hands. 'I can't.'

'Who will then? Your aunt?'

'I will. My aunt's offered but he won't move out there.'

'What about home help or whatever they call it?'

'We haven't got the money. *Especially* if I went to Ann Arbor.'

'But Cassie,' he said, with a sickening sense that he would not be able to argue things his way, 'you can't give up college. We'll work something out.'

'There's no alternative. My father's getting worse, Michael. Not better, and not even the same. Worse.'

'But he must have insurance.'

'Yes, he does. And it would pay for three hours of home help a week. It's too late to increase the cover – he couldn't afford the premiums anyway. Any extra money he ever had went to Marshall College.'

'I'm surprised he didn't make you go to school there,' Michael said bitterly.

'He wanted me to,' said Cassie with a small, wry smile. 'It's the one time I didn't do what he wanted.'

'Well, you're making up for it now,' said Michael angrily. 'Can't he see you should go to college? Isn't he concerned about you?'

'He's too ill, Michael. He needs me. And I'll go to college – it'll just have to be a little later on. I can take courses at North Shore.'

'It's not the same, Cassie, and you know it. You'll be smarter than your teachers there. And what about us? What am I going to do in Ann Arbor without you?'

She lifted her eyes and held his. 'You'll be fine, Michael. It's what you always wanted. New things, new people. And you'll always know where I am,' she added, trying to smile.

'Why don't I stay too?' he asked suddenly. 'We'll both go later. I can work in the drugstore, find something else if Alvin hasn't got enough for me to do. Then in a year or two, we'll both go to Ann Arbor.'

She was shaking her head. 'No, you've got to go. You've worked too hard to blow your chances now. It's what you've wanted for a long time. You can't stay here.'

'Sure I can,' he said, warming to the idea. 'I'll get my own place.'

'On what? Two fifty an hour? Alvin may want you to take over some day, but until you do he's going to pay you peanuts. He has to – it wouldn't be fair to Marilyn any other way.'

'Forget Alvin,' he said brusquely, feeling he was floundering. 'I'll get another job. You'll see.'

'No you won't,' she said flatly.

'Why not? There are *some* jobs around.'

'Because if you do that, Michael, I'll break up with you. And you'll just have wasted a whole lot of time when you could be at college.'

'You wouldn't do that,' he said with bewilderment.

'I would,' she said.

He saw she wasn't bluffing, and he felt a sudden, terrible hurt. 'I thought you loved me,' he said, with a croak to his voice.

192

Cassie lowered her eyes and said softly, 'I do, Michael, I do. That's exactly why you've got to go.'

Then Cassie broke down. She clenched her fists and put them over her eyes as her shoulders heaved, and Michael heard the sound of choked, shuddering sobs. He went and knelt down besides her chair, then put his arms around her, saying, 'It will be all right, I'll come back all the time, it's not that far.' And to himself he cursed the parson, finding his dislike flaring into hatred.

That last month of summer before he went away was the first time he'd felt depressed since the aftermath of his mother's death. So much of the anticipation he had felt about leaving had been tied to Cassie's coming with him that now he felt only an emotional deflation at the prospect of going. When he saw Cassie he didn't want to talk about college, since she wouldn't be there to share it. And when they made love at the Half, he found he said little, focusing so intently on the brute, carnal taking of her that it unnerved her, once in fact being so rough with her that she cried. 'Talk to me,' she'd say as he moved towards climax, but he was too busy trying to take part of her *into* him, as if that would let him take her with him when he went away.

Two weeks before college began, Michael was reading the bewilderingly large catalogue of courses the university had sent when his father appeared in the doorway of his room.

'You going to be okay for money in Ann Arbor?'

'I guess so. I've got the student loan now.'

'You sure that's going to be enough?'

'I've saved quite a lot from the drugstore. If I have to I can always get a part-time job.'

'You shouldn't work while you're going to school.'

'Why not? You did.'

'Maybe that's why I don't want you to have to.'

'I'll be all right.'

His father looked slightly exasperated. 'I know you'll be *all right*. That's not the point. And how are you going to get back here? The bus will take you hours – you'll probably have to change two or three times.'

If it weren't for Cassie this wouldn't be an issue; did his father really think he'd be coming back a lot? He must have read Michael's mind, for he said gently, 'Normally I wouldn't expect to see much of you. But Cassie told me. Seems to me you'll need a car if you're going to see her very often.'

His father was suggesting he needed a car? This from the man who hated driving? 'I can't afford a car,' he said harshly.

His father's eyes widened a little and he was silent for a moment. Then he said, 'What if you had the money?'

'How's that?'

'Your mother left you some in her will. Don't get all excited – it's not that much. But it ought to stretch to a used car. You were supposed to get it when you turned twenty-one, but I think in the circumstances she'd have wanted to release it early.' And then he added, 'Your mother would have liked that girl.'

He was due to leave the day after Labor Day, and spent the weekend working in the store. On Sunday afternoon Ronald came in and bought an expensive pocket comb, a bottle of Brut aftershave, and a large bag of Brach's red-and-white striped peppermints. As he took his change from Michael he said, 'You have a good time down there.'

'Thanks.'

'She'll be just fine.' He gave a small, chesty laugh.

'What?' Michael was too surprised to let fear censor him.

'I said, *you'll* be just fine. See you, little buddy.'

Michael had Monday afternoon off, and planned to take Cassie to the Half in his father's car, but when he went to pick her up she opened the door and put a finger to her lips. 'I'm sorry,' she said, 'I can't come out.'

'What's the matter?'

'He's feeling faint. I can't leave him.'

He swallowed his disappointment as best he could, and the next morning she came to the house to see him off – his father was driving him down to Ann Arbor. As they pulled away he looked back. Gary was already heading for the house, but

194

Cassie stood in the driveway, in the shade of the big maple tree, waving and waving until they turned the corner and were out of sight.

AFTER ALL THIS buildup, his first year proved strangely anti-climactic. At first, his thoughts stayed so much on Cassie back in Stillriver that he had trouble taking in his new environs. He missed her terribly, but was angry with her, too – how could she have let her father ruin her life? *And mine,* he thought bitterly. And he worried that, trapped in Stillriver with her friends and Michael away, she would somehow become vulnerable to what he feared most. *She'll be just fine.*

But within a month of starting college, he discovered that his worries were unfounded. 'Hey Mex,' he said as cheerfully as he could, when on his second trip back to Stillriver he ran into Ronald's little brother by the barber shop. They talked sports for a while until Michael managed to work the conversation around to Ronald.

'He's making good money now,' said Mex, and Michael tried his best to look pleased by this. 'He says he's never met a bigger bunch of airheads, but the Gulf people pay him double what my dad did here.'

'What Gulf people?' asked Michael sharply.

'Gulf of Mexico. He's down near Galveston. I thought you knew that.'

With Ronald out of the picture, Michael found his worries about Cassie evaporated, but his missing of her remained. He lived in a small, clean room in a large new dorm that he grew to detest for its soullessness. He worked hard but found his mathematics course very difficult; most of the class seemed to know more than he did and to learn more quickly, and they were mainly freshmen too. The rest of his courses were lectures, held in large halls with hundreds of students, the only human interface the smaller sessions conducted by graduate teaching assistants. Of these, the only important course for an aspiring pharmacy major was chemistry – which he found straightforward but painfully dull, for he found he could take no interest in a micro world invisible to him.

An old high school classmate named Ward Alison, now working at a second-hand car dealership in Burlington, sold him a used Honda Accord for a good price, and it served him well, getting him to Stillriver in a little over three hours and never breaking down. During the week he spent most of his time, when he wasn't in class, working in the library. So he made only a few friends – friendly acquaintances really – and was lonely much of the time. By spring, when Cassie was finally able to visit him for a weekend (her aunt, the parson's sister, visited from Oregon and offered to look after the parson for a couple of days), he realized there were people on his own floor he hadn't even spoken to.

In his dorm they made love for the first time without any fear of getting caught, though his single bed and the cramped confines of his room eventually drove them outside. He took her to dinner in an Italian restaurant, a first for him, since although there were pizza parlours in Atlantic County, there was no risotto within a hundred miles. 'My aunt took me to one once,' Cassie said shyly. 'But it wasn't as nice as this.'

He told her about his classes, and confessed how hard he was finding mathematics. 'It isn't much fun,' he said, and Cassie looked concerned. 'And I can't stand chemistry.'

'Keep trying things,' she urged him. 'You'll find something you really like.'

He worried she would start to get bored with her visit, since it exposed how little he had explored either the campus or Ann Arbor. He said as much to her as they went back to the dorm. 'When you come next year it will be different,' he added. 'To be honest with you, this year it's seemed like either I was in Stillriver visiting you, or working hard here and *missing* you.'

Cassie didn't say anything. Later that night they made love in the dark while a party went on noisily along the corridor, dope fumes wafting down the hall. They lay quietly together afterwards, listening to the noise of talking and music. Then Cassie removed her arms from his, got out of bed and turned on the lamp on his desk. 'What's the matter?' he asked dozily, for he had been half-asleep.

'I don't know how to tell you this,' she said quietly. She was naked, and went and took one of his T-shirts out of the drawer.

'If you're cold why don't you come back to bed?' he said, but she put on the T-shirt and sat down on the one chair in the room.

'What is it?' he asked, growing alarmed.

'I won't be coming here next year,' she said, in the same flat, dull way she had announced the year before that she would be staying behind.

And it was for the same reason – the parson. 'This could go on for ever,' he protested. 'Your father's got you trapped there.' The parson may have become an invalid, but he seemed to be hanging on to life – and to his daughter – with the vigour of a healthy man.

Cassie shook her head. 'It's not going to last for ever.'

They argued back and forth throughout most of the night, or rather Michael argued, since Cassie stuck firmly to her decision. Finally, as dawn neared, they agreed to stop talking about it and she came back to bed, though he could not resist saying, 'I hate to see you wasting your life. You've got to get out of there and see something of the world.'

She turned over, so her back was towards him. 'I live in the world, too, Michael. And it's not a bad world. I like Stillriver, I always have. And I keep busy.'

In the summer he found that she certainly did. Her father was a demanding, complaining patient, whose chronic discomfort meant you couldn't ask, 'How are you feeling today?' if you ever wanted a cheery answer. Yet somehow Cassie managed not only to tend him – which meant give him his pills, cook his meals, do his laundry, make his bed, and most of all keep him company – but also go half-time to North Shore, the community college twenty miles north, and get 'A's in both her courses, sing in the church choir, bake and sell salt loaf bread to the bakery downtown, and help coach the girls' high school basketball team. Even Michael had to admit that Cassie didn't act like a victim, though her busyness meant that often when he went home for the weekend he only saw her for a couple of hours. He wasn't getting all of her, he thought bitterly, and he certainly wasn't getting much of U of M.

He found the drugstore unchanged, which he supposed indicated that he was the unchanged one, something he had not expected before going to college. Fine weather through June and July meant the store was very busy and there were scarcely any lull times on the floor. It was Marilyn's turn to be ill – she got pneumonia and was out three weeks – and he found Alvin relying on him heavily to oversee the summer staff.

As if in reward for this, he found himself increasingly taken into Alvin's confidence, commercial rather than personal. He began discussing the daily take with Michael, showing him through the newly-acquired computerized tills how much came from liquor (by law only served from the till in the back) and how much from the register nearest the newspapers and cigarettes.

He'd call Michael up behind the drugs counter when he was filling prescriptions, not to give him lessons in pharmacological science, but to show how he ordered the bulk medicines (beta blockers, insulin, Valium), what they cost wholesale and what their mark-up was. He explained too how over the years he'd resisted the urge to expand, feeding any growth from cash in hand rather than the bank. Alvin was half talking aloud, half giving a tutorial. Although Alvin's temper had not been entirely displaced by his ulcers, Michael realized he was no longer scared of his boss.

At home his father seemed even more absorbed in his books and local Indian history than before, while Gary was entering adolescence with a burst of facial pimples and a smart-ass manner that got on Michael's nerves. His brother was doing badly in school but didn't care; he and his friends seemed to have no interest other than smoking dope. Michael doubted his father knew just how much marijuana Gary smoked, then wondered if he should tell him about it. But it didn't seem his business any more; he no longer felt a paid-up member of the household, seeing summer as just an interim period before resuming his new life at college.

With Cassie, he struggled to dovetail their schedules so they could see each other more often, but it was difficult – he worked most evenings in the drugstore, and on the rare free night they couldn't stay out very late because of the parson. They saw a lot of Donny and Nancy, having supper together early at the root beer stand or eating barbecue Donny's mother made at her house. Both Donny and Nancy were at Central and at last going out together; in fact, they seemed so wrapped up in each other that college had made little impression on either of them, and Michael was surprised to find that both assumed they would be coming back to Atlantic County after college. 'Don't you want to go somewhere else?' he asked Donny as they drove out to join the girls at Nancy's parents' farm.

'Yeah, I would,' said Donny. 'I thought maybe after graduation I might travel a bit. See Chicago, maybe try to get to Florida. If I can save up enough.' He looked thoughtful. 'If Nancy wants to come, that is. And if there's time.'

When Michael was working split shifts he and Cassie would sometimes drive to the Half, make love on a blanket by the creek, then walk through the woods, ending up in the large meadow where, like his mother long ago, Cassie would pick wild flowers. He taught her the names of the ones she liked best: milkwort with its tiny buds, the blue tubes of great lobelia, and late in the summer closed gentian, which were protected and couldn't be picked. The Half was where he most liked to take her, since they could make love there, though it didn't seem to have this resonance for Cassie – twice, to Michael's fury, she brought Ethel and Daisy along on their trips there. And Cassie seemed equally happy to stay in town, where they would walk around or go swimming: they would go down to the Channel and dive in, then swim over to South Beach. Michael's agoraphobic reaction to the lake had pretty much petered out, and overall the number of panic attacks he suffered (he'd heard a psychology major down the hall call them that) was blessedly low. And he discovered from Mex that Ronald was still in

Texas, making good money, with no known plans to come back. So that summer there were no clouds on his horizon, other than the looming separation from Cassie when he went back to school. While the hot days lasted they had, as Ethel liked to say when rapturous from gardening with Cassie, 'the bestest time'.

At the beginning of his sophomore year, Michael switched from a dorm to a room in a house with three other guys who'd had their fourth fall through. He didn't really know them at all, and through the autumn it stayed that way. They were all juniors, and had known each other since their freshman year. They had a wide circle of other friends, including lots of girls with whom, unlike Michael's circle in high school, they *did* sleep. They were perfectly civil to Michael, but for the first time in his life he was conscious of being patronized – older and more sophisticated, they seemed to see Michael as a hick, a small town boy at sea in the big wide world. He did not feel he could dispute the justice of this view.

His distance from them was magnified by the fact that none of them knew anything about pharmacology or math or geography ('is Waukegan in Michigan?' asked Sam, the poli-sci major from New York), and none of them seemed to care about what they didn't know. So Michael's new passion was a private one, for he had discovered a new love, in engineering. He wasn't sure why he felt this way, or why he had lost his passion for mathematics. Partly, he knew deep down, it was recognition that he would never be outstanding at math, never lose the feeling that his peers got there more quickly and understood more than he seemed able to. But it was also that the purity of mathematics lay in its abstraction, and the purity of engineering was abstraction made real. It was the very applied nature of the discipline that he loved, using concrete tools to unravel the mystery of the arch, though the mystery somehow still remained, however thorough the explanation.

So he kept himself to himself, working hard in his courses, especially engineering. He continued to go home virtually every weekend to see Cassie. To his fury she had dropped out of North Shore that autumn, claiming she couldn't be away from home at rigidly designated times, claiming too (preposterously, he thought) that she couldn't find cover on the regular basis needed for her to go to class. Yet she managed to stay involved in all her other activities, and sometimes even helped out at the drugstore, working with Marilyn when Marilyn's niece took time off. He tried to keep arguing with her about this, urging her to re-enrol, but instead of flaring up at him, as she would have in the past, now she simply gave up arguing back.

It was proving difficult to sleep together, since Cassie's father was increasingly dependent on her, and his father never seemed to go out any more at weekends – on the one night he had supper at the Fells' and the house should have been empty, Gary got the flu and was at home in bed. At one point, Michael calculated, he hadn't slept with Cassie for over five weeks.

He had Christmas to look forward to, however, since the parson was planning to visit his sister in Oregon – Cassie would go with him for a week, then fly home while he stayed a second one. They would have the parson's house to themselves, Michael told himself when he felt frustrated late that fall. So he could not mask his disappointment when the parson proved too ill to travel. 'Is sex that important to you?' demanded Cassie. 'You actually get to see more of me this way.' He wanted to say, *Yes, it's that important*, but knew she'd find this insulting. He wished she shared his relentless carnal hunger, and couldn't understand why she didn't mind when they couldn't make love. But then, he could not understand her apparent contentment with her whole situation. He was unhappy with it, he told himself, on her behalf.

One Saturday night in January, on a rare weekend when he hadn't gone home, he found himself alone in the house in Ann Arbor watching *Saturday Night Live*, when there was a knock on the door. Opening it he found a girl named Sophie Jansen, a senior and friend of his housemates, standing on the porch, shivering in the cold. He explained that nobody was home and she laughed. 'You count, don't you?' she said, and walked past him into the living room.

He had never talked with her before, but had admired her from a distance. She was breezy, confident and extremely attractive. Sophie had streaked blonde hair which reminded him of Mitchell's daughter in the lumber store, only Sophie's had a shiny, cleaner sheen to it, and it was shoulder-length. Her eyes were bluish-green, and her nose was small and curved – 'People say it's cute,' she had once laughingly declared in his hearing, 'but I do wish it were straighter.' She moved with an obvious confidence, yet seemed without the self-consciousness about her looks, really a kind of arrogance, that had characterized so many of the pretty girls he'd known in high school, like Anthea Heaton (though in her case it was prissiness as much as conceit that rankled), or Cathy Stallover, of course, who wouldn't even say hello half the time to the boys in her class.

Contrastingly, this girl (*woman*, he corrected himself; she seemed to him a woman) seemed so easy with herself that she didn't feel the need to act superior. She was funny, too; he had heard her one night make his housemates laugh with a story about her father, a wealthy contractor in Indiana – something about the money he'd spent on a present for her mother, jewellery that cost the earth but looked like the cheapest paste.

She took off her coat now, then reached down and unzipped her boots, which came to her knees and were a rich mocha brown. He offered her a beer and brought a six-pack out from the kitchen, and soon they were drinking and talking as he sat in the rocking chair and she curled up on the sofa with her legs tucked under her. He was conscious of her unseasonable tan, and the fact she wasn't wearing tights or stockings (*no wonder she was cold*, he thought), and of how the light from the standing lamp next to the sofa picked up the light gold hairs on her arms, and that her toenails were painted shocking pink.

To his pleasant amazement, she asked him questions about himself, and he told her about Stillriver, about the littleness of the place, and the importance of the drugstore, and how strange Ann Arbor seemed to him. He explained too his gradual but growing conviction that he was missing something, and that it wasn't Stillriver. Some new and wider life existed, somewhere around him in this vast, new place. There were so many forms of new life, but he couldn't seem to find them.

He admitted how he knew the others must think him simple and hickish, with small town stamped all over him like dye, but he couldn't help it – 'After all,' he said, to her amusement, 'that's exactly what I am.' But Sophie didn't seem to think it the end of the world to come from a small upstate Michigan town, and he felt encouraged by this, trying to concentrate on what he was telling her, rather than on how she looked to him. For she seemed larger than life, this sudden, vivacious irruption into his dull, solitary Saturday night. With a little urging from her, he told her more about himself, how he didn't like pharmacy or chemistry that much, and how he did like engineering, which he was only just discovering in *Introduction to Civil Engineering (101)* and how he didn't think he wanted to go home after college, even if Alvin and Marilyn were expecting him to.

And then he realized he had been talking almost two hours with Sophie Jansen, who was a senior, a philosophy major, the daughter of a very rich man, and hadn't slept with any of his housemates (he knew this because they all wanted to but had not succeeded) and he had not once mentioned Cassie Gilbert.

And feeling he had probably made a fool of himself, and slightly high from the three beers he'd had, he made his excuses awkwardly and went to his room, while Sophie said she'd sit and wait for the others to come back. He lay on his bed, which was just off the floor, wearing nothing but a pair of Stillriver High shorts (purple shorts with gold lettering, the school colours) because of the warmth of the house – his housemates were not frugal with utilities – and reading *Dune* with just the bedside lamp on, listening to a tape on the cheap system he'd bought the year before in Muskegon.

'Is that Steely Dan?' She was in the doorway, swaying slightly. He nodded, and she came into the room. 'Mind if I listen for a while?'

Before he could even reply, she came and sat down on the edge of the bed. She had a little bead purse wrapped around her wrist and she opened this now and took out a short, thin joint and a throwaway lighter. She lit the j and inhaled sharply, holding her breath until she let it out with a rush and smiled, passing the joint to Michael.

He thought, *I promised to call Cassie*, but the phone was in the living room, and as he took his second hit on the joint and felt the first mild tingle on his bare legs and sensed the first hint of the mental reconstruction he experienced when stoned, he realized he wasn't going anywhere. *I'll call her tomorrow.*

They smoked the whole joint, Sophie sitting cross-legged on the bed beside him, rocking slowly back and forth to the music. When the tape ended they waited for the other side to begin and Sophie gave a big, contented sigh. As the music started she said in a low voice, 'Turn over on your stomach and I'll give you a back rub.'

I have to say no, he told himself, then thought for no apparent reason of his second grade teacher, Miss Summers – *dry as dust* his father had said of her – and he discovered that he had already rolled over on his stomach and Sophie had begun to touch him, lightly at first, her fingertips in slow circles across his back. Then she pressed more firmly – her hands were surprisingly strong – and kneaded his long, thin back, leaning on his spine at one point until he heard a small crack. 'Good,' she said, 'you're relaxing.'

And he was, the sustained eroticism overcoming his self-consciousness and mild alarm, and he began to enjoy these new sensations – Cassie had never given him a massage – and lose himself to the blurred sensations of the soft music, the dope, and this sexy woman's hands. She gently spread his legs and kneeled between them, rubbing the backs of his thighs, and then working for a long time on the backs of his calves.

'It's warm in here,' she said. He felt her weight lift off the bed and, turning his head, saw her stand up and lift her lilac dress in one quick movement over her head and toss it onto the floor. He had a glimpse of her breasts and then she was back on the

205

bed, rubbing his back again with long, smooth strokes. Now she was sitting on him while she squeezed the muscles of his shoulder blades with each hand. He felt the strong bulge of her mound as she leant forward, and her breasts brushed lightly against his back. She sat up over him and her thighs gripped the outside of his own thighs as she tucked her fingers in under the top of his shorts and started to work them down. 'Something's getting in the way,' she said with a light laugh. 'Time to turn over.'

He did slowly and with some embarrassment as she sat watching him, for his excitement was visible. 'Don't be shy,' she said, and he lay back with his hands folded under his head as she leant forward and slowly worked his shorts off, leaving him exposed in full, erect glory.

She reached and held him there with one hand, then looked at him with a sly, lascivious smile, and he smiled weakly back. Then she swung her calf, curved and richly tanned, over him and sat on top, still holding him with one hand. She arched her back and he looked at her breasts, which were round and full but somehow unusual, and then he realized they were as tanned as the rest of her. He watched as she lowered herself carefully, her lips set with determination, and suddenly he was inside her. She said *oh oh* in a small voice that seemed to come involuntarily from somewhere deep inside, and he felt her warm and wet and clenching as she contracted her muscles around him.

He climaxed almost at once and shuddered as she continued to move up and down, milking him. 'Sorry,' he said, finding it hard to look at her.

'Don't apologize,' she said, lifting a forefinger like a teacher. 'That's just the beginning.'

What have I done? he asked himself, then looking up was struck by how pretty she was, the face of someone in the movies almost, easily the prettiest girl in *her* high school class.

To his surprise she stayed the night. Each time after they made love, he expected her to get up, put on her thin dress and head for the door, but there was never any indication she was planning to leave. Once he even asked, 'Do you want to go?'

'Go?' She looked taken aback. 'Why?' she asked, laughing. 'Are you expecting another masseuse in the morning?'

At some point his housemates came back, making a beer-soaked racket of their own, but Sophie had closed his door by then, and they were left undisturbed. They dozed intermittently until finally in the very small hours they both fell soundly asleep, and he woke up to find it snowing outside and Sophie Jansen draped all over him.

And though it was morning she still didn't go. With Cassie, making love had always been in the strict, carnal sense so *simple;* whenever he had tentatively suggested even the slightest experimentation, she would say, 'Okay. I guess.' Then from Michael: 'We don't have to. I was just wondering.' And Cassie would smile: 'It's just I like so much what we do already I can't see it being better any other way.'

But this woman seemed so focused on the physical pleasure of it all: as she did this, or then did that (and some of it was utterly, astonishingly new to Michael), she would sometimes pause and ask him how it felt, or was it better this way, or nicer that. But it had nothing to do with emotions. How could it, with a woman he'd met the night before?

'Breakfast,' she announced late in the morning, and made him share a shower, then took him out to the International House of Pancakes in her zippy Saab convertible.

'You like to eat,' she declared as she watched him down waffles, bacon, sausage, and two eggs over easy. He blushed slightly. 'I like that,' she said, lighting a cigarette as he finished his orange juice. He had eaten non-stop, with the adolescent greed of his younger brother, but it wasn't hunger that drove him so much as not knowing what to say to this woman.

For he felt guilt like flu. He hadn't called Cassie yet and dreaded doing so. How could he let her down like this? Why had he succumbed so easily? He looked across at Sophie, tough and confident, and felt to his great dismay the same hunger stirring that she had tapped all night. *How can you?* He asked himself.

She drove him back to his house and asked him to come see

her in her apartment that evening. When he stuttered something about the homework he had, she took a piece of paper and a pen from the glove compartment. Scribbling furiously, she handed the paper to him. 'That's my address,' she said. 'It's an easy walk. If you change your mind I'll be there tonight. I'm not going anywhere.'

Entering the house, he found his standing with his house-mates had changed, literally overnight. Someone must have seen him leave with Sophie that morning, for now there was an air of excitement among them, one of them suppressing a giggle, Sam the poli-sci major looking at him wide-eyed. He had a feeling they would be paying him more attention in future.

He called Cassie just before supper, feeling nervous about how he would sound on the phone. He had prepared himself for questions about what he'd been doing and why he hadn't called. But she didn't ask them, and sounded preoccupied, almost flat and uninterested in what he had to tell her. Her father was worse, she said, and now had an oxygen cylinder in his room.

When he hung up he felt as irritated as he did guilty. He had an engineering quiz the following day, and he went through his notes for two hours until he realized he was fully prepared – nothing was difficult when you *wanted* to understand it. It was only ten o'clock and he decided to take a walk. As he went round the block he thought about Cassie, the grey quality to her voice on the phone, and he thought about how they made love – decorously almost, gently and lovingly, and with the adroit-ness of the young they would usually climax simultaneously, then collapse in a drowsy contentment – and as he thought of this he was also beset by images of Sophie from the night before, the sheer voluptuousness of her, her sassy badinage, the complete immersion in the sensuous. And he walked right past his house as he finished his circuit and found himself ten minutes later in the studio apartment where Sophie lived, an enormous room with a kitchen in one corner and a new television in the other. Five minutes after this he was in her oversized brass bed with his clothes off while she gave him a full body massage followed by what, years later, the cards posted in the newsagent's windows in the poorer end of Ealing described as 'personal services'.

He knew it was wrong, and what bothered him from the start was not so much the act of infidelity but the dishonesty. He told himself that if he and Cassie had been sleeping together more regularly, Sophie would never have happened. He couldn't tell Cassie about Sophie because it would hurt her, which was partly true, but he also knew he didn't want to risk losing Cassie, for he saw his future with her, missed her, wanted her with him. Yet he wanted – as a grown man occasionally, inexplicably succumbs when passing a Dairy Queen – the ice-cream too: the smooth vanilla and light mocha concoction called Sophie.

And with Sophie, he didn't have to lie. The third time he went to her apartment, late on a weeknight when he came back from the library, she got up after they had made love and put on a blue kimono, then poured them tall glasses of lemonade, and came and sat down on the end of the bed. 'So,' she said, as he sipped his drink, 'what's your girlfriend's name?'

She was smiling as she spoke but there was no banter to her tone. He thought of lying but said simply, 'Cassie Gilbert.'

'Cassie?' she said. 'That's a pretty name. Tell me about her.'

So he did, not elaborating very much, but giving the bare facts – her inability (or unwillingness) to leave Stillriver, her pious prick of a father.

'Is she pretty?' He nodded and she added, 'Beautiful?'

He thought for a moment. 'I think so. In a kind of graceful way.'

'Instead of in a sexy way, you mean,' she said, theatrically cupping her breasts in her hands. He laughed, and she said, 'You do sleep together, don't you?'

Not much these days, he wanted to say, but it sounded too corny. He nodded.

'Do you love her?'

He didn't wait to answer. 'Yes.'

'Then what are you doing here?'

'I don't know.' She looked at him questioningly, and he said, 'I was invited.'

This made her laugh. She stood up and took off her kimono, and he looked at her golden-coloured skin and found himself becoming aroused. 'Interrogation's over,' she said. 'I'm coming to bed.'

If it had remained only about sex he might have managed to stop seeing her, and for the first week sex and sex alone was what she seemed to want from him. He felt guilty after each time they made love: 'Post-coital tristesse,' Sophie said lightly once, when she saw his hangdog look as he lay spent beside her on the big brass bed. But it was ephemeral regret, for the simple reasons that he liked Sophie from the start, and because physically he couldn't seem to get enough of her. He found the smallest things incredibly exciting: the way she put her hair up in a ponytail twist right before she came to bed, the transformation she underwent each morning as she lovingly applied eyeliner, and the way in which her lips, thin and pursed when she listened, suddenly exploded captivatingly when she opened her mouth to talk or laugh.

She must have liked him too, for soon they were meeting outside the bedroom, and doing things together that had no sexual component. She was certainly rich – or her father was, and was generous to her – and she paid for everything: meals in restaurants, the wine they drank, tickets, even gas (though not when he was driving home to Stillriver – 'That's one you'll have to pay for yourself'). When he tried to contribute she wouldn't allow it, and if he protested, she said firmly, 'Don't go all macho on me. If I couldn't afford it I'd let you know, don't worry.'

Most of her friends were seniors, but they saw them rarely – when they did, he felt treated with a mild amusement that he supposed preferable to hostility. She spent a lot of time at his house, for her friendship with his housemates was unaffected; the only change was now they talked to Michael as well. Usually, however, he and Sophie slept in the privacy of her apartment.

She loved paintings and took him to museums in Detroit; she loved music and took him to concerts – once in the same week they saw a visiting orchestra, a chamber concert, and Jackson Browne. 'And which did you like best?' she asked slyly.

He paused. 'The chamber music.'

She looked at him with saucy disbelief. 'Really?' He blushed slightly and Sophie said, 'I love Jackson Browne.'

'Me too,' he admitted, and after that was determined always to tell her what he truly thought. For she never patronized him – that is what he especially liked about her – and if he said something truly stupid would tell him so. He learned about many things by being with her: some were useful, like under-standing the menu in a French restaurant; some just interesting (he had never seen a copy of *Architectural Digest*); some just plain fun (he had never eaten croissants or tuna steak or scallops before).

He called Cassie only slightly less frequently, and tried to make his life sound as uneventful as hers. Her news seemed so *limited,* confined to the square mile around her that was the town. In the past, he had known there was some bigger world outside he wanted to explore; now that he had seen some of it, it cast Stillriver in a dimmer light. The news he had he didn't feel able to relate, since so much of his activities now were with Sophie. Yet strangely, when he was out with Sophie, he often wished Cassie were there, too. It was not some bizarre fantasy of a *ménage à trois* – it had nothing to do with sex. He was doing so many new things – visiting galleries, eating curry for the first time – and he wanted to share his new life. So he could not help mentioning during one of their phone conversations that he had gone to a Jackson Browne concert.

'Really?' she asked excitedly. 'Wasn't it expensive?'

'A friend had an extra ticket,' he lied.

'That's a good friend,' she said quietly, and for the very first time he wondered if she perhaps intuited more than he had thought.

When Donny came down from Central one weekend, Sophie agreed to make herself scarce, but when Michael came home to greet his friend he found him talking and laughing with his housemates and . . . Sophie.

'I couldn't help it,' she said later. 'I had to see if he was really like you described him.'

'And is he?' he asked, trying to remember what stories he had told her about his friend. Fishing exploits, drunken carousing on the beach, what else? Presumably they all seemed completely small town to her.

'He is and then some,' she said. 'That,' she added, 'is one Main Street guy. You think you're a hick, but you're not like that at all.'

'He's my best friend,' he protested.

'You can't have it both ways,' she said, looking at him coolly, 'telling me how much you want to see the world but then getting defensive about your roots.'

And Donny had said, 'I like your friends. That girl Sophie, she's a humdinger.' He looked at Michael with a mock-avuncular eye. 'I think maybe I won't mention her to Nancy. Who knows who she might tell?'

Michael told Cassie he was going for the weekend to Indiana with friends, and she was encouraging. 'The Hoooo-sier state,' she said with a giggle.

He and Sophie flew in the Piper Cub of a Michigan alumnus, who had spent the week being entertained by development officers of the university and was now flying back to Indianapolis. A friend of Sophie's father, he had a hired pilot and drank four Bloody Marys while they bobbed up and down in a late-winter sky.

The first night they went to a hockey game in a vast arena, where they sat in a box with Sophie's parents and two other couples, eating *tournedos* and chocolate cake in a private room during the intervals. Sophie's father, Herb, was a short and stocky man, who wore an immense college graduation ring and a Rolex Oyster on his wrist. His wife was expensively dressed, formally polite to Michael, and remote – not only with him, but with Sophie and her father as well.

After the game they returned to the Jansen residence, a vast brick ranch house, and Michael sat up with Sophie and her father for a nightcap, then made his excuses and went to bed. Since he didn't have a clue where Sophie slept, he lay there, hoping she would come to him, then woke up as the sun rose over the swimming pool outside his room.

'Sorry,' said Sophie at breakfast. 'I stayed up talking with Daddy.'

When her father joined them it was clear he had already been up for hours. His wife brought him a plate with eggs, bacon and toast. 'Sophie says you're majoring in engineering,' he said, pouring himself coffee. 'Any particular kind?'

'Civil engineering. I like bridges.'

Herb looked interested in Michael for the first time. 'Is that what you want to do then, design bridges?'

'I think so.'

'You *think* you want to design bridges. Better make up your mind.' He started carving up his eggs with his fork, dipping a piece of toast into the yolk. '*We* build bridges, you know,' he said, his eyes on his plate. 'All over the Midwest. You want a summer job to see what it's like, you let me know.'

Sophie looked at Michael and said, 'He's got a job already, Daddy. He works in a drugstore.'

Herb looked up from his eggs for a moment. 'I don't get it,' he announced. 'You want to be an engineer, or a soda jerk?' He shrugged and resumed eating. That was the last time during the weekend that he paid any attention to Michael.

'He liked you,' Sophie said. They were driving back in a rental car on Sunday afternoon, though they planned to stop for the night at a motel outside Elkhart. On Saturday night Sophie had again sat up with 'Daddy', so Michael was looking forward to stopping.

'He might have, until you said I was working in the drugstore this summer. I think I was supposed to jump at his offer.'

'Relax. My father wants people to jump at everything he says. You'll get used to him.'

When they got back to Ann Arbor the next day, there was a message on his door telling him to call Cassie. When he phoned she sounded subdued.

'I thought you were coming back yesterday,' she said.

'I know, but we decided to stay an extra day.'

'Oh,' she said. 'I was hoping you'd call.'

'I'm sorry,' he said. 'I didn't feel I could call long distance on someone else's phone.'

There was a long silence. 'What's wrong, Cassie?'

'Nothing,' she said, but her voice was faint.

'Is your father all right?'

'He's the same,' she said, and he could barely hear her. Then suddenly she asked, 'Who's Sophie?'

He hesitated before replying, then rushed his response. 'One of the friends I went down with. Why?'

Her voice went faint again. 'Just wondering,' she said. 'When I called, whoever answered the phone said you'd gone to Indiana with Sophie.'

Thanks, guys. 'Yes,' he said, 'but she wasn't the only one there,' and thus for the first time told an active lie, rather than one of omission.

'Are you coming up this weekend?'

Sophie had asked him to a party some other senior was giving on Saturday night, so he hesitated. 'Sure,' he said finally. 'I'll come up Friday night.'

It unravelled more quickly than he wanted or expected. The parson was asleep and they sat at the kitchen table while he explained his frustrations, how it was hard coming back so often, how he felt he wasn't doing justice to his coursework – he even talked a little about his new passion for engineering – and how maybe they would both profit from a break.

'You're saying you want a break? You mean from me?'

'Not you, Cassie,' he said, already manipulating in his head the words to come. 'Just from the routine, this coming and going. It would be different if you could come down to me sometimes.'

214

'You know I can't do that.' She picked up her coffee mug with both hands and stared at it.

'Of course I do. I just meant there wouldn't be this strain.'

'I don't feel any strain,' she said. 'I look forward to the weekends, you must know that.'

'Shoot, half the time I'm here you're busy doing something else. If it isn't your father, it's choir practice, or basketball.'

'I have to keep busy,' said Cassie, looking hurt. 'This break, how long do you mean it to be?'

'Just until school's out.'

Her eyes widened. 'That's almost three months.'

He shrugged. 'I know. It won't seem that long once it's over.' *What the fuck does that mean?*

'But I'll miss you,' she protested.

'I'll miss you too, Cassie. But I think it's for the best.'

'I need time to take this in.' She looked vacantly at the mug. 'Tell me, are you planning to see somebody else while you take this "break"?' There was now some edge to her voice.

'That's not the idea.'

Her father called out for her. 'Cassie, may I see you please?'

'You haven't really answered the question,' she said as she stood up and went out of the room. He waited until she came back in about five minutes, but she said he had better go, as she would be some time still with her father. He said he'd phone her in the week. When he kissed her goodbye she suddenly hugged him fiercely, then turned and went to the parson's room.

3

HER LETTER CAME that Wednesday, and proved a relief.

> *Dear Michael,*
>
> *I have been thinking about our conversation (and thinking of little else!) and am still not sure what to make of it. I know your life is different now, and I have never wanted to get in the way of what you* wanted.
>
> *But maybe I have been. And maybe you do need the time by yourself to feel you are getting the most out of U of M.*
>
> *See? – I don't know what to say. I think it's probably best if I wait to hear from you. Which you know I hope I will.*
>
> *All my love*
> *Cassie*

He felt only mildly guilty about this, since he saw their separation as temporary. Sophie was a senior, and he had never kidded himself that their relationship would last beyond the end of the semester. She was going east after graduation, possibly to study psychology at NYU, or to work in television if she could find a way in. And to some extent, what he'd told Cassie had been true. He *was* exhausted by the weekly trip, then once in Stillriver didn't usually get to see that much of her anyway, and found it very difficult to study at home, since Gary always played music and always played it loud. If only Cassie would get herself to Ann Arbor, he decided, all would be well.

Now he could concentrate on his work, and he did, doing well in all his courses, exceptionally well in the second-semester course on civil engineering. At Sophie's urging he took a history of architecture course, a basic survey he enjoyed up to a point. He liked its historical sweep, moving from a semi-troglodyte dwelling to the work of Robert Gehry in the confines of an undergraduate term, but the focus was relentlessly aesthetic, and he found himself wanting to linger over the mechanics of what he was being asked to appreciate in purely visual terms. Materials fascinated him, and for his term paper he wrote on the usurpation of brick by steel in the development of early skyscrapers, finding himself perversely taking the side of brick. Steel had suddenly allowed a surge skyward, but he found a grace in the modest twenty-storey vertical limit that was lost when height became the dominating aspiration.

He sensed a disappointment on Sophie's part about his persisting interest in the composition of the building blocks themselves rather than in debates about, say, the durability of postmodernism. For the first time he felt an effort had been made, so subtle as perhaps to be unconscious on her part, to shape him. There was never an open argument, but rather an unprecedented if slight tension, an undeclared skirmish of wills. This had never happened with Cassie; their disagreements had always been out in the open.

They went to Indianapolis again and he began to see how far Sophie, too, had travelled from her roots, because for all his money Herb Jansen was a rough diamond, or, as Sophie herself remarked, a rough *owner* of diamonds. Michael found that once he appreciated this he liked the man much more, yet Sophie seemed slightly irritated by how well he now got on with her father. This time Sophie went to bed while he sat up listening to her father's stories. Herb had worked in the Army Corps of Engineers in his twenties, on rebuilding projects in post-War Germany, which had left him with an admiration for the Germans, then stirring economically for the first time since the War. 'You have to see Europe,' Herb insisted. 'Wherever you end up, you have to see Europe.'

The small prickles with Sophie didn't have much effect on his enjoyment of the time he spent with her. Physically, he still could never get enough of her, and their other activities together (she was developing a near-obsession with foreign films; when he felt peculiar at the start of a movie one night, he realized it was because it was the first one in weeks he'd seen without subtitles) continued to give him a sense of an expanding world, even if it was he and not the world that was growing. He was determined to enjoy this last term with her as fully as possible, and though aware of his own duplicity nonetheless continued to think how much he had to tell Cassie about, how much new he would have to share with her. So he was stunned when, after a supper of takeaway Chinese food and most of a six-pack in Sophie's apartment, about three weeks after Cassie's letter had arrived, Sophie announced that she wanted to sleep alone that night.

'Any reason why?' he asked, since neither schoolwork nor exhaustion had ever prompted his removal before.

'You know,' she said, leaning over and putting a hand on his knee, 'in two months time I'll be leaving.'

'I know that.' He felt better with her hand on his knee, but she removed it and sat back.

'It's been so much fun I don't think either of us is looking forward to its ending. And I *hate* goodbyes.'

'Well, we don't have to say goodbye yet.'

She ignored this. 'You know, all that teary stuff and "promise you'll write" and "I'll always love you". Ugh,' she said with a small shudder.

When he didn't speak she continued. 'So I've come to the conclusion that it would be easier for both of us if we decided to stop early.'

'Really? You mean *now*?'

She nodded. 'Why wait? Let's take our medicine and get it over with.'

'But will I see you?'

'Of course you will. That's the whole point. This way we'll be friends while we get used to not being lovers.'

And truth was, he did see her almost as much as before for a time, though within two weeks he realized that he rarely saw her alone any more, and that she treated him now in much the same fashion as she had always treated his housemates – friendly, even sassy, but very much as one of the boys, with an absolute understanding that sleeping with her was out of the question. And he remembered their conversation over the plastic plates of fried rice, egg rolls, and Chinese spare ribs, and shook his head in wonderment at how smoothly, cordially and effortlessly she had dumped him in the space of a minute and a half.

He felt more stupid than hurt. To his surprise, his house-mates stayed friendly, for with the loss of his stunning bedmate he had expected relegation to his earlier low status. They made no cruel jokes about Sophie's abandonment of him, indeed seemed happy to welcome him into their own informal club which, it turned out, they jokingly called *PFSJ* – the Pining Friends of Sophie Jansen. He usually spent weekend nights with them in the local student bars, or else studied in his room and listened to music. He missed Sophie, though more, he was slightly ashamed to realize, for their rich sexual life together and the new experiences she had underwritten than for her company.

He immersed himself in his work, especially in a term project for engineering, hypothetically redesigning the Mackinaw Bridge as a steel truss job, working for the first time to assess caisson construction under several hundred feet of water. His engineering professor had him to dinner at his house with his wife and children, and went out of his way to encourage him – to Michael's immense, private excitement, the professor got him access to the department's Cray supercomputer. In four and a half minutes Michael had calculations made that would have taken three weeks on one of the department's lumbering microcomputers.

It was, curiously, in those four-and-a-half minutes as he waited for the Cray to finish that he discovered something was missing – someone, actually. It wasn't Stillriver, for his hometown was rapidly receding from his day-to-day thoughts, and it certainly wasn't family (he only rarely phoned his father) and it wasn't the drugstore: he'd work the summer for Alvin, but increasingly Michael saw himself as an aspiring engineer rather than as the future owner of a pharmacy.

No, it was Cassie he missed, though he had trouble admitting this even to himself. He was the one, after all, who'd insisted on a 'break', and if he were to visit earlier than he'd told her he would, Cassie might not think he was returning with his tail between his legs, but he would. There would be plenty of time in summer, he tried to tell himself, to make amends with Cassie and start again. But then he woke up in his Ann Arbor room early one Thursday morning in May, with an image in his mind of Cassie, wearing her down vest, striding forward and suddenly laughing with her flashing smile at something he had said. And he thought, lying in bed alone, *I could love her anywhere.* And that night he returned to Stillriver, where he ate supper in the kitchen with his father and Gary, helped with the dishes, then tried to reach Cassie on the phone. The parson answered and said that she was out, then would not be drawn on when she would be back. So Michael went upstairs to read, feeling as if he were fourteen again and his mother had just died.

He was washing both his car and his father's when he heard a vehicle stop. 'What are you doing here?' It was Donny's face poking out of the pickup's window.

'I should ask you the same thing.' Donny's semester wasn't over either.

'Nancy's mom's birthday. We're having a dinner tomorrow night. I know you'd be welcome.'

He shook his head. 'Thanks, but I can't. I'm hoping to see Cassie.'

'Cassie? I thought you broke up.'

'Who told you that? We were just taking some time off.'

'Is that what she thinks?'

'I sure hope so.'

Donny frowned, which Michael didn't like.

'What's wrong with that anyway? Is there a problem?'

Donny put his hand on top of the steering wheel and looked abstractedly out into space. 'That depends.'

'On what? You know something I don't?'

'Oh Lordy,' said Donny, as if some small family scandal, long thought buried, had inconveniently resurfaced. He wiggled his fingers on the steering wheel. 'You might as well know that her old admirer is back.'

He didn't need clarification. 'Since when?'

'Just after Easter.'

'And?'

'Beats me, bud. I know they've seen each other, but don't ask me what that means.' He squirmed slightly, then sat up straight and looked directly at Michael. 'Truly, I don't know. But I'd be surprised if there were much more to it than going to the movies once in a while.'

'So what's the problem then?' said Michael, though he felt distinctly unrelieved. 'I can't get mad if she goes to the movies with somebody when I'm stuck down in Ann Arbor.'

'I know you won't get mad, and Cassie won't get mad, and that's all reasonable and fine. But the problem is Ronald. Mex told me he's crazy about Cassie. He said Ronald came back from Texas as soon as he heard you two had split up.'

'But we *haven't* split up,' Michael protested. 'So who told him that?'

'Mex, I guess. It wasn't exactly a secret. You weren't coming back weekends any more and Cassie kept bursting into tears in public. So Ronald quit his job and came back – didn't even work his notice. Mex said it's all Ronald seems to think about, how to show Cassie he's not some animal, how to impress her with his gentle qualities. Mex said—'

'Enough of what Mex said. What's your point?'

Donny nodded, as if understanding Michael's impatience, but then said, 'So maybe you'll get mad at me instead, is that it? Because I hate to tell you, but Mex told me that Ronald said if you so much as take a sniff within a hundred yards of Cassie he's going to pound you into mush so fine a dog could only find it by its nose.'

Michael shrugged, more to steady his nerves than to make a display of nonchalance. He struggled to keep a quaver out of his voice as he spoke: 'I'd have thought it was up to Cassie as to who she wants to see. Especially if they've just been going to a movie or two.'

'*Fuck*.' Donny hit the steering wheel with a closed fist.

'Why are you swearing at me?'

Donny put his head in his open, other hand, like Rodin's Thinker transplanted to the Midwest. 'I'm not swearing at you,' he said, his voice muffled by his outstretched fingers. He lifted his head up and looked at Michael with an expression of almost amiable resignation. 'It's just I knew you'd say something like that.' He reached forward and put the truck into gear. 'Be careful, all right?'

On the phone Cassie's tone was unaccommodating and aloof, but she agreed to meet him the following day. Feeling uncertain, he went for a drive in order to be alone, intending to visit the Half, until he saw the vanilla pickup truck do a U-turn and follow him, openly but a good quarter-mile back, out Park Street and across old 31.

He told himself not to be paranoid, but he didn't like the idea of an encounter with Ronald in those remoter parts of the county, where a population density of roughly two citizens per square mile meant that if you needed help, there wasn't much available. So he swung back west towards the lake and drove into Fennville, skirting the fair grounds, and driving out on the strip that was rapidly developing as an offshoot of the interstate's traffic. A Travel Lodge, two new gas stations, a Dunkin' Donuts, pizza takeaway, and a retail outlet for Clarks shoes. There were strict speed controls here and very little traffic: it wasn't hard to see the pickup four or five hundred yards behind him.

This is crazy, he told himself. Was he sure it was Ronald behind him? Was he sure it was the same truck he'd first seen as he left Stillriver, twenty minutes before? He couldn't be positive, and felt momentarily better. But when he took the slip road onto the interstate and accelerated as he joined the highway he was startled to find that the pickup truck gathered speed and followed him.

Not so funny now, he thought, not at all sure what to do. Then he remembered Kenny Williams's account of how the year before, driving back from a trip to Grand Haven, he'd outmanoeuvred a couple of drunken, ageing rednecks who'd been following him. The road was virtually deserted, and Michael accelerated for some time until he caught up to the traffic in front of him, then drove at a steady sixty-five behind a Subaru and an enormous eighteen-wheeler. Ronald was now only about a hundred yards behind him. Just before the exit for Three Forks road, Michael passed both vehicles, then tucked in so tightly in front of the eighteen-wheeler that its driver flashed his lights at him. As they neared the exit, Michael suddenly veered off onto it, and turned to watch as the vanilla pickup, by now passing the truck, struggled to slow down and cut over to the exit ramp, but had its way blocked.

He was *following me*, he thought. But his elation at his escape was quickly dispelled by the realization that it was a purely temporary victory. With the gloominess of a man whose medical test results have turned out bad, he drove home by back roads, entering Stillriver on the sandy track that came down from the higher land of the Meadows and through the site of the old dump.

His father looked at him curiously as he came through the kitchen door. 'You okay?' he asked, and in his anxiety Michael almost forgot to nod.

They had arranged to meet at Nelson's boathouse, and when he climbed the stairs he found Cassie already there, standing against the railings and looking out at Stillriver Lake. It was an acid day in May, clear and sun-filled but with a stinging wind off the big lake that made the air sharp enough for Michael to feel cold, even in a sweatshirt. Cassie looked cold too, and her fingers were pink in the chill.

'Hi,' he said lightly as he came and stood beside her. She turned and looked at him questioningly, and he smiled. She looked back again out over the lake and said nothing.

Oh no, he thought, and tried to launch into his prepared recital. 'Cassie,' he said. 'I made a mistake.' But the rehearsed words flew out of his head like a freed bird, and he struggled to put his racing thoughts into a sentence. 'All I'm asking for is another chance,' he finally declared.

'How do I know you won't make *another* mistake?' she asked. Her voice was dry.

'You don't,' he admitted, and they both fell silent. Across the lake a man came out onto his dock and unhitched a rowboat, clambered in, and began to row slowly across the lake towards them. 'Except I won't,' said Michael at last. 'I know now what you mean to me. I don't want to lose that.'

'You know *now* what I mean to you. It seems you didn't know before.'

This was delivered unemotionally. If Cassie had been angry he would have known how to react. He would have set himself the task of appeasing her hurt, certain that her anger was the natural reaction of someone who still loved him. But he couldn't decipher this flat certainty of tone.

'What does *she* think?' asked Cassie.

'There isn't any she,' he said, and she gave him such a forceful *oh really?* look that despite the technical truth of what he was saying, he couldn't pretend that had always been the case. 'Not any more,' he said, sounding feeble even to himself. 'It's not an issue.'

Cassie gave a small groan and looked up at the heavens in mock-despair. 'Not an issue. You say you've made a "mistake". I ask what's going to keep you from making another "mistake". And all you can say is it's not an "issue".' She shook her head. 'It sounds as if she dumped you, whoever this Sophie woman was, and you think, "That's okay, I'll just run back to Cassie."'

Donny must have spilled the beans to Nancy after all. 'That's not true.'

'Back to me, sitting here in Palookaville – that's how you think of it now, isn't it? – with nothing better to do than wait for you to decide I'm not so bad after all.'

'That's not true,' he said again.

'Maybe it isn't.' Her voice lifted for the first time. 'But how can I tell? I don't know what to believe any more.'

'Be fair.'

'*Fair?* Like you were to me? Listen, I know people change and things happen and life doesn't go on in the same way for ever. But I didn't think things had changed between us.'

'They haven't.' When she didn't reply he said, 'Let me prove it. Please, Cassie. I've missed you. Say you'll see me again.'

'I'll see you, Michael, but I'm not sure I want to sleep with you. Not for a while anyway.'

'That's okay,' and then an awful thought entered his mind. 'Is that because you're sleeping with someone else?'

'No,' she said, sounding disappointed by the question.

'Donny said Ronald Duverson was back in town. He said you'd been seeing him.'

'*Fuck* Donny.' She almost spat the word, which he had never heard her say before. 'Honestly, you men. Is that all you ever think about? I went to the movies with him, all right? He sent me flowers on my birthday – look at you, you didn't even send a card. He walked me home once from basketball practice. And yes, sometimes he's called me on the phone. So what? Why is it Donny's business anyway?'

'It isn't,' he said, trying to reduce her anger.

'And you can't talk either. You haven't told me the truth about anything, and all you want to know is whether I've been sleeping with anybody else.'

'It was just that Donny said Ronald was in love with you.'

'*In love with me?* Did Donny use those words?'

'No.'

'I didn't think so. So Ronald's got a crush on me, so what? I *like* Ronald. I know what you're about to say – and yes, I know his reputation. But he has never been anything but sweet to me. Gentle, and polite.'

'Tell that to his last victim.'

She was shaking her head impatiently. 'He hasn't been in a fight in months.'

'How would you know? He only got back from Texas last month.'

'Because he told me so. He said he's not going to fight any

more. And half the problem is that once people think you'll fight they like to pick them with you.'

'Oh, I see. That's why he has to fight so much.'

'I just told you he's stopped. Give him a break.'

Sure, he thought, *and let him do the same for me.* He could see the vanilla pickup truck in his mind's eye.

'Anyway,' Cassie said, 'I don't want to talk about Ronald. Maybe he is "an admirer", but that doesn't mean I reciprocate the feeling. If I were in trouble I could count on him, but I just like him as a friend.'

'So you'll see me again?'

'Yes, I will,' she said firmly, 'and doubtless you'll get me into bed again, too. I love you, Michael. But understand one thing. Next time, if you get tired of me, you better have the decency to tell me. Because if you disappear again I don't think I could bear it.'

Michael reached over and kissed Cassie until, eventually, she kissed him back. There was a thump from below and Michael looked down. The man in the rowboat was holding onto Nelson's dock with one hand and the oars with the other.

'Excuse me folks,' he said, 'but do you have permission to be here?'

4

IT HAPPENED AS quickly as an accident. Michael was sitting reading the want ads in the *Burlington Daily News,* when he heard a door slam in the driveway, tipped down his paper to see, and found Ronald Duverson coming at full run towards him. He managed to stand up but then found himself paralysed, unable to move away from Ronald's first punch, which hit Michael so hard that he felt a hammer had been driven into his cheek.

Oddly, he didn't fall down, stunned into immobility by the force of the blow. Then *bam!* Again, this time the other hand slammed suddenly into the hollow between his right cheek and jaw, loosening a tooth. Blood spurted out of his mouth like water from a playground fountain.

This time he did fall, backwards against the deckchair he had been sitting in, hitting his head against the thin wooden frame, then sliding awkwardly and hard onto the stone patio. He rolled instinctively onto his front and something hit his back with the dull force of a sledgehammer. Then he was hit again and again in rapid succession, a tattoo of punches against his back and the back of his head. There was the briefest of pauses, then he felt an explosively fierce pain in his side and heard something crack as he was kicked in the ribs.

He wanted to roll out of the way but under the barrage of hammering blows he couldn't move at all. He thought, *This isn't going to stop. He is going to kill me and I can't do anything about it.* Fear of dying overtook his fear of pain.

'*Stop it,*' came a loud voice with bass finality. It sounded much like his father, Michael thought hazily. And then he heard the unmistakable click of a breech closing – smooth, machined, well-oiled.

'You touch him one more time,' the voice announced from somewhere above, 'and I'll pull this trigger.'

The only response from Ronald, who had not said one word or uttered the briefest phrase, was a snarl.

'You go get into your truck and get out of here. Right now. I'm going to count to three, and if you're not in that cab by then I'll shoot. So help me God, I will. *One . . .*'

And Michael heard, as he slowly rolled over, wincing as his back touched the patio, the sound of boots running across the paving stones and onto the driveway. Then a door slammed, an engine started, and the tyres squealed as in a movie and Ronald was gone.

Michael listened as footsteps came down from the porch. He sensed his father's great arms reaching down to encircle him, then winced as he was hoisted up in one powerful heave. His father steadied Michael, then half-pushed and half-carried him up the porch steps, as Michael tried to pick his feet up and keep them from hooking onto each step. Then they were in the house, staggering through the kitchen like marathon dancers, then through the dining room and into the living room, where his father released him and Michael fell onto the sofa and passed out.

Cool, the water felt so cool and fresh. He came to and found his father working carefully on his face with a wash rag. 'Cuts and bruises,' said Henry. 'You've looked prettier, but I don't think anything's broken. How's your ribcage?'

Michael felt down and didn't wince until he pushed hard. But then he flinched with the sudden sharpness of the pain. He was cross with himself for checking – he didn't want to reveal how much it hurt. 'Could be cracked,' said his father. 'The only way to tell for sure is to get an x-ray. I'll take you over to Fennville tomorrow. First though, I'd like Doctor Fell to have a look. I called him but he's up fishing on the Pere Marquette. Back tomorrow.'

Dr Fell – his father's closest friend, the attendant physician throughout the family's history: delivering Michael, then Gary, tending their mother as she slowly died before their eyes. A historical intimacy that Michael hadn't chosen and didn't think he could stand right now. 'There's no point having an x-ray,' Michael said harshly. 'They don't do anything for cracked ribs these days. Taping it is pointless.' His father looked surprised but said nothing. Michael was beginning to understand how badly he had been beaten up. A growing sense of humiliation was taking hold, and he wished he could be alone to lick his wounds. He desperately wanted to cry, but was equally determined not to cry in front of his father. 'I don't need Doctor Fell, either. Let him fish.' Suddenly he snapped, 'I just want to be left alone!' Anger seemed the only way to avoid tears.

'I've got to report this. That kid was trying to kill you. If I hadn't come along . . .'

He left the sentence unfinished, for Michael was shouting again: 'Don't call Jerry Dawson whatever you do. If you call him, I'll deny it.'

'Why?' Henry sounded genuinely baffled.

'I just don't want you to call him. *Please.*' He struggled for arguments to keep his father from calling anybody. He was desperate now. He felt thoughts racing by him, and like a frantic commuter running for his train, jumped onto the latest one to enter his head. 'I'll tell him *you* beat me up, that's what I'll do.'

Michael could see his father was shocked by this, and he was shocked himself. Part of Michael yearned to take the words back, and to admit how bad he felt – not physically, because for all his soreness and hurt he could sense he would recover quickly. It was his impotence that really hurt.

Now Henry spoke slowly, with a show of calmness. 'Let's talk about it tomorrow. You get some rest now. I'll get you a blanket – you can sleep here tonight.'

Sunday he found he could stand and, after a fashion, walk around the house, though his ribcage was very tender and if he jarred his feet at all, the bones in his cheek burned with soreness. Gary came home from his sleepover and stood in the kitchen as Michael sucked soggy cereal from a spoon. 'What truck did you hit?' his brother asked.

'*Gary*.' Their father called him out to the living room and when Gary came back he made no further remarks. It was only after supper, when Gary had gone upstairs to listen to music, that his father brought up the subject of Jerry Dawson again. He spoke with a mixture of decisiveness and resignation. 'Tomorrow morning I want you to come with me and see Jerry. And I want you to tell him the truth about what happened. I didn't bring you up to be a liar.'

When Michael didn't argue his father seemed satisfied, and went to bed early. He was sleeping soundly at four in the morning when Michael tiptoed down the stairs, carrying his duffel bag, uncertain which was bothering him more – the pain brought by his movements or the worry that he'd wake his father up. Once outside, he opened and closed his car door carefully, then sat catching his breath and waiting for his ribs to produce only manageable amounts of pain. He reversed quickly out of the drive, then drove at speed through the empty streets of the town. It was only when he was halfway to Fennville on the interstate that he realized he was running away.

But he had no choice. He felt frightened and, at the return of his old friend Fear, depressed. Having spent so much time fighting the incapacitating effects of fright, he had begun to think he had won not just the battle, but the war. His panic attacks and his odd fear of violence had begun to seem so irrational that they lost their ability to unnerve him. His early fear of Alvin had been entirely forgotten; even his greater fear of Ronald Duverson had come to seem overblown, almost ridiculous.

But it wasn't ridiculous at all. He felt the bruise on one cheek with his fingers, then turned on the car's interior light and looked in the mirror at the mauve mess of his face. That wasn't evidence of neurosis; that, he thought, lightly tracing over his wounds, was real. He had been right all along to be scared.

And he was still scared now, driving through the night, climbing the hills before New Era, seeing a solitary light in a farmhouse in the dark valley below, then descending down through the beech and birch forest. If he stayed in Stillriver he knew that Ronald would just come and do it again – he could visualize Ronald running at him, and even in the mere imagining found himself agitated, taking short, jerky breaths as he gripped the steering wheel and drove on.

The only way to stop Ronald would be to file a complaint with Jerry Dawson, and for reasons of humiliation rather than fear, he couldn't face that either. It was bad enough that his father had witnessed his son being beaten half to death, but two hours after an interview with Jerry the whole town would know. That's how it worked; he'd seen it happen enough while working in the drugstore, how by an unseen bush telegraph anything dramatic that happened got sent racing through the loose-lipped inhabitants of the town, moving from point to point until there wasn't a man, woman, or child alive in Stillriver who wasn't in the know. And after that, how could he stand behind the counter at the drugstore all summer long, knowing that the locals coming in knew what had happened, and worse, knew that he knew they knew? *That's Henry Wolf's boy, the one Ronald almost beat to death*.

News, know, knew – for a moment the words thundered like a symphony in his head, but the effect of every word was *exposure,* the certainty that his humiliation would be public. But worst of all, worse even than the public humiliation, would be facing Cassie. He had never thought one way or another about whether he deserved Cassie, simply thought ever since meeting her that life had at last stopped playing tricks on him, and had decided to do something nice. *Nice?* More than that – wonderful. But now he felt for the first time he *didn't* deserve her; suddenly they seemed divided by a river he didn't know how to cross. Oh sure, she might act understanding, would probably urge him to press charges and ignore the inevitable resulting talk. But how would she help him recover the man-hood he'd left lying on the paving stones outside his father's house? What would he do when he went walking with her and Ronald suddenly loomed ahead, walking towards them menacingly? Just thinking of that made him feel impotent and incapable.

So faced with this combination of humiliation and fear, what else could he do but run? He had to get away, find time and some place to recompose what seemed to him to have been shattered – his very sense of himself. He'd collect himself, however long it took, and then he'd see Cassie, be her man again instead of a pathetic, whimpering kid. *Maybe the parson will die soon,* he thought hopefully as he skirted Muskegon, *and then Cassie can come to Ann Arbor. Once she gets away as well everything will be fine.* And he hung onto the prospect like a drowning man grabbing a buoy, since he could find hope in none of his other thoughts, only shame and fear.

Back in Ann Arbor, he lay low in the house for the first day, going out only to visit the student health service, where the doctor was nosy but nice, and produced the painkillers Michael wanted. He kept his bedroom door closed and his housemates left him alone. He called Sophie and overcame her slight wariness by explaining it wasn't her he wanted. Two days later she called back with a name and number her father had supplied, and that same day he wrote Alvin to explain he wouldn't be back that summer, gave a mail-forwarding address to his housemates as well as strict instructions not to reveal his whereabouts to anyone. Then he left Ann Arbor and drove north along the eastern, Lake Huron side of the state, until he found the construction site seven miles outside Alpena, where he and seventy-three other males were going to erect a small box-girder bridge across the Thunder Bay river.

The first week was spent wheelbarrowing a hand-dug mix of shingle and sand from the riverbank to a vast mound at the back of the site. Sore and stiff from Ronald, he struggled at first to do the job. He barely spoke to any of his workmates, turning in right after supper and sleeping like the dead until roused with the others from his bunk at dawn. By the second week he was less exhausted and by week three he felt himself growing stronger from the exertions of the job, so much so that he declined the offer of a move to a softer position plotting river depths.

Later, much later, when he was living in New York, where such things seemed commonplace, he could look back on his first two months after Ronald and see that he must have suffered some kind of breakdown. But he had no such insight at the time, and lived in a kind of mental cocoon, as if something had been broken inside him, which only he could heal. He received one short letter from his father, forwarded from Ann Arbor, which simply said he hoped that Michael was all right and that he was welcome home at any time, and two from Cassie, which he did not open.

By August he had gained eight pounds, none of it fat, and was able for the first time to think about what had happened to him. The process was helped when two of his workmates staggered back one Saturday night from a bar in Alpena, where they had been beaten up by a bunch of farmhands from the Thumb. To his astonishment they revelled in their injuries, and laughed about how badly they had lost the fight. From this he acquired for the first time some perspective on what had happened. *It is not the end of the world*, he told himself. Now he could think about those few minutes when he had almost lost his life, and although the humiliation still ran deep and the fear his memories brought was awesome, neither were quite as crippling as before – when he gave up fighting them he found that eventually they subsided, unable to live off their own energy when deprived of his.

And as the job ended he understood that he would go home before returning to college. He would see his father and Gary, show that he was all right now, and also see Alvin and Marilyn, though he dreaded this, since he knew he had let them down. But chiefly he wanted to see Cassie, and yes, he hoped he could win her back again. Of course she might despise his cowardice; she might even greet him with contempt, since he had run away. There was no ducking that. What had she said? *If you disappear again I don't think I could bear it*. But once he had explained the mixture of shame and fear that had driven him away he was hopeful of her understanding, for she had always been understanding in the past. And though Ronald Duverson might well come round to beat him up again, unless he actually killed Michael there would be no way this would scare him off

233

from seeing Cassie. Michael tried not to think about this 'unless'.

It took him four hours to drive to Stillriver after he collected his final pay cheque, and he arrived late in the afternoon, when the sun was low, its rays filtered in resinous, powdery skeins through the branches of the spruce in the backyard. His father was in the deckchair, reading the paper and drinking a glass of ginger ale. He stared as at an apparition while Michael walked across the drive, climbed the porch stairs and went into the house. Inside Michael deposited his bag in the kitchen, collected one of the wooden chairs and a beer from the icebox, then went outside and sat down beside his father.

'I didn't expect you back,' said his father.

'I need to see Cassie.'

His father looked at him. 'Don't you know?'

'Know what?' he asked, suddenly feeling a sickening dread.

'The parson died,' his father said, for the first time saying the quaint title without ironic intonation.

'I'm sorry,' he said, though he wasn't. 'I didn't know. Is Cassie all right?'

His father looked pained, and then he told Michael the news, confirmed later that night when Michael at last read Cassie's letters. She had left town, and gone to Texas with Ronald Duverson. They were married now.

Five

1

HE WAS ONLINE at home, working at the dining room table, trying to download an ancient simulation package that would let him calculate the impact of increased water flow on the downstream side of the bridge. Increased water flow? Christ, he thought, if the dam gave way you would be talking about a flood, a wall of water whooshing down the Still.

He worked for some time, entering the measurements he'd taken at the bridge of the cracks in its three supporting piers and making various educated guesses about the rate of water flow. It was clear from his calculations that the upstream side of the bridge, through a combination of high water level and the strength of the current, needed replacing. And that was happening. But what he now saw clearly – thanks to a case study of an even smaller river in Idaho – was that any significant increase in flow (say twenty per cent) would make both the downstream side of the abutments and the central piers vulnerable, and thus put the whole structure in danger. Increased rainfall might not be enough, but the contents of a town lake less than ten miles away should do the trick nicely. The Fennville dam had better not give out.

He called Gary's yet again, and still got no answer. It was four days since he had run out of the house, and Michael was worried – this was now more than a weekend trip away to see some friends. He got into his rental car and drove down to Cedar Street, but there was no car in front of Gary's, nothing to indicate that he had come back, even momentarily.

He wondered whether to call Maguire and tell him that he still didn't know where Gary was, but he could see nothing but downside in doing this – for his brother, and possibly (though he couldn't have specified why) for himself. Yet since there seemed no point waiting for the police to come to him in search of his brother, he decided to go and talk to Jimmy Olds.

In the past the police station had consisted of a room in the Town Hall, a small, windowless room in the back of the building with a yellow linoleum floor, a desk, and a chair on which Jerry Dawson would hang his gun between patrols, sit with his feet up on the desk, and smoke cigarettes – Winstons, invariably purchased from the drugstore.

Now a new station had been built across Main Street with a firehouse-style garage in front, which held two gleaming squad cars. Michael walked past them into a suite of offices in the back. He found Jimmy Olds in one of them, sitting at a PC, filling out a form.

'Jesus,' he said with disgust as Michael came in. 'George Coffin's dog bit a man on Beach Road. Jerry Dawson would have shot the dog, or maybe just shot the man, but I have to fill out a form.'

Michael sat down. On the wall behind Jimmy hung a clipboard holding a stack of Wanted posters and a roster sheet showing the schedule for the week. Out the back window he could see an old classmate named Emma Taggett pinning sheets up to dry on her clothes line.

'There,' said Jimmy, as he banged <Enter> with a forefinger, then turned to face Michael. 'You here for a progress report?'

'Is there any?'

Jimmy shook his head. 'We were trying to narrow down the possible suspects. You know, close down some categories. The problem is we're having trouble keeping any categories *open*. We've gone through students, and friends, and neighbours, and haven't turned up anything.'

Michael said, 'I still wonder if it couldn't have been some vagrant, just passing through town. But Maguire insists it was planned, so it must have been someone my father knew.'

'He keeps looking for a connection between your father and the Marines, but there isn't a lot to go on. At least not that makes sense to me. I can't believe your daddy had much time for the likes of Raleigh Somerset.'

'Of course not. It's all because of Gary. You must have heard his prints were on the bat.'

Jimmy scratched his cheek then unwrapped a stick of gum and put it in his mouth. 'I wouldn't worry very much about it. I explained to Maguire that your brother might not have your brains and yes, he's had his moments, but there's nothing really *bad* about him.'

'Did Maguire accept this?'

'Yeah,' said Jimmy, 'in as much as he accepts anything a dumb-ass small town cop like me has to say. Don't be fooled by Maguire; I know him from before. He's real nice and acts all friendly, but he's an ambitious son of a bitch and ruthless on account of it. If you ask me, he's got his own agenda, which has more to do with rolling up these local Marines than—' And he stopped, in awkward recognition of what he had been about to say.

'Finding my father's killer,' said Michael to finish Jimmy's sentence, waving a hand dismissively to show he had not taken offence.

'Anyway,' said Jimmy, 'Maguire will talk to your brother again, I have no doubt, but then that'll be it.'

Michael took a deep breath. 'The thing is, Jimmy, I can't find Gary.' Jimmy looked at him with surprise. 'And if I can't locate him pretty damn quick, I bet Maguire will issue a warrant for his arrest.'

Jimmy's expression was now impassive, but his jaw was working hard on his gum. 'So what do you want from me?'

'I want a little time to look for him before Maguire goes public with anything. My brother left a note for his friend Bubba. I thought I'd start with him. You know where he lives? And does he have a last name?'

'Braithwaite. Bubba Braithwaite. He lives way out on M-nineteen, past old thirty-one. Hang on a minute.' He got up and went over to a bookshelf behind Michael. It held stacks of reports, a volume of the township's ordinances, some ringbinder manuals, and a phone book. 'Here he is,' he said, opening the phone book and locating the right page. 'Three-four-three Meisenheimer. M-nineteen turns into it. He's on the left side of the road, about two miles past de Goreyands.'

'I got it. Thanks.'

Michael started to get up but stopped when Jimmy jabbed a finger in his direction. 'I'll give you until Monday. If he doesn't show up by then we'll start looking ourselves, and letting everybody know we're looking too. That fair?'

'More than fair. What are you going to tell Maguire?'

'As little as possible.' Jimmy snorted. 'He won't hesitate two seconds to hold you if he thinks you're getting in the way of his investigation. And God help me if he thinks I've contributed to it.'

'I'm not trying to obstruct anything. I just want to find my brother.'

'Sure,' said Jimmy, extracting his gum from his mouth with his thumb and forefinger, then examining the soft cream-coloured plug. 'I'm trusting you, Michael, on account of we go way back. And I liked your daddy.'

'I won't abuse your trust.'

'Sure,' said Jimmy again, reinserting his gum, and beginning to chomp slowly. 'And if you tell Maguire about this conversation, I'll deny it. And then he'll lock your ass in jail. And still come after me.' His expression said *we're all victims together*.

He went home and ate a roast beef sandwich slathered with mustard, then drove out Park Street towards the Back Country. Instead of crossing over onto M-19, however, he turned left, and drove north along old 31, thinking he'd better cover the most obvious ground first. He passed smallholdings and cherry orchards, a maple syrup stand, and went down the deep dip past Ferguson Park, a small picnic area in a stand of paper birch on the east side of the road. His mother would sometimes stop here so they could pick watercress out of the creek that bubbled through this stretch of low land. Climbing again, he looked sharply when the road levelled off, saw the sign, *Lashings Depot*, and pulled in.

The place was set back about fifty yards from the road. Harold's house sat in the shade of a patch of maple trees to Michael's right, but the office shack and the store barn, a vast aluminium affair, were out in the open, with a big turnaround for the trailer trucks that came in to collect the fruit. Behind the barn three deep square pits had been excavated, lined with black polyurethane, then filled almost to the top with brine solution. Here, by the ton, cherries were dumped. Within a week the fruit lost all its colour, ready for the insertion of artificial dye; Gary always said that once you'd seen this method of preparation, you would never eat another maraschino cherry in your life.

Michael found Harold standing in front of the office, staring gloomily at the pits and their bobbing seas of cherries. He was a tall, balding man in his sixties, mild-mannered, as Michael remembered, patient, soft-spoken if a little reserved. But now he seemed cranky.

'Gary's brother, right?' he said, taking off his glasses. He didn't offer to shake hands. 'What can I do for you?'

'I was hoping you might have seen my brother.'

Harold looked mildly incredulous. 'Shoot,' he said abruptly. 'I've got four tons of cherries sitting out there, with a Mexican kid who don't speak English and a retard I got from the Labour Exchange. And apples start in two weeks. I wish I *had* seen your brother so I could give him a piece of my mind.'

'He said he'd stopped working here. Did something happen?'

'I spent a lot of time on your brother. I worked him hard, but no harder than I worked myself. I wasn't ever exactly sentimental about him and neither was my wife, but he had a future here. Why else would I have made him partner?'

'What happened? Was it after my father's murder?'

Harold shook his head. 'It began before then. Otherwise, I might understand it. Everybody was shook up by that murder, so who knows how a son feels?' He added more gently, 'Well, I guess *you* know.'

'What exactly did Gary do?'

'It's more like what he didn't do. Last fall I ended up doing half the apples myself. He said he was sick – sick for two weeks. Next thing I hear he's been over at Scotch Haven at some hootenanny with his Michigan Marine friends. *Marines.* Shit, I got drafted and never went anywhere except Oklahoma, but even I know a real army from this bunch of a-holes.'

'He doesn't do any work for you in winter, does he?'

'There's nothing much to do. Me and Mary spend three months in Florida, and I don't even open the shed door until the end of March. Spring's no big deal – we get ready but the hours aren't very long. But your brother kept not showing up, or showing up late, or showing up drunk. You can't have that. And I don't care what he does on his lunch break but I can do without those friends of his coming by.'

'Who were they?'

'He never introduced them, which was fine by me. One tall, thin guy with a kind of crooked mouth.'

Mouth like an asshole. 'Did he have a tattoo?'

'Probably. Then another big fat fellow. *Dirty.*'

'Bubba something?'

'Yeah, that's him. I actually thought I was going to have to break up a fight. Some other guy shows up – I bet you know him, he used to live in Stillriver – and he gets into an argument with this Bubba creature, and soon as you know it the two are squaring up. And your brother's just standing there, and me as old as I am, I get to go out and say, "Go on, get, before I call the state police". They didn't come around after that. I told Gary I just wasn't having it any more. And then he complained, saying he had rights. That was the last straw. "What do *rights* have to do with running a business?" I said. "Especially a business you're supposed to be part of." And he got huffy and went home early and that, Michael – I remember you now – was the last time I saw your brother.'

'This other guy, what's his name?'

Harold took off his cap and scratched the thinning hair on top of his head. 'That's what I'm trying to recall. He was a big guy too, but kind of goofy-looking, with eyes that looked wide open. But boy was he mad. I thought he was going to hit *me* for a minute.'

'Raleigh. Raleigh Somerset.'

Harold eyed him with surprise. 'How'd you know that?'

Michael shrugged. 'Intuition.'

'Well, you intuitioned right, that's all I can say.'

There was a small crash and they both looked towards the shed where a Mexican kid driving a forklift looked mortified at the crate of cherries that had slipped sideways off the two thin metal tines. The big wooden box lay on its side as fruit spilled out, rolling like cerise marbles all over the concrete apron in front of the shed. Harold shook his head. 'I'll let him clean it up. Teach him to slow down with that thing.'

He paused and looked around him, as if to reassure himself that what he had built here was real. He shook his head wearily. 'You know, your brother used to talk about you a lot. How you'd got away and done what you wanted to do. So I told him: "If this isn't enough for you, then go try somewhere else." But you can't have it both ways. Or am I missing something?' he asked Michael with genuine wonder.

Michael drove east and a little south and was soon in flatter, dustier country – there were no orchards here. He was in the poorest part of the county, a pocket where a vast tongue of sand from the lake extended inland for many miles. To the north lay the hardwood forest, which stretched up through Canada; to the south, the rolling orchard land of Sheringham's; west, the place where sand belonged, the dunes and beaches that attracted tourists; and east – well, that was another county.

He went along Meisenheimer Road, past de Goreyand's place, a small, neat farmhouse with green shutters shaded by an immense oak, then past acre upon acre of asparagus, by now let to seed, vast hairy plants blowing in the day's light breeze. He couldn't find the place. There was no numbered mailbox, no fence, no turn, nothing to show where Bubba lived. He wondered if Jimmy Olds's estimate of two miles past de Goreyands was wrong, and carefully tracked a good four miles of road past the Belgian's vast holding.

Finally, in frustration, he stopped at a farmhouse where three large mongrels circled his car and barked until a man came out of the kitchen and walked over to him. When he explained who

243

he was looking for the man gave him a dubious look, but then supplied precise directions. 'Mind his track,' he said as Michael turned to go. 'It's usually passable this time of year, but with the rain we've had you could get stuck. You might want to walk in.'

He found the turn at last, an unmarked single-track road with high grass in the middle crown. It meandered across dry meadow until it climbed a slight rise and moved out of sight of Meisenheimer Road. After a quarter-mile the track began running gradually downhill, into a light copse of pale pin oaks and jack pine. The dry sand of the meadow gave way to softer, moister terrain, then suddenly mud. Before his wheels spun Michael pulled over, crushing dozens of ferns underneath the wheels. He was fairly confident he would be able to turn round.

Even in the shade of the wood stand it was hot, and blue flies circled him as he walked quickly along the track, picking his way around the churned-up mud. His view on either side was blocked by choke cherries lining the track; at a bend, a red-headed woodpecker suddenly flew off high and right, and turning the corner Michael saw a long, brown-and-white trailer ahead of him, sitting high up on concrete foundation blocks. As he approached he heard the deep bass of a stereo. He climbed up a homemade set of wooden steps to the trailer's front door and knocked on the window pane, trying unsuccessfully to peer through the closed lace curtain. There was no doorbell so he knocked again, but no one came to the door.

He climbed down and walked around one side to see if there was a back door. Behind the trailer, an area roughly the size of a basketball court had been cleared out of the pine woods, which gave a faint eucalyptus scent to the thick, moist air. At its far end, under the protection of a boarded lean-to, sat a Dodge pickup truck and two motorcycles, a big Harley and a smaller Japanese model. Next to a corner of the trailer there was a barbecue – recently used, Michael concluded from the blackened serving fork sitting on its rack, spattered with congealed grease the colour of skimmed milk.

There was no back door. Michael stood and looked at the vehicles and wondered what to do. *Someone* was inside; the thump of the bass was even more pronounced here. He stood on tiptoes by one of the back windows and tried to see in, but the height of the trailer was even greater here, as the land sloped gently downhill.

Spying a spare breezeblock, he lugged it over and deposited it carefully on the ground, then climbed up on it to look inside. The room he looked into was dark, and it took several seconds for his eyes to adjust. Two figures were sitting on the sofa against the far side of the room. He saw a handsome face, almost pretty, clean-shaven, darkly tan. It was a young man, Hispanic, with thick black hair parted in the middle and long enough to reach his shoulders. Next to him on the sofa sat Bubba, wearing a vast, old-fashioned man's undershirt. Despite the *thump thump thump* of the music, the two were watching television, or possibly a video – Michael could only see the back of the set. As the music stopped between tracks, Bubba slowly lifted an arm, reached over and lightly caressed the hair of the youth next to him.

It was a gesture of such obvious and simple affection that in a different context it would have seemed entirely unsexual – like patting the head of a favourite Labrador, or ruffling the hair of an eight-year-old boy. But the Hispanic boy was not eight years old.

He was spying, Michael realized, there were no two ways about it, and suddenly he felt both prurient and exposed, perched on a breezeblock outside Bubba's trailer. He got down gingerly but quickly and walked as quietly as possible round to the front of the trailer, wondering what on earth to do next. *Did that mean what it looked like?* He wondered. *Is that what Gary gets up to?* It would not come entirely as a surprise. Michael had worked in so many all-male environments that he knew a macho front – guns and fights and boys' bravado – could often signal a womanless life. Having had the short end of the stick with their mother, Gary had never had the benefit of any female surrogates; his father had not remarried and there was no Marilyn to take an interest in Michael's younger brother.

If it were the case, would this account for his father's change in his will? Henry had held his generation's conventional view about homosexuals – it was not a lifestyle he would have chosen for his son – but for all his disdain for groups and his cynicism about causes, Michael's father had never been a bigoted man. There had been a tempered tolerance there, which made Michael think it was something else that had precipitated the new instructions for his father's lawyer, Atkinson.

He walked back along the track, jumping in surprise when he flushed a grouse gorging on the choke cherries. He sat in his car for several minutes with the door open and the radio on, then he pushed hard on the horn, giving it half a dozen long blasts, and got out and walked back to the trailer. This time as he approached the front door opened and Bubba came out and stood at the top of the steps. He had added to his costume and now was wearing an enormous pair of blue jean overalls, with the white T-shirt on underneath, and the same tan work boots Michael remembered from Gary's house. There was nothing to suggest he had company, or what he had company for.

He didn't seem pleased to see Michael. 'You just get here?'

'Yep. I parked up the track so I wouldn't get stuck.'

Bubba scowled. 'So what do you want?'

'I'm looking for Gary. I thought you might know where I could find him.'

'You thought wrong.'

'All right,' said Michael. 'If you say so.' He turned to go, and added, 'I thought you two were friends. Guess I got that wrong, too.'

'We *are* friends,' Bubba protested.

'Then help me find my brother, will you? If he doesn't turn up soon, the police are going to issue a warrant for his arrest.'

'Arrest for what?'

'Arrest for my father's murder,' he said, though he decided not to mention the baseball bat. 'Sure, it's ridiculous, and no, I don't think Gary had anything to do with it. But why has Gary run away? Maybe he's scared of Maguire, but this disappearing act isn't going to help.'

'Maguire's not after your brother. It's someone else he wants.'

'Somerset?'

'That's right.'

'What for?'

'Gary hasn't told you anything?'

No, he thought, strictly speaking he hadn't. But he wasn't going to admit that to Bubba. 'Oh,' he said, 'you mean about the dynamite.'

'That's right,' said Bubba. 'Maguire was in charge of that one and he thought he had Raleigh dead to rights. He was fit to be tied when Raleigh got off. Who wasn't?'

'I thought you and Raleigh were brothers-in-arms.'

Bubba snorted and spat, an inch-long plug of saliva that fell like a wad of goose shit onto the grass. 'You've got the wrong idea, mister. There are plenty of things I believe in, including the right to bear arms. But I'm not a racist.'

Michael wondered where the Mexican boy was. 'And Raleigh is?'

Bubba looked at him as if he were irretrievably stupid. 'Do fish swim? Pigs fuck? Of course he's a racist. You ask me, Raleigh's no different than a Nazi. Anything out of the ordinary, Raleigh wants them in an oven.'

'Like gays,' said Michael to be provocative.

Bubba didn't flinch. He stared at Michael and said, 'It's usually the Jews he likes to go on about.'

'So why did you have anything to do with this guy?'

Bubba shrugged. 'You might laugh at this, but to begin with it was all kind of *social*. I like guns.' He gestured back towards the trailer. 'I got a lot of them inside. Some of us would get together and practice target shooting at Scotch Haven, then drink a couple of beers at the Spring Valley Tavern. Your brother was one of them. Raleigh would be there, too, always talking politics. Then one time he brought somebody along from downstate who started talking, and the next thing you know we're a branch of the Michigan Marines. No big deal – it's still mainly target practice and drinking beer, only now we sometimes had enactments.'

'Enactments?'

'You'd call it war games, I guess. You know, one guy would set out and the rest of us would track him down. Or we'd do survival weekends. You get set down in the national forest, miles from nowhere, they'd blindfold you on the way, and then see how you got on. Shelter-building, making fire with flints, catching fish with a hawthorn hook – survival skills. It was a lot of fun,' said Bubba with a small, recollecting smile.

'How does that get you to dynamite?'

Bubba looked at him thoughtfully. 'It doesn't. That's what I'm trying to explain. The problem was always Raleigh. He wanted *action* – we always had to be rehearsing *for* something. Not just the end of the world,' he said with his cartoon giggle, 'but real things. Like taking an IRS man hostage, or defending your house from the state police.'

'And the dynamite?' he insisted.

'That was a *big* mistake,' Bubba said appreciatively, then suddenly realized what he was saying. 'On Raleigh's part. I never knew anything about it.'

'Did my brother?'

The gradual warming he had found in Bubba during the course of the conversation abruptly came to a halt. 'Time for you to go. I'll keep my eyes peeled for your brother.'

'Where should I be looking?'

Bubba said, 'How long is a piece of string?'

He bought a new filled gas can and a quart of oil at the Shell station, grateful that he no longer knew anyone working there. At home, he got the old mower out and soon had it started. He had hated cutting the grass as a boy, but now found the simple monotony of the chore calming. As cars passed, sometimes the occupants stared, and he tried to ignore them, though he found it hard not to stare back. *Yes*, he wanted to stop and tell them, *even when your father's been murdered you still have to cut the grass.*

When he had first been sent out of the New York office on projects, Streatley (who was as close to a mentor as he had) would ask on his return from the field, 'So what did you learn?' And forced to take stock, he would find that usually he had learned more than he imagined. He performed the same exercise now, hoping to reduce his persisting bafflement.

So what had he learned from his day's forays? Bubba didn't like Somerset and *vice versa*, and Bubba seemed less involved in Marine matters than Michael had expected, or feared, since clearly Bubba and Gary were pals . . . or whatever. The games side of the Marines had served as a lure to the kind of gun-owning outdoorsmen who would enjoy something more organized than their usual hunting and range practice activities. Throw in the odd diatribe about gas taxes and the gun control lobby, and this hardly constituted subversive activity. But then there was the dynamite, which manifestly crossed a line. Michael couldn't figure out how either Bubba or his brother had got that far if their involvement in the Marines were as innocent as they claimed – but then, if Gary were entirely in the clear, why had he panicked at the mention of dynamite, and taken off?

Then there was the matter of Maguire, who according to Jimmy Olds was single-minded and relentless behind the friendly manner. But what exactly was he pursuing? If both Bubba and Jimmy Olds (improbable bedmates) were to be believed, Maguire was pursuing his own agenda, a continuation of his previous pursuit of the Marines. And that was peculiar too, for Maguire obviously had some pre-existing relationship with Gary that was Marine-linked; yet neither Gary nor Maguire had mentioned this to Michael.

He wasn't really sure where to head next. He could try and track down the other figures from Gary's bungalow – asshole mouth, the guy drinking beer, the other one whose face he struggled to visualize. But he wasn't at all sure he'd find out anything new from them. He had the feeling that if anyone could function as a spokesman, it would be Bubba – he remembered how asshole mouth had turned to him when Michael got annoyed in Gary's bungalow.

No, increasingly, everything and everyone, including Bubba,

seemed to point in Raleigh Somerset's direction. Michael had trouble aligning his recent sighting of him at the Homecoming Parade – large and swaggering in his fatigues – with the big, child-like adolescent who had been his classmate for, how long? Two years at least, maybe three. Would Raleigh even remember him? After his experience with Bubba, he did not want to show up unannounced. But he didn't want to phone ahead: Raleigh might well tell him to stay away and leave him alone. And if Raleigh were involved in his father's murder did Michael really want to go to his house, expected or not?

He had to get to him somehow. He went inside and got online again with his laptop. He found the Marines' site again and discovered an updated page with a fresh list of meetings, courses, and forthcoming events. *Unarmed Combat, Rifle Range, Survival #1* and *Survival #2*. Then two talks being given in Muskegon: *The Right Way to Bear Arms, Local Politics and Federal Danger*. And a list of get-togethers: dinners, picnic lunches, barbecues. It was here he discovered that on Saturday, two days hence, there was a barbecue for the Atlantic County branch of the Marines (families welcome). Tickets would be sold at the door, the charge was $7.50 a head ($2.50 for children under twelve) and the venue was the backyard of the Spring Valley Tavern.

AT SHERINGHAM'S, SOME of the local farmers had been invited, and they were among the first to eat, sitting on the patio at long trestle tables that had been covered with blue table cloths, eating baked chicken with lemon wedges, and corn on the cob, wrapped in dishcloths to keep it hot, which Lou had boiled in a vast cauldron over a portable tank of bottled gas.

Michael stood above them, leaning on the wooden rail of the deck that had been extended out from the living room. The view from here, on the back side of the house, was quietly beautiful: the land sloped gently down from the hilltop into a miniature valley studded by lines of peach trees, which gently undulated to the base of another rolling hill in the distance. The light was fading in the minute, indistinguishable increments of dusk, for the setting sun was itself out of view behind the distant dunes of Lake Michigan to the west.

Donny came out of the sliding door with a fresh can of beer. 'I'd better go with you,' he announced, rejoining Michael, who had just been explaining whom he'd seen while searching for Gary, and where he planned to go next.

Michael was relieved enough not to argue. 'I wouldn't mind.'

'I'm not sure Raleigh will be any help. It doesn't sound as if he and Gary have been on the best of terms.'

'That's what I can't make out – why Bubba and Raleigh had a falling out, and whether it had anything to do with Gary. But you know, where Maguire sees a dangerous terrorist, all I can remember is a no-hope dickhead who used to get on every-body's nerves.'

'He's still a dickhead, only now he's a nasty one.'

Michael laughed. 'Maybe we should have been nicer to him in school.'

'We weren't mean to him. We just didn't take him seriously. That's what Raleigh wants – to be taken seriously.'

'Speaking of seriously, I've run tests on the Junction bridge, and if they don't protect the abutments and the downstream side of the central pier, then even mild flooding might knock it down. If the dam goes, I'd say the odds of the bridge surviving are minimal.'

'I'll tell Cassavantes, but the water's come down a ways since last month, so he'll say we can take our time. He'll do the downstream piers eventually to cover himself, but only after enough time's gone by so it looks like his idea.'

'Well, let's pray for *no* rain then,' said Michael with a sour laugh. 'Let's eat.' They went down the stairs from the deck, took plates and filled them with chicken and corn, green beans topped with sautéed almonds, sliced tomatoes drizzled with vinaigrette, and potato salad laced with chive. Cassie and Nancy were walking in from the orchard, talking intently while Cassie's kids ran in front. Suddenly Nancy hugged Cassie excitedly and Michael realized Cassie must have shared her news.

Which he had learned when he'd picked up Cassie and the kids an hour before. He had wanted to talk to her about Gary, and ask her advice about where to look next. But she was beaming as she got into his car. 'What's happened? You win the lottery or something?'

'Almost,' she said, then explained that she'd got a one-year contract to fill in for the no-show teacher from Lansing.

'I never thought I'd see the day when you stepped into Miss Summers' shoes,' he said, and saw her smile dissolve.

'I thought you'd be pleased,' she said.

'I am, Cassie.' He reached over and took her hand. 'I'm thrilled for you.'

But he wasn't, and her announcement served to crystallize his own uncertainty about what would happen next. He was back, he told himself, to pursue the matter of his father's death; equally, he knew he was staying for a while because of Cassie. *For a while.* What did that mean, precisely? Somewhere inside him there lurked a fantasy – he saw it now for what it was – that he would win Cassie back, then take her (and yes, the children) off to some other world where they would reassemble and reconstitute some new family life.

And where exactly does this scenario play out? he asked himself for the first time with sceptical force. Ealing Broadway? Of course not. Then where? A construction site in Dubai, on the Gulf where an English-language school could be found for Jack and Sally, and the saltwater winds made the heat bearable? That would be fine and dandy for the five months of his assignment. Then where? Turkey maybe – they always needed help with bridges – or another foray into the water-lands of western Sweden, some inland lake two hundred miles from Stockholm?

What kind of life would that be? He was used to it, but what about Cassie, who had never been east of LaGuardia Airport? Or her children, who after the hellish years with Ronald needed the one thing he couldn't provide: stability? Yet what alternative was there to an itinerant life? He'd been left a lovely, large and ageing house to live in, tax-free and unencumbered by mortgage, but otherwise had only about four months of savings left. Whatever small economies he practised (get rid of the rental car, buy own-store brands) he would be out of money shortly after Christmas. And then what? His services might be valued by Donny, but he couldn't imagine Jack Cassavantes feeling anything but threatened should he, Michael, declare himself locally available. And however deep his knowledge of concrete bridges might be, what could he offer in expertise that was needed by the Michigan State Highway Department, who were not themselves exactly novices in the use of the material?

This bleak, internal argument continued as he watched Cassie guffaw when Jack gave her first one peach, then another, and then another – windfalls he picked from the ground. Michael looked at her, still girlishly angular in her blue jeans and white sneakers, and remembered the happiness of that time so long ago when they had first become lovers. A time when the future was promising but not pressing, because the present was so powerfully alive. A time between the depression and fear of the first year after his mother's death, and the advent of Ronald Duverson. A time that could have continued on to this very evening, he told himself, had he not destroyed it by running away. There was no one else to blame: not the parson, not Cassie, not Sophie Jansen or Sarah Perkins, not his father, and no, not even Ronald. Michael had done it all himself.

So he was determined to destroy nothing now, though he had no idea what he could build. *I don't build bridges; I fix them.*

Around him there was laughter and loud, joking voices, fuelled by the bottles of wine set on the table. Cassie was down at the end, between Lou and a woman who looked familiar. Donny was talking baseball with his eldest son. Michael recognized Janie Waters, a tall but uncoordinated girl who had played on the basketball team with Nancy and Cassie, and Archie Willard, who had been a quiet kid who liked to play chess.

He sat down and ate by himself while contemplating his lack of a clear future. One of the Sheringham girls cleared his plate, then put a bowl of peaches, covered with sugar and cream, in front of him. He ate two helpings of the fruit, which was marvellously tart and sweet at once, and drank his third glass of Californian Chardonnay, yet he couldn't shake off the morose mood that was dragging him down like a weight.

'Hello, Michael.'

He looked up to find the familiar-looking woman sitting down across from him. He looked at her closely. 'Anthea?'

'Don't make it so obvious you aren't sure. I haven't aged *that* much,' she said with a brittle laugh. But Anthea Heaton had, and she looked a good ten years older than the rest of her classmates. She wore a pink tank top that showed the tanned freckles beneath her throat – he remembered how her skin would spot each summer in the sun. But she wore more make-up than he recalled ever seeing on her former, teenage face, and her skin was somehow puffy and wrinkled at the same time. She looked as if in the years since high school she had lived hard.

'I didn't know you'd be here,' he said. 'I thought you lived in Florida.'

'I'm in Grand Rapids now. With Julie and Eddy.'

'I don't think I ever met your husband.'

'Eddy's my son. My husband's still in Florida.' Michael smiled blandly, and she said, 'I'm divorced, Michael.'

'Ah,' he said, 'so am I.'

'But not unattached, I hear,' she said with a small smile.

'Have your folks still got the house?' Fromm Street, with the swing sofa on the front porch.

'It's just my mom now. Daddy passed away three years ago.'

She told him about the breakdown of her marriage, speaking in a light tone that failed to disguise her resentment: how her husband, a property developer of much energy and no scruples, had started staying out late or not coming home at all, until Anthea gave him an ultimatum that another woman had won. How she and her husband had then fought over the value of the house during the divorce negotiations, their respective avarice separating their appraisals by over half a million dollars. How the children were adjusting 'pretty well' to life in Grand Rapids, which to Michael suggested they were complaining every day about their reduced circumstances, lamenting the absence from their lives of expensive restaurants, large bedrooms, and the unavailability of waterskiing in Michigan's winter months.

It seemed a sad, sour tale, and he sensed the difficulty she had in finding anything positive to say about her 'fresh start' in Grand Rapids. Her emotions were still living in Florida. And as Michael realized this, he started to feel depressed again, until suddenly he heard Nancy Sheringham's voice, booming from the end of the table: 'I *don't* believe it.'

She was staring up at the deck of the house, and Michael turned around to look. A man and a woman were standing looking down from the railings, both smiling, the woman very shyly. They were casually but stylishly dressed: she wore a white cotton skirt and pink sweater, the man a blue sports coat, white chinos and an open-necked dress shirt. They looked distinctively fresh, like a clean-cut couple modelling in a mail order catalogue. It was Kenny Williams, Michael realized, almost twenty years older than when seen last, but with the same wavy head of hair and the same confident smile.

The couple came down the stairs and Michael saw that

Kenny's partner was pretty to the point of beauty, and much younger than the rest of them. *She can't be more than twenty-five*, he thought. Donny caught his eye and raised his eyebrows in rueful appreciation of Kenny's continuing appeal to attractive women.

'You'll recognize some of us,' said Nancy, after hugging Kenny and shaking hands with the girlfriend. Kenny turned and looked down the tables, smiling at Donny and Brenda, and giving a surprised wave when he saw Cassie. 'There's Anthea Heaton,' he announced loudly, and she blushed furiously beneath a taut smile. Kenny paused for a beat, like a veteran comedian. 'Bet you're glad asparagus season is over,' and there was a sudden explosion of laughter from the rest of them.

'Michael!' he exclaimed when he saw him. 'Now here's a face I haven't seen for a while.' Nancy was trying to steer him towards the food. 'I'll come back to you and catch up.'

Michael tried to talk some more with Anthea, but she seemed distracted now, and after a minute excused herself just as Kenny sat down with a full plate next to him. Kenny looked protectively towards his girlfriend, who was talking with Cassie and Lou; satisfied that she was being looked after he turned his attention towards Michael, who said, 'Last time I saw you, you were planning to go to law school. Did you?'

Kenny nodded as he chewed a chicken breast. 'I'm a lawyer, in private practice now, but I used to be in the federal prosecutor's office. Have they got anywhere with your father's case?'

Michael was startled but not offended by the bluntness. 'You mean the police?'

Kenny nodded. 'When I heard about your father's murder, I rang the DA in Muskegon. He said the cops didn't have any leads at all. Is that still true?'

Michael looked around him. There seemed no reason not to tell, so he explained about the baseball bat and the fingerprints.

'The prints of a child? Maybe somebody borrowed the bat. You know, in a sandlot game.'

'That's what you'd normally think. But Gary swore he hadn't

taken the bat out of the basement for years. And I doubt my father lent it to somebody.'

'Weird,' said Kenny. 'Any other evidence?'

'A smudged footprint on the porch. But nothing else. Who-ever did it planned the whole thing carefully. And that's what's so odd. Otherwise it just looks like a psycho – somebody moving through town, something like that.'

Kenny said, 'I mean, Stillriver's changed; what place hasn't? But it's not a violent place. The worst you get is a fight in the bars on Saturday night.' He wiped his mouth on a paper napkin. 'Or outside the Dairy Queen. Remember that?'

'I do,' said Michael levelly. He knew that Kenny didn't know what Ronald had done to him – no one there other than Cassie knew – but he still felt an ingénue's blush start to fill his cheeks when Ronald's name was mentioned.

'He was a bit of a freak, you know,' said Kenny, with the perverse admiration of an ex-prosecutor. 'He'd stand out anywhere. He could kill somebody. What am I saying? I hear he *did* kill someone.'

'He's in jail in Texas.'

'That explains it. I wondered what Cassie was doing back here. Boy, I never understood that one.' He looked down the table where his girlfriend was still talking with Cassie. 'Anyway,' said Kenny, 'the DA, when I talked to him, said something about a paramilitary connection. But what would the motive be?'

'That's what I still can't figure out. My father had no interest in paramilitary goings on.' He didn't mention Gary.

Kenny looked thoughtful as he bit on his chicken breast. 'I had something to do with those people when I was with the feds. The Wayne County bunch.'

'McVeigh's people?'

He nodded. 'Most of the branches have fizzled out, but the worry isn't about the old Militia so much as the members who've gone underground.'

'Are there many of those?'

'Not a lot. And not up here, I think. Though Raleigh Somerset, you know who I mean?' When Michael nodded, Kenny said, 'He was downstate near me but he's back here now.'

'He's the paramilitary connection your colleagues are so interested in.'

'He was in your year at school, not mine, so when I saw the name I recognized it but couldn't really remember him. Then one of the agents showed me a photograph, and I thought, "I remember that big doofus."' He laughed lightly. 'But he's hard core. He knew McVeigh. We got onto him when he went to Germany. First time I ever heard from Interpol.'

'Why was he in Germany?'

'To make contact with neo-Nazi groups there. He knew the country – he was stationed there in the army before he got discharged.'

'Honourable discharge?'

'No.' He lowered his voice. 'Psychiatric condition. As I remember, one quack diagnosed him as paranoid schizo-phrenic, the other as psychopathic. Combine the two and it's still called crazy.' Kenny paused and looked at Michael. 'Strictly speaking, I shouldn't be telling you any of this.'

And Kenny looked embarrassed enough that Michael changed the subject. 'Did you drive up here to see your mom?'

'No. She moved down to Arizona three years ago. The winters were just getting too much for her. I came up because I'm thinking of buying a place on the beach. If I can afford it. Prices are going through the roof. At least that's what Larry Bottel says,' Kenny added with a smile. 'So it must be true.'

'I never expected Larry to stay in Stillriver. I always assumed he'd want a bigger pond to fish in.'

'Oh, I don't know,' said Kenny, 'he's doing very well. It's not just summer houses, either: a lot of people are retiring to Stillriver. It's got a nice way of life, after all. Shoot, sometimes I wish I'd stayed here.'

'I think you'd have given Steve Atkinson a run for his money.'

Kenny grinned. 'It's a little late now to start practising small town law. I'd probably be real bad at it.'

'Are you married now?' asked Michael, nodding towards Kenny's friend at the end of the table.

'No. And that's the other thing. No one I'm likely to meet is going to want to live in Stillriver. Jackie over there, she's not going to be satisfied with a social life where the weekly big event is the bandstand concert. Though she was nervous about coming here tonight.'

'I can't blame her for that, meeting a lot of strangers—'

'No, not about that. She was nervous because she said she'd never been to a real farm before. So I told her the wild animals get locked up at night.' He laughed with the confidence of someone living worlds away from his background but still at ease with it, and Michael envied him this equanimity.

Janie Waters was sitting on Kenny's far side, and now she turned round and started talking with him, so after a minute Michael got up and strolled out into the peach orchard, where he surprised Donny's eldest boy and another kid smoking cigarettes behind a tree. He laughed and turned back, and when he got to the patio found that the farmers had gone home, and the small group of his former classmates were sitting together. He looked at his oldest friends and felt a sudden sense of estrangement, thinking how most of them had stayed in or around Stillriver, and how even those who had left, like Kenny Williams, seemed able to return and reinsert themselves without effort into the place of their upbringing.

As he approached they seemed to suppress a collective giggle. 'Am I dressed that funny?' he said with a smile, but felt slightly miffed.

Donny shook his head. 'We were just talking about your father. You may not know it, but the police interviewed every one of us, anybody who'd ever been his student.'

Nancy Sheringham spoke up. 'It turned out that when they asked us if we could remember anything he really felt strongly about, we all said the same thing.'

'What was that?'

And then in unison all of them chanted, 'Potawatamee.'

259

The local Indians, who, unlike their fierce Iroquois counterparts in other parts of the state, had posed no resistance to the early settlers in Atlantic County, timber cutters and then farmers, in the years before the Civil War. The small tribe had fished and hunted the land before the white arrivals, and then been pushed out of the valuable properties by the lake when the timber mills went up and the ships came in to dock, settling for a land grant in the 1850s out in the Back Country where they sort of survived by hunting, fishing, foraging and farming (badly).

Nancy asked, 'Do you remember the state requirements in Michigan history?'

'How could anyone forget them?' Michael replied. A whole term of tedium, learning which was the biggest county in the state (he couldn't remember), the average alfalfa yield per acre, the population in the UP of non-Caucasians (roughly twelve).

'I think your father found it as boring as we did. And we learned we could always get him off the subject if we said the magic word.'

'Which was Potawatamee,' said Donny.

'He'd be off at the mention of the name, telling us stories. "One-eyed Joe" – you remember that one,' said Nancy, and Donny, Cassie and Janie Waters nodded. 'One day he even corralled the school bus and took us out to the Indian Cemetery in Elbridge.'

He had taken Michael there too. It sat on a hill next to the old Baptist church, at a crossroads about eight miles west of Fennville. The church was shaded by large maples and a sole surviving elm, but the cemetery was an exposed two-acre square of bleached grass and dust. The headstones were wooden crosses, painted white, and unnamed.

'We thought we were pulling the wool over his eyes. But on the very last day of school when we came into class, on everybody's chair there was a copy of a pamphlet he'd written on the Chippewa. He'd signed every one *with thanks to my inspirations*. He'd known all along exactly what we were doing. But he didn't mind.'

Nancy paused and looked at Cassie, then again at Michael. 'He never taught you, Michael, so you wouldn't know, but he was a great storyteller in class. And he had a great sense of humour.'

His father? Wry to be sure; a dry appreciation of the inevitable idiocies and minor comedies of small town life. But not what you would call a *great sense of humour*. Surely not. *Surely?* 'I never heard that before,' he said.

Nancy shrugged. 'No reason you should have. You were always touchy about being a teacher's son.'

His eyes widened and he looked at Cassie, who smiled at him reassuringly. Then Kenny filled the silence with a story about the night Nancy had got locked in the Burlington High School bathroom, and other stories followed this one, moving across the table like semaphores in the cool night air, while Michael remained behind with the Potawatamee and his father.

They left a little after midnight, collecting the kids from the TV room upstairs, where along with half a dozen other small children they had crashed out in sleeping bags. Jack woke up just long enough to be deposited on the back seat, then promptly conked out again. Sally walked proudly under her own steam to the car, but was asleep by the time Michael had pulled out of the Sheringham's half-moon drive.

He drove the back way home, through Happy Valley, and as they clonked over the wooden bridge above the thin stream of the Still's south branch, Cassie suddenly exclaimed, 'Look! Can you pull over?' He did, where the hill crested on the north side of the valley. Cassie opened her door and went and stood by the front of the car, and Michael followed, mystified, into the cooling night air. He found her leaning against the hood, gazing upwards. He looked up and saw why: a lush and lilac-coloured radiance spread like purple milk spilt across the sky.

'Northern Lights,' she said. 'I haven't seen them in ages. You couldn't in Texas.'

'Why's that?'

She laughed as she locked her arm with his. 'Why do you think they're called *Northern* Lights?'

'I saw them once in Sweden,' he said.

'I'm impressed,' said Cassie, pinching him lightly on the arm as she had done in the early high school years of their romance.

'I would have been too, but I didn't know what they were.' And he pinched her back.

They got back in the car quietly. As he drove off, Cassie said, 'It was nice to see Kenny.'

'It's funny how things changed. When we were kids he was always confident, but you couldn't help thinking of him as younger. I didn't have that sense at all tonight. It was almost like the return of the conquering hero. He's done real well for himself.'

'He's not the only one,' she protested. 'You have too.'

'Not in the same way,' he said. He had chosen something else. He could hear Sarah's angry voice – *You're throwing away your career. Do you really expect me to come with you and help you do it?* He hadn't and she didn't. He sighed with the thought, then changed the subject. 'By the way, where did Anthea Heaton go? One minute she was telling me about her terrible ex-husband and the next she'd disappeared.'

'She went home to her mother's. I think Kenny upset her.'

'What, about the asparagus? She took offence at that, after all these years?'

'Not that. I think she was hoping Kenny would show up on his own, especially since Nancy had made a point of telling him Anthea would be there.'

'Can't he bring his girlfriend if he wants?'

'Sure he can – even if she is young enough to be his daughter. I know all about where I can buy designer clothes in Detroit now. Very useful.'

What was this about? Cassie was never catty. He said, 'Anthea's single now, that's the problem isn't it? If she were still in Florida in her million-dollar house with a Hispanic maid she wouldn't care less about Kenny's girlfriend.'

'You can't exactly blame her, can you? She's got two kids, no husband, and not much of a job apparently.' Cassie paused, and then added in a low voice, 'Sounds familiar, doesn't it?'

Michael felt they were close to the edge of something he didn't want to fall into, so he stayed quiet. He drove into town, passed the wireworks and parked outside Cassie's bungalow. He got out and opened the back door, gingerly lifting Jack out as Cassie did the same for little Sally. Inside, he put Jack into his bed, and when he came back into the kitchen waited for Cassie to return from Sally's bedroom. 'Can I get you a drink?' she asked when she came back.

'I better not. It's late and I'd probably fall asleep.'

'You can do that too, you know,' she said, looking at him in the pale light of the kitchen's overhead bulb.

He understood at once; he had been waiting for such a sign for weeks now. But he shook his head slowly, smiling to lessen the blow, which would be to her pride – he didn't believe she really wanted to jump on his bones this late and both of them dog-tired.

'Let's not do it this way, okay?' he said. 'Let's do it at my house, when the kids aren't around and you're not tired and I'm not tired and we haven't just had an argument.'

'You don't like my house?' she asked sharply.

'Not much,' he said. 'But I love you.' He stopped for a second, suddenly realizing this was the first time he'd used the words in almost seven years. 'And if that means I have to like your house I'll do my best. Though I don't think you like it much either.' He mimicked her, but gently. '*I always liked your house. Big rooms. High windows.*'

Cassie smiled faintly. 'You sure know how to make a girl feel wanted.'

'You know you're wanted,' he said, and ignored her deprecating snort. 'I'll see you tomorrow.'

'Maybe,' she said as he turned to go.

'You'll have to hide then,' he said as he went through the door. 'Because I'll be looking for you. Goodnight.'

And as he drove down the darkened street, then down the slope of Luke Street, heading for home, he hoped to himself that she did know how much he wanted her. And that she *didn't* know how vulnerable she seemed right now. He had known her vulnerable before – God knows, you had to be vulnerable to run off at the age of twenty with Ronald Duverson. But she had never seemed this fragile or exposed to Michael, and he would have congratulated himself on his hard-won maturity, demonstrated by his not taking advantage of her, had he not wished so much that he had.

3

BOURBON AND BRANCH, a highball – whatever it was nowa-days called, Michael was rewarding himself for taking the garbage out (the twins could no longer provide this service) by drinking a large bourbon and water with half a tray of ice cubes, when there was a knock on the back door and Steve Atkinson came in. Today he was wearing a canary yellow golf shirt with *Atlantic Country Club* monogrammed on its breast pocket, and checked trousers.

'Hi Steve. You want a drink?' When Steve looked at Michael's glass of bourbon, Michael said, 'There's iced tea if you want it.' He was doubly embarrassed: to be found drinking in the middle of the day was bad enough, but it seemed especially shameful to be discovered by a former rummy.

'Thanks. I just had some lemonade.' Steve sat down at the kitchen table and put down an envelope. 'We've had a reply,' he said solemnly.

'To what?'

'My letters to that postal box in Detroit,' he said, his tone indicating he felt Michael should have known. He pushed the envelope towards Michael. 'Go on, read it.'

Michael picked it up and extracted a single sheet of paper, on which was typed neatly:

Dear Mr Atkinson,

A thousand apologies for not writing before but I have not been myself altogether well (hospital) and only just am recovered enough to write you back.

I was so shocked to hear of Henry's awful murder. Please tell me as any progress by the police is made.

Now to business. I will need to explain the situation and would like to see the sons of Henry in person, assuming they are available (I don't even know their names!!). I

265

*would plan to arrive in the next week or so – God willing
my health allows – and will phone you beforehand. No
need to worry about hotels – my great nephew will find
one for me on the internet!!*
   Yours sincerely
    Patricia Minsky

'We've found her,' said Michael.

'It's more like she's found us. Look at the letter.'

Michael looked questioningly at Atkinson, who said, 'See
any return address on it?'

Michael shook his head, then examined the envelope.
Nothing there either. 'Jesus. You think this is for real? Or some
kind of joke?' For he had begun to think that if he didn't find
his brother soon or uncover any real leads about his father's
murder, he would have to go to Detroit. *And do what?* He
knew no one in that city, and knew nothing about his father's
life there over fifty years before. But now it seemed the life was
coming to him in the almost mythical figure of Patsy. Unless the
letter was a hoax.

Steve lifted a big hand like a traffic cop. 'Don't get down
about it. Chances are she's just real old – at least that's how it
reads to me. So keep your fingers crossed.' He looked at
Michael's glass. 'I wouldn't mind that iced tea now.'

Spring Valley would have been called a hamlet if its inhabitants
had used the word, for it was a scratchy collection of half a
dozen houses, a gun shop that sold game and fishing licences,
and the eponymous tavern, behind which sat a disused one-
room schoolhouse, superseded decades before by the advent of
school buses to ferry the few children to the schools in
Walkerville. It was in the old playground of the school that the
local Marines barbecue was being held.

Known as The Fights, the tavern itself was not a place that in
their younger years either Donny or Michael had thought it
prudent to frequent, since anyone with long hair, dark skin, an
educated way of speaking, or just the possessor of a face

someone didn't like, would not often stay unmolested for long.

They were early, and decided to go inside out of the bright sunshine for a beer, Donny with some reluctance. They stood against the long, battered pine bar, drinking bottles of Stroh's, alone in the room except for a farmer eating a microwaved hotdog by the window, and the bartender, who mopped the floor with a laxity born of knowing that in twelve hours' time he would have to mop it again.

'You know,' said Michael, 'my father used to stop here sometimes when he'd been out at the Half. I always thought he was crazy, but it must be different during the day. I guess the only trouble here's at night.'

'Let's hope so.'

Three cars pulled up at once outside the tavern, and their occupants got out and walked around the tavern to the playground behind. 'Shall we go now?' asked Michael.

'In a minute. First tell me one more time just what you're hoping to accomplish.'

Michael sighed, for he wasn't entirely certain himself. 'I thought I'd ask Raleigh if he knows where Gary is. I'm pretty sure he'll say no, but I want to ask him anyway. And I'd like to get a feel for what this organization of his is like. Kenny Williams made him out to be crazy. I'd like to see if that's the case. But there's no reason to get all agitated. I'm sure most of these people are pretty normal.'

'I'm not concerned about these people.' Donny drained his bottle of beer and put it gently on the bar. 'It's you I'm worried about.'

'Don't worry, I'll behave.'

'You used to be Mr Easy Going. I'm not so sure any more.'

If he had hoped for manifest evidence of extremism, Michael was immediately disappointed. It was just an ordinary barbecue, it seemed to him, with a lady in baggy green shorts selling tickets from a table at the near end of the playground. They paid, and waited in line for hamburgers and corn. There was only soda to drink.

There was no sign of Raleigh, and though Donny nodded at a few faces, Michael knew no one there. They ate their hamburgers standing up, as the men – Back Country types, from the looks of their overalls and work boots – talked in small groups among themselves, their wives sat at picnic tables and the kids played on the swings and jungle bars of the playground.

Then suddenly he saw Raleigh, tall and muscled in green fatigues and a white T-shirt with lettering on it. Next to him was a short, middle-aged man with curly ginger hair, dapper in a maroon sports jacket, white shirt, and brown tie. The two of them stood on the edge of the playground, talking intently. Then Michael saw Raleigh signal to somebody in the crowd, a spoon was rapped against a glass, and the crowd grew quiet as the mothers hushed the playing children.

Raleigh held up his hand for silence and Raleigh's companion moved towards the crowd of guests. The man had a pie-shaped face with wide, flat cheeks and small eyes. The effect was of an odd Scandinavian-Asiatic mix, like a Swede with Inuit blood. But when he opened his mouth the slight oddness of his face was forgotten in the mesmerizing appeal of his voice. For though pitched a little higher than average, it was buttery smooth, with crooner-like modulation and a timbre the aural equivalent of velvet.

'Hi everybody, I'm Herman Kohls of the Wayne County branch of the Michigan Marines, and I'd like to thank you all for having me here today. A television reporter was trying to interview me last week – I say *trying* because I've learned they're always going to twist whatever you say – and he asked me where I would be going this weekend. When I explained that I'd be travelling up here, he said, "That seems a far way to go for a barbecue".'

There were easygoing chuckles at this, and one of the wives at the picnic tables clapped.

'But the fact is, I wouldn't miss the chance to meet you for all the television reporters in the world. And I hope I'll get the chance to visit with each and every one of you this afternoon and thank you for your support.

'You know, this country was founded by small communities like this one. Rural, farm communities with people who had fled oppressive governments and were determined to lead their own lives with their own religion, their own families, free from interference. These are values we all share, and I think that more than ever it's important that those of us who share these values seek each other out.

'Somebody once asked "What's in a name?" I'd say quite a lot, for if I were going to put a name to what unites us, I'd say that we are Christian Patriots. Capital C, capital P, and they sure don't stand for Communist Party. I think we know too who our enemies are, and I don't mean rowdy neighbours next door.

'But I'm here to listen to you, not to lecture you – that's the last thing you need on a bright sunny day like this one. So I want you to enjoy yourselves, and remember what binds us all together. And for you men, our next training session, Raleigh here tells me, will be Thursday night, out at Scotch Haven – have I got that right, Raleigh? Good. Now let's bow our heads for a minute and say thanks and then . . . let's eat!'

After this, someone brought Kohls a plate of food, and he stood holding it with one hand while the men in the crowd gradually went up to him one by one to pay court and say hello. Raleigh stood next to him, making introductions, and Kohls was uniformly cordial, greeting people as if he had met them before. He exuded the air of a cheerful undertaker at a local party, where everyone was a potential customer.

Seeing an opening, Michael went over, closely followed by Donny. This close up, he could read the words on Raleigh's T-shirt: *The tree of liberty must be refreshed from time to time with the blood of patriots and tyrants – Thomas Jefferson.*

'Hello, Raleigh. Remember me?'

Raleigh looked at him suspiciously. 'Can't say I do.'

'I'm Michael Wolf. Gary's brother.'

Raleigh looked startled by this but didn't respond. Michael asked, 'Is Gary here today? I was hoping to see him.'

Raleigh shook his head emphatically. Michael turned to

Kohls. 'Hi, Mr Kohls, I'm Michael Wolf and I wanted to say hello.'

'Herman, call me Herman.' He seemed to sense something was amiss. 'Are you from around here, Mr Wolf?'

'Born and bred. But I've been working overseas for the last few years.'

'Well, it's nice to see the world, I'm sure, but nothing beats Michigan. What's home base for you now?'

'England. I work out of London.'

Kohls nodded neutrally, but seemed to digest this carefully. 'I hear they've got some problems over there too.'

No, Michael wanted to say, *Utopia has been discovered and it's in Ealing.* 'How do you mean?' he asked, keeping his tone cheerful.

'There's a coloured problem there too, isn't there now? Not so bad as here.' He looked at Raleigh briefly and gave a small smile. 'That's because they haven't got so many to contend with.' He laughed at this, a sharp cackle. The mask of undertaker's unctuousness had slipped, replaced by an embalmer's cocky certainty that his clients were in no position to complain.

Michael said, 'I think it's fair to say the royal family has yet to be integrated. Still lily white as far as I can tell.'

'That depends on how you define lily white. There's a Hebrew strain in there somewhere, according to what I read.'

What was it Sarah had laughed about? For all her comparative sophistication, she had been a gushing fan of the British royals, especially Princess Di. Hadn't Princess Anne married someone who was one thirty-second Jewish? Or a sixty-fourth? Enough blood at any rate to warrant a mention in the English press. But this couldn't be what Kohls had in mind. 'Since they're head of the national church,' said Michael, unsure about the correct nomenclature, 'I think it's pretty unlikely they're Jewish. If that's what you mean by Hebrew.'

'Hebrew, Jewish, the Chosen people – call them whatever you like. Funny things about the Jews. If they're so special, why do they hide it all the time?'

'How's that?'

'Well, take that royal family over there. They're called Windsor now, aren't they? But they didn't used to be. If you look carefully – they don't publicize this much themselves – they used to be called Saxe-Coburg.'

'So?'

'A Jewish name, I think you will find.'

'I thought it was German,' he said, vaguely remembering some reference by Sarah to the Queen's German ancestry. One of the minor royals, to Sarah's intense disappointment, had turned out to have a Nazi father.

'If it was just German, then why change it?'

'The English did fight two wars with the Germans.'

'Nah,' said Kohls dismissively. 'Sachs – that's Jewish. Co-*berg*, that sounds pretty Jewish to me.'

This reasoning occupied Michael momentarily; he had too little knowledge of the royals to be on firm ground disputing it. Then a larger sense of absurdity overwhelmed him, and to Kohl's obvious surprise and Raleigh's disapproval he burst out laughing. 'That's crazy,' he said, suddenly sobering up.

'Are you suggesting I'm a liar?' Kohls asked coldly, his voice suddenly a full octave lower. Michael realized others were now watching them.

'No sir,' said Michael in a folksy, Back Country way. He paused to heighten the effect. 'Just an idiot.'

'What are you?' Kohls demanded. 'A reporter?'

Michael shook his head. 'I'm a civil engineer.' When Kohls looked sceptical, Michael gestured at Donny, who was still standing behind him, looking increasingly uncomfortable. 'Ask him, he'll tell you.'

'If you're not a reporter then what are you? Why are you here?' A light bulb seemed to go on in Kohls' head, for he suddenly looked triumphant. 'Are you one of those anti-defamation boys? If you are, you're a long way from home.'

'I told you, I'm from around here. Stillriver-born and bred. My father taught school here.' Michael pointed at Raleigh. 'He even tried to teach this guy here, though my father was forced to admit defeat. He said that when the Lord was

271

passing out brains, young Raleigh must have stepped out for a beer.'

Kohls could not suppress a giggle, but Raleigh's expression froze. 'You know,' Raleigh said slowly, 'I didn't like your father and I didn't like you. I still don't like you.'

'Meaning you've grown fonder of my father?'

Kohls laughed again at this, which seemed to anger Raleigh even more. Kohls said, 'Son, you make me laugh. You must be a Jew. You even *talk* like one.'

Raleigh looked at Donny. 'Washington,' he said, 'take your smart-ass friend and go.'

'Okay,' said Donny, with obvious relief.

'Pleased to meet you, Mr Kohls,' said Michael, sticking out his hand, but Kohls, as if sensing trouble, had already moved on to greet a more promising group of supplicants. *Good to see you, how you doing?*

Raleigh called out sharply in the direction of the tavern. 'Barry! Hey, Barry! Come here a minute.'

Donny began walking fast towards the front of the tavern and Michael struggled to keep up. Donny turned and looked behind them, then murmured, 'Hurry,' in a low, tense voice.

'What's the problem? Raleigh's not going to do anything now.' He too looked back and saw a familiar figure leave Raleigh and run into the back of the tavern. He recognized the figure's face. 'It's asshole mouth,' he told Donny.

'What?'

'Why is he here?' Michael wondered out loud.

'Tell me later,' said Donny. 'Let's go.'

Michael followed him to the truck but took his time getting in, even after Donny had started the engine. He refused to be cowed by Raleigh Somerset.

'Come *on*,' Donny pleaded, just as Barry – Michael was relieved not to have to think of him as *asshole mouth* any more – came out of the tavern's front door. He was wearing a football shirt with 88 emblazoned on it and carried a shotgun, broken at the breech, but with the brass tops of two loaded shells clearly visible. He stared at Michael, and when he started

272

to come down the tavern's front steps, Michael's bravado dissolved, and he jumped into the truck and slammed his door just
before Donny pulled out sharply, spraying dust behind them.

Donny was furious. 'Shit, you remind me of Kenny Williams,
pulling that kind of smart-ass act.'

'What did I do?'

'What was the point of all that?'

'Don't tell me you agree with that guy back there?'

'Of course not,' said Donny with obvious frustration as he
took a bend in the road at high speed, the wheels slipping
slightly on the gravel. 'But why stir things up? I don't want
anything to do with it.' He sighed as he looked in the rear-view
mirror. 'Not that it looks like I have a choice any more. Thanks
to you.'

Michael turned his head and looked back in time to see a red
Trans Am slip sideways at the same bend behind, straighten
and continue at high speed towards them. 'Shit, you reckon
that's Barry behind us? The guy with the shotgun?'

'Looks like it,' said Donny, craning his neck for a better view
in the mirror. 'Though I'm pretty sure they're just trying to
scare us.'

'They're doing a good job, I have to say.'

Donny nodded, biting down on his lower lip and concentrating on driving. 'The problem is, their idea of scaring us
– *just funning*,' he said in a hick drawl, 'could *just* get us killed.
Buckshot's buckshot, whether they're aiming deliberately or
not.'

'So what do we do?'

'I want to get off this road. He's slowed down a bit, probably
because he thinks he knows where we're heading. If I go
straight at the Hesperia Road he'll figure we're heading for
Stillriver. There's a short cut through Black Lake he might take
to cut us off at Four Corners. So,' said Donny, 'we'll fool him
and go east. *Away* from Stillriver.'

'Back by the Half?'

'Exactly.' And then Donny looked at Michael and they both
nodded simultaneously. 'Let's go there,' said Michael.

As predicted, when Donny went straight at the Hesperia Road, the Trans Am veered sharply right, towards Black Lake. Donny slowed the truck gradually, all the time scanning the mirror, then did a series of three-point turns until they were heading back the way they came. A right, followed by a left, and they were on the old sand road, still unpaved after all these years, that went by the Half.

'Slow down,' said Michael, 'it's been years since I was there and I'm not sure I'll know the turn.' But he recognized the dip they slowly descended, for there was a highway sign saying **DANGER: FLOODING**, and he remembered how a prolonged spell of rain would cover this part of the road in water. The stand of poplars was still there, though now full-grown, casting shade over the road.

He peered carefully ahead. 'There!' he suddenly shouted, and Donny pulled sharply left, onto a track now almost completely overgrown with ferns. After the first bend he had Donny stop the truck. 'Come help me,' he said, and they both got out and walked back to the road. Donny had a pocket knife and started cutting swathes of the ferns. He handed a bunch to Michael, stem first, then cut himself another bouquet and they both used the ferns to sweep away the telltale tyre tracks that revealed where they had turned off. After a minute they stood and examined the road. 'That should do it,' said Michael.

Back in the truck, they drove slowly along the track until the forest gave way to a large square of open meadow, full of garden lupins and mint the colour of lavender, and dotted by the occasional conifer – Scotch pine, Jack pine, and Douglas Fir, remnants that had escaped the saw when these acres, years before Henry bought them, held several thousand Christmas trees. 'This track circles back to the road,' said Michael. 'Keep your eyes peeled – there should be a spur that goes to the rear of the property.'

And at the back edge of the meadow they could just make out the signs of an even smaller track that went through ferns and more wild mint into higher grass and brush. 'If we can get through that,' said Michael, pointing to a mixed stand of tag alder and birch saplings, 'we'll be near the crick. There's a place to park there.'

'You built a parking space back here?'

Michael laughed. 'No, it's just some flat land where we used to leave the car.'

They bumped and scraped their way through the under-growth, scratching the sides of the truck, once hitting a tree stump so hard on their underside that they both sniffed for a telltale smell of gas from a ruptured fuel tank. Nothing, only the faint, sour odour of stinking chamomile. Just as Michael began to fear they were lost, hopelessly enmeshed in woods, they found themselves in a small circle of low grass, stunted by the lack of sunlight. There was just enough room to turn round.

They got out and stood, listening. 'What's that tinkling noise?' asked Donny.

'Come see.' They walked to the end of the clearing, then over a curved and gentle ridge of soft earth, covered with soft needles from a fully-grown Balsam pine. Michael pointed to the far side of the ridge, where a creek not much more than a yard wide bubbled noisily. It was only inches deep and on its sandy bottom the current had traced whorls and miniature ravines no thicker than a baby's finger. The sand was bronze with streaks of cerise; it glowed like petrified wood.

'Water's high, believe it or not,' said Michael, remembering how he and Cassie used to make love on a blanket not fifteen feet from where he now stood. They'd bring sandwiches, then lean down on their knees and drink straight from the tiny creek. 'Usually by this time in summer it's almost dried up.'

'Where's it go?'

'Into the Still, I think. At least that's what Pop always claimed. But then he said there were fish in it, too. I never saw any. He made up a story about a big brown trout he called George. There was a log down there a ways which formed a little pool. He claimed George slept there at night. I must have been twelve years old before I didn't believe him any more.'

He followed the rivulet downstream, with Donny trailing. Soon they were in woods so viscous-thick with leaves that they couldn't even see the truck, less than a hundred feet away. Amazingly, he found the miniature log jam still there, clogging up the creek; the pool that formed in front of it was almost three feet deep. Michael stood staring at the darker, deeper water here, his head full of memories: of Cassie and the soft cooing noise she made when they made love; of the time they'd been experimenting with Cassie on top, and she'd suddenly screamed – out of excitement he'd thought at first, but actually because a garter snake was trying to join them on the blanket.

There were childhood memories too: of chasing Gary through these very woods in some elaborate game of tag; of his mother on the bank by the creek, unpacking sandwiches, the sound of ice cubes clunking out of a thermos's mirror-bright insides; of his mother's post-lunch walks through the meadow and her eventual return with a bouquet of wild flowers – thyme and purple Meadow-rue and wood nymphs from the swale by the crick, all wrapped with a veil of Queen Anne's Lace.

Suddenly Donny's voice cut in, hushed and urgent. 'Look at that.'

Lifting his head, Michael expected to see a deer, or partridge, something worth keeping quiet for. There was nothing. Then looking past Donny's outstretched hand he saw, behind the trunk of an enormous maple, a small, olive-coloured pup tent. Its canvas roof was sagging badly.

'Let's get out of here,' whispered Donny.

'Why? I want to know who this is. He's trespassing on my land. Or Gary's land anyway.'

And he stepped quickly over the crick and began walking quietly towards the tent. Donny followed behind, whispering more than once, 'I wish I had my gun.'

As they approached the tent they could see the blackened stumps of a small camp fire. The tent's entrance faced away from them, and as Michael began to circle around he stubbed his toe on a rock and stumbled, almost falling down.

Some Indian I'd make, he thought, just as a shout suddenly came from out of the tent. 'Who's there?' It was a strained voice, panicky and thin.

'Come out with your hands up,' Michael shouted back. Donny looked at him as if he'd gone crazy. Then a figure crawled slowly out of the front of the tent, trying to hold its hands in the air.

Michael said more softly, 'It's all right, Gary. There's nobody here but us chickens.'

GARY MUST NOT have graduated with honours from Survival Training #1 *or* #2, for by the time Michael had found him he hadn't eaten in forty-eight hours. Now he sat looking drained and exhausted while Michael put two pork chops under the broiler, French fries in the oven, and a square block of frozen peas into a saucepan of boiling water.

Gary had hidden his car deep in brush in a far corner of the Half. Not willing to chance another effort to run away, Michael had driven it and Gary back to the house while Donny drove in his own truck and tactfully went home. The brothers had barely spoken in the car, and when Gary started to explain, Michael had told him to wait until they were home. But now, once started, Gary barely drew breath, so relieved did he seem to spill the beans. He seemed tormented, something Michael couldn't understand until Gary had told most of his story.

There had been exercises in Mason County, held in the national forest not far from Dr Fell's hunting lodge, about two miles from the Pere Marquette river. Hostage-freeing, counter-terrorism – various simulated manoeuvres to prepare for all the potential crises that the participants presumably agreed would one day threaten this part of the Wolverine state.

Then, as if automatic weapons fire were not exciting enough, someone had the bright idea of enlivening things with explosive. One highly illegal hand grenade was produced – a souvenir from the Vietnam era – and used on the edge of a swamp, but to what was unanimously felt to be disappointing effect. So two weeks later, when Raleigh Somerset revealed to a core elite of trusted Marine members a cache of ten sticks of dynamite, a couple of micro-detonators, and six hundred feet of slow-burning fuse, the excitement was hard to contain.

On the appointed day in April, when six large tree stumps

from a once-harvested part of the forest were targeted for destruction, the weather turned nasty: freezing rain fell in high, harsh winds throughout the day. To Raleigh's fury only three of his nine 'inner circle' cadre showed up, including Gary and Bubba. Unwilling to proceed with such a small participatory audience, Raleigh had conducted an indoor seminar on small arms instead, then asked Gary to stay behind when the others went home.

Raleigh said he had a small request, though it struck Gary that his casual manner of asking was belied by the pains he'd taken to make sure they were alone. Would Gary store the dynamite for him until the following month, when the day's aborted exercise would finally take place?

Flattered at first, Gary happily agreed, but soon found himself wondering what to do with the small wooden crate Raleigh entrusted him with. He couldn't very well store it in his rented bungalow, since he had a wide-ranging circle of hard-partying friends and acquaintances who were in and out of his place, sometimes even when Gary wasn't there. Not to mention the vague but even more disturbing concern that he might somehow – by dropping the stuff, by storing it in the wrong conditions (too hot, too dry, too something) – blow himself to smithereens. He ruled out his father's house on the same grounds. *That was big of you*, thought Michael.

This left the Half. Ten and a half acres of mixed woods and meadow gave plenty of hiding space; the only visitors other than Henry Wolf and Gary were occasional hunters who ignored the No Trespassing signs in search of their buck. But hunting was out of season, and there was no reason to think the dynamite wouldn't be safely gone by June, much less by the opening day of deer season in October.

At this point Michael interrupted. 'Why did Raleigh ask you to keep the dynamite for him?'

'He told me he couldn't store the stuff at his place because he was being watched.'

'Do you think he was?'

'Maybe. He left Wayne County in a hurry last year, and who

knows what trouble he got into down there. Though Raleigh is paranoid at the best of times.'

At first, Gary couldn't decide where to hide the dynamite on the Half. There were no buildings on the land, and he didn't dare leave it in the brush, however well covered. Equally, he didn't want to bury it – inevitably there'd be traces of his excavating. He ended up (Michael could tell Gary still thought it a clever solution) by wrapping the crate in waterproof plastic and hauling it halfway up one of the overgrown Douglas Firs, where it sat concealed in a bunch of evergreen branches from all eyes except those already in the know. And Gary was the only one in the know.

All would have been well, had there not occurred one of those freak coincidences in which Gary, describing it, clearly saw the hand of a harsh and punitive Fate.

Adlard Ferguson ran one of the few independent timber businesses left in the state of Michigan, and specialized in the selective harvesting of land the big boys – Weyerhaeuser in particular – did not find worthwhile cutting. He was assiduous if not particularly prosperous, and it was in the normal course of business that he wrote Henry Wolf, as he had written him every year, to ask if, as the owner of a small land parcel in the east end of Atlantic County, Wolf would consider allowing Ferguson's team to cut down no more than one hundred trees on his property, such trees to be selected ahead of time and chosen only with Wolf's approval. In return, Ferguson would pay Henry a one-off fee of $1500 and a ten per cent royalty on his own gross revenues from board length sold post-sawmill.

Every year before Wolf had replied with a polite no, but now, whether out of interest in the money on offer or just out of some arbitrary curiosity, Henry considered the offer, and even, most uncharacteristically, drove out to the Half to look at what he might be willing to allow Ferguson to cull.

And it was during his survey of the timber on his land, (which naturally focused on the taller, more lucrative specimens) that Henry discovered, obscured by branches, a wooden crate sitting halfway up a Douglas Fir, attached to a rope that ended in a neat loop on a branch a dozen feet above the ground. Curiosity piqued, Henry then managed, by standing on top of his automobile, to reach and untie the rope, then lower the crate onto the roof of his car. Unwrapping its plastic cover, he pried open the crate's lid with a screwdriver from the car's toolset and found himself looking at what were indisputably ten sticks of dynamite.

Here Gary stopped his account for a moment, as if in awe at the freak chance leading to his father's discovery. 'I never thought he could get that angry,' he said, looking slightly sick at the memory. He added that in the face of Henry's explosion he had not even tried to lie, coming clean with the whole truth at once.

'So what did Pop do?'

'He'd left the dynamite at the Half, in the brush by the clearing.'

'Yes, but what did he do?'

Gary wouldn't look at Michael. 'He went to see Raleigh.'

Raleigh hadn't been home, but Mrs Somerset, the former sweet girl called Louise Grade, had gone to Stillriver High School. So she told Henry happily enough that Raleigh was in Weir township, addressing Marine members on the pressing topic of counterinsurgency. Michael's father must have been in a near-frenzy of anger, because he wasn't willing to wait to see Raleigh, but drove straight to Weir to find him.

Since Michael had never understood why his father had attended Marine meetings, this explained a lot.

Once at the meeting in Weir, his father had doubtless listened impatiently to Raleigh's codswallop declamations, then confronted him. Gary reported that his father had called Raleigh stupid, and Michael could almost hear the specific locutions: *You were always a horse's ass when I taught you, Somerset, so I'm not surprised to see the saddle still fits.* Something along those lines.

'Why didn't you go with him?' Michael asked Gary.

'He didn't tell me he was going. The first I knew about it was Raleigh asking me how I could be so dumb as to let my father know about the dynamite.' He paused momentarily. 'Then I took the crate back to Raleigh's house.'

'Was that the dynamite the police found?'

Gary nodded. He still wouldn't look Michael in the eye. 'Four days later. That's when Maguire arrested Raleigh.'

And then Michael understood. 'Quite a coincidence. What did Raleigh make of that?' Gary didn't say anything. 'Raleigh must have thought Pop had turned him in. Didn't he?'

His brother nodded slowly. Michael kept talking. 'Is that why you became an enemy of Raleigh? Harold told me Raleigh had a ruckus with Bubba, but it was you Raleigh was after, wasn't it? Bubba was trying to help *you*, wasn't he?'

Gary said, 'Since you seem to know it all, why ask me?'

'Well, Pop's not going to explain anything any more, now is he? And if I understand all this, Raleigh thought Pop turned him in, which gives Raleigh a motive to kill Pop. Doesn't it?'

Gary looked out the window. 'Pop didn't turn Raleigh in. Not that he wasn't tempted, but he told me he wouldn't because he thought I might get arrested, too.'

'How do you know he didn't change his mind?'

'I tell you, I know. Pop didn't tell Maguire anything – he never even met Maguire.'

'How can you be so certain?' He sensed this was worth pressing.

'Easy. I know Pop didn't turn Raleigh in because *I* did.' And then Gary's mouth wobbled and he burst into tears.

Michael comforted his brother as best he could, but his thoughts were racing as first he put an arm around Gary, then got him some paper towel on which to blow his nose.

Eventually Gary stopped sniffling and said, 'We had a softball game last summer, out at the snowmobiles resort.'

Michael said, 'So?' more patiently than he felt.

'I took the baseball bat with me, and I used it in the game. I don't know if anyone else did.'

'That explains your prints on it. You might have told me that, you know.'

'You don't understand. The bat disappeared. I couldn't find

282

it when I went home that night. I didn't think much about it – it was just a baseball bat – and then it shows up again.'

Michael went and put some ice cubes in a glass, then poured himself two inches of bourbon. He took a large slug of it as Gary said, 'He's trying to set me up.'

'Who? Raleigh?'

'Who else? He killed Pop because he thinks Pop told the cops about the dynamite. I thought he'd kill me, too, but in a way it's worse than that – he's trying to hang me for Pop's murder instead.' He looked close to tears again. 'I guess it's no more than I deserve. I might as well have killed Pop myself.'

'Listen,' said Michael sharply, 'you've said that now. I don't want to hear you say it again. Not to me, or anybody, and especially not to yourself. Otherwise this thing will eat you up inside.' The corrosive effects of obsession. *I've been there myself. A complete waste of the soul.* 'You have to let it go.'

Gary took a deep, hyperventilatory breath, then nodded as he stared at his hands.

Michael asked, 'Was this why you ran away?'

'Yes,' he said without hesitation. 'As soon as you said the bat was back I knew what Raleigh was trying to do.'

'But why go to the Half? Why not get out of Dodge altogether? Set out for Detroit, or Chicago? Why not *really* hide?'

Gary looked thoughtfully at Michael. 'I don't know. I just ran. I can't say I thought it out.'

And it was exactly the calm, confessional tone of his voice and the plausibility of his confusion that made Michael feel his brother was no longer telling him the truth.

'Listen,' said Michael again. 'I think for the time being you'd better stay here. We need to talk to Maguire, but until we do you better not stay at your place. We can go by later and get your things.'

He seemed happy with this and as Michael put his dishes in the sink, Gary said, 'I need to let Bubba know I'm okay. I've got one of his rifles and he may want it back.'

'Sure,' said Michael. 'Anybody else? Barry?'

'No.' This was emphatic. Michael thought of Barry coming out of the tavern with the shotgun. No point scaring his brother more than he was scared already, but it was good that he knew Barry was not on his side.

'Why don't you go upstairs and lie down for a while?' Michael suggested. 'I'll get you some sheets and a blanket.'

And twenty minutes later, his kid brother was sound asleep while Michael washed his dishes and thought about what Gary had related. Or rather what he hadn't told him, since running out to the Half didn't make sense, whatever frazzled state he'd been in. Could Raleigh really have killed his father? Thinking of him at the barbecue – how he angered so readily, the ill-disguised viciousness of Kohls' party line – Michael had no real trouble seeing Raleigh as a murderer, given the right situation. But would he really risk a life sentence, if not the death penalty, to exact revenge on an old man whose supposed ratting on him didn't work? And would Raleigh really kill someone so brutally? Why not just use a gun?

He went outside and walked slowly around the house, enjoying the smell of the fresh-cut grass. In the flower patch behind the house he looked at the old flower bed and saw that a few carnations were out, garishly pink. Memories of Cassie planting flowers in the back came to him, and of Ethel helping while his father looked on, bemused. Ethel would have slept in the flower bed if they hadn't ordered her home at suppertime.

And then suddenly he understood; it was as if the small patch of garden had been dramatically bathed in illuminating light. He went into the house at a run, through the ground floor and up the steep stairs, taking them two at a time, and went straight into Gary's room without knocking.

His brother was sound asleep and stirred only when he shook him by the shoulder. 'What is it?' asked Gary. 'What's the matter?'

'Tell me, did you do any gardening here this year?'

Gary sat up and rubbed his eyes. 'What are you talking about? I only mow the lawn. I *hate* gardening, you know that.'

'There're flowers in the back, where Mom used to grow

them. And Cassie too. They weren't there when I was back in May. So who planted them?'

'How should I know? How can you be sure they're not old flowers?'

'Because they're *annuals*, you nitwit. You have to plant them every year.'

Gary shrugged, as if to say, *fine by me if you want to make a fuss about it.* 'Well, whoever planted them, it wasn't me.' He shook sleep from his head and looked at Michael with exasperation. 'What's this about, anyway?'

But Michael wasn't listening any more. He was thinking hard, and wondering with a certain satisfaction what Maguire's face would look like when Michael told him he knew whose prints were on the bat.

Six

1

'POP,' GARY HAD once asked, 'what's a Rubicon?'

And his father, in a rare bad mood, had snapped, 'Something you'll never have to cross.'

Would that were true of me, thought Michael, smiling a little ruefully at his own predicament, and looking down from the corner window of the thirty-ninth floor. He reckoned he had fifteen minutes before McLaren would grow impatient and come looking for him. The son of the company's founder, McLaren had his father's aggressive bluster but none of his talent. Another reason for Michael to be out of central office. And then he wouldn't have to fire Streatley, whose drinking was out of control.

Fifteen minutes to decide. He looked down at the street, the familiar calming view where it had all started. In his first days at the firm, he would retreat here, to this corner window of the open plan, look down and see hansom cabs across the street from the Plaza Hotel. At lunchtime he would sneak the horses peanuts he bought from a hotdog stand on the corner.

He had come to New York fresh out of college. During his last two years at the University of Michigan, he had buried himself in his work, concentrating on civil engineering to the exclusion of any other subjects save the ones necessary for the BA requirements. The members of the Pining Friends of Sophie Jansen had graduated ahead of him, so he had few friends, and though he had dates with girls, he missed Cassie so much that he was incapable of starting a significant relationship with anyone else. To the girls he went out with he was consistently nice and equally uncommitted: the last one, a chemistry major from Petoskey named Jessica Mint, who was so smart and so good-looking that he couldn't believe he didn't feel more for her, told him he had a reputation as someone you shouldn't think you were going to get very close to. He could not dispute this, since even sleeping with girls didn't bring them into his heart, or move Cassie out of it.

So most of his time was spent alone and working, trying to reduce his obsessive thinking about Cassie. *Why did she have to marry him?* he asked himself again and again. He could understand her going away; he could even try to understand her going away with Ronald. But why marry him? He felt that having been knocked to the ground, he had been kicked in the teeth for good measure.

He went home rarely, and when there avoided walking anywhere near Cassie's house, which Donny told him had been rented out. He also avoided the drugstore, though when he did encounter Marilyn she was always friendly. Even Alvin was polite, though visibly disappointed when Michael told him he had switched his major to engineering. He spent as little time in his father's house as possible: instead he drove around the Back Country, hunting in winter with Donny for rabbits on the Half or, in warmer weather, fishing with him on the Still near Happy Valley. In his senior year he even spent Christmas in Ann Arbor.

After graduation he headed, as if directed, straight for New York and his first full-time job. He had been very lucky to get it, the sole person hired that year by McLaren with only a Bachelor's degree. Why had he been so insistent on New York? It was not a question he could ever satisfactorily answer, not even eight years later as he looked down on Central Park and got ready to see McLaren. He supposed the fact that Sophie Jansen had gone there influenced him, for if even Sophie – high priestess in Ann Arbor of *The New Yorker* magazine and *Vanity Fair,* the embodiment of self-confident style in Michael's undergraduate eyes – felt the need to flock to the Mecca called Manhattan, who was he to think of going anywhere else? And it seemed the place where the other world he was always searching for might be found; the place, as he understood it, where taste was dictated and disseminated to the rest of the country.

His job was as low level as you could get. The 59th Street

bridge was being renovated, and he was assigned the job of reviewing cylinder tests made on the concrete and tension tests performed on the steel. The task was not unimportant, and it was specified in detail by the City, but his duties were simple and mind-numbingly dull. He worked in the open plan among the engineering draftsmen, whose cubicles were divided by shoulder-high partitions. Michael didn't even have a cubicle of his own, so junior his standing, and was expected to use any place unoccupied that day by a more senior colleague.

Most of the more senior engineers were family men and lived outside Manhattan – Yonkers, Queens, the near suburban towns of Long Island – arriving in the morning from their commutes already looking tired, rushing out like clockwork in the evening to catch their trains. Two or three of them, however (including Streatley, his immediate boss), were happy to take him under their wing, and it was from them that he found his vocation. There were no opportunities to work on the historical wrought iron bridges he loved ('they're all dinosaurs, I'm afraid' Streatley had remarked, though he was partial to them too) and there was little inspiring in his second assignment – tracking the repetitive construction of multiple box-girder bridges over a Connecticut interstate. But informally Michael was learning from these engineers all about the detailed application of pre-stressed, reinforced concrete, and that was to prove his bread and butter.

He never got entirely used to working on the thirty-ninth floor, and the height of Manhattan's buildings seemed somehow preposterously unnatural, almost unreal. Where he lived, on the other hand, was entirely too real for his liking – a basement room in the Flushing house of his former housemate Sam's ageing aunt. His landlady, Mrs Gennaro, was polite but unfriendly. He had the use of the kitchen, and could watch television in the living room, but both were available on the clear understanding that when she entertained (which was often – a continuous flow of relatives and neighbours came for home-cooked meals of pasta and roasts), then he should make himself scarce. He had his own key to the house, but with no separate entrance felt quite unable to bring anyone back. Not that he had friends to entertain, much less a girlfriend to share his bed.

Each morning he walked to the Flushing subway, rode it to Grand Central, then walked north to work, alternating between Park, Madison and Fifth Avenue. Lunch was a hotdog across from the Plaza, then back to the office where he studied manuals on stressed loads and looked at the *New York Post*; evenings he usually went straight back to Flushing, where he read engineering monographs borrowed from the office library and watched Mrs Gennaro's television when she didn't have company.

In his last two years in Ann Arbor, his fear had been manageable, suppressed as it was by his immersion in engineering and by his longing for Cassie. Here in New York, both in the office and at Mrs Gennaro's he felt safe, in the same way he had felt safe as a boy, playing with marbles in his bedroom upstairs. But he was as scared the rest of the time as he had been after his mother died. New York – its scale, its pace, its almost breathtaking *hardness* – was scary; it made him feel vulnerable, almost fragile. Possibly it was a delayed reaction to the beating he had taken from Ronald. *Coward*, he often said to himself, and he found himself sensitive to any possible physical confrontations, often going to absurd lengths to avoid them: crossing the street if he saw a drunk lurching ahead of him, wary and nervous when anyone grew boisterous or aggressive anywhere near him.

Sometimes in the morning he would look at himself in the mirror, stripped to the waist for shaving, and wonder, *Why should you be scared? This is a man's body.* For he had filled out in his last two years of college, helped by two summers of construction work, and he now stood a little over six feet and weighed 175 pounds. But he felt that inside this impressive shell a small boy remained in residence.

He finally did something about it after an incident one evening in a crowded bar near Lincoln Center, where he had arranged to meet two of his older colleagues from work. When he came in, he couldn't see them, so he bought a Scotch and water at the bar, next to a group of big guys in suits. Spying his colleagues at a table in the rear, he made his way past this bunch, and one of them – a Bruce Willis lookalike but bigger, with a gold chain around a turtleneck – accidentally backed into him, spilling some of Michael's drink. When he turned round Michael assumed he was going to apologize.

'Don't worry about it,' said Michael amiably. 'No big deal.'

The guy eyed him with a long, hard stare. 'You better hope it's not,' he said, unsmiling, until Michael shrugged, feeling himself blush, feeling he would rather do anything than confront this man, sensing his lower legs beginning to tremble and his throat grow so tight that he could not have spoken if he'd wanted to. After another stare, the guy snorted. 'I'll let you slide, jerk-off.'

This tipped the balance, and he decided to do something – anything, however uncharacteristic – which might allay his feeling of utter powerlessness, for he was determined not to have the fear any more, reasoning that if he did not rid himself of it now, he would end up serving a life sentence. Through a casual mention from a former college boxer at work, Michael started going to a boxing gym in the West Forties. There a trainer named Malley set Michael his initial regimen. He was a small man with an unmarked face and big ears, but his hands looked like a short order cook's, full of welts, red scar lines, and odd puffy bits of skin around the fingernails. He had fought professionally and trained a few mildly celebrated boxers thirty years before. Now he ran the gym, and looked after newcomers like Michael.

For a month he wouldn't let Michael in the ring with anyone, confining him first to the heavy bag, then the speed bag, then to shadow-boxing under his careful instruction and eventually some sparring against Malley himself, holding up oversized mitts. When he finally let him fight, Michael was knocked down twice near the end of a two-minute round by a Hispanic kid who made apparent his contempt of the businessmen who used the gym (this seemed to include Michael) and had already hit Michael with a low left hook right into his cup protector.

But he got better quickly, though Malley now threw him in with lighter fighters. He felt less scared on the streets, more confident, and more aggressive – once he thought he saw the same medallion man from the bar near Lincoln Centre, and followed him half a block, until a man turned round who was unknown to him. *What was I going to do?* he asked himself. Somebody pushed him on the subway and he pushed back; a cabby gave him the finger when he was slow crossing Madison Avenue and he walked over and asked the cabby if he wanted to get out of the cab (he didn't).

In the gym he fought with a new ferocity, especially when matched against what Malley called the East Coast White Kids, the preppies with their fading jock powers and social cockiness. Put in the ring with a fresh-faced kid who worked for some astronomical salary at a brokerage house, Michael knocked him down with a barrage of punches – jab, right hand, jab jab, jab, right hand – then almost hit him again as he was getting up. 'What is your problem?' the kid had said as he climbed slowly out of the ring, and Michael felt his aggression melt away, replaced by embarrassment.

It was after this that Malley took him aside. 'Did something bad once happen to you?'

'Why?'

'Well, how do I put this? I just get the feeling you're here for the wrong reasons.'

'I'm not a weirdo,' he said indignantly.

'I never said you were, and believe me, we get plenty of those in here. Psychopaths who don't mind hurting people, psychotics who enjoy hurting people, repressed homosexuals who like the smell of other guys' sweat. I can recognize them all right, but you I can't make out.' He looked around the gym. It was getting late, and there were only two Hispanic kids hitting the speed bags, and a cop Michael knew to say hello to jumping rope.

'Sometimes,' Malley continued, 'we get guys in here who've been bullied. They come in because they feel humiliated, and they want to kill the world in a return match. Frankly, sometimes you seem that way to me, but you're too big to bully. So where did all this anger you've got stored up inside come from?'

'I wasn't always this big.'

'Maybe,' said Malley doubtfully. 'Something's pushing you, that's for sure. Maybe you don't know yourself.'

'I know all right,' said Michael.

Malley waited for a moment, but when Michael said nothing else he shook his head. 'Whatever it was, if I were you I'd let it go. I don't think you're really cut out to be a hard guy. It's not in your make-up.'

'Really?' said Michael testily, feeling slightly aggrieved.

'Take it as a compliment.'

'I need to know I can look after myself.' He had a flashing image of himself, flat on his stomach, lying on the paving stones outside his father's house, as Ronald Duverson tried to beat him half to death. *Half?*

'Look after yourself? You can look after yourself. Look, even Mike Tyson got beat up in jail, so if it's a guarantee you want, forget it – there's always somebody who's tougher.' He looked at Michael gently for a moment, then said, 'Take my advice.'

When he didn't continue, Michael felt forced to ask: 'What advice?'

'Try to forget about whatever happened to you. But if you can't, and you ever come up against whoever fucked you up the first time, don't fight back right away.'

'What, and let him do it again?'

'Of course not. But in a fight like that there're no rules, so don't act like you're in a ring and someone's about to call time. Try instead to surprise the son of a bitch. One way or another, do something unexpected.'

After this Michael stopped going so often to the boxing gym, and when he did he usually just hit the heavy bag and skipped rope. He began to realize that he had been confusing machismo with masculinity; as if he had decided that his physical humiliation by Ronald Duverson was keeping him from becoming a man; as if he could only be a man by acquiring the ability to hurt Ronald as much as he'd hurt him. He had hoped that as his physical confidence grew, he might also feel confident enough to forget about Cassie Gilbert, and he even bought a pop psychology book, which said it could help rid him of unwelcome thoughts. But it must not have worked very well, since shortly after reading it – about a year after he arrived in New York – he saw Cassie, at 12.38 one Thursday lunchtime as he walked down Madison Avenue in the fifties on the west side of the street.

Having yet to adopt the New York precaution of not looking at strangers, his eyes that day swept across Madison and came to rest on a young woman with shoulder-length hair, blue-black and from his vantage point very straight and shiny. He watched with interest that turned to disbelief as the figure raised a hand to sweep back the fringe that came down over her forehead, and when she turned sideways to him he saw the familiar straight nose, the thin-lipped mouth and short, pointed chin. The woman nodded (she must have been with someone) and then as she nodded again her teeth clamped down on her lower lip. He had stopped walking by then, fixated on the female figure, but now the woman was obscured by people passing by, and he could only see her overcoat, which was a long, blue wool one. He wondered when Cassie had bought that. When the crowd cleared he couldn't see her at all, and he raced to his corner and waited for the light, then rushed across the street and stood at that corner, looking up and down Madison Avenue and east and west along the side street. But she had gone, and he had walked back to work feeling absolutely desolate until on 49th Street he saw her *again*, between Madison and Fifth, and this time he had run and caught up to her, and when the woman turned at the sound of his running footsteps he had seen a highly attractive young woman who wasn't Cassie Gilbert.

That was not his only sighting, and they were all upsetting, even when the misidentification only lasted for a second – catching a glimpse of shoulder-length hair on the subway, or an obscured face in the elevator up to work. The worst happened in a steakhouse off Broadway, where he'd been invited by the senior engineers to someone's farewell dinner. He'd been impressed by the refrigerated anteroom where sides of beef were hung to age like punching bags. He'd sat with the others, eating a pork chop (cheaper than steak) and nursing a beer when he looked over at the bar and saw, there on a bar stool, Cassie again, wearing a silk lilac blouse and a short, sexy skirt. *She never used to dress like that.* She had low leather boots on, and at one point as she reached down to tug on one of them, Michael saw her hair was shorter now and looked rougher and drier than the soft, full strands he had known, though he figured that might be the effect of the light in the restaurant. His throat was constricting and his chest seemed to be filling up. *How did she find me here?* he thought, with the excited joy of a small boy on Christmas morning. He was about to get up and go to her, had actually risen in his seat – he sensed his colleagues looking at him, wondering what was up – when to his consternation he saw that she was with someone, a tall, muscular man in a blue suit standing next to her bar stool. When he realized the man was Ronald Duverson (*Why is Ronald wearing a suit?*), his happy excitement turned to a terrible feeling of heartbreak, and then the maitre d' walked over to the couple, spoke in the man's ear and began to lead the two of them to their table, and Michael saw that it wasn't Cassie or Ronald after all.

And he realized then that his chief burden was no longer his sense of shame and humiliation, or a fear of physical violence. It was something far darker and deeper than that, a soul-withering loneliness, an overpowering sadness he still felt about losing Cassie, and the seeming impossibility of building a life without her.

2

IT WAS STREATLEY who came to his rescue. Streatley was his boss, a tall and rangy man, given to wearing loose-fitting suits and white shirts, usually without a tie. A native of Salem, Oregon, he had a flop of straw-coloured hair that made him look far younger than the ten years he had over Michael. He had studied after college for a year at Imperial College in London, and to Michael he was a glamorous figure at first, for he also had an impressive array of working experience on construction projects all over the American West – Nevada, Utah, Idaho – and was vividly articulate and funny about it. He had only returned to central office, here high up in the General Motors building, when his wife became pregnant. Six months after their daughter was born, his wife had left him for a director of television commercials, and Streatley found himself trapped in a middle manager's corporate position (and in Manhattan) by the legal demands of child support and the natural wish to see his daughter.

Streatley liked to drink, and had no compunction about drinking with colleagues, even if, as in Michael's case, they worked for him. With corporate niceties he had little patience: 'We are on the cusp of a new age, an era of corporate rationalization, mass redundancies, and careers cut short at fifty by the insatiable requirement for younger, cheaper blood. I can play the game, knowing however dutiful I am, however "professional" my conduct, I will still one day face the very same axe that I have wielded so fiercely on the company's behalf. Or I can say *fuck that,* drink with the people I like, chase the woman I want, and figure that even if I get the chop a couple of years earlier than might have been the case, I sure as hell enjoyed myself while I could.'

Streatley was in a characteristically buoyant mood when he

stopped before lunch one Tuesday by the desk Michael had for the day, and asked him if he was busy that evening.

Michael did not need long to consider this, since he faced a typical evening: some reading in his room, before watching *Hill Street Blues* with Mrs Gennaro. 'Not really,' he said.

'Then could you do me a big favour?'

'What's that?'

'Join me at Costello's.' A bar and restaurant near Grand Central where newspapermen, especially from the nearby *Daily News*, hung out. Streatley loved it because the food was good and Hemingway had been a customer. 'I've got a date with a girl named Maura Hobbs. She's got a friend and says the friend has got to be there too.'

'What's the friend like?' asked Michael, able to see where this was headed.

Streatley shrugged. 'I'd like to tell you she's gorgeous, but the fact is, I've never met her before. Maura says she's rich. Do you like rich girls?'

'I don't really know any,' he said truthfully, since he'd learned the week before that Sophie Jansen had moved to Los Angeles to work for a television production company.

'Well, I would if I were you. My grandfather used to say, "It's just as easy to marry a rich girl as a poor one." But believe me, it's not. Anyway, come see for yourself.'

'What's her name?'

'Sarah. Sarah Forbes. Something like that.'

In fact her name was Sarah Perkins and when Michael arrived she was sober (which was more than could be said of Streatley and Maura Hobbs), and looking impatient. She also seemed to Michael more than pretty, almost beautiful, with high, wide cheekbones flanking a soft, small nose, and small round blue eyes. Her hair was straight, long, and light brown with blonde streaks, and her arms and face were tanned the colour of a ripe peach, the tan mottled with hints of sunburned red. She was short, no more than five feet four, with an athletically trim figure except for her breasts, which, he could not help noticing as she stood and leant forward to shake his hand, bordered on the oversized.

As Streatley got drunker and Maura followed him, Michael could not really have said what he and Sarah talked about over the next three hours. It was small talk to be sure, mainly about their jobs (Sarah worked in an advertising agency on the accounts rather than creative side, not far from the General Motors building), but he felt that with any topic she answered so truthfully, so directly, that it gave an interest to the otherwise commonplace. There was also a formality about her, which seemed novel, quite unlike the easygoing, casual manners of the Midwest. But it didn't put him off, for it didn't seem affected, or pretentious. It was just formal.

When they said goodbye to the other couple, who piled unsteadily into a cab headed north to Streatley's apartment in Yorkville and/or Maura's studio on Fifth and 104th, Michael turned and asked hopefully, 'Can I see you home?'

'Not unless you want to meet my parents,' she said with a laugh, then explained that she still lived with them in New Canaan, almost an hour's train ride away. So he offered to walk her to the station.

When they came to her track he stopped and said, 'It was very nice to meet you,' wondering how he could ask her out again.

'Really?' she said dryly.

'Really,' he said with some surprise. 'I mean it.'

'Then why aren't you asking me out again?'

He was surprised Sarah Perkins didn't have a boyfriend until she explained that she had recently broken up with her child-hood sweetheart, one Oakley Hale, whom she'd known since birth. Her parents were unhappy about this, she confided (she had dumped him), for Oakley's parents were friends of the family.

She knew Manhattan better than Michael did (which wasn't saying much) and their early dates covered the obvious locations – the Metropolitan Museum, MOMA, feeding the ducks in Central Park. They even went to a jazz club once, in the West Village, but it was very expensive, and when Sarah herself admitted afterwards she didn't really like jazz, they tacitly agreed to confine most of their dates to the movies. She was mad about them, and here Michael was happy enough to go along, especially since her taste was for the major releases he liked and might have seen in Burlington or Ann Arbor. There, movies were the gateway to fantasies of the big time world; since Sarah was actually living *in* that big time world, he found it surprising that she insisted on going to the movies so often.

But in fact he soon found Sarah was far less adventurous than he. She was a creature of confirmed habits and strong if conventional tastes: she was tidy, and wore expensive skirts and crisply ironed blouses for work, with middle height heels and charcoal stockings; the effect, perhaps because of its very corporate demureness, was amazingly sexy. Her casual dress was equally unrelaxed. True, she wore blue jeans, but they were Calvin Klein, and the sweaters she wore were from Bloomingdale's, her boat shoes from L.L. Bean. There was something so conventional about this – as if someone had opened the back pages of *The New Yorker* and, pointing to the ads, said, *Dress like this* – that he found it oddly alluring, and it made him want to sleep with her very much.

It was because of Sarah and sex that he got out of Queens. For once they started going out, they quickly discovered they had no place to sleep together. A hotel would for him be unaffordable; for her, he sensed, too tacky. Mrs Gennaro's was out of the question, and so, Sarah made clear to him, was the Connecticut house of her parents. Then just as he felt near breaking point – tired of the midnight clinch under the Grand Central clock, finding his interest in one of the friendlier secretaries at work growing – Sarah announced that her friend Valerie, Bryn Mawr classmate, was out of town that weekend and they could borrow her place. Sarah would tell her parents she was staying with Valerie.

In the cab to Valerie's she was quiet, and he resisted the impulse to put his arm around her. When they arrived she got out while he paid the driver. When he joined her under the building's awning she was staring abstractedly down the street, which was full of the weekend traffic of jostling taxis and partygoers, horns blaring and headlights flashing as they bounced along the pot-hole pitted surface of Columbus Avenue. He stood with her for a minute, sensing she was making a decision. At last she took his arm and led him into the building.

For all her usual assertiveness, she proved very shy in bed, undressing before Michael and quickly hopping in, where she pulled the sheet up over her breasts and tucked it under her arms. When he joined her, she was tentative at first, as if unsure how to proceed. Although she kissed him back, she seemed oddly inert. Gradually, by caressing her gently while kissing her hard, he found her becoming aroused, then increasingly excited, until she climaxed abruptly and noisily from his stroking hand before he had even entered her. When he slowly moved into her, she seemed to steel herself, and closed her eyes, as if the better to lie back and think of New England.

He made a point of coming quickly, then got up and poured them glasses of the wine he'd brought along, then slowly teased out from her the brief details of her sexual history. She had lost her virginity as a freshman at Bryn Mawr to a cadet from the Naval Academy, but had otherwise only ever slept with one man: the worthy Oakley Hale. Doubtless Oakley had his points – the photograph Sarah showed Michael revealed a handsome, athletic figure with tousled hair and Pepsodent teeth who had played lacrosse for Yale – but he could not have been a ball of fire in the sack, since Sarah seemed unaware that what she called with only mild irony 'the act of love' was something women were allowed to enjoy as well.

This surprised him. With Cassie sex had been an exploration for them both, unrestrained yet never more important than their simple urge to be with each other, to share *everything* – sex, yes, but also food, and ideas, and feelings. But with Sarah, her sexual awkwardness was curiously pleasing, since it allowed him to lead in a relationship where otherwise he felt he always followed – it was Sarah who knew that Sixth Avenue was really the Avenue of the Americas, that there was only one 57th Street gallery open on Sundays, that Tompkins Square was not the place for a late evening stroll, and that New York taxi drivers really did expect twenty per cent as a tip. It was nice to know that at least in the bedroom he was the one in the know.

It turned out that Valerie's roommate was moving, and for an extra hundred dollars a month above the rent he paid to Mrs Gennaro, Michael could move in. So he transferred his few belongings from his grim room in Queens, where Mrs Gennaro insisted on keeping two weeks of his two months' deposit, and installed himself in his new bedroom in Valerie's apartment on a dicey block off Columbus in the high west nineties. Valerie had a boyfriend in Brooklyn and often stayed there, leaving Michael the whole apartment to himself – or rather to him and Sarah, who now stayed over one or two nights a week, still telling her parents she was staying with Valerie.

He was Sarah's boyfriend now, he supposed, though there was no immediately greater intimacy between them. Nor did he discuss much about his past with her, as if their initial exchanges of information were, for her purposes, more than adequate. She knew there had been a girl named Cassie in his life, and it was Cassie in fact who provoked the first display of Sarah's irritable side. They had been in a fern bar near Lincoln Centre, having lunch one Saturday, when he had compared the way Sarah ate her hamburger – politely, bird-like – with the almost ravenous gusto Cassie had brought as she used to chomp her way through hers. 'Don't compare me to her,' Sarah had said crossly, 'I don't like being compared.'

But he couldn't help it, noting to himself the contrast between Sarah's indifference and Cassie's almost pedantic interest in everything he did. 'Why can't you use an electric razor?' Cassie had asked when he'd nearly cut half his lip off one absent-minded morning; 'You have to tell Alvin,' after he'd mentioned suspecting one of the summer help of stealing money from the liquor till; and later, with concern, 'Are you still

303

skipping breakfast in Ann Arbor?' Oh, Sarah knew – thought it 'cute' in fact – that as a teenager he'd worked in a drugstore, and yes, she could probably remember if asked that his father taught high school. But after receiving this kind of basic information she asked no further questions; so after a while he stopped talking about his past. *If she's not interested in me*, he thought, *then why is she seeing me?*

Unwittingly, her roommate Valerie supplied the answer. He was asleep in his room and alone in the apartment, having come home early with what he feared was the flu. Valerie came in at 5.30, far earlier than his usual arrival, just as the phone rang, and she picked it up before he had time to shout hello and let her know she was not alone in the apartment. He only half-listened as she chatted cheerfully with some friend. Then she declared, 'I think he's kind of cute.' *Oh, so who was Valerie keen on?*

'Of course he's not right for her,' she continued. *Who was this unsuitable guy?*

'He's from the smallest town in America, apparently. That's half the reason she's fallen for him.' She paused to listen, then giggled. 'No, it's not just the sex. He's smart and she says he can be very funny too. You'd never think he was an engineer. But her mother would die a thousand deaths. And pray to God that Sarah was just slumming it for a while.'

The phone conversation helped clarify his position in Sarah's life. She was not very interested in his past because it was of no use to her in her liberation struggle with her mother. What mattered was what he stood for now. He was a symbol, a vehicle for rebellion. Slumming it indeed.

Yet the emotional distance this revealed was not in his view necessarily a bad thing, even if he concluded that his 'love life' was a far cry from the complete romance he'd had with Cassie. He was not in love with Sarah Perkins, and wasn't even sure how much of the affection he had for her was simply the desire for company. She was smart, she was direct, she was attractive, she was fun (now) in bed – and besides, the woman he loved had gone with someone else. *I've got to get on with my life*, he told himself. And when he sometimes questioned why he was seeing Sarah Perkins when he knew he didn't love her, he would conclude that she was his hope for getting over Cassie. *I can't do it on my own.* And if this were a very cynical way of proceeding, Valerie's *précis* of Sarah's motives didn't indicate any fairytale romance going on in Sarah's mental neck of the woods, either. If Sarah were serving his purposes nicely, he had little to feel guilty about, since apparently he was suiting hers.

One evening Valerie put in a rare appearance at the apartment, to announce that she had become engaged and was going to live with her fiancé in Brooklyn. Michael was depressed by the news. 'I don't want some roommate I don't know,' he said to Sarah. 'I'm not in college any more.'

'Take the whole place yourself then,' said Sarah.

'I can't afford it.' He had never seen any point pretending he had more money than he did. *Why bother?* he told himself, especially if Sarah thought she was slumming it anyway.

'I know you can't. But if we split it . . .?' She was staring at the Vermeer print in the corner as she said this, which distracted him until he suddenly realized what she was suggesting.

She moved in six weeks later; in the interim Streatley cautioned him against just such a step. 'What are you, twenty-four? You're way too young to be shacking up with somebody. Sow some oats kid, then settle down.' He laid off the topic only when it became clear Michael wasn't going to change his mind. The week before he had seen Cassie again, for the first time since he had met Sarah; she was waiting at a bus stop on 57th Street. He had almost got on the bus with her until she turned round and he was face-to-face with a woman probably thirty years older than Cassie. Fed up with the false hope these phantoms kept stirring, he decided that if anything were going to get Cassie Gilbert out of his head for good, it would be a firm commitment to life with someone else.

Sarah was too terrified to tell her parents that she was living with someone. 'What's the problem?' Streatley demanded. 'She's a grown-up. What do her parents care?'

Michael shrugged. 'Her parents are still upset that she dropped her last boyfriend. Who rejoices in the name of Oakley Hale.'

'They'll get over it,' said Streatley. 'But it's you I'm worried about. This WASP business is harder than you think.'

It never got easier. The wedding was held in the Episcopal Church of New Canaan. His father and Gary flew in two days before the wedding, staying in a Ramada Inn on the Greenwich side of town. He saw little of them since they spent the next day sightseeing in the city. At the wedding reception Gary had too much to drink and was sick in some bushes at a corner of the country club grounds; Michael's father was polite, but talked more to a distant Perkins in-law from Cincinnati than to any of the other, closer Yankee family.

Streatley was best man, and gave a long and only mildly drunken speech, contrasting the high WASP setting of the wedding with Michael's humbler origins in what Streatley repeatedly called The Great Plains. Michael laughed throughout most of it, though Sarah told him later she thought it was ungracious and, in parts, bordering on the vulgar.

They honeymooned in Bermuda, a wedding present from his in-laws. It was much farther north of the Caribbean than he'd realized and correspondingly colder, even in summer. He returned to New York with his bride, conscious that in some indiscernible way, New York was his home, and that he should now become a New Yorker – after all, Sarah's parents were in the *Social Register*.

He tried his best, but within eighteen months he realized he had made a big mistake. The biggest mistake of his life? *The biggest one since I ran away and lost Cassie.* Of Cassie he had heard nothing until, well after his own marriage, he learned from his father that she and Ronald had a little girl now, named Sally. He spoke so rarely with his father that he was surprised to hear him mention Cassie's name. *But why not*, he thought, *I'm married now. He probably thinks it doesn't hurt any more.* But it still did, and though he no longer saw her on the street, Cassie still figured in the fantasy life he found he often retreated to.

He had thought that marrying Sarah would somehow serve to bring them closer together, as if the legalization of jointly handling life's small duties and obligations – paying the rent, filing taxes, taking the garbage down the hall to the building's incinerator chute – demanded a similar sharing of emotional life. But it didn't. There were no explosive arguments, and no sudden epiphanies, just an increasing process of disenchantment (mutually suffered, he was certain) in which he and his wife slowly found themselves not so much at odds, but operating with completely divergent views of what was meant to be their joint future. The first indication of this drift had come when he decided to study at night for a graduate degree. Streatley had been emphatic about it: 'Look, whether you stay with this firm or do something else, if you really want to make it as an engineer you need at least a Masters.'

Sarah was less convinced, arguing that he should study for an MBA instead. 'You could be a senior executive in any kind of business, not just engineering,' she said, sounding excited. He took a Masters in Engineering anyway, and did it in two years, which almost killed him. Sarah complained with some justice that she never saw him, and he later calculated that in that two-year period they had gone to the movies together exactly once. He went to class three nights a week and studied on all the other nights; in his second year of study the firm allowed him half a day off each week to work on his thesis, a treatise on how iron bridges could still be constructed economically in an unfriendly world. *Imaginative and well argued*, came back the report with an 'A' grade, *but entirely impractical*.

He didn't expect Sarah to share his enthusiasm for bridges, or for engineering in general, but he thought there had been a tacit acceptance that it was what he wanted to do. Instead, he sensed increasingly that she didn't care what he did to make his living, or indeed whether he truly enjoyed it, provided he could make it in New York. And here lay the crux of the growing problems between them, as his fifth year in New York arrived and he found the early excitement he'd felt about his new life entirely gone. With his graduate degree, he had received two promotions at work, and begun to earn reasonable money – enough so that his father-in-law's generosity seemed a nice bonus, rather than a lifeline out of credit card debt. But the work he was doing – managerial, financial – was not what he'd ever envisaged for himself. He knew what he cared about, and that was bridges, and he wanted to help make them work first-hand.

He liked New York a lot for what it was, a *city*, utterly urban, of extraordinary energy and diversity. He respected its riches, and tried to take advantage of them, but deep down, compared to what really seemed to stir him, he simply did not feel passionately enough about the place to make it, in his heart, his home. Oh, it was wonderful enough that you could find seventy-three different kinds of restaurant in a ten-block radius, or that there were more art galleries per head of population than anywhere on earth, or that every conceivable kind of performing art could be found, conducted at the highest possible level. He loved the brash brightness of its inhabitants – the fact that so many people read books while they took the bus or subway to work; the way that you couldn't make assumptions about them – he'd had an ageing cab driver use the words *deracinated* and *rebarbative* in the course of a ten-block ride. He fully believed that Central Park was an unrivalled urban piece of greenery and accepted that Hester Street pro-duced the best pastrami, and that in all likelihood there were more poets in three blocks of the West Village than at the Iowa Writers' Workshop. He admired these riches, but he didn't *need* them, and he would have felt guilty that he didn't love his wife enough to stay in New York and do what he didn't want to do, had he not known that she didn't love him enough to go with him.

He did his best to be with her in spirit, nonetheless, and it should have been easy enough to make that journey, con-sidering the distance he'd come from Stillriver, his distance from his father and brother. He knew that sophistication acquired as an adult need not be skin-deep, if the acquirer's earlier skin is shed fully enough. *You can take the boy out of the small town, but you can't take the small town out of the boy.* But that wasn't always true. Time and again, he would meet people who appeared seamlessly integrated into New York life yet, when asked, would turn out to hail from Wichita, or Duluth, or Boswell, Indiana.

But increasingly he felt he was trying to become something for which he had no real aspiration. He felt this especially in the upper class milieu of his in-laws, where it was what he hadn't done and what he didn't know that created the gulf. He hadn't gone to Choate or Groton or whatever the name was of the prep school Mr Perkins had attended and always complained about; he hadn't gone to an Ivy League college or, failing that, the University of Colorado at Boulder because of its proximity to first-class skiing; he didn't make his living either on Wall Street or from designing solar heating panels for houses in Vermont; he'd never heard of paddle tennis or Plymouth Gin.

He supposed he could learn about gin and even, God forbid, take a paddle tennis lesson or two, but there seemed no point trying truly to assimilate. For there remained deep within him something of Stillriver, which he not only couldn't remove, he didn't *want* to excise either. It was something that wouldn't let him go. And there was something else that wouldn't let him go: the memory of Cassie Gilbert.

He sometimes wondered what a shrink would make of Cassie's enduring presence in his mental life, for his mother's flat statement that *calf love never lasts* had proved entirely incorrect, at least as far as he was concerned. Here he was nearing thirty and his first love from teenage years still had a hold on him of almost mesmeric power – how else to account for the weird sightings of her that had plagued him here in New York? He assumed any analyst's diagnosis (did shrinks diagnose?) would be a straightforward case of persisting immaturity: *You haven't grown up, Mr Wolf,* he could imagine them saying. Which might even be true to a certain extent, though he preferred to think that Cassie had been his second chance at Eden, after the original Fall from grace when his mother died. But where his mother was now reduced to a few images he held like slides in his head, Cassie was alive to him, Cassie kept him going, Cassie was his refuge from the life he now so much regretted.

His increasing unhappiness at work did not go unnoticed by Streatley, who bought him lunch at P.J. Clarke's one Friday, and insisted they each have cocktails, something frowned on in the office.

With the first gulp of his Martini, Streatley said, 'You're getting sucked in, you know that, don't you?'

'How's that?'

'You'll have your own office soon, then they'll make you a director. One day you might even get on the board.'

'You think that's what I want?'

Streatley drained his drink and signalled elaborately to the waitress for another. 'I don't know. But it looks like what you'll be getting.'

'And if it's not what I want, what can I do about it?'

'That's where I come in.' Streatley leaned back while the waitress put down a paper napkin and his new drink before him. 'Ah,' he said appreciatively, after his first sip. 'In theory, I remain your superior,' he said.

'That goes without saying.'

Streatley waved a hand impatiently. 'This isn't about turf. You know me better than that. The only reason I mention the fact is that I may still be in a position to help you. But not for much longer. One more promotion and you'll be beyond my helping you.' He gave a slightly tipsy chuckle. 'Beyond anyone helping you, perhaps.'

'What do you think I should do?'

'Make up your mind,' said Streatley, and his voice was suddenly sharp. 'You can be a senior executive, wield great power, make excellent money, and become what I have signally failed to become. Nothing wrong with that.'

'Or?'

'Or, you can get your ass out of the General Motors building, wear a hard hat at something other than the office Christmas party, and be an engineer. As I said,' he added wearily, 'the choice is yours. But I don't want you to end up where you don't want to be. *Unlike me.*'

'Christ,' said Michael, trying to lighten the tone, 'you sound like something out of a movie. You know, *On the Waterfront* – "I could have been a contender."'

Streatley shrugged sadly. 'Who says life can't imitate art? Now tell me when I can meet this friend of your wife's.'

At Christmas he got the usual card from Donny and Brenda and one from Nancy Sheringham, with a photo on its front, taken the summer before, of her and Lou and the three girls in front of a tractor in the orchard behind her house. On the inside of the card she wrote her usual report:

> *We're all well and hoping this year will see a Michael Wolf presence in the state of Michigan! Corn was especially good this year, and peaches too.*
>
> *Little news to report except my girls keep growing fast! Donny and Brenda are fine, and we saw Kenny Williams last summer with a new girlfriend (her dress was as high as possible – and you could almost see possible!) Had an early Xmas card from Cassie last week – her aunt (remember the one in Berkeley?) has moved to Austin, which is nice since Ronald is away working a lot. Your daddy says Gary is doing well at Lashings but says you're no better communicating with him than you are with us. Shame on you!*
>
> *But love from all of us and Merry Christmas to you and Sarah.*
>
> *Nancy*

Three weeks later a supervisor at a steel truss bridge in northern Montana broke his back when his jeep overturned on black ice. 'That's a wonderful part of the country,' said Streatley meaningfully when he told Michael what had happened. 'I need somebody to go for two months and fill in.' And then, almost as an afterthought, he said, 'There's one in Texas, too. The crew engineer's wife died and he's got to go look after his kids.'

'Texas? Why didn't you say so?' and before Streatley could ask any questions Michael nominated himself to fill in.

He got her number over the phone from Nancy Sheringham, who asked no questions. He figured it was eleven o'clock in the morning in Texas and Ronald would be at work. He dialled and hung up two times before he dialled again and forced himself to wait.

When he heard her voice say hello, he found it hard to speak. 'Cassie,' he said in a whisper.

There was a long pause. Then she whispered back. 'Michael. Oh my God. Michael, is that you?'

3

HE WAS THREE weeks into a major job in the Hill Country, and instead of spending the first long weekend home in New York made an excuse to Sarah and went to Austin, where Cassie had arranged to visit her Aunt Judy, the ex-hippy who had moved from Berkeley.

He usually stayed in inexpensive chains – Best Western, Motel Six – but now splurged out on a long, light room in the Pedernales Hotel. It was big enough to have a sofa and two armchairs grouped around a table at the courtyard end. Two French doors opened out onto a small balcony overlooking a courtyard filled with potted trees and climbing plants and wood pigeons cooing in its high corners. He drew the curtains and tidied up the room. From the minibar's fridge, he took out two wine glasses and a bottle of California Sauvignon he'd bought that afternoon near the university's campus. When he heard the light tap on the door he didn't have any idea what to expect.

It was the same Cassie, though of course it wasn't – she had grown up like he had, and was entirely a woman now, no longer a girl on the cusp of adulthood. Yet her hair was still shoulder-length, with the same bangs in front framing her clear, ever-so-slightly long face, which was smiling at him a little nervously.

'Come in,' he said, trying to sound relaxed, standing aside and watching as she walked in. She was wearing cream linen trousers with a cherry-coloured top. On her ring finger she wore a thin gold band. *What did I expect?* Nothing this stylish and smart; he'd hoped she'd come in threadbare clothes, looking pinched and exhausted, impressed by the hotel.

They sat down and he gave her a glass of wine, while they made halting small talk. She showed him pictures of the house in Bryan, a long bungalow of white aluminium siding, with a catalpa tree in the front yard; the whole place looked hot. And pictures of her daughter Sally, in diapers, a little blonde girl crawling in a sandpit. There were no photographs of Ronald.

They talked for an hour, or rather he listened as she talked, first about her courses – she was excited to be studying again, happy at last to be getting the education she had always planned for – but then mainly about Stillriver. Out of touch, he learned how many acres Nancy Sheringham was now farming, that Mr Wagner, the twins' father, had cancer, that Donny was working for the county on road crews, and that Anthea Heaton had married a flashy guy in sales and moved to Florida. She talked endlessly, it seemed to him, and innocently, steering so far clear of any emotionally-charged topic – from the worst of them (Ronald) to the mildest (his father) – that he felt like a man brought to a feast, who's only allowed to drink water.

She's going to go soon, he thought, *and we haven't talked about anything.* He knew that he could leave things as they were, try and accept that people change, their lives diverging like the roads in the Frost poem he had liked so much in high school. But what struck him was that Cassie's personality didn't really seem to have altered. Yet if she were the same, were her *emotions* the same, too? Was her friendly but thin and distant conversation now the true extent of what she wished to say? Maybe she wasn't holding anything back, because she no longer had feelings for him that she needed to repress. At the thought of this his spirits sank, and he sat, feeling fatalistically passive, waiting for her to announce her departure. She put both hands in her lap and tipped her head down, so he had trouble at first making out what she said. 'Sorry?' he said.

'I said,' she declared loudly, lifting up her head, 'do you want me to go now?'

'No. Of course not.'

'Well, conversation's getting a little stale, don't you think? "And how is Johnny Ferguson, seen much of him? And whatever happened to Missy Carpenter, is she still in Michigan?"' This was more like it, that slightly sassy sense of humour, which had always kept her good nature from becoming saccharine. 'Aren't you even going to ask me how I *really* am?'

314

'I don't know what you mean,' he said, not allowing himself to hope.

'Can't you even pretend to care? Does knowing me back then count for nothing at all now?' She had drunk two glasses of wine.

'Oh, Cassie,' he said, with a sense of despair that he would not be able to make himself understood. 'Of course I care. It's all I care about. Why do you think I'm here?'

'I don't know why you're here.'

'Well, I don't know why you're here either,' he said like a schoolboy, and when she stuck her tongue out at him they both laughed. He said, 'You know, I was hoping you'd come here tonight looking terrible and tell me how miserable you are. But instead you waltz in wearing fancy clothes and looking like a million dollars.'

'Don't tell me about fancy – how do you think I feel in this hotel? I couldn't afford a cup of coffee downstairs from the looks of it. And these,' she said, pointing to her trousers, 'these aren't even mine. I borrowed them out of my cousin's closet. My aunt didn't mind; she knew I didn't have anything to wear.'

'Well, I don't usually stay in places like this. I'm more a motel man myself.'

'You're just saying that. You're from New York, you must be used to the high life.' There was a slight challenge to her voice. 'You like the glitz, don't you?'

'*What* glitz? I live in a two-bedroom apartment on the eighteenth floor of an ugly building in an ugly block. I go to work on a hot, overcrowded subway and spend all day high up in a bland tower doing work that could be done anywhere – anywhere pleasant, I mean, with grass and trees and nice people. Except the owner thinks New York is the hub of the world.'

'Well, isn't it?'

'It is for an awful lot of people, or they wouldn't have gone there in the first place. I thought it would become that way for me, but somehow it's passed me by. What about you?' He looked at her. 'Do you like Texas?'

315

'I'd rather be in Stillriver. That's the difference between us. You might not like New York but you wouldn't want to be in Stillriver.'

'Oh, I don't know.'

'Don't pretend you miss the place.'

'I don't any more.'

'What, you don't pretend, or you don't miss the place?'

He laughed, then said quietly, 'What I miss isn't there any more.' He looked at her intently and she started to blush. He got up from his chair and stood in front of her. He leaned down and she looked at him with what seemed a tentative eagerness. He put his face an inch away from hers. 'Let's say hello again. Then we can really talk.'

And he kissed her softly on the lips, and she kissed him back, putting her hands behind his neck to hold his mouth in place. Breaking away, her mouth broke into a sly grin. 'Listen, before we talk about *anything*, there's one thing I need to know.'

'Yes?' What was she going to ask – about Sarah, or something about Ronald? He felt curiosity and dread at the same time.

'Can you afford some room service? I didn't eat any dinner – I was too nervous about seeing you. And right now I could eat a horse.'

And then she told him how, when she had first known her father was beginning to die, she took comfort from Michael and the prospect of joining him in Ann Arbor, the prospect of a new life. She may have seemed happy in Stillriver to Michael, but she was as intent as he was on finding this new life. Therefore when Michael had taken his 'sabbatical' from the relationship she had been terribly upset, made worse when gossip got back to her about another girl after Donny's visit to Ann Arbor. Yet when Michael came and asked her forgiveness, she had been so relieved to have him back that she had given it completely, so frightened was she by the prospect of losing both her father and him.

As for Ronald, he had been constantly, almost dutifully

helpful. He had never pushed, but would show up unobtru-
sively, like a faithful retainer, seemingly when needed most –
once he had carried the parson to bed when he had collapsed in
the hallway. He'd been soft-spoken, gentle – there was never
any hint of all the things that gave him such an awful
reputation. He understood that people didn't trust him, and
accepted that he was not the kind of fellow people would find
suitable for the daughter of a clergyman. But he seemed
genuinely remorseful about what he called his 'hell-raising'
days, and equally keen to demonstrate that he wanted to better
himself: go back to high school, even attend college ('if any
college would have me,' he'd say with a self-deprecating grin).

Ronald had been there for Cassie, which if Michael had been
there as well would not have mattered so much – Ronald might
have wanted more, but he would have remained only a friend.
But in the emotional wake of her father's death, when the
strength she had shown for so long looking after the parson was
no longer needed and indeed had seemed to desert her anyway,
she was suddenly vulnerable to anyone who offered to look
after her. And where was Michael? *Where had he gone?* His
father didn't know, his roommates in Ann Arbor wouldn't tell;
it was a complete mystery. She only knew he wasn't there for
her, and he couldn't even be bothered to tell her why. In those
weeks she *hated* him.

And this seemed to have made her think that in time she
could love Ronald. She tried to explain to Michael how
different a person he was in her presence, how like a lost little
boy he could become. And yes, there was some physical
attraction on her part – there was no point denying it – for he
was strong, with a man's body well beyond the boyish stage of
adolescence. But actually when she first started seeing him
seriously (which Michael took to mean when she first started
sleeping with him), it was more out of her fearfulness at being
alone in the world, and out of anger at Michael for deserting
her.

Here Michael interrupted for the first time. He had watched
as Cassie ate ravenously, a cheeseburger with fries and a side

salad, a dinner roll, even an ice-cream sundae, enjoying herself with the mixture of gusto and grace he remembered, licking her fingers and laughing when she spilled a drop of ketchup on her blouse. Now they lay side by side on their backs on the bed.

'Why did you go to Texas?' he asked. 'He could have worked in Michigan, worked with his father again if he'd wanted to.'

'I think he felt he'd do better down here. In Texas he hadn't been in trouble, not yet. And I was desperate to get away. Right then Stillriver to me meant my father and, I guess, it meant you. I didn't think I was going away for ever, just for a while, until the hurt stopped being so bad.'

'But then why did you *marry* him? It was all so quick.'

She looked at him calmly. 'Because I was pregnant. Call me old-fashioned, but I didn't want to have an illegitimate child.'

He was dumbstruck. 'But what child?' Mentally he counted years. 'Sally's not old enough.'

'I miscarried just before Thanksgiving that same autumn. Nobody knew I was pregnant, except Nancy. I know she never told a soul. Thank God my father wasn't alive to hear about it.'

'Golly,' he exclaimed with genuine wonder, for a question had been answered which he had carried around for years – since the day, in fact, when he had returned to Stillriver at the end of that summer and learned as he sat on the patio next to his father that not only had Cassie gone away, not only had she gone away with Ronald Duverson, but she had *married* him. Now he understood why, and he could respect it. She had married disastrously in Michael's view, but for the right reason. But then (the cruellest twist of all) she had lost the reason. *Jesus*.

Life in Galveston was fine at first. Well, tolerable at any rate. Ronald worked in the same dock-building business as before; having said he'd finish high school, he didn't even try. But he didn't interfere when Cassie enrolled in the local junior college, especially since she could pay her own tuition (as well as contribute to the household bills) from the money she got renting her father's house. Ronald was still nice to her, and she no longer felt quite so adrift, for she now had a goal: she wanted to teach school. Not that life was perfect: 'You see,' she said and hesitated, 'I missed you. I still hated you, of course,' she added with a quick smile, 'but I missed you too.'

'What did you miss?'

She thought for a moment. 'I could always be myself with you. You never seemed to want me to be anything but what I was.'

'And Ronald did?'

'Yes, he did. He had some idea of me that wasn't me, if you know what I mean. It was so intense.'

'What, did he put you on some kind of pedestal?'

She nodded. 'He thought I was a lot more special than I was. He seemed to think I should be what *he* thought I was, not what *I* knew I was. He had a clear idea of what I should and shouldn't do; he still does, actually. He doesn't like me to drink, not even wine – he thinks it's unladylike (he can drink of course, because he's a man). If I wear a shirt and jeans – you know, like I always dressed – he gets upset. He thinks I should always wear a skirt and blouse.'

Then, over two years since moving to Texas, she got pregnant again. And Ronald changed. She felt sick, really nauseated, almost all the time; there seemed almost nothing she could get done, not even the simplest chores around the house. Yet just as she needed him most, Ronald started staying out – working late, he claimed, but as far as she could tell, spending hours in the bars. He wouldn't come back drunk, so she wondered if maybe he was seeing other women. But then she realized the answer was simpler than that. He had started fighting again. One day he had come home with a cut above his eye, and a big yellowing bruise along the side of his ribcage. He claimed he'd had an accident stringing anti-erosion net in the Gulf, but his explanation was so unnecessarily involved that she didn't believe a word of it. Then he spent a night in jail after hitting somebody in a cowboy bar and Cassie, worried sick when he hadn't come home, had to bail him out in the morning. Fortunately the guy he'd hit hadn't pressed charges, or she'd have been really stuck – she was six months pregnant at the time.

'What made him start fighting again?' asked Michael.

She shrugged. 'For a while I thought it was me. Funny how you can blame yourself for almost anything if you set your mind to it. We'd had a scan and knew I was going to have a girl. Ronald was incredibly disappointed.'

'That's terrible,' said Michael. 'If you're not going to be happy with either sex you shouldn't have kids at all.'

'Of course not,' said Cassie, 'but I thought it had just been standard men's talk – you know, *I'll teach him to play football and show him how to shoot a gun.* That sort of bullshit, if you will excuse my eloquence. I never dreamed he'd actually *resent* a girl. I couldn't understand it – I still don't. But you asked me why he started fighting again, and part of me thinks it's because he just can't help himself. You see, the odd thing is I've always believed that Ronald actually *hates* men. These days everyone talks about men who hate women, or men who love women, or even men who love men. But they forget that some men hate other men. And Ronald's one of them.'

'What caused that?'

She hunched her shoulders in a shrug. 'I know his father beat him something terrible when he was little. Never Mex, just Ronald. I guess he thought Ronald could take it. And he could, I guess, though I think it damaged him a lot. But who knows?' she said impatiently. 'I've never thought upbringing explains everything.'

Ronald lost his job in her third trimester, claiming his boss had been cheating him on his pay, though she heard from a girlfriend that in fact they'd had a fight and that, again, Ronald had been lucky to have charges dropped. He found work through a friend, but it was in Bryan, several hundred miles north, and she was in no shape to supervise a move or move herself. So he commuted at weekends until after she'd had Sally; when they joined him in Bryan, they lived in a small tract house on the town outskirts, not even near the university, a bleak place neither desert nor swamp nor Hill Country.

And since then life had been absolute hell.

'Is he violent to you?'

'No. I wish he was, because then I'd have left him.'

'What is it then?'

'He doesn't really care about me; he only cares about some idea of me. He'll go whole days without talking to me, and as far as Sally goes, he hardly ever takes any interest at all. I mean virtually none.'

'Has Ronald got somebody else?'

'I don't think so. Yet he's obsessed that I might. Considering how little interest he takes, you'd think he wouldn't care, but the opposite's the case. It's so bad I've learned not even to smile at a man or say hello in case Ronald flares up. Once he thought the boy loading my car with groceries at the supermarket was being fresh – the kid couldn't have been more than fourteen years old – and he grabbed him so hard I thought for sure he'd break his arm.'

'So why don't you leave him?'

She said nothing, and Michael propped himself on one arm and leaned over and kissed her. She responded gently with her lips, and he kissed her again until she opened her mouth and kissed him back more passionately. Slowly he moved an arm behind her neck as he continued kissing her and lay his other hand firmly on her belt, then moved it lower against her mound. She stirred at first, then reached down and moved his hand away. She broke off their kiss and said, 'Don't maul me, please, Michael. You know we can't.'

'Why not?' he whispered, as if afraid to express himself too clearly.

'It's all different now,' she said.

He sighed. 'Of course it is. For both of us. It's bound to be.'

'You act like that doesn't matter. Like we were back in high school all over again.'

'I don't want to make love to a memory,' he said. 'I want to make love to you.'

She sat up on the bed and began putting her sandals on. 'I have to go now.'

He didn't say anything. She turned her head and looked at him but he looked away. 'Don't be like that,' she said.

'I'm not sulking,' he said. 'I'm just scared I've spoilt everything.'

'You couldn't have done that if you tried. You haven't changed that much.' She reached for her handbag and slung it over her shoulder. 'What should we do tomorrow?'

Tomorrow? He cheered up at once. 'We could go swimming out at Barton Springs. It's beautiful.'

'I'll pick you up,' she said. 'I may bring Sally. It depends on what Aunt Judy's up to. Babysitting a two-year-old's not every-body's cup of tea.'

'That's fine,' he said, closing his eyes with the happiness of the prospect. When he opened them again he found Cassie's face leaning down over his. She kissed him lightly, then with sudden ardour until he started to reach for her.

'That's enough for now,' she said with a small laugh, pushing his outstretched arm away. 'I'll see you tomorrow. Sweet dreams.'

The next day they drove to Barton Springs but didn't swim, standing instead barefoot in the shallowest part of the springs. They watched as some local teenagers went in, horsing around with an exuberance that made Michael feel older than he was. And it was with a sense of many years having passed that he stood with Cassie in the limestone springs, and told her what had happened to him since that memorable early evening when he'd heard a truck door slam, looked up from his paper, and saw Ronald run across the yard straight at him.

He took his time, working backwards from his current situation. He told her about his work, how he had managed to extricate himself from office 'success' before it had destroyed his love for engineering altogether. And he told her about Sarah, and how through no fault on either side, they had grown apart. *'Grown* apart?' he queried aloud. 'Hell, we were never close to begin with. That was our mistake.'

'So why did *you* get married?'

'Not because she was pregnant, that's for sure. I don't think she really wants children – it would be better if she'd just say it, instead of always finding reasons to delay. I don't want to raise kids in Manhattan anyway, and she won't hear of living anywhere else.'

'You still haven't answered my question. Some things don't change.'

'Sorry,' and he took a deep breath. 'I suppose I married her because I thought I would get a new life that way, one that would let me get over you. But it didn't work.'

She reached over and took his hand. 'It didn't for me, either.'

Which brought him at last to Ronald and the truth about what had happened. He had been steeling himself to tell her, for it still seemed to him a tale of cowardice and fear, one that never failed to fill him with self-loathing. But he omitted nothing from his account of Ronald's assault and his flight from town, and when he finished she was staring at him, part in wonder, part compassion.

'But why didn't you tell me? Did you think I'd be ashamed of you? Did you think it was like cavemen fighting over a girl, that I'd want to go with whoever won? Did you think I'd believe you were less of a man because Ronald could beat you up?'

He shrugged. 'Maybe a little bit.'

'But you weren't brought up that way. You weren't a Bogle boy, after all. Your father was a gentle man.'

'But a strong man, too. Nobody messed with him.'

'You sound like a school kid. Did you really think that would matter to me? How could you think that?'

'Actually, I didn't really think that of you, Cassie. It was even worse, if you have to know. I wasn't thinking of you at all, I was thinking of me. It's like something snapped inside me. I felt I had to run away or I'd go mad from the fear of it all. That, and the humiliation.'

'What humiliation? Ronald's a violent man. You're not.'

'I can't explain it – it was so many different things. There was the fear, like the fear I had after my mother died, only worse. And then the place, the town, it seemed so wrapped up with what had happened to me that I couldn't bear to stay. And what would have kept Ronald from doing it again? Every day if he'd wanted to; I couldn't have stopped him.'

'You should have gone to the police. Stillriver's not exactly the Wild West. Jerry Dawson would have done something.'

'That's what Pop told me to do. But then everybody would have known. I know it was just pride, but I couldn't bear the thought of that, not when the whole town knew me from the drugstore. It was already bad enough that my father had witnessed it.'

'Why?'

'You know we were never close – after my mother died he wasn't any help to me at all. I learned not to need him – and then he goes and saves my life.'

'He's your father. He would have wanted to save you.'

'I couldn't bear the thought of owing him anything.'

Cassie still looked confounded. 'That's just nuts.'

He looked quickly at her, then away. 'I probably *was* nuts for a while, Cassie. That's what I'm trying to tell you. And by the time I'd got sane again, and come back, you'd gone. I waited too long because I was too scared, and off my head, and then it was too late.'

She nodded as if she understood. But then she said, 'Some day you're going to have to forgive him, you know.'

'Who? Ronald?' he demanded.

'No, dummy,' she said, and touched his arm with a soft, flat hand. 'Your father.'

'Forgive him for what?'

'For always trying to help you. Because if you don't forgive your father while he's still alive, you'll never forgive yourself.'

The job in Texas lasted four months, and although he had told Sarah he would be back half a dozen times during the duration of the project, he managed only two visits to New York. He saw Cassie six times instead, all of them in Austin except for one brief lunch outside Bryan, where they propped Sally in her stroller with a bottle of milk and a cookie while they ate barbecued ribs on the back deck of a roadhouse. The little girl was beginning to talk, and he could only pray that she wouldn't mention his name in front of Ronald, who had seemed satisfied, according to Cassie, with her explanation that the requirements of her teaching certificate course included several weekend seminars at the University of Texas in Austin.

They never had much time together, so they didn't go to the movies or attend concerts, or do much of anything that might get in the way of talking to each other in a mutual pact to fill in the gaps inevitably created by eight years' separation, learning more about what had happened to each of them in that time, and through an unspoken agreement trying to discover how far apart they might have grown. They walked, usually around the Texas campus, or sat in restaurants and coffee shops, often leaving their meals largely uneaten for talking so intently. She always seemed to have a book on the go, in addition to the heavy reading load she had for her education classes – after stopping when she had Sally, she now was studying to be a teacher.

'What do you want to teach?' asked Michael. Would it be English, or Social Studies or, God forbid, religious studies?

'I want to teach little ones,' she said. 'First grade, second grade; that kind of age. That's what I'd be best at, I think.'

And he realized that, focused as he was on degrees and qualifications, he'd assumed she'd want to teach high school or even junior college. He was learning how little he knew about children and was astonished by her patience with Sally, who was tricky – strong-willed and precociously defiant. He liked how Cassie handled her; she managed to convey an unconditional love with a firmness that kept Sally from exploiting that love.

Sensing his new excitement at finally getting out of the office, Cassie asked him all about his work, and one Sunday he drove her out from Austin into the Hill Country, where he had planned to show her one or two of the bridge sites. But she insisted on seeing all five of them, peppering him with questions about pre-stressed concrete, about the difference between tension and compression, and about that first abiding question that had drawn him to engineering: *How does it manage to stay up*? At one site, she'd looked puzzled and, when he asked why, she'd pointed to the large concrete Butler's Tray they were erecting and the small stream it spanned – one of the lesser tributaries of the Pedernales. 'Why so much bridge for so little water?' she'd asked.

And he'd explained it was flood country, where water would course through the low swales and gulleys at almost unbelievable speed. 'In the last flood,' he added, 'that little crick gained five feet in height and spread three times its width in just eight hours.'

'*Crick?*' she said mockingly. 'Bet they don't use that word in New York.'

He smiled but went on, gripped by the image of what the bridge had to be prepared for. 'Someone at work saw the same thing wipe out a bridge in Alaska. That was glacier, what they call a GLOF, but the effect's the same: the power of the water is incredible, it just scours all the retaining sides and sweeps it right away. And then you get translatory waves.'

'What are they?'

'The speed of the flow gets so great that it *translates* into a wave it makes itself. It's like a mini tidal wave.' He suddenly remembered Streatley, standing at the bar of a saloon near Grand Central, describing one he'd seen in Colorado: 'There'd been fourteen inches of rain in three days and I was standing on the riverbank, watching the water race by, when some old boy from the crew showed up and shouted at me to get my ass out of there. I couldn't see what the problem was but I figured I'd humour him so I retreated to higher ground. Five minutes later this enormous wave about five feet high shoots by, covering the entire river and all of the bank where I'd been standing. If I hadn't moved I'd be swimming still – or more likely, not swimming, if you catch my "drift". So after that I was happy to let that old boy tell me what to do.'

Cassie was looking at him curiously. 'Have you ever seen one?' she asked.

He shook his head. 'You have to remember where I've been

326

working. They don't have many translatory waves in midtown Manhattan.'

She would not sleep with him, which frustrated Michael in a physical sense, but did not otherwise worry him. For it gave a weight to what they were doing – no one could call their relationship an adulterous affair when adultery was not part of the equation – which sleeping together might have undermined. That, at any rate, is what he told himself, hoping it didn't mean that she cared less than he did. And then at the end of their fifth assignation, as they kissed each other goodbye outside her aunt's house, Cassie lingered longer than usual.

'What is it?' he asked, worried something was wrong.

'I just wish I was seeing you tomorrow. And the next day. And the day after that. I miss you all week long.'

'So what do you want to do about that?' he asked, trying to sound calmer than he felt.

'What do you think?' she bandied back.

'I asked first,' he said with a brittle laugh.

'I want to do what you want to do,' she said, and before he could protest that she was ducking his question again she added meaningfully, 'that is, if you want to do it.'

He looked at her, still hesitant to make the first real declaration. Cassie said, 'You're making me shy. I wish you'd say something.'

He thought of New York just then, of the apartment he had come to loathe, of the office and its claustrophobic effect on him. An image of Sarah came into his head, neat in weekend clothes of pink Lacoste shirt and a khaki skirt with a trendy belt, standing on the deck of her parents' summer house in Cape Cod. He didn't feel any anger or resentment towards his wife, but he didn't feel any warmth either. All along, there had been a certain coldness between them, one which may have suited their purposes in the past but did no longer. As he looked at the warm, talkative and *confiding* woman before him, he could not imagine being able to live that New York life again.

A worried look was beginning to emerge in Cassie's eyes, and her teeth were clenching her lower lip as she watched him thinking. He mimicked her, chomping down on his own lower lip, and they both laughed as he put his arms out and held her by her shoulders. 'I want to do it,' he said in a light whisper.

And her eyes widened, and grew slightly teary as she nodded and said, 'I do too.'

Slowly they began to plan – how he would separate from Sarah, she from Ronald, and then live together. His assumption was that he would continue to be outsourced by Streatley, and in the first instance Cassie and Sally would join him in accommodation near his project, possibly in western Montana, if Streatley could fix things, until he found a settled job some place they both wanted to live.

As the job outside Austin neared completion, he found Cassie increasingly tense, at first, he thought, because she was half-afraid he might disappear again. But then he realized it was another kind of anxiety altogether, and he could only conclude that she was nervous about the next step – the one each would have to take on his or her own – of telling Ronald she was leaving him.

On their last night together, a warm spring night in May, he booked the same room in the Pedernales Hotel, and they had steaks and salad from room service, and most of two bottles of California Cabernet. She had been working her aunt's vegetable patch, and wore blue shorts and a simple white blouse that showed off her new tan. She'd bought a mobile phone, and they arranged when he would call her next from New York, and discussed how best to have her join him in six weeks' time in Montana.

After dinner he turned the radio on low to a classical station, and as he lay down on the bed she kicked her sandals off and sat down beside him, slowly rubbing his back. He thought fleetingly of Sophie Jansen, but then sat up and leaned over towards Cassie. He kissed her softly, and was surprised at how readily she opened her mouth, sliding her tongue forward, slithering in against his. This time, when he drew her down onto the bed, she didn't resist, and they lay sidewise, arms around each other. They kissed, and he turned her so she lay on her back, while he leaned over her. He kept kissing her but slowly moved his hand down to her shorts, working her zipper down, then unbuttoning them until he could move his hand in and lay it gently on the soft bulge of her panties.

Her breath quickened, and she drew her mouth away. 'We shouldn't,' she said, but then let him kiss her some more as he rubbed his hand slowly against her. When he drew her panties down with his thumb, she stirred, and made to draw her mouth away from his again, but didn't. Reaching down he found her slick with wetness, and he moved his index finger until he found the small wet button of her and gently stroked it. She brought her own hand down and lightly grabbed him through his trousers, then closed her eyes as he took his own hand away and slowly pushed her shorts and underwear down to her knees, then began to unbutton her blouse.

As she unzipped him he stopped kissing her for a moment, and took his shirt off, then pulled her clothes down from her knees over her bare feet, pushing them off the bed onto the floor.

Cassie put a wrist over her eyes. 'If you think I'm going to say no now, don't worry, I'm not.' He smiled as she opened her eyes, looking at him seriously. He stared back as he finished unbuttoning her blouse, then, as Cassie sat up and took it off, he reached over for the half-full wine glass on the bedside table. He offered the glass to her but she shook her head and he drained it instead.

He felt distinctly high from the wine now, and dizzy when he stood up and pulled back the bedclothes on his side. Cassie matched him, and they met naked under the covers in the middle. She took the lead now, kissing him firmly and insistently, touching him with her hand while he licked her breast. Then she moved her mouth away, put her head down on the pillow, and looking away from him she said quietly, 'I never did stop loving you.'

Emotion seemed to sweep over him like a wave swamping a still pool. It was so powerful a feeling that he felt his sexual excitement diminish, then go away altogether, and he went completely limp in Cassie's hand.

There was nothing he could do to revive it. Cassie tried, with her hands first, then, mounting him, with the wetness between her legs. She kissed him as she tried, and stroked him, but the harder she tried the less he felt close even to a half-mast state of arousal, and as his own frustration grew and he felt the wine's effect inducing a torpor, he grew further away from being able to make love to her.

Cassie laughed, making light of it, but he felt ashamed, and kept apologizing, despite her saying that it didn't matter. He drank another glass of wine as they talked some more and then tried, fruitlessly, again, and he found himself lying on his stomach babbling gently, *I'm so sorry, Cassie. I'm so sorry*, and she was saying, *Sh-sh-sh,* and stroking his arm as he fell asleep.

And when he woke with the covers off in the middle of the night, the room pitch black and quiet except for the low hum of the air conditioning, he found himself feeling cool and alert and almost brutally, rod-like erect. But when he reached for Cassie he found her pillow empty. *Why did she go?* he thought, and then he felt her hair brush lightly against his stomach and suddenly felt himself taken there, barely lipped as he was drawn into her mouth and the soft flickering of her tongue.

He reached to bring her up to him but she pushed his arms back and moved her head up and down, gently tonguing him and holding him with her hand at his base, which was wet and slick with her saliva, and as she kept up the gentle, insistent movement of her tongue he suddenly surged and came, then stopped moving altogether and stretched his limbs out, completely spent.

She got up and went to the bathroom, closing the door behind her before turning on the light, which showed in a pencil line of yellow underneath the door. When she came out again into the dark room, he listened as she began to put her clothes on.

'Cassie?'

'You go to sleep,' she said in a whisper, and he heard her step into her shorts and button her blouse, then snap her sandals on standing up.

'But Cassie—' he began.

'I have to go,' she said, and sat down in the dark beside him, stroking his hair with a hand he could not see. 'I can't show up at Aunt Judy's at breakfast time.'

'I'll call you about Montana,' he said, feeling drowsiness set in again.

'I know,' she said quietly. 'You sleep now.'

'I love you, Cassie.'

'And I love you, Michael. More than the moon and the stars.'

The letter arrived at work and caught him completely by surprise, five minutes before he was due to sit down with Streatley and find out when he was going to Montana. Sarah didn't know he would be away again, but he felt no dread about the prospect of telling her, since she had not seemed especially pleased to see him when he'd flown back from Austin ten days before. She was engrossed with her work, staying late at the office on several nights to work on a new account who, she said, was proving difficult to please. At the weekend they had seen a movie and had dinner with Oakley Hale and his latest girlfriend, then gone home, where they'd got in bed with the TV on and made love, without much passion on either side, he felt, but without any repeat of his difficulties with Cassie.

He had called Cassie as arranged on her mobile, but the first time she couldn't talk because Sally was crying, and the next few times he tried her mobile was switched off. He had planned to call her that very morning, but then he saw the familiar handwriting on the letter.

Dear Michael,

You need to know that I will not be coming to Montana. Don't even think that it's because I don't want to – it's because I can't. And I can't see you any more.

I wasn't sure that night in Austin, but I am now. I'm

pregnant again. I can't explain it to you except to say I did not have a choice.

Yes, I have thought about a termination, but I can't bring myself to do it – it's always seemed like murder to me. And it would only be for my sake and not the child's. That would ruin us in time.

This is the hardest letter I have ever had to write. I seem to cause nothing but hurt to you and I can only say how much I am hurting too. Please believe me when I say I love you, and I always will. And for ever know that's true.

Cassie

At first he could not believe it. When he had lost her before there had been at least the promise of a new world in New York. It was a false promise and life had for so long seemed to be closing in around him in a suffocating, numbing cloud, until he had found Cassie again, found fresh air and seen light, out there and available. And now he feared that the hope that had returned to him was extinguished.

She would not answer the phone – not her mobile, not the home line he tried during the day. Once, in desperation, he even phoned in the evening, but when the gruff voice of Ronald came down the line, he hung up. He tried calling her from work, and secretly from the apartment. He could not concentrate on anything except trying to reach Cassie to find out what had happened.

For her explanation was so simple that he could not accept it. *Why can't she get rid of it?* he asked himself at first, but gradually saw that she would never do that – not out of any theological conviction, or any Right to Life fervour, but simply because that was the gentle way she was.

But then he thought, *So what if she's pregnant? I don't care. She can leave him just the same. I'll raise his children. The parson managed to die,* he thought, *couldn't Ronald extend me the same courtesy?* He could not understand how Cassie could stay with Ronald, not if she loved Michael as she said she did. Had Michael done something wrong? Why had he failed to make love to her? Had he put her off through his impotence? Even in his anguish he could see the ridiculousness of his frantic search for explanation, and soon his complete bafflement turned to anger. *Cassie has nothing to feel guilty about towards Ronald. She should feel guilty about me. She's left me in the lurch.* Lurch? He felt he was on the edge of an abyss.

Why had she slept with Ronald? Why hadn't she been more careful? What did she mean, *I did not have a choice?* He had a thousand other questions, too, and the more he obsessed the more he spun a fantastic web of invented situations, betrayals, downright lies. Nothing would blow away this web except talking with her. And she wouldn't answer the phone.

He went so far as to contemplate flying to Texas to confront her, and he might have, had he not had to go to Michigan, to a wedding in Charlevoix of a girlfriend of Sarah. The woman was marrying the son of wealthy people who summered in northern Michigan, so he and Sarah had long before decided to spend a night first in Stillriver, where Michael had not been since before his own marriage, and where Sarah had never been at all.

It was not a happy visit. Sarah seemed inclined to find fault from their arrival; she saw nothing in the town she liked, or when she did, it was compared disadvantageously to what she'd seen before back east – the beach had fairly nice sand, *almost like Cape Cod;* Main Street seemed a little drab; there was a sail boat in the marina *almost like the ketch we saw last summer in Maine.*

Even his father's house, with its high gable and looming wooden beauty, was spoiled for Sarah by the smallness of its lot. *This isn't New Canaan*, he wanted to say, where a citizen's standing seemed measurable by the square footage of his lawn, but when he tried to explain to Sarah how the town had been built – how important neighbours had been; how unnecessary a big yard was when just outside the town limits the wilderness began and there was all the space you'd ever need or want – he could see she had switched off.

Gary, long out of high school and working for a fruit

middleman, had lasted ten minutes in Sarah's sports-clothed presence, then made his excuses and gone out for the evening. His father had been polite, and made them dinner, but conversation was awkward and after some wine Sarah seemed bored. 'It's a very pretty town,' she declared, 'but *very* white.' They were all three sitting outside on the patio with their coffee after dinner.

Henry shrugged his shoulders. 'There was a black family.'

'*Was?*' she said teasingly.

Henry smiled. 'They died,' he said, and she laughed. 'There used to be Indians, but they haven't lived here for a hundred years – they were driven into the Back Country, but have pretty much died out. There are a lot of Hispanics. It used to be entirely migrant; they'd pick asparagus in spring, go work in the west for summer, then come back for apples in fall. Now a lot of them live here year-round. Why do you ask?' he said to Sarah, though in fact there hadn't been a question.

'I was just curious,' she said brightly, and when they finished their coffee they all went to bed early.

His father hadn't put them in the master bedroom, saying a little gruffly, 'I thought you might prefer your old room,' where he and Gary had put another twin bed in for their stay. Michael was relieved not to sleep in what had been his parents' room.

Sarah slept badly, and complained early in the morning about the noise – true enough, the Bogle boys had partied until late at night, as if in her honour, then left for work at dawn with a poor man's symphony of slammed car doors and noisy exhausts. After breakfast his father drove her out to Sheringham's to buy corn – Michael begged off, since the last person he wanted to see in the presence of his wife was Cassie's best friend, Nancy Sheringham.

When they came back Sarah asked to walk around town, and they set off down Calvin Street, heading towards Main Street and the Dairy Queen. Two blocks on, Sarah stopped at the corner and pointed. 'Is that the church you went to down there?' He nodded. 'Let's go by it,' she said, and he could think of no plausible reason to say no.

They walked slowly down Henniker Street, as a breeze gently stirred the maple leaves of the dense network of branches that formed a canopy over the street. 'You're quiet today,' said Sarah. 'In fact you've been quiet the whole trip.'

'It feels funny being back,' he said.

'Memories. Always tricky,' she said quietly. 'What was the name of that girl you used to go out with here?'

'Cassie,' he said, feeling the blood rise in his face. Sarah was watching him carefully, which made his blushing worse. 'Cassie Gilbert.'

'Did she live in town?'

He stopped in the street, midway between the church and the parson's house. 'She lived right there,' he said, and turned and looked at Cassie's old house. It had been freshly painted, and green shutters had been added to the downstairs windows. In the sunlight, it looked trim and picture-perfect.

'You never told me she lived in Texas.'

'You didn't ask,' he said, wondering how she knew this. Maybe Nancy Sheringham told her just now. No, she wouldn't have betrayed him, however indirectly, not after giving him Cassie's phone number in Texas so many months before. Maybe it had been his father. But why would he have mentioned Cassie?

She took a deep breath. 'Did you see her in Texas, then?'

'Sure. Why not? She's married.'

'So are you for what that's worth. You know, sometimes I've wondered whether you aren't still in love with her.'

'Have you now?' he said, keeping his eyes on the street.

'Are you?'

He looked across at the Episcopal Church. 'I suppose I am a little.'

'Did you sleep with her in Texas?'

'No,' he said glumly.

'No?' she asked incredulously. 'I'm supposed to believe that. Why on earth didn't you?'

He felt stung by the superior look on her face. On this one occasion, when he wished they could draw close to each other, his wife seemed a million miles away. Conscious that his words might bring about the end of his marriage, he said, 'Because I couldn't.'

To his surprise she gave a cheerful burst of laughter. 'At least you're honest,' she said. 'I can't say the same myself.'

'What do you mean?' he said, and found her looking at him knowingly, almost provocatively. 'Are you having a thing with somebody?'

She smiled, and it was a proud smile, of a lover perfectly happy to be discovered, such was her satisfaction in her illicit alliance. 'I don't know if you'd call it a thing,' she said carefully, and turned away sideways from him.

'What should I call it then?' he asked. Her coyness was infuriating. He grabbed her by the near shoulder. 'Goddamnit, answer me.'

'Why should I?' she said angrily, and wrenched away from him. 'You've already supplied enough answers for both of us. But no, I haven't been to bed with Oakley Hale, and not because he said no. I could have.'

Suddenly his jealousy evaporated like a puffball exploded by a gust of wind. She could have given up any name – there was nothing especially ridiculous about Oakley Hale – and he would have had the same reaction, since his jealousy was so thin and *pro forma* that it could not survive the actual materialization of a rival. Relief flooded in, and he just kept himself from laughing. 'Maybe you should have,' he said.

'What, slept with Oakley? Thanks a lot. Nice to know you care.'

She was looking across the street at the Episcopal Church. A car drove by and somebody waved – he didn't recognize them. An old acquaintance, or a tourist being folksy-friendly.

'Actually, I don't think you do care,' said Sarah levelly. 'But I tell you this: if we're going to stay married then I don't want you to see that woman again. Ever. And I want you to quit travelling.'

'Maybe we should move.'

'Move? Where to? Stillriver?' She looked at him incredulously. 'You do what you want. But I'm staying in New York.'

He didn't know if his marriage was going to survive, but he found it hard to care, so hurt was he by Cassie's letter and her continuing refusal to talk to him. And when she finally picked up the phone with a caution he could almost feel, three weeks after he had returned with Sarah to New York, she sounded flat, distant, uncaring.

She wouldn't enter into any conversation about why she had changed her mind – 'You got my letter, that's as clear as I can be' – and in his torment he was reduced to begging her to see him again. She said no, and when he called again, and then again, she continued to say no.

He turned down the Montana posting, simply not having the emotional strength to cope with a major project, and also rejected Streatley's offer of a cable span job in southern Colorado. At home, Sarah was working even longer hours, or seeing Oakley Hale at night – he didn't really care enough to find out which was the case. They passed each other at odd hours in the apartment like distant roommates, each intent on their own single life; they shared a bed, but went to it, and rose from it, at different times.

And then, as his mixture of anger, sense of betrayal, and simple heartache seemed about to burst, Cassie announced she was coming east. An elderly cousin had died in Philadelphia, and she could arrange things so she flew back to Texas through New York. There wouldn't be much time, she said; possibly only an hour or two, but he booked a motel room anyway, adjacent to the airport, virtually in the shadow of its runways.

It was a depressing place, three stories of yellowing brick and plastic panels painted bright, uncheery colours, with smoked glass in the window frames. His room was over the parking lot, and he waited by the window, watching the unrelenting line of aircraft taking off in the distance, each one pushing black smoke out of its jet burners as it lifted off the runway, each one shimmering in the unseasonable heat of a warm October day.

She was almost an hour late, and came into the room in a rush, wearing a dress the colour of charcoal, fresh from the Philadelphia funeral. 'I'm so sorry Michael, but the plane got delayed, so I haven't got much time. I can't miss the flight home.'

He nodded, imagining the reception from Ronald if she did. 'You want a drink?' he asked, but she shook her head. 'Something to eat?'

'I'll get something on the plane.'

She sat in the one armchair by the window and he sat down on the bed. 'Cassie,' he said unsteadily, 'I've missed you so much.'

She nodded pleasantly, as if he were an older relative praising her performance in school. 'I've missed you, too,' she said, sounding friendly but oddly formal. He wanted to say, *Cassie, it's me. You don't have to talk like that. It's me.*

'When's the baby due?'

'I'm just at twenty weeks. Pretty soon they won't let me fly.'

'Well, I'm glad to get in under the line,' he said sharply.

She looked at him anxiously. 'Michael,' she said, but he wouldn't look at her. He heard her sigh. 'I shouldn't have come. This is just painful.'

'Painful?' He gave a small groan. 'Pain is not seeing you. Pain is your not wanting to see me. That's painful.'

'I told you, it's not that I don't want to see you. It's just that it's best for us both.'

'How can that be? I love you and you love me.'

'There's another life for me to worry about now, Michael. I can't do that to him.'

'Who, Ronald? After all he's done to you.'

'I meant the baby.'

'How do you know it's a boy?'

'From the scan. Ronald wanted to know.'

I bet he did, thought Michael bitterly, remembering how much Cassie said Ronald had wanted a boy the first time round. He said to Cassie, 'I don't care what sex it is or who the father is. I just want to be with you.' He heard how strained his voice had become.

'Maybe you don't care, but Ronald does.'

'What do you mean?'

'Ronald thought at first this baby was yours.'

'What?'

She looked away, towards the window and its hazy view of LaGuardia's runway. 'When I got pregnant he asked me if the baby was his. I said of course. He asked if I'd been seeing anybody else; in fact he asked specifically if I'd been seeing you.'

'Why would he think it was me? As far as he knows, we haven't seen each other in eight years.'

'He saw Donny when he was back in Stillriver for his mother's funeral, and Donny told him you were working in Texas. So he put two and two together. And got five, which is typical of Ronald.'

'And what's he think now?' asked Michael, though he was too miserable for even the thought of Ronald's fury to agitate him. He added, 'It's not as if it even *could* be mine. You know that's not possible.'

Her mouth managed a wry smile. 'Give me a little credit. We did have sex education, remember?'

'Well, can't you tell him we never made love? You don't have to tell him why we didn't.' He began to laugh at the absurdity of it, and said, 'Better not tell him what really happened.' He grew sombre again and asked, 'But why were you sleeping with Ronald anyway?'

For the first time Cassie grew animated, even fierce. 'I hadn't been, damn you. Night after night he asked me to have – *relations*.' She laughed bitterly and briefly at the coyness of the word. 'I always said no. But how could I keep doing that fifty nights running – I did get to forty-seven – without his thinking I was seeing somebody?'

'Who cares what he thought?'

'I did,' said Cassie, and for a moment Michael thought she was about to cry. He hoped she would, because then he could comfort her, then he could hold her again in his arms. But she stiffened. 'I cared because I was scared of what he might do to me before I had a chance to get out. And because . . .' She stopped, then said, 'So I gave in. I felt I had to. And later, when he asked about you, I told him that if he didn't believe me, then when the baby's born we can have a DNA test. That convinced him I was telling the truth, I think.'

'How reassuring,' he said sarcastically.

Cassie looked exhausted. When he sighed she smiled at him, but only briefly before looking at her watch. He suddenly realized that in a moment she would be leaving – her smile didn't mean a thing. 'Don't go yet. Please, Cassie. Listen to me – please listen to me.'

'I'm sorry, Michael. I shouldn't have come. It just makes it worse.'

'You don't love Ronald, you told me so yourself. You can't stay with him.'

'I have to, Michael.' Her voice was dull. 'The baby's his.'

'But what about me?' He was pleading now like a child, but couldn't help himself. He'd lost his dignity a long time ago, to the same man. 'How am I supposed to live without you?'

'You have before and you can again,' she said crisply. She got up and he watched with disbelief as she walked to the door and opened it. In another moment, she was going to be out of his life for ever. 'Please,' he pleaded, 'just stay another five minutes.'

She turned and looked back at him. He couldn't tell if there was hurt or concern in her eyes. She seemed to be speaking with enormous self-control. 'I would if I thought it would do a single bit of good.'

'Oh, Cassie,' he said, getting up and moving towards her. When he kissed her she kept her lips firmly closed, but then hugged him suddenly with surprising strength. It was a last hug; he could tell that.

'You'll be all right,' she whispered. 'I promise.'

'More than the moon and the stars?'

She detached herself and wiped her cheek. 'Goodbye,' she said, and then was gone.

*

It still hurt him, staring down once again at the hansom cabs, ready to see McLaren; hurt him more than the first time he had lost her, for now there was no fear or humiliation, just the ache as he tried to accommodate himself to life without her.

And without Sarah, who had moved out of the apartment and in with Oakley Hale three weeks after Cassie had said goodbye. 'I know you're depressed,' she had announced, not without kindness, 'and I'd stay if I thought it would help. But it's not me that's hurt you this badly. I have a pretty good idea just who it is. All I can say is, I hope you work it out.'

And so, as he walked to McLaren's office to tell him that no, he didn't want the deputy director's chair, and yes, he would like the overseas posting please, with the Asian-European business they had merged into, he felt he was starting all over again, looking for the second time in his life for a new place to heal old wounds. Only this time there was no expectation or excitement in his decision; no hope, really, when he looked hard at himself. *Still*, he thought, *at least I won't have to fire Streatley.*

4

IT WAS BRIDGES that saved him, he realized, two years after he threw out the anti-depressants that the doctor on Park Avenue had prescribed but he had never taken.

Michael had started in London, trying to integrate the company there with their new McLaren masters and preparing a thorough survey of all the projects underway in the belt stretching from Europe through the Middle East as far as the Philippines. He lived in a studio apartment in the Barbican which was owned by the company; he could walk to work, and each day he liked to focus on his way there, with an outsider's eye, on the surprisingly human, unfrightening scale of London. *This is a city I could learn to love*, he thought, but although he was supposed to ease his way into field work gently, six weeks after Michael arrived a site supervisor in the Philippines had a heart attack and Michael was on a Manila-bound flight forty-eight hours later.

He lived on the edge of the site, half a mile from the end of the bridge under construction, in a Portakabin lifted up onto breezeblocks. Evenings at this remote and steamy camp were mental torture: he avoided drinking himself insensate since he had to think clearly on the job, but there was little else to divert his attention away from his own unhappiness. Even reading didn't help since he found it impossible to concentrate. Fortunately, the mornings – from the first post-breakfast move to work – brought relief, as he could at last stop thinking about himself and focus on the job.

The work went well until an unexpected and unseasonable monsoon hit, with flash flooding that wiped out three hundred feet of causeway on either side of the bridge and six weeks' worth of work. Two of the local guards hired to protect the site were caught by the flood in grassy lowlands as they drove back from a weekend's leave in Manila, and drowned. Michael and his number two, a gruff veteran named Jock he didn't know very well, pulled the bodies out of the car after the waters had receded. One of the dead guards had become wedged between the front and back seats, and it took almost half an hour to extricate him; when at last they got him out Michael looked at a face that seemed eerily peaceful, the skin softened by its immersion in water, and he realized the guard had been little more than a boy, with a few dark hairs on his upper lip the evidence of his efforts to grow a moustache.

After this Michael and Jock became friends, usually meeting up in the evening for a whisky, or two, or three. Jock had worked on every continent except South America and his company was a welcome distraction, since he told stories unprompted and Michael could listen for an hour or two without thinking about himself and his own misery.

After the job ended, he had six more weeks back in England, helping to run the office while awaiting his replacement as manager. During this time he conducted a small affair with a PA, also divorced, who worked on his floor. They told each other very little about their respective pasts, made no plans more foresighted than afternoon arrangements to meet in the evening, and spent most of their time together in bed. Sex remained pleasurable for him, but he no longer found in its physical excitement even a glimmer of the brave new world he had once found in Sophie Jansen.

He travelled to Scotland for a holiday and met up with Jock and his wife, Annie. They spent five days along the west coast of Scotland, travelling at the driving equivalent of an ambling pace, stopping frequently to look at birds and wild flowers, spending the night in B&Bs and once in a castle hotel. They ate well, drank sparingly, and talked almost exclusively about the wildlife and wild flowers they saw each day. Michael was relieved to find that he could enjoy being in the natural world again. For the first time in years, he lived without any anxiety, since there was nothing he cared enough about to fear losing. Sometimes at night, lying in his bed with the light off, unable to sleep, he saw the calm face of the Filippino guard as in a visitation, and would envy him his apparent peacefulness.

When he returned to London he discovered that the PA had a new boyfriend, and that Streatley, of all people, had arrived to run the London office. Celebrations seemed in order, and he was lucky to make his flight to Riyadh two days later since, thanks to Streatley's exuberance in something called the Gaslight Club, Michael had almost spent the day in jail instead. He landed in Saudi Arabia with a hangover (as close to alcohol as he was to come during the two months of his stay), a certificate of baptism, and a security clearance – the chain of bridges he was being paid to assess sat near an American military installation.

The Saudi job was a highway bridge built in the 1970s which had developed delamination problems, accelerated by salt in the air from the Gulf, which it adjoined. It would be easier to knock it down and build again, but also far more expensive, so Michael spent three weeks devising a program to save the bridge through strategic concrete reinforcements and an epoxy-coated beam, only to realize belatedly that no one *wanted* to repair it – national pride and the interests of the construction industry demanded that a new and bigger bridge be built. Yet it was in devising his unwanted plan to save the old bridge that Michael discovered his metier. For he learned that he much preferred repairing old bridges to helping build new ones. He became a particular expert on reinforced concrete degradation and its repair, on delamination and spalling, and the effects of corrosion which always weakened, sometimes fatally, the structure of a bridge. He was careful and deliberate in his work, but privately took pride in his ability to take one long look at a bridge and know in most cases just what was wrong and how bad the problem was.

This stood him in good stead in other countries, where the civic authorities were more eager to save money than boost national pride. A steady succession of jobs came Michael's way, chiefly in the northern climes – Sweden, Germany, briefly in Finland – which he preferred. His divorce with Sarah came through two years after he left New York, when she initiated proceedings in order to marry Oakley Hale. It was perfectly amicable, chiefly because he didn't have the money to fight a protracted case. When the dust cleared, he was left with $11,000 to his name; so much for marrying an upper-class girl.

But he was making better money now, and though he continued to work almost entirely for the McLaren company, he became an independent consultant, and his freelance market value meant McLaren had to pay him a day rate more than twice that of the salary he had been drawing. With new savings and the money from the divorce, he scratched together a sufficient down payment to buy the two-bedroom flat in Ealing. Michael liked it precisely for its dullness, the civility of his neighbours, the way it brought the privacy he wanted without (as in New York when he first arrived) making him feel anonymous. He liked the English as well; they had a quiet scepticism that complemented his own persisting, glum detachment.

He was not unreceptive to the individual cultures he worked in, and tried in each location to learn something about the people and the country he was seeing all too briefly. He acquired a working knowledge of German, and once spent Christmas in Lapland, among reindeer and seven feet of snow, where he had a fling with a woman of independent means from Cohasset, Massachusetts. But it was difficult to soak up much culture, since he had enough responsibility for the projects not to be able to stray far from them, and he was not being paid to broaden his life experience. He knew the postcards he sent home to his father and to Nancy Sheringham must sound deep, exotic notes, but he found it hard to take pleasure from his travels when his personal life remained rootless and solitary.

His sense of isolation was heightened when Streatley married a much younger English woman, had twin daughters, and promptly took the pledge. Envying his friend the pleasures of a domesticity he was convinced he would never have in the normal way, Michael briefly looked at abnormal avenues, and actually considered the acquisition of a mail order bride from

Thailand, or perhaps the Philippines. He reasoned that such a marriage would be no more artificial than any relationship he could now have with a western woman, and probably more honest than one he tried to forge on a supposed basis of love. The cynicism of this only partly deterred him; what really stopped him from acting on it was the recognition that he would simply be extending the loveless nature of his own life and inflicting it on someone else.

As well as sending postcards, he rang his father on Christmas and his birthday in autumn. Reluctant to talk about himself, Michael used these occasions to ask about Stillriver, though there was a sadness in his father's recital since increasingly, inevitably, it comprised news of death and decline: Alvin died of pancreatic cancer, Larry Bottel's father dropped dead while opening the bakery one morning, Marilyn had a stroke. Gary had moved out of the house upon at last acquiring a girlfriend, and to Michael's ear his father sounded lonely. He thought of inviting him overseas to visit, but his schedule was uncertain, it was hard to block time out, he wasn't sure there would be room in his flat – and when each of these excuses looked thin, he decided that it would be an awkward, possibly unpleasant experience for them both.

And then, returning in January from a small job in Dorset (it lasted less than a week in fact, since it was almost immediately clear the bridge in question was beyond repair) he found an old-fashioned air letter waiting for him, addressed in a slightly shaky hand it took him seconds to recognize as his father's.

> *Dear Michael,*
>
> *Letters are unfashionable these days, but I'm of a generation who call long distance only in emergencies and this email business is beyond me.*
>
> *All is well here, though we had a heavy winter and the snow stayed on the ground past Easter. The windows need attention and a lick of paint or two on the shutters is*

probably in order, but otherwise the house is in pretty good shape with less obvious signs of decrepitude than you might find in me.

I saw Nancy Sheringham last week in town to visit her best friend and she sent you all the best. There's been a lot of rain lately so she is optimistic about the season. I am going to Fell's for supper tonight as the Doctor caught a large Chinook in the Pere Marquette which he plans to barbecue. The water in the lake is very high – so high the Fells have had to sandbag the area around the A-Frame. The scholarship they set up in Ricky's memory is going to a nice girl whose folks live in one of the new houses out on Park Street by the iron bridge. She's planning to go to MSU.

It was nice of you to phone at Christmas and I was glad to hear that work continues to go so well. Thank you also for the recent postcard – I'm glad you're able to do jobs nearby. Actually, I hope very much that at some point you will be able to stop travelling altogether (except for fun) and settle down a bit. Obviously only if you want to – so I suppose I am saying that I hope some day you'll want to settle down.

I know in my own case having a family completely changed my life. It let me start afresh (which I needed to do) and brought me great happiness. When your mother died, even in the worst moments I had people other than myself to worry about and take care of. That is the danger of living on your own, I suppose – that after a time you not only don't care, you can't.

Not that I always feel I provided enough caring to either you or your brother. Actually, maybe with Gary I cared for him too well – he's had so much trouble making a go of life by himself. With you, on the other hand, after your mother died you could have used more caring, of that I'm sure. Old Marilyn could not have been enough, kind to you though she was. I thought she and Alvin could help you in ways I couldn't, but this may just be a backwards-

looking excuse for not doing enough. I hope not.

Well, enough of this old man's musings, which you should know come only with a father's pride and love. It would be nice to see you this side of a blue moon.

Your Pop

Michael was unsettled by this letter, and touched, for it was more revealing than anything his father had communicated before. But it also raised questions which only his father could answer. Who was Nancy Sheringham's best friend, a position always occupied in the past by Cassie? Why had his father needed to 'start afresh'? And why was his father suddenly talking about what happened after Michael's mother died?

He decided he should reply, and thought at first he would phone his father, then reinstitute contact on a more frequent basis. Then he changed his mind – he knew his father disliked the phone – and decided instead to write him back, perhaps initiate a regular pattern of correspondence. But he changed his mind again, deciding that vicarious communication wasn't good enough. When the next jobs – a short one in Ireland, then a longer one at Jock's behest on the west coast of Scotland – were finished, he decided he would go home for a while. *Home?* Well, it was close as anything else he had at the moment.

And he would have gone, too, flown to his hometown of Stillriver and seen his father if, on that misty morning as he wiped rain from his face and peered at the beam encasing above his head, while the local kid steadied the rowboat as best he could, his mobile phone had not rung. And he'd exclaimed *Christ*, wishing he had turned the phone off as he fumbled with the flap of his oilskin and retrieved the plastic instrument from deep beneath his fisherman's sweater, and then said, '*Hello.*' Then '*Hello?*' more loudly as he struggled to hear over the slapping waves against the side of the boat, until the faraway voice broke through and he did hear – heard with unmistakable clarity that his father had been murdered the day before in his bed.

Seven

'I KNEW WE'D have to talk about it sometime,' said Cassie.

Michael had left a message for Maguire to call him, then gone spontaneously with Cassie and the kids to the beach to take advantage of this late day of full summer – blue, cloudless sky, the temperature in the low 80s, a breeze off the lake meaning it was tolerable on the shore, though outright hot in the Back Country, where people would be wiping off sweat and fanning themselves.

They had walked down from the house, Jack still young enough to be excited, Sally pleased in her owlish, undemonstrative way. At the Dairy Queen Michael had paused, but Cassie shook her head no – later on. Barefoot, they found the black macadam of the street sticky as fudge and too hot for walking, and moved with their towels and Jack's array of toys along the sandy sidewalk, past the cottages of Beach Road until they reached the State Park. On the beach itself, the countless mini-moguls of soft, white sand were also too scorching to stand on, so they ran hot-footed down to the shore, twisting among the families, couples, bikinied girls and teenage boys who had staked out positions with towels.

They walked north a few hundred yards on the cooler, wet sand of the shoreline, their feet splashing through the low incoming surf, past the boundary of the park to the point where the dunes and beach grass began and the sandy beach narrowed. Above the dunes and away from the lake, the first houses sat on a ridge of sand, shaded by stands of pine and birch. Less private than their South Beach counterparts a mile south across the channel, they had the same stunning views of the lake and of the setting sun each evening, though the advantage of being closer to town was debatable.

They picked a spot and put their towels down on the rockless beach near an accumulation of driftwood. Michael took off his shirt and tried to suck in his stomach until Cassie tickled him and his new paunch ballooned. 'I'm fighting fit,' he said. 'I just don't look it.'

'I'm no spring chicken myself,' she said, but in fact she had kept her figure, the only sign of ageing a slight thickening in her thighs and a group of veins, bunched like grapes, on the back of one calf. Of course she was changed, he realized, even from the woman he'd known six years before, much less the half-girl, half-woman of their early romance. But he *liked* the changes, the evidence of age and wear and a life hard-lived.

Am I getting old and soppy? he wondered, until Jack interrupted his musing by splashing water his way. In the manner of small boys, he couldn't stop, and was soon kicking water at Sally, despite his sister's telling him not to. When she took revenge by splashing him back, more effectively than he could manage, his mood soured, then turned visibly murderous. He scooped a handful of wet sand and threw it straight into his sister's face. Sally burst into tears and Jack reached for more, readying to throw it just as Michael reached out and held him by the arm.

The little boy turned in furious astonishment, trying to twist out of Michael's grip. He was surprisingly strong. 'Let me go! Let me go!' he shouted.

'Drop the sand, Jack,' he said, trying to keep his voice calm. Cassie stood some distance behind, looking worried.

The boy was still enraged, still struggling. 'Let me go. You're not my daddy.'

Michael held Jack away from him, not loosening his grip, then leaned down to speak. 'I know I'm not your daddy. And you're not my son. But that doesn't mean you can throw sand at people.'

The boy's anger was subsiding enough for him to think about this. Michael took a chance and let him go. Jack clenched his fistful of sand, hesitated for a moment, then turned and hurled it out in a fine brown spray over the water.

'Thank you,' said Michael.

The boy looked at him suspiciously. 'Do you know my daddy?' he asked.

Michael looked again at Cassie, now close enough to hear this. Her face looked pained and tense. 'I used to,' he said.

'I don't,' said Jack, and suddenly ran out into the water. Michael watched him go, then turned to Cassie. 'I'm sorry, I wasn't trying to hurt him. Or play Daddy.'

'That's all right. He needs somebody to tell him. I mean, somebody male.'

'Does he remember Ronald?'

She dug a toe in the firmer, moist sand of the shoreline. 'He says he does, but he was only three when they put Ronald inside. I think he *wants* to remember him.'

'He's got his father's temper, anyway.'

'*Don't say that!*' she snapped. Then said more calmly, 'I told you he was never violent to me.'

'You did.' He remembered their first conversation in the hotel in Austin. 'I didn't know whether to believe you.'

'It was true all right – *then*. But that changed.'

'When?'

'After I stopped seeing you.' That new, bitter laugh. 'And *after* the DNA test, which said Jack was his. Doesn't make much sense, does it?'

'Did he hurt you?'

'Not half so much as he scared me.' There were tears on her cheeks, which she tried to wipe casually away. He resisted the temptation to take her hand. 'The worst thing was,' she said, looking out to where Jack was now chasing Sally in the shallows, 'she saw a couple of times.'

'Who, Sally? Saw him hurting you?'

She nodded, seemed to hesitate, then said slowly, 'When the police came and told me they'd arrested Ronald, told me that he'd killed someone with his fists – a driver he got into an argument with – my very first thought wasn't *how terrible*. Or *the poor victim and his family*. Or even, *what am I going to do with a husband in jail and two kids to support?* No, my first thought was *thank God*. Because now he couldn't kill me.

That's how scared I was.' Tears were running freely down her face, and this time he took her hand. Sally, by the first sandbar, saw this, but then shyly looked away.

'When did you decide to leave Texas?'

'After I went and saw him in prison. It was a four-hundred-mile drive. I told him I'd wait for him and be there when he got out – he'll get paroled if he doesn't kill somebody while he's inside. But he told me not to bother. He said it was over between us, said I shouldn't wait for him. So I didn't. I went to see him one last time and told him I was coming back here, coming home.'

'And what did he say?'

'He said that was fine, and that I shouldn't worry about him.'

This sounded so unlike the Ronald Michael had known that he looked hard at Cassie, who determinedly kept her gaze fixed on her children playing in the water. 'Is that all he said?' She was biting her lower lip with her front teeth, and still crying. 'Cassie?' he added softly.

When she nodded, looking very wobbly, he decided not to press the point. 'Nancy said he got ten years. Is that right?'

'No. He got six.'

'And he's been in for three?'

'Yep.'

'So when's the soonest he can get out?' He was thinking hard, making calculations and plans – where could they go? Ealing wasn't very likely, was it? Still, they had *some* time.

Cassie said, 'He had his first parole hearing in early May.'

'He did?' He asked more sharply than he wanted to.

'He got turned down.'

'How do you know?'

'He called me. He didn't seem surprised.'

'Well, that's good to know. When's the next one?'

'Next May. But he's not very optimistic.'

'You can relax. Even if he gets out then, which I doubt, he'll have his own life to worry about. He's not going to bother you, not if he's said that you shouldn't worry about him.'

She didn't look reassured at all. She shook her head, but now she turned to face him, and although there were still tears in her eyes there was something composed and sad in her expression. 'He said he wanted me to start a new life and he wouldn't bother me, unless . . .'

'Unless what?'

'I started seeing you again.' She sighed. 'I know I should have told you right away. But it was so nice to see you, and I was worried it would scare you off.'

'Don't worry, Cassie. He'll be on parole – he's not going to want to go back to jail.'

But the haunting look in her eyes remained. 'Cassie,' he said, 'you've got to tell me exactly what he said. I need to know.'

'I told you what he said.'

'Tell me *all* of it, Cassie. Go on. I know you.'

She nodded, sighed again, but this time with resignation. 'He said,' and she spoke in a low, flat voice, '*if you start seeing Wolf again, this time I'll finish the job. I'm not having him raise my son.*'

He was so astonished he could not bring himself to speak, and he could sense that he was at least a little scared. It had been so long since he'd felt that fear that it took a moment before he recognized the signs: his heart began to go *thump thump thump* and his breathing turned shallow and fast, and he felt what seemed to be his blood racing around his arms and hands. He thought, with a kind of astonished appreciation of the situation, *Someone's killed Pop and left a swastika on the wall, and now this son of a bitch wants to kill me.* 'So,' he said, in an immoderately loud voice that caught the two kids' attention right away, 'Who wants an ice-cream cone?'

When they reached the house Gary came out onto the back porch looking relieved to see them, for since his return from the Half he had been manifestly nervous whenever Michael left for long.

'Maguire called,' Gary announced. Michael looked at Cassie. 'Said to tell you he's going to Fennville on his own. Whatever that means. He'll call you later.'

Cassie shook her head knowingly. 'He won't get anywhere with Ethel. What I don't understand is how you know the fingerprints on the bat are hers.'

'Like I told you, the flowers out back. No one else would have planted them. Plus, Mrs Jenkins said Ethel had been running away; I'm pretty sure someone's been in the basement, and Ethel's small enough to squeeze through the window. And her hands are *tiny* – Maguire thought the fingerprints were a child's. Add all these together and it doesn't take Sherlock Holmes to come up with Ethel.'

An hour later Maguire phoned again, sounding more annoyed than contrite, and five minutes after that Michael and Cassie were in the car heading towards Fennville, leaving the kids in Gary's care. Michael expressed mild apprehension abut this, but Cassie wasn't worried. 'They'll be fine. Jack thinks he's great and Sally's nose is so deep in her book she'll forget we're not there.'

Near the bottom of Happy Valley, just before the wooden bridge, Michael turned left, and they followed the smaller road – sand, but levelled smooth and hard-packed – up a rise of adolescent apple orchard to the east.

The poorhouse, also known as Fennville Acres, had been expanded, with a new ground floor wing of yellow brick and smoked glass windows running along one end of the wooden gingerbread house, which had been built in the nineteenth century for the indigenous poor. Michael parked and said, 'I'll be back.'

'Don't be silly,' said Cassie, opening her door and hopping out.

'But Maguire said only me.'

'What does he know?' Cassie seemed completely confident. 'She's not going to talk to you either. If I come with you now it'll save you fetching me.'

The front hall had a bleached oak table and metal folding chair behind it, but was otherwise empty. Michael looked in vain for anyone, shouting hello up the pine staircase, then down along the corridor of the ground floor. So, like trespassers with good intentions, he and Cassie moved cautiously through the front hall and finally found a woman orderly in a white uniform, drinking a cup of coffee in a tiny room next to the kitchen. 'You looking for Mr Maguire?' she asked.

'That's right.'

'He's in the backyard.' She added knowingly. 'He's being read to.'

They went out the back door and stood on a rickety porch, which had a railing missing several posts. They looked out over a roughly cut lawn; it ended at a small red barn, which had a field of higher grass behind it, separated by a sagging fence of barbed wire. In the middle of the lawn, Maguire was standing impatiently over a deckchair, which was occupied by a small figure whose legs barely reached the ground. On closer inspection it was a woman of middle age, dressed in the shorts and baggy T-shirt of a teenager, reading aloud from a book she held in her hands.

As Michael and Cassie approached, Maguire looked at them with a mixture of relief and irritation. 'I don't know why you got me over here. She says she's never left this place since her brother put her in a year ago.'

Cassie looked down at the chair and laughed.

'What's so funny?' demanded Maguire. He seemed even younger when he was cross.

'Hello there,' said Cassie. The face of the woman in the chair broke into a grin. She kicked her bare feet together like a gleeful toddler, and said, 'Hello Cassie.'

Cassie laughed again and Maguire looked ready to explode.

'You've got the wrong twin,' Michael explained gently. 'This is Daisy.'

'But she said she was Ethel,' protested Maguire.

'Daisy!' said Cassie with mock sternness.

Daisy looked up at Michael. 'Ethel didn't want to be bothered,' she said.

'So you stepped in, huh?' asked Cassie, and Daisy nodded. 'And where *is* Ethel?'

'She's in our room. She didn't know you'd be here, Cassie, or she'd have come down.'

They left Daisy with her book, and walked towards the house, with Maguire demanding to know how old Daisy was.

Michael said, 'She must be nearing fifty. Don't you think, Cassie?' She nodded.

'*Fifty?* She was reading a Nancy Drew mystery when I got here,' said Maguire.

'There's always been something childlike about her,' said Cassie. 'She's probably read more books than all of us combined – not just kids' books either – but in most respects you'd have to say she's simple. They both are actually.'

They found Ethel eventually, in a small alcove bedroom high up in one corner of the house. Michael and Maguire had to duck as they entered to avoid hitting their heads on the sloping cedar ceiling. She was lying on her back on one of two beds positioned on either side of a dormer window, which only slightly reduced the claustrophobic impact of the room. 'Well, Ethel,' said Cassie, 'this is nice.'

Ethel put down the gardening magazine she was reading but did not sit up. To an outsider she would have looked identical to Daisy. It was the bluish tinge on her jaw that gave the game away to Michael. Ethel had always needed to shave.

'It was nicer on the ground floor.' Her voice was deeper than Daisy's by about half an octave.

'Why did you move, then?'

'*They* moved us. I used to be able to open the window and step outside. Can't do it way up here.'

Cassie sat down at the end of Ethel's bed and said with an easy authority, 'You two sit over there.' Maguire and Michael obediently sat on Daisy's bed. 'You used to go out a lot, didn't you, Ethel?' asked Cassie in an encouraging voice. Ethel nodded, and Cassie went on. 'Back to Stillriver sometimes?'

Ethel nodded again, but more slowly. She said, 'Benny didn't like it. Told me not to.'

'So where would you go? You were gone overnight sometimes, weren't you?'

Ethel's expression set tensely.

'Ethel, honey,' said Cassie, 'you're not in trouble. That's not why we're here. You know you can trust me, don't you?'

She waited and eventually Ethel spoke. 'I trust you, Cassie.'

'Good. Now when you would go back to town, did you sometimes go to Michael's Daddy's house?'

A nod. Her eyes were moving randomly.

'Was he there?'

Another nod.

'Did he see you?'

Ethel looked sideways at the wall and its yellowing wallpaper pattern of geese. 'He saw me one time. He'd left a window open in the basement and I spent the night there. He found me.'

'What did he say?'

'He said "Hi Ethel. You don't look very comfortable sleeping down here." I came upstairs and he let me use the bathroom. He gave me breakfast and then he let me garden in the back. I planted seeds, Cassie,' she said proudly, 'just like we used to do. Then he drove me back here. He promised he wouldn't say nothing to Benny.'

Cassie nodded. Then she asked with almost exaggerated casualness, 'Did you ever happen to see anybody else at the house?'

Ethel's eyes darted back to the wallpaper geese. 'Not that time.'

'What about—' Maguire interjected, but stopped when Cassie gave him a look that could cut ice. She leant forward and touched Ethel gently on one knee.

'Tell me about the other time.'

Now Ethel's eyes were focused on the ceiling, and she spoke as if remembering for the first time. 'I was sleeping in the basement again. Mr Wolf hadn't told me not to and the window was still open. It wasn't cold and I found a tarp to lie on in the corner by the boiler. He must have left it there. I was asleep but I woke up when I heard someone come down the stairs. Then the light went on. I thought maybe it was Mr Wolf, come to put something away, and I thought I'd tell him I was there, but then

I thought it would scare him. And then I figured maybe it wasn't Mr Wolf, and that scared *me*, so I stayed still and listened to the rustling.'

'Rustling?'

Ethel looked quickly at Cassie, then looked again at the sloping ceiling above her head. 'Like leaves in the wind. Rustling. Then he put something down. It went *tonk*. *Tonk*,' she repeated, with obvious relish at the sound of the word. 'Then the light went out and the person went back up the stairs.'

'What did you do?'

'When I couldn't hear footsteps I got up and turned on the light, just like he did. I found what he'd put up against the wall. It was a baseball bat. It wasn't there when I came in. I didn't move it,' she added anxiously.

'It's okay if you touched it.'

'I might have touched it,' Ethel conceded. 'But I didn't move it.'

'Then what did you do?' asked Cassie.

'I left. I climbed out the window where I'd come in.'

'Tell me, Ethel, did you get a look at the person in the basement?'

She shook her head. Michael grimaced and Maguire gave a small moan of disappointment. Then Ethel said, 'I only saw him outside.'

'What?' Michael exclaimed.

Ethel was nodding. 'I was about to cross the street to our house when I heard somebody come out on the back porch. So I hid behind the fence. Then I saw *him* cross the street and cut through Mrs Decatur's backyard.'

'Who was "him", Ethel?' asked Michael.

'I only really got a look when he went under the streetlight.'

Cassie took over again. 'Did you recognize him, Ethel?' she asked.

'Was he the man who did the bad thing?' asked Ethel.

'You mean to Michael's father?'

'Yes. Was he the one?'

'Probably.'

She looked at Cassie. 'Would he do the bad thing to me?'

'No way.' Cassie was emphatic. 'Nobody knows you saw him. He doesn't even know. But did you know who he was, Ethel?'

Ethel was looking at the geese. 'I think I did.' She paused and Michael heard a deep intake of breath from Maguire. 'But I can't remember his name.'

'Would you know him if you saw him?'

'Maybe.'

'Would you know his name if you heard it?'

'Maybe. Sometimes it's on my tongue tip. Then it goes away. I keep thinking capitals.'

'Capital letters?'

'No. State capitals. Don't ask me why, that's just what I keep thinking.'

'Albany,' said Maguire.

'Springfield,' said Michael.

Ethel began to look anxious and Cassie held up her hand. 'Hang on, let's do this systematically.'

'We need a list,' said Michael.

'Where we going to find that?' demanded Maguire.

'Let's start in Michigan, and go state by state,' said Cassie. 'Was it Lansing?' Ethel shook her head.

By common agreement they moved south then east with the states, finding that between the three of them each state capital was eventually unearthed. Indiana, Ohio, Pennsylvania, New York, New Hampshire, Vermont (they argued over that one, but neither Burlington nor Montpelier rang a bell for Ethel), Maine, Massachusetts, Connecticut, Rhode Island. Then they headed south, and with Maryland Maguire suddenly started to look excited. 'Hurry,' he said.

'Annapolis,' said Cassie.

'Go on!' Maguire suddenly shouted.

'North Carolina is . . .' began Cassie, and Maguire spat out '*Raleigh!*'

They all looked at Ethel, who suddenly beamed, delighted that they all seemed so happy.

'Raleigh Somerset,' Maguire insisted.

Ethel kept smiling and Maguire clapped his hands. 'That's our boy,' he said and stood up, while Cassie patted Ethel on her knee again and said, 'Well done. Let's go down and find Daisy, should we?'

'Wait a minute,' said Michael. 'There's something I don't understand.' Cassie and Maguire looked at him expectantly. 'So Raleigh has the bat and he . . .' – he struggled with words – '*uses* it. And then he puts it back later and Ethel sees it. Even touches it, which accounts for her fingerprints. But then how come the bat's not there when the police arrive the next day?' He looked at Maguire. 'You told me yourself that both you and Jimmy Olds searched the entire house the day after the murder.'

No one said anything – Maguire looked tense and seemed to be thinking hard. Then Cassie turned back to Ethel, who, having sat up on the bed, now stared down at her knees like a shamed child. 'Ethel honey,' she said gently. 'Did you take the bat with you when you left that night?'

Ethel refused to look at Cassie, who repeated softly, 'Did you?'

'I wanted it,' Ethel said plaintively. She looked up at Michael. 'We used to play with it.'

Michael nodded, and Cassie said, 'But then you put it back, didn't you?'

'That was later,' said Ethel. 'You had come home, Michael. I saw you at the Homecoming Parade. And I thought you might be needing it, so that night I put it back. I didn't tell you because I was scared after the bad thing. I knew I shouldn't have taken it.' She looked utterly forlorn.

'It doesn't matter, Ethel,' said Michael. 'You had nothing to do with the bad thing. We all know that.'

They went downstairs as a group and at the bottom Cassie said, 'I'll take Ethel outside with me and find Daisy. After all this, I need to visit with them for a while.'

Maguire said, 'That was real good upstairs. You should have been a policeman.'

Cassie looked at him coolly. 'You should have been one too.'

362

'Ouch,' said Maguire as Cassie went out the back door. Michael ignored this and Maguire said, 'You going home now?'

Michael gestured toward the yard in back. 'We'll spend a little time with Daisy and Ethel first. What about you? What happens now?'

'I'm going to find Raleigh Somerset, and put him in an identity parade. Then when that Ethel creature identifies him I'll have a warrant all set to search his place.'

'You almost had him once before.'

Maguire looked at him sharply. 'That's right. Six sticks of dynamite. But no fingerprints. This time I've got two forensics guys you wouldn't believe – if there's *anything* in his house linking Raleigh to your dad they'll find it. And I bet there is.'

'I hope so. I can't see you convicting him on the basis of Ethel's knowledge of state capitals.'

Maguire gave a tight-lipped smile. 'She's just the thin end of the wedge. I've got our killer, I'm sure of that; now I just need the rest of the wedge.'

Ethel was tired so Michael and Cassie cut short their visit, promising to come back the following week. In the car both were quiet as they came down to Happy Valley and crossed the wooden bridge.

'It's hardly rained at all since I came back,' said Michael, 'but the water's still high here.'

'Spring was the wettest for years.' Cassie sounded abstracted, as if talking to a tourist, and they drove in silence for a few minutes, while Michael wondered why he didn't feel more relief that there was now a prime suspect in his father's murder. Probably because if Raleigh had killed his father, it was for a completely pointless reason – revenge for something his father hadn't even done. The motive for the murder still seemed hard to accept. *Would you really beat a man to death for telling the police you were in possession of explosives?* Apparently, if you were a racist semi-Nazi psychopath like Raleigh, you would.

Gary would be right to blame himself, and Michael worried

about how his brother was going to live with the guilt. It was a peculiar feeling, worrying about his brother, especially as it overrode any sense of completion or relief that the mystery of his father's death now seemed solved.

Cassie sighed, and glancing over as he drove past the charter school, Michael saw her top teeth clamp down on her lower lip, a certain sign that she was considering something. 'What's the matter?' he asked.

'Nothing,' she said unconvincingly. Then she sighed again. 'I guess that's that then.'

'What do you mean?'

She opened her window with the power switch in the console between them. 'Well, you came back to find out who killed your father and now you know. So I suppose you can go now.'

'That's just stupid.'

'Is it? Tell me why.'

And he found himself unable to reply – every answer he considered fell apart in the face of his knowledge that he would have to call London soon and accept the Dubai assignment. He didn't feel he had any choice; he couldn't just sit and wait for the money to run out. Desperate to say something, he finally asked, 'What do you want for supper?'

'Come again?' said Cassie. There was contempt in her voice. 'Did you really just say that?'

'I'm sorry,' he said, and he pulled over suddenly and parked under the big elm at the entrance to the charter school.

'Don't worry about supper,' she said curtly, 'I'm going to pick the kids up and take them home.'

'I didn't mean that,' said Michael, wishing the words were back in his mouth. 'I didn't know what to say. But instead of me coming here, why don't you come with me?'

Her face filled with an expression of fixed intensity. 'This is home. Why don't you come here?'

'I can't, Cassie.'

'Why not?'

He stared over at the school, where several teachers' cars were parked – they would be preparing for school's opening on

Tuesday. He was going to say that he couldn't make a living in Stillriver, but found himself saying quietly instead, 'Too many ghosts. I can't seem to shed them.'

'If you'd said to me, it's too slow here, too small, or you can't find work here, then I'd understand. I wouldn't even argue with you; those are reasons. But *ghosts?* That makes it sound like you're just running away. That you don't *want* to be over in Europe, it's just you can't find your way back here. What are you scared of? Why do you pretend you don't like this place? What is all this garbage about how much it's changed? Sure it's not the same – there's more money, more retired people, more tourism. *So what?*' She was almost shouting now. 'The big lake's still there, the beach is the same, the channel hasn't gone away, there are still two branches to the river, the Back Country remains poor as poor can be, asparagus and cherries taste remarkably like they did when we were teenagers, and your daddy's house still has big rooms and high windows. So just *what* are you complaining about?'

He said as calmly as he could, 'I don't see why you won't think about coming over there. You're not like Donny. He acts sometimes like going to Grand Rapids is as big a deal as flying to Paris. For Christ's sake, you've travelled.'

She was shaking her head before he had even finished speaking. 'You know, you never see things from other people's point of view. You haven't changed at all in that respect. Say I did come with you – to where, by the way? From the sound of it you don't even know where your next job will be. A London suburb where I don't know a soul? Or a site in Germany? Or, where did you say? Dubai? I'm not xenophobic, you know, but visiting a place is a lot different from living in it. But say I did come. What if it doesn't work? Maybe the kids turn out to be miserable. They're not exactly fluent in Arabic, you know. Or you discover I'm a lot different from what you thought. Or I find out you're not the man I used to know. What then? Where would I be then, Michael? No job, no husband, no home. You'd be fine – you'd just move on to the next job, and probably the next woman. But I'd have *nothing*. And if I stay here, even if I don't have you, at least I've got *something*. At least I have this place.'

Michael put a hand up to his face and sighed. 'God, I hate Stillriver sometimes. I could cope with Ronald getting in the way; I've had years of practice with that one. But not this town.'

'Bullshit. Now let's go,' she said, 'I need to get the kids.'

They drove back to town in silence, and when he turned the last corner for home he saw Maguire's car further down Luke Street, moving in the opposite direction. 'What is he doing in town?' he asked. 'I thought he was going straight out to Raleigh Somerset's.'

It was Gary who held the answer. 'We've had a visitor,' he said, coming out onto the porch to greet them.

'Yeah, I saw his car going down the street as I came in.'

'Oh, him,' said Gary, flushing slightly. 'He came by to tell me what Ethel had said. I guess I don't have to worry any more about that bat.'

'So you know about Raleigh?'

'Maguire told me. I just hope they have enough to take him to trial.'

His brother seemed strangely unexcited by the news – probably, Michael decided, because he'd already been thinking Raleigh had done it.

'And guess who came by?' Gary didn't wait to let Michael speculate. 'Mrs Minsky.'

'What? Patsy?'

'Across the street,' said Gary, and as he pointed Michael turned and saw one of the new, foreshortened Cadillacs, a gleaming gold model, parked in front of Benny Wagner's.

'She's staying *there*?' he asked incredulously.

'Sh-sh-sh. She might hear you.'

Cassie whispered, 'What's she like?'

'An old Jewish lady. Nice though.'

I like the 'though', thought Michael.

'And you know what? Pop lent her some money years ago and it's come good.'

'How's that?' asked Michael suspiciously, since for all he

knew, Mrs Minsky was running an elaborate scam, duping the unwitting heirs of a name plucked at random from the obituaries column of the *Atlantic County Herald*.

'She gave him a small percentage in her company in return for the loan – this was way back mind you, before he even came up here. She sold the company to a competitor and the competitor's about to go public.'

'How much?' asked Michael, uninterested in the history of the transactions.

'A fortune!' Gary seemed unable to contain himself. 'My shares are going to be worth a hundred and fifty thousand dollars.'

Not a fortune, thought Michael, especially in the spendthrift hands of his younger brother, but nothing to be sneezed at either, especially by an older brother with far less money to his name than Gary seemed ever to realize. 'What have you got to do?' he asked, still playing older brother.

Gary looked surprised. 'Nothing. Nothing at all. I own the shares – well, I will as soon as Pop's estate gets through probate. And you hold some shares, too. You've got money coming as well.'

'But why weren't there any certificates left behind by Pop?'

Gary shook his head in amazement. 'That's just it – he never had them. She held them for him. He told her to look us up if something happened to him. And she has.'

Cassie spoke up for the first time, looking reprovingly at Michael. 'You never can trust anyone, can you? She just sounds an honest woman.'

'I guess so,' said Michael, trying to take this all in. 'She sure must have some story to tell.'

AND IT WAS a very pretty story. She told it very well, consuming two glasses of iced tea during her recital, which took place the following afternoon, only half an hour after Jimmy Olds had phoned to say, dutifully rather than enthusiastically, that Raleigh Somerset had been taken in for an identity parade.

Patsy had first known Henry because Henry's mother had been her own mother's best friend. 'Close,' she said, and rubbed her index finger against the side of her thumb. 'Close as this.'

She sat at the kitchen table, wearing a raincoat of orange cotton, belted loosely at the waist, declining Michael's offer to hang it up. For an old woman she was tall, though it was hard to pin down just how old she was – Michael thought she could be sixty-five or eighty-five. She had a pleasant, pixie-like face with no cheekbones and light green eyes, and she was heavily made up in an old lady's powdery way. As she spoke she seemed slowly to relax, putting her arms on the table. But she kept her coat on.

Henry Wolf had been an only child, and had grown up alone with his mother. His father had 'gone away' before the Second World War. To help his mother, Henry had left school early to go to work, then enlisted in the army in his early twenties and served in Korea. Once out of the army, he had finished high school while working a night shift on an assembly line, then gone to college, courtesy of the GI Bill. His mother's death virtually coincided with his BA, and it was then that Henry had moved to Stillriver and begun to teach school in 1957. He'd had no family left at all, and few if any close friends. 'He was always a bit of a loner,' declared Patsy, fingering her wedding ring as if it were an *aide-memoire*.

'Did you ever meet my mother?'

Patsy looked at him and smiled like an indulgent grandmother. 'No, and what a shame. She must have been a lovely person.'

'You didn't go to their wedding?'

She took a sip of iced tea with great care, as if it might burn her mouth, then twiddled her ring again. 'Unfortunately, I couldn't attend. There was an illness in my family.'

It would have been an interesting encounter, he thought – the gentle lady of his memory, and this urban *yenta*, whom he found himself starting to like. 'My brother Gary told me you said there are some shares my father held in a company of yours.'

'Of course,' Patsy said, with a smile that showed she was expecting this. 'It's quite simple, really. And presumably pleasing to you.' *Presumably* was pronounced elaborately, almost ironically.

It seemed Patsy's family had begun a wartime business manufacturing small steel components for armaments. After VJ Day, they'd switched to supplying parts to automobile manufacturers. In the following years, the car business boomed, but the family business didn't. By the time Henry Wolf left Detroit for Stillriver, the business was in decline; by the time he had married Michael's mother, things were even worse, and Henry had made an emergency loan of five thousand dollars – out of general kindness, perhaps, or the specific recognition of how close his mother had been to Patsy's.

She didn't know how Henry had come into this kind of money, Patsy quickly added, pre-empting any questions from Michael. *My mother?* he wondered, as Patsy moved on. In 1967 the business had changed tack again, and began producing less heavy-duty auxiliaries – they made ashtrays for cars, for example, and a better kind of rear-view mirror. A major contract with Ford Motors meant they were soon in a position to laugh about their former hard times (when five grand made a life or death difference) and in the following decades they had expanded, diversified, prospered, and, inevitably, been bought by another, much larger privately owned firm.

'Why didn't you just repay the loan then?' asked Michael, sounding a little ungracious even to himself. He managed a small smile.

'Well, it was business,' said Patsy, expansively gesturing with an open hand, 'and *not* business. Like I told the detective.'

'What detective?'

'The young fellow in charge of your father's case. You know, Mick something. An Irish name.'

'Maguire?' he asked incredulously.

'That's him. Nice young man.'

'When did he come and see you?'

She shrugged. 'Ages ago. It must have been in July.'

Thanks detective, thought Michael angrily, remembering Maguire's cross words over the phone when Michael was still in Scotland: '*Why didn't you tell me about Patsy?*' Whatever Maguire's agenda was, it didn't seem to involve helping anyone else. *Atkinson and I have been looking for this woman since May and Maguire didn't even mention that he found her two months ago.*

Patsy was saying, 'I'm afraid I wasn't much help – I think he must have decided whoever hurt Henry had nothing to do with Detroit. Anyway, we wanted to thank your father and so we converted his loan into a small position in the business. To be frank, very small, but one that grew in time. Believe me, we asked him repeatedly if he wanted to cash in, but he always said no.'

'Why?'

She looked surprised by this. 'I haven't the faintest idea.' As if to say, *He was* your *father*. Which of course had always been the problem.

'Anyway,' said Patsy, and she went on to explain that after the imminent flotation – which was already underwritten – the shares would be worth at least the amount quoted so ecstatically the previous afternoon by Gary. And with that Patsy clasped her hands together, lifted her head and beamed. *End of story.*

Michael sat in silence, thinking hard, until he realized Patsy was about to get up and leave. He didn't want her to go; there seemed so much unsaid still, so many questions he wanted to ask. 'Let me take you for a drive around town,' he said. She looked about to shake her head, so he added quickly, 'You can't come all this way without at least seeing the place where my father lived.' Again she hesitated. *'Please.'*

Outside she handed him her keys. 'Let's go in my car.' So he drove the Cadillac quite slowly, going down Calvin Street under the canopy of the maple-lined avenue. At the Dairy Queen corner he turned onto Main Street, and cruised like a teenager showing off his father's car. Where two months earlier high sunlight had flooded the street like the flesh of a white peach, now the lengthened shadows of early September cast dark squares and oblongs. At the marina he circled around, then retraced their tracks through town. He pointed out the former drugstore.

'I used to work there,' he said, and when she looked curious, explained, 'when I was a kid.'

Back at the Dairy Queen, he turned down Beach Road and drove past the summer cottages that lined the street until he turned at the entrance to the State Park. He paid four dollars for a day pass, resisting Patsy's offer to pay, and parked in the vast asphalt lot on the edge of the beach, which was almost full. Before he turned the engine off, he pressed a button and lowered the windows all the way down.

'That's town,' he said lightly.

'Very nice,' she said politely, as if finishing a sandwich he had made.

'What you expected?'

She seemed determined not to look at him. After a moment she said quietly, 'Frankly, it's not at all what I thought it would be.'

He felt a twinge of irritation. What did this woman want – Grosse Point transplanted to Atlantic County?

She cleared phlegm from her throat, and said, 'It's much *nicer* than I thought it would be.' She turned her head towards the dunes on North Beach, and to his surprise he saw there was a tear on her cheek.

He waited, and in time she turned her head back. 'You have no idea how many times I visualized all this. How many times

I had a picture in my mind of where Henry lived. Your father. But I had it all wrong.'

'Why is that?'

'Because it's *pretty* here. It's lovely. In my head, I thought it would be small and dry and horrible.' She laughed wryly.

'Tell me,' he said, 'why didn't you ever come up here? It's not that far from Detroit.' She seemed uncomfortable with the question, and as he looked searchingly at her he thought he saw the answer. 'Or was it that my father didn't want you to?' When Patsy's expression seemed to confirm this, he asked, 'Why was that? What was he hiding from?'

Patsy shrugged and wiped the tear from her cheek. Michael sighed. 'Mrs Minsky, I am not trying to upset you. I am just trying to get to grips with my father a little better than I ever did when he was alive. They think they've got the guy who killed him now, and I realize nothing you and I talk about holds a candle to that, now does it? But I would like to know about my father's past.'

'It was so long ago,' she said in a whisper.

'Can't you tell me the truth?'

'I haven't lied to you,' she snapped.

'I didn't mean you had. But please understand, I don't know anything about my father's life before he came here. I don't even have a photograph of him from then.'

She played again with her wedding ring. It circled once, then twice around her finger as she seemed to consider what to say.

Michael said, 'Did you know my grandfather? He couldn't have just disappeared.'

Patsy spoke without hesitation. 'Oh no, you're mistaken. That's exactly what happened to him. He went back to Poland before the War for a visit, wrote your grandmother that he was going to stay there for a while, then war broke out, and that's the last she ever heard from him.'

'Did my grandmother take it pretty hard?'

'Not emotionally, if that's what you mean. My mother told me it wasn't a happy marriage. But financially – I mean, think about it, your grandmother had a little boy and she spoke bad

English and it was still the Depression. I don't know how she got by.'

'Your mother must have helped,' Michael suggested.

'Yes,' she said, nodding, 'I think she did. Your grandmother took in laundry for people. I know that. Henry once told me he'd rather sleep rough than ever iron another sheet. He was helping your grandmother by the time he was four years old.'

'So my grandfather never came back. Did he die in the War?'

'I assume so. It would have been a miracle if he'd survived.'

Michael looked at her for a moment, trying to understand. Then he felt as if a light bulb had gone on in his head. 'Wait a minute, was my father's father a Jew?'

'Of course,' said Patsy simply.

He thought of the swastika on his father's house and Jimmy Olds's bizarrely prescient query: *Was your father some kind of Jew?* 'My father never told me that.'

'Why should he? I don't think it mattered much to him.' Patsy looked at him and added sharply, 'What's the problem? You look like you swallowed a goldfish.'

'So my father was a Jew?' he said. His father had run away from *that*? Michael felt a terrible sense of disappointment, both because the secret seemed so mundane, and because his father's concealment seemed so fundamentally at odds with the essential honesty Michael had always perceived in the man.

Patsy looked at him oddly. 'Don't tell me you're an anti-Semite.'

'No, no,' he said hastily. 'But why did my father run away from it?'

'I don't think he did. Anyway, most people wouldn't say he was a Jew, because his mother wasn't.' Her voice suddenly rose. 'Listen, I don't care what your father was. As far as I'm concerned, your father was *wonderful*. When I was a girl he was my hero. And later on he gave me five thousand dollars that saved our business when nobody else gave a damn whether we sank or swam.' Her lips were pinched tight and there was real anger in her voice now. Michael said nothing and she seemed to calm down. 'Your father wanted to make a new life for himself.'

'You mean a new self?'

She shrugged. 'I suppose you could call it that. That meant Detroit was out the window. In a funny way, it meant I was too, and my mother, and anyone who knew him before. But *religion* wasn't the issue. That's not what he was ashamed of.'

'So what *was* he ashamed of?' Michael looked at her so intently that Patsy started to blush. He was tired of pleading and let the question sit between them, waiting for an answer. Patsy squirmed slightly, then took her handbag, a small flat lozenge of shiny black leather with a gold clasp, and opened it. Peering down, she extracted a packet of Tic-Tacs and offered Michael one. When he shook his head she popped one in her mouth, and sat sucking for a moment.

When she spoke it was in a low, almost offhand voice, as if otherwise her emotions would betray her. 'There was an accident.'

'What kind of accident?'

'A car accident.' She started twisting her ring again. 'Your father was driving.'

'Who did he hit?'

She looked at him. 'He didn't hit anybody.'

'Well, who else was involved?'

'Your grandmother. His mother,' she added redundantly, looking slightly stunned by her own recollection. 'They'd been up along the Huron shore for the weekend and were driving back late at night. Your father was tired, and he must have nodded off. They went off the road and down an embankment; I think the car rolled over. Your father didn't have a scratch on him, but your grandmother got thrown from the car.'

'And?'

'And she was killed.'

'Jesus. He killed her by falling asleep at the wheel?'

'Yes.' She paused and spoke more slowly. 'I'm tempted to say it could happen to anyone. I know there've been times I've almost nodded off. Haven't you?'

After a moment, Michael agreed. He remembered driving once, late at night, to Stillriver from Ann Arbor, exhausted from finishing a term paper but too eager to see Cassie to wait until morning. He'd almost gone off the bridge in Grand Haven, which scared him so much that he felt *too* awake during the remaining sixty miles home.

'Like I say,' Patsy continued, 'it's tempting to think it could happen to anyone, but the fact is it was *his* fault. He should have pulled over, or sung to himself, or whatever it took to stay awake. But he didn't. The only consolation was that she was asleep when it happened. She wouldn't have known what hit her. Not that there was any consoling your father.'

Michael sat stunned, trying to sort this new answer into the complicated mosaic of his life with his father. Detroit – no wonder he'd loathed the place. And driving – Henry had *hated* driving, inexplicably, almost phobically. Now Michael knew why.

'I was worried for a while that your father might go crazy, and in a way he did. His grief was terrible: his mother was all he had in the world. But his guilt was even worse. He told me he couldn't bear it. And the next time we talked he said he had to leave. He couldn't live with himself if he stayed in Detroit. He said he wanted to begin again, have a fresh start. That's when he came to Stillriver.'

'Is that the last time you saw him?'

She nodded and said with a trace of wonder, 'Over forty years ago.'

'How much were you in touch? Or has all this happened only since he died?'

She shook her head. 'No. He lent me the money a few years after he came here. I wrote him in desperation but I never expected him to be able to help, not five thousand dollars' worth anyway. After that, every few years I'd get a Christmas card with a message on it. It was never very long – I knew when you were born, when your brother was born, when your mother died, and then the year your father retired. He never had much more news than that. Until I wrote him a few years back and told him about the sale – we got bought out and I wanted him to know. After that we started to write, though still only occasionally. And then last winter he called me.'

'On the phone?'

'Yes. He wanted to let me know he'd changed his will.'

'Did he say why?'

'I suppose in case anything happened to him, I should know who to contact.'

'No, sorry, I mean did he say why he had changed the will?'

She turned and looked at him with softer eyes. 'He wasn't mad at you, if that's what you think.'

'He left me the house,' he said quietly. 'I've got nothing to complain about.'

'He was very proud of you. I think he felt bad you'd been divorced, though he told me he'd never thought she was the one for you.'

'He was right there.'

'You had a girlfriend he was very fond of – he mentioned she was back in town. Have you seen her?'

He nodded. *Yes*, he thought, *but not for much longer*.

'It was your brother he was worried about. He said Gary was in and out of trouble all the time. According to your father, he'd need the money more. As I told your brother yesterday, you should both sell your shares as soon as they're traded. There's nothing to be sentimental about – it's not as if we own the company any more.'

'That was in winter. Did you hear from him after that?'

'No. I wrote him in April about the flotation. But I never heard back, until the lawyer wrote to say he'd been murdered. What a terrible thing.'

They sat in silence, looking out over the lake. A front was approaching from Wisconsin in a tumbleweed-shaped pack of dark cloud. The people on the beach were packing up their towels and coolers and hurrying up through the sand to their cars. Michael sighed, then turned on the ignition and drove slowly out of the State Park.

When he got to Benny's B&B he pulled over and parked. As he handed over her car keys, Patsy broke the silence. 'Could a

376

not-so-old old lady give you some advice?' She didn't wait for an answer. 'Your brother thought the world of your father; he doesn't need to know what happened. Don't you think?' she said, turning her head to look at him in a friendly but dispassionate way. 'As for you, I'd hate to think that what I've said would lower Henry in your estimation. He was a fine man who made a mistake. I'd say that he more than paid for it. And I'd like to think you'd forgive him, because I know for sure he never forgave himself.'

She opened the side door and began to get out. 'Mrs Minsky,' he said, 'could we give you dinner? My brother and me, and maybe that friend of mine you mentioned?'

She smiled again and he started to think of where to take her. 'That would have been very nice,' she said, 'but I've got an engagement already.' His face must have shown his surprise, for she explained. 'I'm seeing Mr Atkinson, your lawyer. Now that he's found me at last, it's like he doesn't want to let me go.' She pushed the door closed, then leaned in through the open window with an extended hand.

He shook it and said, 'Would you like to come to breakfast?' He gestured with his head towards his house across the street. 'It's not exactly far away.'

'That's very kind, but I'm leaving at the crack of dawn. I have to get back to the family.' She drew her hand back through the window. 'It was very nice meeting you.'

He got out of the car and watched her walk towards the front steps of Benny's B&B, wondering why she had come all the way up to see him and Gary if she didn't want to get to know them.

Of course. She had wanted to put faces to the two sons of Henry Wolf because that was as close as she would ever get to seeing Henry Wolf again. She didn't really want to *know* Gary or Michael – she wouldn't, in his father's phrase, even break bread with them. It was his father's ghost she had chased halfway up the lower peninsula, not the living, breathing figures of his sons. *He was my hero.*

THAT EVENING IT began to rain: first patchily in an intermittent spray; then heavily, even tumultuously, in thunderstorms that lit up the sky with silver; finally steadily, relentlessly, from a solid ceiling sky of grey.

Cassie had taken the kids to a movie in Fennville with Nancy Sheringham and her youngest daughter. 'Will I see you tomorrow then?' he had asked, trying to keep the anxiety out of his voice. There was silence at the other end. 'Please,' he had added.

'Yeah,' she'd said quietly, and put down the phone.

So after a supper of sandwiches he sat in the living room reading while Gary made financial calculations on a yellow legal pad he had found in their father's study. Michael had said nothing to Gary about his own conversation with Patsy, other than to confirm that she seemed above board and their inheritance real enough. He had been distracted, anyway, by a call from Donny, to whom Michael related the latest developments in the murder inquiry. Donny sounded surprised by the news of Raleigh's involvement. 'I told you he was nasty, but I never took him for a killer.'

'Who did?' said Michael. 'The revenge of the nerd. Just like in the movies. But I still don't really understand it. Do you kill an old man you think has squealed on you, even if you've got off? And why put a swastika on the house?'

'Well, let's hope Maguire gets him to tell all.'

Then Michael reminded him about the Junction bridge and its downstream vulnerability. Donny had yet to speak with Cassavantes. 'I will tomorrow,' he told Michael. 'Don't you worry about it; you've got more important things on your plate.'

When he came back to the living room, Gary looked up from his pad. 'Will I have to pay those bastards tax on it?'

'Which bastards?' asked Michael, knowing full well.

'The feds. How much will they get?'

He resisted the temptation to bait his brother. 'Nothing. We're way below the inheritance ceiling. That's something like six hundred grand. Pop wasn't *that* rich.'

Gary grinned. 'It seems a lot of money to me,' he said, and Michael didn't say anything. *Let him enjoy it while he can.*

It was still raining the next morning. Michael had heard a car leave Benny Wagner's just as the first light slanted in through his bedroom window, and getting up he saw that Patsy's car was gone from the yard across the street. Outside the grass was slick with rainwater, and the leaves on the trees hung limp and sodden. Deep puddles had formed in the small dips of the street, and there was a sleek basalt shine to the new patch of asphalt at the corner.

When Cassie and the kids came over in the late morning, they decided to have an indoors day. Michael made roast beef for lunch, with sautéed potatoes and green beans, and then Jack and Sally took ice-cream cones into the living room and began a seemingly endless game of Stratego with Gary while Michael and Cassie read the papers, deferring any continuation of their conversation by the charter school. He wanted to tell her about his father, too, but felt it would have to wait until things were clearer between the two of them. *Clearer?* It wasn't clarity he wanted; it was closeness.

The rain stopped briefly in mid-afternoon, but by evening it was coming down hard again. 'It's arrived too late to make much difference to the farmers,' said Cassie, 'but just in time to spoil Labor Day for everybody else.'

Yet liking or loathing the rain seemed beside the point in the face of the sheer amount of it. After sixteen hours of non-stop precipitation, Michael felt a mixture of oppression and alarm. He was used to climatic extremes, which was perhaps why he found himself so worried now. For this was not a county accustomed to natural disasters. Tornadoes never really liked a lake; they preferred the milder, flat prairie of the country further south. Snowfall, too, was comparatively moderate, unlike the southwest corner of Lake Michigan (where snow got trapped like flour in a sieve), or the Upper Peninsula two hundred miles north, which had a winter landscape straight out of Jack London – snowshoes were a necessity rather than an affectation, and the inhabitants of remote cabins could be snowed in for weeks.

Usually the rainfall in Atlantic County was moderate: thirty-six inches a year, roughly half that of some other places on the same latitude. But Michael reckoned that they had received the average monthly rainfall due the county in the last twenty-four hours alone. When Cassie and the kids left he stayed up to listen to the forecast on the Blue Lake station, though his thoughts were mainly on Cassie's goodbye. 'We need to talk,' he'd whispered as she'd gathered up the kids.

'I don't see what there is to discuss,' she said crisply. 'Just tell me your leaving date a little ahead of time so I can start to adjust. *This* time I'd appreciate a little warning, if only for the sake of the kids.'

Blue Lake radio announced that flood warnings were in force in the counties that stretched along the shoreline on the western side of the state, from South Haven to Traverse City. Atlantic County was mentioned by name, and although there was no specific mention of the Still river, Michael went to bed feeling uneasy. For he had seen catastrophes before, seen them creep in like uninvited guests showing up for the weekend – though unexpected, they behave well and prove no trouble, until they try to burn the house down Sunday morning.

He woke now in the dark to an intermittent burring sound. For a brief second he thought he was in Scotland, on the job, and that something terrible had happened on the site. It was only as he jumped out of bed in his boxer shorts and T-shirt that he got his bearings, and recognized the noise of the old-fashioned telephone in his parents' former bedroom.

'You awake?' It was Donny.

'I am now.'

'It took you so long I was about to phone Cassie's. Listen, the dam's close to going, and I thought you'd want to be there. Christ knows what's going to happen.'

'Pick me up in five minutes.'

'Call it ten so I can make us some coffee.'

He had promised to take Jack to see the dam, but it sounded as if it would be too late for that now. He would make it up to the boy somehow. He and Donny drove in silence out of town, sharing coffee from the thermos's cup. When they went over the Junction bridge, Donny shook his head. 'I told Cassavantes what you said about bracing the downstream side of the central pier. He said he'd "take it under advisement". What the hell does that mean?'

'It means that if the dam goes we might lose the bridge.'

They took the interstate to Fennville and the rain came down in thin sheets which, as Michael rolled the window down, sailed through the dark air like spitting icicles. This time Donny didn't approach the dam through the park on the far side. 'It's probably flooded over there. No time to get stuck.' He parked instead in the empty lot next to Cameron's hardware store, and they picked their way along the soggy bluff for a quarter of a mile until they could look down on Fennville Lake as it was gradually illuminated by the light of the imminent sunrise. Michael was wearing his waterproof jacket from work and thick corduroys, but his hair soon grew soaked because he hadn't been able to find his hat. Jack had been wearing it as a joke; it dwarfed his little head like an oversized sombrero. *I have to teach him to put my things back where they belong,* he thought. And then, *When are you planning to do that?*

Michael looked around the lake shore, as morning arrived through the misty air without colouring the scene at all. It was surprising how big the circle of water looked from this high vantage point, and surprising too how unchanged it seemed from his earlier visit with Donny. But what had he expected? Surging, frothing waters? A tidal wave propelled across the surface like a billowing sail filled with wind? Something like that – anything other than this slow, almost imperceptible rise.

He looked down at the dam. The clay section was closest to

them, with the level of the lake now within a foot of its restraining lip. The far side of the dam was slightly higher and made of concrete; where he and Donny had walked casually along it on their earlier visit, now a group of men stood in a long chain, passing sandbags down to two brave souls who stood stacking them on the imperilled clay edge. One of the workers from the concrete end ran skittishly across the clay lip until he jumped with visible relief up onto a knoll of grass, where another group of workmen stood, almost directly below Michael and Donny.

They all seemed to be staring out at the lake, and Michael peered out at the water, wondering what they were looking at. Gradually a figure emerged from the lake's mild mist, swimming slowly in a black wet suit with goggles and a long flashlight held aloft in one hand. Reaching shore, the frogman clambered out and stood awkwardly, catching his breath, his black flippered feet splayed out. He climbed up onto the grassy point where the watching group stood and pulled back the rubber hood of his wet suit, then began talking urgently to a burly balding man, who was wearing a knee-length raincoat of luminous orange that reminded Michael of New York traffic cops in bad weather.

'Well, if it isn't Brixton,' said Donny.

'Which one's Brixton?'

'The guy in the wet suit. He was a SEAL in the navy; he likes to show off his diving prowess. Cassavantes is the guy talking to him, the guy in the orange.'

'Shouldn't you be down there? I don't want to get in your way.'

'I'm on the Home Guard – for Stillriver. But come on, let's go down.'

They worked their way down the bluff and through the crowd of helpers, who had stopped stacking sandbags and were staring glumly out at the water while they drank steaming coffee out of Styrofoam cups. Donny nodded to most of them and sometimes stopped to say hello; eventually they came to Cassavantes, who was still talking to the former SEAL.

'Boss,' said Donny, 'this is Michael Wolf, the guy I was telling you about.'

Cassavantes nodded but didn't shake hands. He was a little shorter than Michael but much broader. 'Oh yeah,' he said, just on the edge of a sneer, 'you're the big time engineer. Problem is, we're not trying to build anything here, just keep it from being destroyed.'

Oh no, a tough guy, thought Michael with an inward groan. In the work he was used to, nobody ever bothered to act tough, since most of them *were* tough, and posturing could get you hurt, either from doing something foolhardy, or from pissing off someone tougher than you and happy to prove it.

'I appreciate that,' said Michael. There was no point pushing it. 'If I can help in any way, just let me know.' He added quietly, 'I have seen a dam give way before.'

'Stick around and you'll get to see another one.'

Michael pointed at the dam itself, no more than forty feet away. 'I reckon the clay end will go first.'

'Do you now? Well, thank you very much – I don't know how I would have figured that out myself.' And Cassavantes turned on his heel and walked off to another group of maintenance workers.

Michael looked at Donny. 'Sorry about that. I should have kept my mouth shut.'

Donny shrugged. 'If you had, he would have complained you weren't being any help. That's just the way he is. You can't win.'

'Okay. But listen, I'm going to go up there again.' He pointed to the bluff where they had been standing. 'Do me a favour: talk to Cassavantes and try and persuade him to get all those guys' – he pointed to the men on the concrete side – 'off the dam.' Then he pointed to the group on the knoll below them. 'And try and get him to move these guys as well.'

'Why? It's the low clay part that's going to give.'

He thought how best to convey a distant yet discernible danger without being alarmist, and without (although this had more to do with his own ego) looking foolish should the danger not materialize. 'You ever see a bathtub overflow?'

'Yes,' said Donny, adopting the expression of superficial passivity with which, as a teenager, he had endured Michael's lengthier explanations of geometry solutions.

'No, I don't mean what happens *after* a bathtub overflows, I mean *as* it overflows.'

Donny looked at him bleary-eyed. 'Listen, I know I'm not Einstein, and it is six thirty in the morning, and I haven't had my second cup of coffee. But if I go up to Cassavantes and start talking about bathtubs, I don't think I'm going to get very far.'

Michael took a deep breath. 'Understood. But my point is dead simple: when a bathtub overflows it tends to do so at one particular point, say the corner down below your left foot when you're lying in it. But pretty soon the water starts coming over the top *everywhere*. And that's what's going to happen here.'

'Meaning?'

'Meaning, those guys on the concrete are going to be standing there staring at the point of overflow and suddenly the water's going to start rising all around them too. Maybe not very fast, maybe just enough to get their feet wet. But conceivably, fast enough to drown one or two of them. I don't know.'

'I got you.'

'And another thing,' said Michael, taking a deep breath. He pointed down towards the far end of Fennville Lake. 'Up that way there are boats and docks and all sorts of crap that's suddenly going to be sucked this way faster than hell. But it's not going to go in a straight line right for the little hole. It's just going to come in this general direction. And I wouldn't want to be standing down there when a speedboat or a junked car or somebody's dumped icebox comes zipping in sideways in my general direction. Not if I'm already standing in three feet of water that keeps me from getting my ass out of the way.' He paused momentarily. 'Understand, I am talking worst case here.'

Donny looked at him and gave reluctant assent. 'I suppose an optimist isn't much use right now.' He turned and walked slowly towards Cassavantes while Michael retreated to the bluff.

Ten minutes later no one remained on the top of the dam, and even the men on the grassy point had climbed higher up, away from the lake. Donny was among the last to come up to the bluff, and he came and stood next to Michael, breathing heavily. 'I don't know,' he said between heavy breaths, 'whether you got me fired or you got me a promotion. But it seemed to work. Nobody's down there anyway.'

They watched as the water crept slowly higher, so tortuously that Michael found himself willing the rising water to hurry up and get it over with. After twenty minutes some of the men grew impatient, and one of them started to go back down the hill towards the dam until Cassavantes curtly called him back. Then Cassavantes himself turned and looked up contemptuously at Donny and Michael. Michael ignored this, trying not to feel self-conscious as he stood waiting for something to happen.

At first the change was almost imperceptible. Near the dam the water, viewed from high above, suddenly seemed to darken, though this might be a trick played by the early light, or stirred-up sediment close to the shore. Ripples appeared on the surface, miniature waves that soon began to revolve, then join together to form a larger whirlpool. As this whirlpool grew, it rotated at increasing speed, and seemed to dip below the level of the neighbouring water, as if it were pulling additional water into itself the way it would suck in a struggling swimmer.

'See,' he said in a loud voice to Donny, and several of the men near him on the bluff looked over. He pointed down. 'It's going all right, but the hole's under the surface. Give it time and it'll come up.'

And suddenly from the upper rim of the clay side of the dam, where the water had been lapping gently a good six inches below its top, a large chunk gave way. The water shot through this gap, falling over the edge as if poured in a generous stream from a jug. The flow was thin at first – less than a yard wide – but it thickened as the gap in the dam's lip expanded sideways. The milk chocolate bulk of the dam began to crumble like delicate cake, small crumbs giving way to bite-sized chunks, then whole wedges, until soon the water cascaded with silky violence over what had been a smooth, sixty-foot blockage of clay.

Within a minute of the first breach of the dam, water was running like spilled ink below it, easily swamping the banks of the river, moving with subtle capillary force among the thin oaks and aspens of the sparse forest. There was a popping noise, then a volley of them, like muffled automatic weapon fire. At first, Michael wondered why anyone would be firing a gun, but then he saw a small stand of tag alders knocked flying like bowling pins, and he realized he was hearing the splintering noise of the tree trunks splitting at their base.

'Come on,' said Donny, without his usual mildness. 'I got to get back before that reaches Stillriver.'

And they ran towards the truck, leaving the other men to watch as the devastation mounted below them. Michael felt as if he were leaving a ringside seat just before the final round.

Donny drove out of Fennville at high speed, slapping a yellow light onto the top of the cab even as he accelerated out of the parking lot, heading east, away from the river, towards the old highway. 'If I follow the water,' he said in explanation, 'we may get cut off.' He managed to go ninety miles an hour on the old 31, then slowed down as he turned west on a loose, sandy road that ran through Weekly's peach farm. Trees stood in leafy lines along both sides of the road, mature stands as well as the dwarves of the new plantations. In one field of older trees, the fruit had not been touched. Unpicked peaches clogged the outstretched arms of the trees, and windfalls lay soft and rotting on the ground, filling the air with a sticky sweetness.

They were on a track unfamiliar to Michael until he saw the high Victorian roof of Fennville Acres, home to Ethel and Daisy. The road surface grew firmer here, with graded packed sand, and Donny's truck picked up speed as they passed the home, then careened downhill through young apple trees to the intersection with the back road between Fennville and Stillriver. They were at the bottom of Happy Valley, and not more than a hundred feet to their left sat the old low wooden bridge. Donny stopped the truck to look, and they could see at once that some of the flooding waters had arrived, for the river had surged into extraordinary life, coming down the Fennville side of the valley in rushing curls of white, like semicircle strips of birch bark. The floor of the wooden bridge had disappeared from sight and the water was beginning to cover the upright struts of the railings on both of the bridge's sides.

'We better get back,' said Donny. 'Cassavantes will be at the Junction. He said if the dam went we'd all recce there and figure out what to do next.'

Do? Thought Michael. In his experience, there wasn't usually anything you could actually do in a situation like this, other than stay the hell out of the way. As they drove on he took a last look back at Happy Valley, which now looked like a vast bowl half-full of water. There was no clear course to the river any more. They drove without comment by Ricky Fell's bend, where the large oak stump formed a memorial of sorts. Donny accelerated down a straightaway and thumped a fist impatiently on the steering wheel. 'I can't believe something is actually happening here. I mean, something *big*.' When Michael said nothing, he added pointedly, 'You're probably used to this kind of thing.'

Michael said, 'There's some excitement you can do without.' He thought of the two drowned men in the Philippines. How small they'd seemed; they looked as if they had fallen asleep.

As they came down the slight, sloping hill towards the Junction, they could see cars and pickup trucks parked on both sides of the bridge. On the bridge itself, a patrol car sat in the town-bound lane with its top light flashing. Michael noted that the water level was very high, but not dangerously so – the dam water was still to come. Donny started to slow down and pull over, when Michael tapped his shoulder. 'Go across,' he said. 'Better to be on the town side, I think.'

On the bridge they stopped as Jimmy Olds walked over, smart in his blue uniform and wearing a brown Mounty-type hat. 'It's coming, Jimmy,' said Donny.

'I know. Cassavantes told me.' He pointed fifty yards along the road, where the now-familiar orange figure stood talking to a small group of men.

'I best get on then,' said Donny.

'Hang on a sec,' said Michael, and leaned his head towards the driver's side window. 'Hey Jimmy?'

'Hi Michael, you come to give us some of your expertise?'

The last syllable was drawn out comically, but the remark was in good humour, and Michael laughed. 'Of course,' he replied. 'And I tell you, if you're looking to get a new model patrol car, just keep this one where it's at. We just saw the Happy Valley bridge under water, and I wouldn't give two bits for this one surviving.'

Jimmy's eyes widened, and he tipped his hat.

Donny put the truck in gear and drove it slowly across the bridge, then pulled over and parked on the road side, only a couple of feet above the shoreline of Stillriver Lake. The rain was coming down hard again, in lashing, stinging bursts pushed by the wind.

Cassavantes appeared on the driver's side, and tapped sharply on Donny's window. He looked angry. 'Thought I told you to get back here right away.'

'I'm sorry, but it was slow coming through Happy Valley,' said Donny.

Cassavantes looked unappeased so Michael asked him about the Junction bridge. Cassavantes said, 'There ain't nothing going to knock down those supports. We've propped it every which way and half the steel wire's been laid for the new concrete pours.'

'But you haven't propped the downstream pier and the abutments.'

'So what?' demanded Cassavantes with what Michael took to be either the bluster of the unconfident or the stupidity of the certain. 'They're downstream.'

Where do I begin? thought Michael, since almost half the time the downstream side went first. It seemed paradoxical, if you assumed the water flowed as usual, but became understandable once you knew the role scouring and erosion of the banks played in almost every flood.

Before he could say anything, Cassavantes' mobile phone

trilled, and he walked away from the truck to answer it. To Michael's surprise Donny fished in his shirt pocket and took out a pack of Winstons, then lit one with the car lighter. In the wet air of the cab, the smoke seemed especially acrid.

'Since when do you do that?' he asked.

'We're not inside, so I didn't think I had to ask permission,' he said peevishly.

'Shit, I don't care. I just didn't think you smoked.'

'That's big of you,' said Donny, and took a long drag on his cigarette. It took Michael a moment to realize his friend was enraged – but was it with Cassavantes for dressing him down, or with Michael? 'You always know, don't you?' said Donny, exhaling a big softball of smoke. 'You think we're all little piss ants compared to your big, sophisticated self. You don't like this place at all, but you might try to hide it a little.'

Michael was bewildered. When he looked at Donny, he found him staring out at Stillriver Lake, his eyes narrowed and his nose wrinkled up high – with him, the sure signs of fury. Michael said, 'Who says I don't like this place? I grew up here.'

'Sure,' said Donny, 'and got out at the first opportunity.'

'What is this about?'

'Say what?'

'You heard me. Aren't we a little old for hidden resentments to come surfacing now?'

Donny took another long drag at his cigarette. 'I'm not hiding anything,' he barked.

'You sure?'

'Goddamnit,' Donny declared, 'I can't talk to you any more. You won't listen to anything.' He took a final drag, gripped the filter like a paper airplane between his thumb and forefinger and sailed it out the window. 'I am sorry about what happened to your father, I am sorry for all the mess of it. Believe me. But honestly, Michael, things are happening to other people too. Not bad things necessarily, not anything like a murder, but lives *do* go on, and things happen in those lives.'

'What are you trying to tell me?' he asked, thinking, *Things? What things?*

But Donny was already shaking his head. 'There's no point.'

'Go on, try me,' said Michael.

'She made a mistake, I know she thinks she did, and like an idiot I made a mistake right after that.'

'Who are you talking about?'

'Nancy of course. Who else? Can't you see *anything* around you?'

'I guess not.' Coming on the heels of Cassie's accusation of tunnel vision, this seemed to be the truth.

'You know, you fucked up too,' said Donny, with the urgency of someone trying to comfort himself. 'But you've had a second chance, and you're taking it, aren't you?'

'It's not that simple,' said Michael, wishing it were.

'Bullshit. Duverson's in prison, you're divorced, what's the problem? You've got Cassie now.' *Do I really?* thought Michael, but he didn't interrupt his friend, who was continuing, 'I wish my life was that simple. But Lou's not in jail and my wife's not about to divorce me. Face it,' he said, with an emphasis he seemed to feel he deserved. 'I'm fucked!'

Michael tried to speak calmly, aware that diffidence might only inflame his friend further. 'You're only fucked if you think that having a dream means you've got to act on it.'

'Look who's talking. You've never got over Cassie.'

'I don't have kids. Before you say "lucky you", think about what it would be like not to have your children. Forget the rest for a second – whether you love Brenda or Nancy, whether you're living the life you think you need to live. Would you *really* be happier without those kids?'

He answered his own question. 'I don't think so. And think, too – instead of picturing how sad you are without what you're so sure you want, try to picture what it would be like if you got it. Don't think about yourself, think about other people. Think of the misery for Brenda – I don't believe you really wish her harm – and even think about Lou (*of course* he's a douche bag, but he's not a *mean* guy), and think about their kids as well as yours. And then finally think how happy you'd actually be, sitting in some one-bedroom bungalow in a place like Walker-ville, with Nancy, all right, but not with your kids, that's for sure. You'd sit there, telling each other how true your love is while everybody else is stinking miserable. And actually, you are too.'

He didn't look at Donny. 'In my opinion – not that it seems to count for much – you happen to have a *great* wife. But even if you had a mediocre wife, whatever that means, it still wouldn't be worth it.'

'Is that how you feel?'

He thought of his Rubicon moment on the thirty-ninth floor and told a lie he could excuse on the grounds it was well-intended. 'If I've learned one thing it's that life doesn't always let you follow your heart. If I had followed it from the beginning, then maybe everything would have been okay. But then again, maybe not. I might be sitting here complaining to you about having spent my whole life in Stillriver with boring old Cassie and why hadn't I slept with Sophie Jansen at U of M when I had the chance.'

'Was that that blonde girl's name?'

'You ought to know. You told Nancy about her way back when, and she told Cassie.'

'Ah, so it cuts both ways,' said Donny.

'How's that?' asked Michael.

'You've got resentments too.'

'I'd have called mine a justified grievance.'

'I'm sure you would. But aren't we a little old for a justified grievance too?'

'And you told Duverson I was working in Texas. That one could have cost me my life.'

'And that one I'm sorry about. With Sophie Jansen I was probably just jealous, and it serves you right for cheating on Cassie. With Ronald, it was an accident. He came back for his mother's funeral and I saw him in the tavern. He'd been drinking and I'd had a few myself, and shit, it just slipped out. When Nancy heard what I'd done, she wouldn't speak to me for six months.'

They sat quietly for a while. 'So,' said Donny neutrally.

Michael said, 'Think of it this way: maybe I've made enough mistakes that I don't want other people making more.'

Donny chewed on this for a moment, then said, 'And maybe I wasn't trying to do you harm by saying something to Ronald. Maybe it was just a dumb-fuck mistake I made. Think of *that* that way.'

'Deal,' said Michael, and they shook hands, not – it seemed to Michael – with any pretence that all was forgiven, but rather as if by a common accord that said, *It's there and always will be, but nothing can be done about it, so let's move on.*

They could hear Cassavantes shouting through the rain as they got out of the truck. 'Right! Everybody come over here and listen up. We got a change of plan.' His voice softened only marginally as people gathered around him. 'You can stop worrying about the bridge.' He looked over at Michael on the edge of the group. 'There's been a landslide upstream, and the whole course has got diverted. It's running into the south branch now and starting to flood the Meadows. It's not coming this way any more, it's headed for town.'

Half an hour later all of them were positioned on the town edge of the Meadows on the high land just east of town, above the trough of the old septic swamp that ran in a half-mile trench towards the wireworks. Here, up in the Meadows' grassland, there was the advantage, in terms of containing the flood, that the relatively level surface of the fields meant the water was moving in a wide, slow arc; the drawback was that it was a lot of ground for them to cover in the rain.

They did their best, and soon all the workmen from Fennville, as well as Stillriver's volunteer firemen, had formed a human chain in front of the slope that moved down to the septic swamp. At one end of the chain stood a vast pile of empty sandbags, long stored for just such an emergency (*stored where?* Michael wondered) and here a dozen men were busy filling bags from a load of sand poured onto a tarpaulin from the back of Kyler's dump truck. Two other trucks had been sent to the State Park beach to be filled by a mush eater that was already scooping sand from the shoreline. Soon there would be sand enough.

But not enough people to manage it. According to Donny, who joined Michael where he stood stacking filled sandbags, Cassavantes had called for help from the unit of National Guardsmen stationed in Muskegon. But the Muskegon river was threatening to swamp the city's business district, and the protection of that was seen as the higher priority; his request was turned down.

'Muskegon's more important than the wireworks?' asked Michael with a cynical laugh.

'And even than the bungalows,' replied Donny in kind.

'Shit,' Michael said. 'That's Cassie you're talking about.' He looked at the wide disc of water stretching towards them across the plain, and shook his head.

'I can't see they're in any *danger* there, can you?'

'I hope not,' said Michael. 'The problem with floods is you can't ever tell. Especially in the open countryside. This is probably the dam water here,' he said, pointing at their sopping feet, 'but it's still raining and there's more to come. Let me have your phone a minute, will you?' Michael dialled Cassie on the mobile but got her answer machine, so he left a message asking her to call him ASAP. It was now ten thirty.

He kept trying her at odd moments throughout the morning, but got no answer. Then he saw Donny walking along the edge of the field towards him, holding his mobile phone aloft. 'It's for you,' he said. 'Hold it steady – the reception's no good.'

He took the phone and said hello.

'Michael?' He could barely hear the voice.

'Cassie? Are you okay? Where are you? I don't want you in your house right now. Go to my house as soon as you can. Are—'

She interrupted. 'We're at Nancy's. Sally and me. Jack's at Donny and Brenda's with their kids.'

'Oh,' he said, slightly nonplussed.

'Listen, I've got some bad news,' she said, and he waited tensely. *She doesn't want to see me any more, she wants me to stay overseas for good, she's decided she doesn't love me.* 'Maguire just called. They held the identity parade, but Ethel didn't pick out Raleigh. She didn't pick out *anybody* – she said the man she'd seen that night wasn't there.'

He was both so relieved that she wasn't blowing him away and so stunned by the news that he couldn't say anything. 'Anyway,' Cassie went on hesitantly, 'I told Maguire I'd tell you. And I thought you might be worried, I mean about the river and where we were. So now you know.'

'Hey,' he said, 'don't go yet.' He tried to think of something to say, though his thoughts were starting to race with her news. 'Are you okay out there?'

She gave a faint, tinkly laugh – a nice one. 'Michael,' she said, 'Sheringham's is on a hill, remember? You go back to work now. I'll see you tomorrow.'

'I love you, Cassie,' he said loudly, hoping she heard him before the connection was broken.

Ethel was wrong, he thought, *but what did that* mean? *That she'd been confused, and possibly not seen anyone at all? Or seen someone else? But if wasn't Raleigh, who could it be?* They were back to square one. Maguire must have been absolutely furious when Ethel let him down, though with other cops present (and doubtless a lawyer or two for Raleigh), he would have had to keep his cool. Now he wouldn't even be able to get his warrant to search Raleigh's house, for without Ethel's identification, what did he have to show just cause to search the place?

By noon volunteers from town began to come along in what seemed to Michael remarkable numbers. There must have been two hundred of them. Most of them were men: he saw all three Bogle boys for the first time in twenty years, Benny Wagner, who nodded from afar, and even Larry Bottel, who spent more time talking to the girls making coffee than he did moving sand-bags. For the first time since coming back, Michael felt happy to be in such public company, since they were concentrated on a shared task that had nothing to do with his father.

394

The diggers came in, too, trying to push makeshift mounds of loamy soil around to diffuse the water. It was miserable work, for the fresh wind off Lake Michigan meant the rain came in at an angle and was impossible to avoid. By two o'clock the floodwater was above the ankle, and by four o'clock the front line stood in it up to their knees. But it didn't go any higher, and reports from town suggested that although the septic trough was now one vast lake, the water had yet to seep into the surrounding neighbourhood. And then shortly after five thirty, the water actually seemed to be going down, very gradually, just as everyone began complaining about how exhausted they were. Soon it was receding visibly.

'I'm surprised by this,' Michael said to Donny when his friend made one of his periodic visits to Michael's place on the line. 'It's still raining, and yet the water level's going way down real fast. What's happening?'

'Cassavantes may know. Let me ask,' said Donny.

He came back a few minutes later. 'Much as our work is appreciated, it's not what's stopped the water coming through. Cassavantes got two front end loaders from Fennville and they've been digging at the landslide. It's taken them two hours but they've managed to reverse the flow back to normal – well, sort of normal. The north branch is flowing again, and apparently flowing real hard.'

'What's he gone and done that for?' Michael demanded. 'The level in the trough wasn't rising any more. There wasn't any danger. Why didn't he ask me?'

Donny shrugged. 'Probably couldn't bear the thought of your being right twice.'

'Well, this way he may lose the bridge.'

'At the Junction?'

'Yes, at the Junction. Shit. That'll take six months to rebuild. Come on, let's go.'

'Where?'

'To see the bridge. You've got your truck, don't you?'

'No, it got co-opted into bringing sand up from the beach.'

'Let's walk, then. It can't be more than a mile.'

Donny shook his head. 'I don't want to walk two feet, Michael. I'm beat. Sorry, but you go look if you want to. There's nothing we can do about it now anyway.'

Michael looked at his friend impatiently, then saw how tired Donny was. He was breathing hard, and his face had lost its pinkish colour. Behind him he heard a boy shout, and suddenly Donny's youngest son – Clayton, who was two or three years older than Jack – rushed by Michael and hugged his father at the waist. 'Hey, what are you doing here?' asked Donny affectionately.

'We wanted to see the flood, Dad,' said Clayton. 'Where's it gone?'

Before Donny could answer, his eldest boy, Jeffrey, rode up on his bike. To Michael's surprise, a little behind him, running to catch up, came Jack, wearing an oversized slicker Brenda must have lent him. He ran towards Michael, but when he saw the frown on Michael's face he stopped short.

'Donny,' Michael said, 'Jack shouldn't be out here. It's not that safe.'

Clayton piped up now. 'It's okay, we're looking after him.'

Michael shook his head and Donny said, 'Relax, Michael. The boys know what they're doing. They're careful.'

'He's only six, Donny. He should be home – it's getting dark soon.' He could tell that Jack was watching him carefully.

Donny said, 'Shoot, Michael, what's going to happen to him? The flood's over, you said so yourself. He can't come to any harm. Let him stay with the boys. This is Stillriver, not New York.'

Michael looked at the strained expression on Jack's face, and he felt his own tension relax as he relented. 'Okay,' he said, 'but Jack, you come here.' The boy looked at him warily, until he saw Michael reach out with his arms. He ran forward to let Michael lift him up and talk to him face-to-face. 'I hate to think what your mom would say,' said Michael, tickling the boy, who giggled. 'You stay close to Clayton and Jeffrey, you understand? And while you're here, do whatever Donny says.' Jack nodded, and impulsively Michael hugged him before putting him back on the ground. 'Have a good time, and for Christ's sake don't tell your mother I said it was okay for you to be here. Or that I said "for Christ's sake."'

Donny laughed. 'Well,' Michael said to him, setting off towards the Junction, 'I'll be back when I'm back.'

'Take my mobile,' said Donny, handing him his phone. 'That way you can call me if you start to drown.'

Michael set off and walked up the slight incline towards the corner of the Meadows, passing the furthest group of men, who had stopped momentarily to rest, smoke a cigarette, and drink half a cup of coffee before returning to the monotonous stacking of sandbags. They looked at Michael with curiosity, but since he didn't recognize any of their faces he kept walking, turning west and downhill towards the ravine that carried the north branch of the Still down towards the Junction and Stillriver Lake. The rain was lessening, though it still stung as it blew in against his face, borne on the harsh wind coming off the big lake to the west.

At the head of the ravine there was a path of sorts, which wound its way down from the upper edge through the dense wild blueberry bushes and scrub brush that thrived in this undisturbed canyon. Michael moved carefully on the sandy path, digging in his heels with every step, grabbing for support from the slithery branches, sometimes actually getting down on all fours when the footing seemed especially treacherous.

Although he could not see the north branch of the Still he could hear it, even in the wind, and as he came up over a small outcropping of rocks, there was a gap in the brush and he suddenly saw the river below him at the bottom of the ravine. It had been transformed. It was wider, naturally, but it was not the expanse of the flood-filled water that struck Michael so much as its accelerating speed. Gone was the usual placidity of the Still, normally closer to a large stream than a river, with slow moving currents that seemed to stop and stand still in deep, dark and quiet pools. The present river was in turmoil, a white, rushing, tumbling mass of water that steamed in the darkening air. The scene resembled pictures of high mountain rivers raging in the Rockies, or the Swedish rivers he had seen, fjord feeders, racing madly to bring their waters to the vast containers of those Nordic lakes.

But now it was this river that wouldn't stop, and as he watched its torrential progress, Michael felt a corresponding urgency take hold. He looked ahead and saw he had very little trail left to descend, and realized, too, that where the river turned at the bend a few hundred yards ahead of him, careening at high speed like a racing car precariously cornering, he would be able to see Stillriver Lake and the Junction.

He forced himself to move slowly, resisting the temptation to join the river in its mad downhill race. Twenty minutes later he emerged from the last trailside bush and found that the trail ended abruptly at the edge of a small cliff, a ledge really, roughly five or six feet above a wide, flat pan of sandy gravel riverbank that adjoined the Still. Though obscured by the bend in the river, the Junction was less than a quarter-mile away; to get there he would have to move along this flat section of gravel, which made him nervous, for it was next to the river and only inches above the surging water level. The water was moving so fast and at such a steep angle down the hill he had just descended that Michael couldn't help but worry about translatory waves, and indeed he soon saw one about a foot high rush past him, sloshing over the gravel. But there was no other way forward, and having come this far he wasn't going to turn around and trudge all the way back uphill. He'd have to move quickly and hope for the best.

He paused to catch his breath. The rain had stopped and he listened as the wind picked up, moving in and out of the trees on the upper reaches of the canyon, clearly audible now above the rushing noise of the river in spate just below him. As a little boy he was frightened of storms, and his mother would come down the hall to his bedroom and comfort him. 'Listen to the wind,' she'd say. 'It's talking to you. Try to hear what it's saying.' But he heard nothing now except the susurrating rise and fall of the wind's breathing. He looked up, as if for guidance, but the sky was darkening and the cover of cloud obscured any early stars. There was no moon.

He felt the mobile in the pocket of his coat, a nylon windbreaker he'd bought in Germany. He wanted to call Cassie again, to tell her the sad news about his father's past, and to let her know that yes, he was going to Dubai, but that he was determined to come back after that. He would be in Stillriver for Christmas with her and Sally and Jack. After that he didn't know – he had to make a living, after all, and he couldn't see how Atlantic County could provide one. But even if he had to go abroad again without Cassie, he would return to her, and to Stillriver. God knows how they would cope with a life that saw him semi-commuting to construction sites four and five thousand miles away; God knows what he would do when Ronald Duverson got out of prison. But this time he was not going to give up. This time he wasn't going to run away.

Time to move. He got down on his knees and turned round, then let his legs hang over the small cliff while he held on by his arms; when his feet finally hit the riverbank he let go, stumbled, then stood up. As he started to walk along the gravel he saw something ahead of him, something low and curled up against the base of the cliff that curved at the bend in the river ahead of him. *An animal? Dog? Bobcat?* He expected it to run away at his approach, but as he drew near the figure moved only a little, and peering ahead in the failing light Michael realized he was looking at the figure of a man.

'Am I glad to see you,' the man shouted when Michael was about fifty feet away.

The voice sounded slightly familiar, but Michael couldn't see the man very well in the failing light. He called out, 'Listen, you better get out of here. The river's still rising and that's no place to sit.' He wasn't going to bother to explain about translatory waves. What was this guy doing here? 'Come on,' Michael added impatiently, 'the Junction's just around the corner.'

'That's real thoughtful of you,' said the man, now slowly getting up. He seemed to be holding something in one arm. 'I appreciate it, truly I do. Thanks a million, *little buddy*.'

Michael stopped walking and stared as the man finally stood up. 'I have to say,' Michael said slowly, partly because he was so astonished, and partly in an effort to stay calm, 'that I'm real surprised to see you.'

'I bet you are,' replied Ronald Duverson, who now stood about eight or nine feet in front of Michael, barring the path towards the Junction, with his arms hanging down by his sides. He wore light brown cut-offs without a shirt; his pectorals were heavily contoured and his stomach flat. There was a tattoo of a lightning strike over his heart. On the ledge behind him there was a yellow slicker, which he must have been wearing in the rain.

Michael said, 'How did you know I was coming this way?'

'I was up there,' said Ronald, pointing towards the Meadows. 'I saw you heading over and figured you were going to come look at the Junction. "*He loves bridges*,"' he said in a mocking imitation of Cassie's voice. 'When you stopped to talk to some kids, I took the opportunity to get down the track real fast. I've probably been two hundred yards ahead of you all the way down.'

'I thought you were doing six years for killing an innocent motorist.'

'Innocent?' Ronald laughed. 'He swung first. Bad mistake in my view.'

'So how the hell did you get out?'

'The door to my cell was opened; I walked down the corridor, out through the yard, the locks went *beep beep beep*, the big door opened, and hey *presto*, I was a free man again.'

'I don't understand.'

'Ever heard of parole, asshole?' Ronald said with sudden venom. Ronald's face had aged and his complexion looked rough, but there was a leanness to his jaw and to the tendons in his neck which suggested the super-fitness regime of a prisoner who has twenty-three hours a day to do pushups. Michael noticed that Ronald had never bothered to get his teeth fixed – the front two were still chipped.

'But you got turned down.'

'I wonder who told you that. Probably another man's wife. Probably another man's wife you've been fucking.'

Michael suddenly understood. 'You *didn't* get turned down, did you? You *got* paroled. You didn't have to escape because they let you out.' He said this almost admiringly, thinking, *how clever*. No law official was going to be looking for Ronald; there would be no APBs out for someone who had the right, however recently granted, to walk the street. And, conversely, those with cause to fear Ronald's release would sleep peacefully, believing that he was still safely behind bars.

'I'm due back next week for my meeting with my parole officer. He's very pleased with my progress since leaving the joint. I haven't got a job yet, but he says I'm making real efforts and something's bound to turn up sooner or later.'

'So you've come all the way up here just to . . . see me.'

'That's a real sweet way of putting it.' His smile was chilling. 'I just missed you the last time you were in town. I didn't think you'd leave so soon. If you'd stayed one more night I was due to come calling.'

'The last time? You mean after my father was killed? But what were you doing here?' And Ronald began to smile again. Then he lifted his right arm to reveal a short-handled sledgehammer, which he held by its tapered wooden handle. As he moved his arm there was a shimmering sound as it brushed against his hip, and Michael saw that his right hand was enveloped in a long latex glove, the translucent kind used by dentists and nurses since the arrival of AIDS, skin-tight around the fingers but loose above the wrist. What had Ethel said? *Rustling* – that was it, and that was the word for the noise Ronald's arm had just made. It had been that sound Ethel had heard in the basement.

Michael suddenly felt sick. 'Oh Christ,' he said softly.

'You see,' said Ronald, as if he were explaining something intricate but anodyne, 'I can fly up here and fly back, pay cash, use any old name I like, and nobody's the wiser. But overseas is different altogether. Even if I got permission, which I wouldn't, there'd be no way to hide the fact I'd gone

401

and found you. But this way, you came and found me, if you see what I mean.'

'You killed him to be sure of getting me back here?'

'Partly,' said Ronald readily, as if conceding a point. 'But partly because I *wanted* to kill your father. I never got him back for the time he saved your ass. He made me feel two feet tall that day.'

'Why didn't you just go back later and beat him up too?'

'Sure, and if Cassie had found out about it she wouldn't have touched me with a bargepole. Fact was, I was sure she'd find out what I'd already done to you. I was holding my breath.' He shook his head briefly at the memory. 'You must not have told *anybody* what I did – Cassie never heard a word before we moved to Texas. She couldn't understand why you'd run off. I knew, of course.' He gave a short, harsh laugh. 'But I wasn't saying anything.'

'That was taking a risk. I could have gone to Jerry Dawson. My father wanted me to.'

Ronald nodded in agreement. 'I didn't think it through. You have no idea how much I wanted to be with her, how long I worked on getting to know her. You started diddling some babe at college and I saw my chance. And then what do you know, you stuff your dick back in your pants and ask for forgiveness. When I saw you kiss her down at Nelson's something snapped.'

'So you killed my father and now you think you're going to kill me.' It felt surreal saying the words; he half-expected to discover that this was a dream too.

'There's no "think" about it.'

'Real fair fight you got in mind,' Michael said, pointing at the sledgehammer. Could he shame Ronald into giving him half a chance?

'There isn't going to be any "fight" about it either. If all I wanted was to beat you, I could kick your ass in about five seconds flat.'

'No,' said Michael. 'With my skills and training it would take at least half a minute.'

It took Ronald a moment to realize he wasn't being challenged. The resulting smile was at once appreciative and sarcastic. 'Cute, that's real cute.'

'So what happens after you kill me?'

'Not much. I go back to Texas, find a job, start my life again.'

He hasn't mentioned Cassie, thought Michael, just as Ronald said, 'If you're thinking about Cassie, don't bother. I'm not going to hurt her. Somebody's got to raise those kids. *I* can't. But I tell you one thing: she's going to know who killed you and why. She's going to know that if she hadn't took up with you again you'd still be alive. And so would your daddy. Sorry about that.'

'When you killed my father, I hadn't seen Cassie in six years.'

'So what? You think I'd ignore the fact you fucked my wife because it happened six years ago? You think I'd *forgiven* you?' He was gripping the hammer more tightly now, the veins in his forearm bulging like implants of rubber tubing.

'If you tell Cassie what you've done, aren't you taking quite a chance that you'll get caught?'

'They won't have any more evidence than they do now. As far as the law's concerned I'm in Texas – I haven't missed a meeting with the parole guy yet. If I'd left any evidence they'd have found it by now.'

'What happened with the bat?'

'You mean why did I leave it? Simple. I needed them to suspect somebody else while I got my ass back to Texas to see my parole officer. I never thought it would take them two months to find it. Jesus, Jimmy Olds is just hopeless.'

'How'd you get it in the first place?'

'Raleigh Somerset. Your brother left it out at his place. Raleigh was determined to get your brother back for selling him out to some cop in Muskegon. Said he had this bat with your brother's prints on it, and he was going to set him up with it somehow. I used it instead.'

'So is it Raleigh's you've been staying at?'

'That's right, but never for long – I can't take a risk that the parole officer finds me out of Texas. Even Raleigh's wife didn't know I was there. Though I had quite a scare yesterday when some detective paid a visit. Fortunately, it was Raleigh he was looking for, not me. I don't know why they think he killed your daddy.' He smirked. 'Maybe the swastika I painted on your place pointed them in his direction.'

'Are you a Nazi too, then?'

Ronald gave a hoot of derision. 'Not me. Though I tell you, in a Texas prison you got to be polite to the Aryan Brotherhood if you want to survive. But I don't believe any of that stuff. No, Raleigh owed me big time, though I expect we're about even now.'

'What have you got on Raleigh, then?'

'I saved his life. Remember? Back when we were kids. You got to remember that,' he said, sounding mildly peeved.

'I remember. You were a hero.'

'I was,' said Ronald, and chuckled. 'The thing nobody ever knew, including Raleigh, is that sure, I saved him from drowning, but I was also the one who pushed him in.' He was laughing heartily now.

'But how did you know I was coming back again?'

'You told your brother, didn't you? He told somebody else, and that somebody else told Raleigh.'

'Who? Bubba?'

'Not that fag. Someone else.'

'Oh,' he said, suddenly certain. 'It was asshole mouth.'

'What did you say?' Ronald demanded.

'Barry. That's his name isn't it?'

'Yeah,' Ronald said impatiently.

He was struggling to form more questions. He didn't want to dwell any more on the bat – there was no point explaining why it had gone undiscovered for so long, for if he brought Ethel into the conversation, God knows what might happen to her. He noted with an odd detachment that he wasn't especially frightened, as if in confronting the source of fifteen years' worth of fear he found that its incarnation could not match the terror of fantasy. Worried, yes, he was certainly that, for he could not see any way out. If he attempted to climb back up the cliff he had just so awkwardly come down, Ronald would hit him in the back of the head with his hammer before Michael had even got one leg up onto the top of the sandy ledge. The alternative – going past Ronald to the Junction – would bring about the same grim resolution. He didn't know what to do.

But it seemed Ronald did, for suddenly Michael heard the faint rustling and watched as Ronald tightened his grip on the sledgehammer speaking with a cold, low menace: 'I think it's showtime.'

And then a third voice suddenly entered the air, young and shrill. 'Leave him alone!' When Michael turned sideways he saw, to his astonishment, that Jack was standing on the ledge above them, pointing with his finger at Ronald. He had left his slicker behind and was wearing only a yellow T-shirt with his jeans. *He'll catch cold*, Michael thought incongruously, then barked harshly at him, 'Go back. Run back up the hill and get Donny.'

The boy looked at him with a mixed expression of hurt and incomprehension; clearly he'd assumed that Michael would be pleased he had followed him successfully along the rocky, dangerous trail. Then Jack turned his head and looked at Ronald, who was starting to sidle over very gradually towards the ledge. Again Jack waved his finger at him, saying, 'Don't you hurt him or I'll tell my daddy.'

Ronald stared at the boy with disbelief and shook his head. Then he laughed and asked, 'And who might your daddy be?'

Michael thought, *He doesn't even know this is his son. For Christ's sake, look at the kid – who else could his father be? Doesn't Ronald recognize him?*

And Jack said, 'His name is Ronald Duverson, and he'll get you if you hurt my friend. I promise, he'll get you.' Ronald looked stunned at first, and stared at Jack, sizing up the little boy he hadn't seen for over three years. For a brief moment, Michael expected the discovery to be too much for Ronald – he'd hug the boy, or want to talk with him. But instead he laughed again, and kept laughing in a harsh series of explosive bursts – *haw, haw, haw* – in which Michael sensed a hysterical note. This increased his own sense of urgency and he shouted at Jack, who was still standing close to the edge of the ledge: 'Go Jack! Get out of here. Do what I say.'

But Ronald, still moving slowly but steadily towards the ledge, had stopped laughing, and said with calm deliberation, 'Don't listen to him, Jack. We were playing a game. It was just pretend. Everything's all right.' And Jack, who had looked ready to obey Michael and run, hesitated for a moment, looking first at Ronald and then for guidance to Michael. And as Michael started to shout at him again to run away, Ronald slid a long arm out, like a snake extending itself with deceptive speed, and pulled Jack's leg out from under him. As the boy fell Ronald grabbed him by the waist, and in one quick movement brought him down with a sudden *wham* onto the riverbank. Stunned, Jack started to cry, while Ronald held him by his T-shirt with his left hand, keeping the sledgehammer firmly in his right.

'What was the point of that?' Michael demanded. 'This has got nothing to do with him and you know it. Let him go.'

Did Ronald look confused? 'I can't,' he said, tightening his hold on the boy's T-shirt.

'Why not? He's yours. You can't hurt that boy.'

'I'm not going to hurt him,' Ronald protested. For the first time, there was uncertainty in his voice.

'Then let him go.'

'I can't,' said Ronald. 'I need time to get away. I'll never get out of here if I let him go. The Junction's just around the corner. There's bound to be people there.'

'Oh, so you're going to take him back to Texas with you?' asked Michael. Ronald shrugged, then lifted the hammer menacingly. Michael ignored this and said, 'You're going to make him watch what you do to me?'

Ronald thought about this for a moment. Jack was squirming under his grip and Ronald looked down at the boy. 'Stay still,' he ordered, then looked back at Michael. 'I don't see as I have much choice.'

'That'll be a nice thing for him to live with. Bad enough to know you're a killer; now he gets to witness the crime.'

'He'll get over it,' said Ronald doggedly, but he was thinking. Michael was wondering what to say next when he saw Jack suddenly twist his neck to gain some slack from Ronald's grip, then turn his head sideways and bite hard into Ronald's ungloved hand.

'*Goddamnit!*' Ronald shouted, letting go of Jack to look at the wound, which was already bleeding profusely. But before Jack could escape Ronald lifted his bleeding hand and slapped the boy viciously across the face. As Jack stumbled and fell down onto the gravel, Michael ran at Ronald. As the sledgehammer started to swing towards him he readied himself for the blow while simultaneously launching a punch with his right hand. It landed high on Ronald's face – he felt his fist hit a cheekbone – just as the heavy hammer hit his shoulder with colossal force, driving him sideways on to the gravel.

Ronald was knocked backwards by his punch, but though he dropped the sledgehammer he didn't fall down. As Michael lay on the riverbank he shouted at Jack, now standing again, 'Run, Jack! Run!' This time the boy didn't hesitate and flew off along the gravel pan towards the corner.

Michael rolled towards the cliff and scrambled to his feet as Ronald retrieved the hammer from the ground. Ronald looked at the escaping boy as if contemplating running after him, but thought better of it and now focused on Michael. He was standing with his back to the river, blocking Michael's access to the bend and the safety of the Junction, swinging the sledgehammer gently with his hand as he took a step forward to work Michael back against the cliff.

Neither man spoke. A minute before their voices, sheltered by the cliff, had rung out clearly in the chill air against the background of rushing river: Ronald's harsh and slightly Texas-flavoured, Michael's resonant and deep like his father's; even the boy's high-pitched tones had been shrilly audible. But now the river roar was almost deafening, a wall of sound modulated only when Michael moved his head in the wind. *At least Jack got away*, thought Michael, for he could see no escape from the kind of mortal hammering that had killed his

father. He thought of Henry Wolf with a sudden, intense compassion, and the irony of dying himself when he was at last
happy to keep living was not lost on him. An image flashed
through his head of the Philippino guards in their final fatal
sleep, but there was no peace in this prospect, and he saw no
reason now to envy them at all. *I don't want to die*, he thought
angrily, imagining Jack running towards the Junction, then
envisaging Cassie and Sally sitting out at Sheringham's.

He had to do something, so he feinted sharply to the right like
a ballplayer in a rundown, trying to avoid the tag, and Ronald
was slightly slow to react. So he did it again, and this time
Ronald simply backed up a little, to make sure Michael could
not slip by him. Michael feinted left this time and Ronald
backed up again, getting closer now to the river. And then
Michael remembered Malley's advice: *Try to surprise the son of
a bitch*. It stayed in his head like a moral injunction, which he
now struggled to translate into action. How? He was thinking
so hard that he didn't notice how Ronald had edged forwards
again, until the sledgehammer came out of nowhere and
smashed into the side of his forearm. He leaped back, trying not
to rub the arm, which felt agonizingly painful – he was sure
some bones were broken. Ronald laughed his harsh, shitty
laugh and looked more confident, though he still kept his
distance to cut off any chance of escape.

And then Michael made up his mind, and did something he
hadn't done since his baseball days, showing off in Little
League. He took two quick steps towards Ronald and then
simply dived – as in a headfirst slide with his arms folded
together in front – right at the man, aiming to hit him waist
high. And even as he felt the sledgehammer break the air and he
prepared to be hit, he was confident that he had found his
target. He hit Ronald like a human torpedo, right in the middle
of his belt buckle, with all of his 192 pounds. As Michael fell
onto the gravel, scraping his face as he hit the stones, and
already feeling the pain where the sledgehammer had struck
home, he heard a frightened shout of surprise as Ronald's feet
scratched desperately at the gravel, then slid suddenly as he lost

his footing altogether, and Ronald toppled backwards into the raging waters of the Still.

Michael rolled over and sat up on his knees, trying to ignore his own pain, and watched as Ronald struggled in the rushing water. Even with the flooding the river was shallower here by the bank, not the depth of a man's height, and for a moment, as Ronald got both feet down and started to rise, Michael thought he might just make it out of the river right away. He looked around for the sledgehammer to protect himself, but then stopped as he saw Ronald, trying to take a step, get knocked suddenly sideways by the current's force.

And then Ronald was swept quickly downstream by the water. Michael stood up, and as his adrenalin masked the pain he began to run, trying to keep up with the figure in the water. But it was hopeless, for though Ronald was moving his arms and even kicking in a vain effort to swim towards the bank, he was now entirely in the grip of the raging river. *He's a goner*, thought Michael as he watched Ronald going pell-mell towards the bend. He strained in the dark to see him, and picked him out as he was caught in a vortex of water that pushed him even further from the bank. As Michael kept running he was startled to discover that he was actually catching up to what his eyes had marked out as Ronald, and as he got closer he saw that it *was* him, stationary in the water. Approaching the bend, Michael found the mystery solved when he saw Ronald hanging on for dear life to a boulder jutting out of the river, about a third of the way across. As he drew parallel Michael saw that Ronald's chest was draped over the front of the large rock, while he clung on desperately to its sides with both hands as the water rushed around him.

There was no way Michael could reach him. He looked fruitlessly around for a rope until he recognized the absurdity of this. 'I'll go for help!' he shouted out across the waters, which seemed even fiercer in the dusk, pouring by him with a rushing, boiling roar. He doubted that Ronald had heard him, so he shouted again, and this time he could just make out his face, pressed against the rock but turning to look his way. 'I'll get help!' he shouted one more time, taking a last look out at the figure on the rock before he turned to run to the Junction. It was getting more dark than dusk now, and he wondered if it was simply his imagination, for the expression he thought he had just made out on Ronald's face, hanging on as the water poured around him, seemed – even now, even in his utter desperation – completely contorted by *hate*.

As he turned the corner he could suddenly see the Junction bridge, its three supporting piers looking inexplicably dark until he realized the water level was so high that the space beneath the bridge was almost filled to the top with river. On the surface of the bridge two patrol cars sat, one on each end, facing each other in the woolly light, their roof lights stabbing red, white, and blue into the darkening air. He could see no human figures near them and worried about Jack's where-abouts, until to his right, on the Stillriver side of the bridge, higher up on the elevated causeway, he saw several people standing in a group, bunched around a lamp. *Kerosene?* he wondered idly. And as he struggled to continue running, feeling stabbing pain in his ribs with each breath and every step he made on the hard gravel pan, he tried to wave his arms and shout. Then the wide beam of a big searchlight played across the gravel until it reached him and hit him full on, momentarily blinding in its brightness. He kept moving as fast as he could, shouting, 'Help, help,' and as he came within about a hundred yards of the grouped men he saw a policeman step towards him, and recognized Jimmy Olds. Jimmy was holding some-thing yellow in his arms, and to Michael's immense relief he saw that it was Jack.

The pain was now constant, but he thought of Ronald holding on desperately, and forced himself to keep running, wondering why Jimmy Olds and the others weren't moving to help, starting to feel infuriated that they were just *standing* there, waiting for him. And then through the noise of his own heavy breathing in the air, and the internal wheezing that seemed to come from his ribs, he heard the figures shouting, and they were saying *Run!* And again, *Run, run!* He thought, *I* am *running goddamnit,* and as he came up the hill to the causeway and neared its rim, three men came out of the dark and helped haul him up. He stood with his hands on his knees, gasping for breath, until he lifted his head when someone shouted, just in time to turn with the others and watch as the river came sweeping towards the bridge below them in one vast, translatory wave, an immense rolling surge that would have carried anything along with it, including, he realized at once, Ronald Duverson. As it reached the bridge he peered into the dark roll of water, curved like an enormous breaker, and sought something human. But he saw no sign of Ronald – no boot, no white and flashing arm, no face twisted by hate – and then the wave hit the scaffolding with a reverberating ring and the water came up and onto the bridge with an explosive *whoosh.*

Then Jimmy was by his side, holding Jack, who was now wrapped in a blanket and shivering. 'There was someone back there,' Michael said, not wanting to say the name out loud in front of Jack.

'I know,' said Jimmy. 'The boy just told us. Who was it?'

'I'll tell you later.'

'I've called up to the Meadows. If he goes back up that way they'll get him.'

Michael shook his head. 'He was in the river. That's why I was yelling for help. He was hanging on to some rocks and I came to get help.'

Jimmy's eyes widened. 'He won't be there now,' he said quietly.

Michael nodded, then looked over at the bridge, where the water was draining away from its surface. Amazingly, the bridge was standing, still shrouded on the upstream side by scaffolding, seemingly untouched by the translatory wave, its beam-and-slab construction not really so different from those of the early simple bridges that had first enthralled him years before. Somebody had moved the big searchlight until its light shone out over the Junction, and Michael suddenly saw that although the bridge had survived and its three piers were still standing, the banks supporting the highway approaches on either side had been completely washed away. The river now flowed both under the bridge and *around* it, through channels it had rudely cut on either side.

The effect was as severing as if the bridge itself had fallen. As he looked at the two police cars now marooned on the bridge, he felt an absurdity to the spectacle that made him want to laugh. Cassavantes' last-minute meddling had taken its toll after all; Michael realized that it would be weeks, more likely months, before this main route to town was usable again. *One bridge out of action*, he thought, *and one man dead*.

He felt something brush against his leg, and when he looked he saw that Jack had got down from Jimmy Olds and was standing next to Michael, looking up at him with an expression at once mystified and beseeching. The boy was still wearing the blanket and Michael tucked it firmly around him. 'I'd pick you up, Jack, but I can't. I think my ribs are broken.'

'That's okay,' the boy said simply, and slid his small hand into Michael's. They stood together, looking down at the bridge, and at the cascading flow already widening the gap between the causeway and the bridge itself. Something was fluttering on the scaffolding on the upstream side, and when Michael stared at it, wondering what kind of debris it could be, he saw that hooked on a pipe's edge was a latex glove, flapping empty in the wind above the flooding waters of the Still.

Epilogue

THEY FOUND RONALD's body the next morning, caught by the rocks at the Stillriver end of the channel, not far from Nelson's boathouse and only about a hundred yards from the channel where Ronald had once 'saved' Raleigh Somerset from drowning. To spare Cassie, Michael identified the body, with Jimmy Olds having to hold his arm as they walked down to the edge of Stillriver Lake – an x-ray had shown that four of Michael's ribs were cracked. As another policeman pulled the tarp back, Michael looked down at Ronald's face, seeing that in death the mouth of his tormentor was taut and unsmiling, his face bruised and purple from the violence of the river.

That day, and in the days that followed, Michael had a growing conviction that the world he had been living in was for ever behind him. Like it or not, he was now in the new world he had sought for so long, a new world that, curiously, he had rediscovered; for it was the world of his childhood and adolescence, the world of his growing up. He had been confident for so long that he would find it elsewhere – Ann Arbor, New York, London, a Swedish island – that it seemed amazing to discover it had always been right here, waiting for him.

This feeling of arriving back where he had begun was accompanied by an entirely unexpected sadness about Ronald's death. Cassie didn't share this feeling, for she was at first plagued by feelings of guilt that she had believed Ronald when he told her he had been rejected for parole. 'If only I had checked for sure,' she kept saying to Michael, until finally, with just a hint of exasperation, Michael pointed out that if Jimmy Olds had been even slightly more on the ball he would have taken the fifteen seconds required to check the National Crime Index database and discover that Ronald was no longer in prison.

At Cassie's insistence, and to Michael's relief, Ronald was

buried in Texas. Mex, his younger brother, did not travel there to attend the funeral. Neither did Jack or Sally; they stayed with Nancy Sheringham during the week it took their mother to bury Ronald and wind up his affairs.

Cleared of any direct involvement in the murder of Henry Wolf, Raleigh Somerset soon found he had other problems. For despite Ethel's failure to identify Raleigh, Maguire managed to obtain a warrant to search Raleigh's place on the grounds that he might find evidence linking Ronald Duverson to the murder of Henry Wolf. No one doubted Michael's account of Ronald's confession, but there was no forensic evidence to prove that Ronald had killed him. When Maguire searched Raleigh's house with two local policemen (though not Jimmy Olds), he discovered nothing relevant to the homicide; but he did find four sticks of dynamite in a wooden box in the basement. Raleigh's fingerprints were all over them.

When he heard this news from Gary, Michael told his younger brother not to bother trying to look surprised.

'What do you mean?'

'You know exactly what I mean. Now I know why you were out at the Half. You could *walk* to Raleigh's from there, plant the dynamite and wait until the right time to let Maguire know about it.'

'What dynamite?'

'Maguire said he arrested Raleigh with six sticks of dynamite the first time.'

Gary shrugged as if to say, *So?*

'You told me there were ten in the crate you buried at the Half.'

'I can't remember.'

'And this time when they got him, they found four sticks.'

'What's your point?' asked Gary sourly.

'Six plus four equals ten.'

'Why would I tell Maguire anything?'

'You tell me. I still don't understand why you told him about the dynamite the first time around. Were you just being a good citizen or did Maguire have something on you?'

414

Gary blushed so dramatically at this – it looked as though cherry juice had suffused his face – that Michael didn't have the heart to press it. Of course. *Maguire knew about the proclivities of Bubba and the boys. He probably threatened to tell Pop. Or Gary's 'girlfriend'. Or the world.*

'But this time,' said Michael thinking hard, 'you and Maguire were on the same side. You told him about the dynamite that you still had because you were scared of Raleigh, scared he was going to try and kill you. You thought he'd killed Pop. You wanted Raleigh put away, and so did Maguire, if not for murder, then the dynamite would do.'

Michael looked thoughtfully at his younger brother. 'And that's why Maguire came by here after he heard Ethel's story. It wasn't to tell you that you were in the clear – that's far too humane a thing for Maguire to do. No, it was to establish that if he couldn't nail Raleigh on the murder charge – all he really had then was Ethel's word for it – he'd at least get him for something. With your help.'

To which Gary replied with a smug and knowing smile.

Certain mysteries remained, though one was cleared up in the week after Ronald had been killed when Michael read his brief obituary in the *Atlantic County Herald*. **RONALD SALEM DUVERSON, 39, FORMER STILLRIVER RESIDENT**, read the small headline on the piece. The middle name made him pause. *Salem?* That was where Streatley had grown up. In Oregon. Then Michael remembered that yes, Salem was the state capital. Ethel's peculiar mnemonic had been correct after all; Maguire had been so keen to nail Somerset that he had stopped too early – at North Carolina and 'Raleigh'.

Maguire himself proved something of a mystery, for despite all the detective's talk about peach trees and his sister's smallholding outside New Era, Michael later learned from Kenny Williams (who had bought the beach property after all) that within six weeks of Ronald's death Maguire was back in Detroit, working for a new federal unit specializing in counter-terrorism. Michael would have liked a further session with the man – he had more than one bone to pick – but by this time Michael had left town, having given countless interviews to the police and having testified exhaustively at the coroner's inquest into Ronald's death by drowning.

The job in Dubai was quick and straightforward – a concrete beam-and-slab job that actually could have been supervised by someone less experienced and cheaper. Jock wasn't needed, really, and though Michael had offered to bring him along, the old man had declined, though he seemed touched by Michael's offer.

The site crew was a mix of Pakistanis and Yemenis who spoke little English, and Michael spent his nights in his air-conditioned trailer reading, resisting the temptation to make expensive overseas calls, writing letters instead. He still found the day-to-day problems of concrete rehabilitation interesting, but they were no longer a substitute passion, indeed not a passion at all. He was happy to discover that what quickened his heart was no longer inanimate.

Returning to London in early December, he found the Ealing flat under offer. Ten days later he had exchanged contracts and managed to sell the buyer all his furniture as well. When he flew out of Heathrow, the only property he owned was the house in Stillriver.

He arrived there a week before Christmas. Gary had long ago decamped to his bungalow, where he celebrated his prospective inheritance non-stop with Bubba and the boys until the day after Thanksgiving. Then, as if someone had thrown a switch, he had driven out with a hangover to Harold Lashing's, made peace, and became Harold's junior partner again.

The house had not been neglected, for Cassie, Jack and Sally had been living in it since the beginning of the month.

Before Michael had even unpacked, Cassie drove him and the kids eighty miles north to Sugar Mountain, the ski resort, where they stayed for two nights in a chalet on the main lodge grounds. There, while the kids spent the daylight hours in ski school, he and Cassie stayed in bed. Making love again for the

416

first time in more than fifteen years, they found their first try tender but awkward – though not so awkward that they did not repeat the process three more times before darkness loomed and they went to pick up Jack and Sally from the bottom of the bunny slope.

They had only a single conversation about Ronald, but it was an important one, for there was something he felt he needed to know. 'Tell me,' he said as they drove on an icy road to Manistee the next day to buy Christmas presents, while the kids went back to ski school, 'Why didn't you come with me when I asked you to, back in Texas?'

'I told you why.'

'Sure, but I can't believe being pregnant with Jack was the only reason.' He said this as mildly as he could.

'Oh, I don't know,' she said with a show of nonchalance. 'I guess it was a lot of things.'

'Like what, exactly?'

'Well, there you were a married man, asking me to join you in God knows where – you weren't positive yourself – while I was about to give birth to another man's child. What if you'd changed your mind six months later? What would I do then? I'd already followed one roughneck halfway round Texas. Did it really make sense to follow another?'

This was the same argument she had made in the summer for staying put in Stillriver. He looked at her dubiously and she lifted her eyebrows, as if to say, *That's the way it was, whatever you may think.*

'There was something else, wasn't there?' he asked. 'You were worried about what Ronald would do.'

'Can you blame me? You were worried about what Ronald would do, too.'

'Did he ever say he'd kill *you*?'

He knew she wouldn't lie outright and she didn't. 'No,' she admitted, 'he did not.'

'Was there anybody he did happen to say he'd kill, I mean, way back then?' He wasn't sure why he was persisting with this, except that he had never fully accepted her coldness in the motel room near LaGuardia, her studied certainty that she had to go away from him. So he was not entirely surprised now to see tears well up in her eyes. He nodded. 'I thought so. It was me he said he'd kill, even seven years ago. Wasn't it?'

She sniffled and nodded at the same time and he reached over and put his arm round her. 'You sent me away because you thought he'd kill me if we got together.'

'That's right,' she said, wiping her eyes with her hand.

He withdrew his arm and drove carefully down the snow-packed road approaching town. There was still one thought in his head that wouldn't go away, an uncomfortable one he could see might hang around in future, like a bedroom mosquito at night, which buzzed infuriatingly close to your ear, then receded while you lay in the silence, waiting for it to come buzzing back.

Cassie lifted her head up. 'You're not stupid, Michael, but neither am I. You must be wondering why I wanted you back here so much last summer if Ronald was still saying he'd kill you if I were with you. I mean, you probably think it was asking you to be a sitting duck, just waiting until Ronald got out of prison and came to get you.'

'It doesn't matter.'

'Of course it does. What you have to understand is, I thought we had at least a year. I didn't know what would happen in that time. Maybe Ronald would calm down before he got out. Or maybe we *would* have to go away – I'd have come to Dubai or wherever if I'd thought there was the slightest chance he'd come harm you. But I needed to know first that you wanted to be with me – wanted me enough even to come back here.'

He pulled into the highway mall parking lot and stopped the car, then put his arm round her shoulders again. 'I'm glad you told me,' he said. And then he did tell one lie: 'Honest, that had never even crossed my mind.'

They went home to find a Christmas tree deposited on the back porch by Nancy Sheringham from the farm. On Christmas Day Gary joined them for presents and a Christmas dinner of baked ham, which Cassie and Michael cooked together. New Year's Eve they stayed in, drinking most of a bottle of champagne and just managing to stay awake until midnight and the new millennium.

In January, after an internal inquiry into the flood of the Still river, Cassavantes was suspended from his job and promptly resigned, moving to Panama to work on Canal-related restoration work. Donny told Michael at once about the vacancy, and there was an ad for the post in the following week's *Atlantic County Herald*.

But having laid the ground by correspondence, ten days after New Year Michael flew to Florida and visited Betty, the widow, who lived pleasantly in a bungalow on the Gulf Coast near Sarasota. She was not crucial to the deal, but it seemed appropriate to pay his respects before flying on the next day to Chicago, where he expected Betty's son to drive a hard bargain. In fact, it wasn't clear the son even knew who he was, or had any memory of Michael's past connection with his father. And as for the retail premises, he seemed delighted that someone was willing to take them off his hands. Having dreaded the negotiation, Michael flew north out of Chicago in a tiny prop plane that wavered in the wind on take-off like a tippy little bird, feeling almost guilty about how little money he would be paying Alvin Simpson's son Phil for the drugstore.

He went to work at once. He was alone most days, redecorating the premises, having company only for specialized tasks – the whole place needed rewiring, the plumbing down-stairs proved beyond him – though occasionally Cassie would come downtown to help after school. He decided to cater unabashedly for the affluent summer clientele and was determined to be open before Memorial Day. He reinstalled the soda fountain, and was delighted to learn on an expedition to Manistee that people seemed willing to part with $3.50 for a hot fudge sundae. He bought 200 beach towels from the previous owner at a knockdown price, along with seventeen cases of sun tan lotion he planned to mark up even more than Alvin had. Finding the old pine racks buried in the back of the liquor cage, he stained them afresh and bought 300 bags of charcoal at a closing down sale in Grand Haven. Most significantly, he lined up the part-time services of two retired pharmacists, one from Burlington, the other who lived in a cottage on the Stillriver Lake side of South Beach.

He looked forward to opening, since he felt it would somehow seal away the recent past and, as far as the store was concerned, atone for the distant one. Surprisingly few people ever talked to him about his father's murder, and he was only aware that many people thought it strange – even creepy – that he was living in his father's house again, because Donny told him so. *Thanks*, he wanted to tell his oldest friend, but decided that if he talked about it with him at all he might as well talk to everybody else.

Yet this niggled enough at him that he thought he had better raise the issue with Cassie. One night as they drew back the bedspread in what he still thought of as his parents' bedroom, he said, 'We don't have to live in this house, you know.'

Cassie drew her white cotton nightgown down over her hips – he was happy to see she'd gained a little weight during the autumn. She climbed into bed, and picked up her book, an Anne Tyler novel, one of many paperbacks of hers that were slowly edging out his mother's hardbacks on the little bedside bookstand. 'I know that,' she said.

'I still don't really understand why my father changed his will and left it to me. I thought maybe he was mad at Gary because of the dynamite, but if you're mad at somebody, you don't usually leave them a hundred and fifty thousand dollars in stock.'

'He wasn't mad at Gary.'

'He might have been if he'd known about the gay thing.'

Cassie shook her head. 'He wouldn't have been surprised. I think he had an idea about that.'

'Really?'

She nodded with certainty. 'One night last year I went to the movies in Fennville and ran into Gary. The Jenkinses were there and seemed to think we'd gone to the movies together. When that old witch saw your father the next day she made some remark – you know, how maybe I was going out with another of his sons now. Apparently your father said, "Sorry, Gloria, you'll have to find your gossip somewhere else. Gary's not a going-out-with-women type." '

'Really?'

'Really. I don't think his will change was about Gary at all.'

'You mean it was about me?'

'Could have been,' said Cassie. She looked uncomfortable.

'In what way? Just what are you trying to say?'

'How can I put this? I know he was glad I was back because he said so. He came round one day just after Christmas last year.'

'You never told me that.'

'You never asked,' she said easily. 'Don't pretend you've told me everything, either. Anyway, he seemed especially pleased when he learned I wasn't with Ronald any more. He said you were single again, too. He didn't say anything explicit, but I got the feeling he was hoping we'd get back together. And maybe that's why he left you the house.'

Michael looked rueful. 'I'm stumped. If that's what he thought why didn't he *tell* me?' He thought of his father's last letter and yet again regretted not replying to it. 'I just don't understand.'

'Maybe he thought he'd tell you in person. He told me you were going to be here for a while in the summertime. You know, on vacation.'

'He did?' Michael was flabbergasted. And he was never able to discover why his father had said this, how he had known that Michael was planning to come and see him. *I will never understand the man*, he thought, but was determined at last to appreciate him. For in clearing up so many other mysteries, he had come to conclude, inevitably he discovered some new ones.

'Anyway,' he said, getting into bed himself, 'you sure you like living in this house?'

'You got somewhere else in mind where we could live?'

'No, it's just—'

'Good,' she said firmly. 'Because I love this house and always have. As far as I'm concerned this is where we're going to live. And raise our children.'

'*Our* children?'

She looked at him with a warmth that touched his spine. 'Don't get your hopes up. I'm pretty old. But those two—' and she pointed towards the hall, in the direction of the bedrooms, once Gary's and Michael's, where Jack and Sally were now sleeping – 'are your children too now. They need a Daddy, you know.'

This helped him, for he had been wondering what role to assume in addition to that of their mother's lover. Ancient family friend? Mild avuncular figure? Sally was precocious, and developing a fine line in sarcastic rebuke: for a brief while she perversely called him 'Pop' until Cassie managed to persuade her to desist. It was March before he knew she thought he was okay, and that only when she confided this to Nancy Sheringham's youngest daughter.

As for Jack, Michael had interested him in fishing, and he planned to take him in summer up the north branch of the Still, wading on its soft, sandy bottom just up from the wooden bridge, now rebuilt, at Happy Valley. Jack knew now that his father had drowned – Cassie reasoned that if she didn't tell him, a classmate at school would be bound to, or a nosy parker like Mrs Jenkins. Jack had not made the connection yet between his father's death and the man who had been threatening Michael on the riverbank; this was one home truth that Michael and Cassie decided could wait a while.

With the boy, Michael tried always to be gentle, and he never lifted his hand to him: if Jack misbehaved he simply talked to him, firmly but without temper. And when Jack hit out – at him, or more often at his sister – Michael would envelop him in his arms until the boy's anger turned.

Such episodes were becoming more infrequent, though when thwarted in some wish or other, Jack could still flare up, with a malign look that would surface in his eyes and seemed to Michael to be pure Duverson. There was hate there, then, of the kind that could kill a man. When he saw this, Michael would suppress his own memories, and his own internal shudder too. For the boy's sake, for the sake of Cassie, and for what he figured was his own sake as well, he would try to love the boy as best he could.

Acknowledgements

THE AUTHOR WOULD like to thank Don Calvert, Pat Elder, Peter Keating and Candia McWilliam for advice and information.